Ab

Susanna Carr has
she read her first M
has written sexy contemporary romances for several publishers and her work has been honoured with awards for contemporary and sensual romance. Susanna lives in the Pacific Northwest with her family. When she isn't writing, Susanna enjoys reading romance and connecting with readers online. Visit her website at susannacarr.com

As a child books took **Robyn Donald** to places far away from her village in Northland, New Zealand. Then, as well as becoming a teacher, marrying and raising two children, she discovered romances and read them voraciously. So much she decided to write one. When her first book was accepted by Mills & Boon she felt she'd arrived home. Robyn still lives in Northland, using the landscape as a setting for her work. Her life is enriched by friends she's made among writers and readers.

Niobia Bryant is the award-winning and national bestselling author of more than forty works of romance and commercial mainstream fiction. Twice she has won the RT Reviewer's Choice Best Book Award for African American/Multicultural Romance. Her books have appeared in *Ebony*, *Essence*, *The New York Post*, *The Star-Ledger*, *The Dallas Morning News* and many other national publications. One of her bestselling books was adapted to film.

Island Escapes

June 2021
Caribbean Kisses

July 2021
Tropical Trysts

August 2021
Hawaiian Nights

September 2021
Moonlit Liaisons

October 2021
Passion in Paradise

November 2021
Seduction at Sea

Island Escapes: Passion in Paradise

SUSANNA CARR

ROBYN DONALD

NIOBIA BRYANT

MILLS & BOON

First Published in Great Britain 2021
by Mills & Boon, an imprint of HarperCollins*Publishers* Ltd,
1 London Bridge Street, London, SE1 9GF

www.harpercollins.co.uk

HarperCollins*Publishers*
1st Floor, Watermarque Building,
Ringsend Road, Dublin 4, Ireland

ISBN: 978-0-263-30268-4

FSC
www.fsc.org
MIX
Paper from responsible sources
FSC C007454

This book is produced from independently certified FSC™ paper to ensure responsible forest management.

For more information visit: www.harpercollins.co.uk/green

Printed and bound in Spain
by CPI, Barcelona

A DEAL WITH BENEFITS

SUSANNA CARR

To my editor, Carly Byrne, with thanks

PROLOGUE

"OUR GUEST IS early, Miss Ashley. Ooh, that boat is sweet," Clea, the housekeeper, said and gave a squeal of laughter that rang through the hall. "You should see Louis running down the dock to get a closer look."

"It must be quite a boat," Ashley said. Clea's husband didn't move fast. No one did on Inez Key. Their families had been here for generations and they followed the gentle rhythm of island life.

Ashley took a step outside and stared at the scarlet red boat. The sharp and dramatic lines seemed obscenely aggressive against the lazy waves of the ocean. The boat said a lot about the owner. Loud and attention seeking. She squinted and noticed that there was only one person on the boat. "Damn," she muttered. "He's single."

Clea patted Ashley's bare arm. "I'm sure he won't require that much work."

Ashley rolled her eyes. "Single guests are the worst. They expect to be entertained."

"I can meet him while you change into a dress," Clea said as she headed down the hill to the dock.

Ashley followed her. "No, thanks. I'm not dressing up for paying guests anymore. Not after that basketball player thought I was included in the weekend package."

Clea gestured at Ashley. "And what is this man going to think when he sees you dressed like that?"

Ashley looked down at the bright yellow tank top that didn't quite reach the frayed cutoff shorts. Her worn sandals were so old they clung lovingly to her feet and her long hair was gathered up in a messy ponytail. She only wore makeup or jewelry for a special occasion. A man did not fall into that category. "That we aren't formal around here."

Clea clucked her tongue and stared at Ashley's long brown legs. "You don't know much about men, do you?"

"I've learned more than I ever wish to know," Ashley said. She'd got her education whenever her father had been around during the tennis off-season. What she didn't discover from Donald Jones, she had learned from his entourage.

She had finally used all that knowledge to secure a generous loan from Raymond Casillas. It had been a huge risk. She didn't trust the aging playboy and knew he was going to find a way to have her repay him with sex. That wasn't going to happen.

Unfortunately, she was behind on her loan payment and she couldn't miss another month. Ashley shuddered, the icy-cold fear trickling down her spine as she considered the consequences. Just a few more rich celebrities seeking privacy on her island—okay, quite a few more—and she would be free of the threat.

Ashley walked down the hill with renewed determination. She strode along the sturdy wood dock, blocking the bright sun with her hand as she took a closer look at her guest, Sebastian Esteban.

The man stood on the deck like a conquering hero waiting to be swarmed by the grateful natives. Her heart started to pound against her chest. She noticed the thick dark hair ruffling slightly in the wind and the T-shirt stretched against his broad chest. His powerful legs were encased in faded jeans. She felt an unfamiliar pull low in her belly as she stared at the gorgeous stranger.

"Huh," Clea said as she walked alongside Ashley. "There's something familiar about that man."

"Is he famous? An actor?" Ashley immediately dismissed that idea. While his stunning good looks would make Hollywood lay down the red carpet for him, she sensed Sebastian Esteban wasn't the kind who would trade on his harsh, masculine features. The blade of his nose and the slash of his mouth suggested aristocracy, but the high, slanted cheekbones and the thrust of his angular jaw indicated that he fought for every inch of his territory.

"Can't say for sure," Clea muttered. "I feel like I've seen him before."

It didn't matter what he did for a living, she decided. She wasn't going to be starstruck. Ashley had intentionally cut herself off from the world when her parents died five years ago. She would probably recognize a few superstars, but she didn't keep up with the current celebrities. Yet she didn't think she could tolerate another famous person who thought basic manners applied to everyone else and not them.

"Mr. Esteban?" Ashley asked as she reached out her hand. She looked up and their gazes clashed and held. Her safe little existence went completely still as the beat of her heart pounded in her ears. Anticipation rushed through her as Sebastian touched her hand. When his large fingers enclosed hers, her world shifted. She saw the glow of interest in his dark eyes as the energy, wild and violent, ripped through her.

Ashley wanted to jerk back, but the stranger held her fingers captive. Her muscles clenched as every instinct told her to hide. But she couldn't move. She was frozen as the dark, swirling emotions threatened to pull her under.

"Please, call me Sebastian."

She shivered at the sound of his rough, deep voice. "I'm Ashley," she said. It was difficult to push the words out of her tight throat. "Welcome to Inez Key. I hope you will enjoy your visit."

Something hot and wicked flickered in his eyes before he released her hand. "Thank you, I will."

As she stiffly introduced Clea and Louis, she reluctantly noticed how Sebastian towered over her, his broad shoulders blocking out the sun. She could feel his masculine power coming off him in waves.

She covertly watched him as he refused Louis's assistance and tossed his backpack over his shoulder. Who was this man? He was wealthy enough to own that boat, but he didn't wear designer clothes. He had no entourage or tower of luggage, but he could afford to stay at her home for an exclusive weekend.

"You'll stay here in the main house," Clea said as they escorted him up the hill toward the white mansion.

Sebastian stood for a moment as he studied the plantation home. His expression was blank and his eyes were hooded, but she felt an explosive tension emanating from him.

Ashley wondered what he thought about her home. The guests were always in awe of the antebellum architecture. They saw the clean lines and graceful symmetry, the massive columns that stretched from the ground to the black rooftop and surrounded every side of the house. The balconies hinted of an elegant world long forgotten and one could almost ignore that the large black window shutters were for protection from the elements instead of decoration.

But no one noticed that her home was falling apart. There was only so much that a slap of paint, a carefully angled table or a fresh bouquet of flowers could hide. The antique furniture, the artwork, anything of value, had been sold years ago.

As they walked into the grand hall, she dimly heard Clea offer refreshments. Ashley glanced around and hoped she had not overlooked anything. She wanted Sebastian Esteban to notice the curving staircase and how the sunlight caught the crystal chandelier instead of the faded wallpaper. Yet the way he quietly studied the room, she sensed that he saw everything.

Ashley stifled a gasp when she felt Clea jab her bony elbow in her ribs. "Miss Ashley, why don't you show Mr. Sebastian his room while I get the drinks?"

She gritted her teeth. "Of course. This way, please."

Ashley bent her head as she approached the stairs. She didn't want to be alone with this man. She wasn't afraid of Sebastian Esteban, but she was uncomfortable with her reaction. This wasn't like her.

Ashley's skin tingled as she climbed the stairs ahead of Sebastian. Her cutoff shorts felt small as she felt his heated gaze on her bare legs. She should have listened to Clea and worn a dress that covered every inch of skin.

But she immediately dismissed that idea. She wanted to hide, but at the same time she wanted Sebastian to notice her. Her chest rose and fell as she quickened her step. Ashley wished she could ignore the fast and furious attraction. So what if she found Sebastian sexy? Any woman would find him desirable.

Ashley didn't look at Sebastian as she flung open the door to the master suite and gestured for him to enter. "This is your room," she announced. "The walk-in closet and bathroom is through that door."

He strode to the center of the room and Ashley knew he wouldn't find fault in his accommodations here. It was the largest room and offered a magnificent view. She had placed the best furniture in the sitting area. The four-poster bed was carved mahogany and was big enough for him to lie in the center with his arms stretched out.

Ashley closed her eyes as the unwelcoming heat flushed through her skin. Why did she have to think of that? She wanted to purge the idea of him on the bed, as he lay on the rumpled sheets, naked and gleaming with sweat. She imagined his lean and muscular arms extended as if he was waiting for her. Welcoming her.

"Am I kicking you out of your bed?" Sebastian asked.

"What?" she asked hoarsely. The vision of her curled up next to him on the four-poster bed bloomed in her mind. She shook her head to dispel it. "No, I don't stay here."

"Why not?" he asked as he tossed his backpack on the bed. The bag looked out of place against the vintage handmade quilt. "It's the master suite, isn't it?"

"Yes." She nervously darted the tip of her tongue along her dry lips. She couldn't explain it to him. That this room, this bed, had been the center stage for her parents' destructive relationship. The affair between her father, Donald Jones, and her mother, his longtime mistress Linda Valdez had been fueled with jealousy, infidelities and sexual obsession. She didn't want the added reminder. "Well, if you need anything, please let me know," she said as she slowly made her way to the door.

He tore his gaze away from the ocean view and Ashley saw the shadows in his eyes. It was more than sadness. It was grief. Loss. Anger. Sebastian blinked and the shadows suddenly disappeared.

Sebastian silently nodded and walked to the door with her. He guided her through the threshold by placing his hand on the small of her back. His fingers brushed her bare skin and her muscles clenched as her skin tightened. He dropped his hand, but she still felt the blood strumming through her veins.

Ashley took a deep breath and hurried away from Sebastian, refusing to look back. She was scared to explore these feelings. She was not used to being tempted while she stayed on Inez Key and this was going to be a challenge. She had hidden away for years, purposely disconnected from the world and was quiet and contained. None of the guests who came to her house interested her, but this man…this man reminded her of what she was missing.

And she wasn't sure she wanted to hide anymore….

CHAPTER ONE

One month later

"SIR? THERE'S A woman here who wishes to speak with you."

Sebastian Cruz didn't look up as he continued to sign papers. "Send her away." He didn't tolerate any kind of interruption while he was at work. It was probably a former lover who mistakenly thought the element of surprise and drama would gain his attention. His employees were experienced in handling the situation and he wondered how the woman had managed to get into the executive suite in the first place.

"She insists on seeing you and hasn't left the reception area all day," his assistant continued, this time with a hint of sympathy for the uninvited guest. "She says it's urgent."

They all said that, Sebastian decided as he scanned another letter before he signed it. It annoyed him rather than made him feel curious or flattered. He didn't understand why these sophisticated women would stage public tantrums when the relationship was clearly over. "Have security remove her from the premises."

The younger man cleared his throat and nervously adjusted his tie. "I had considered that, but she says you have something of hers. She wouldn't tell me what it was because it was a private matter. She's here to get it back."

That was impossible. Sebastian frowned as he scrawled his name on another document. He wasn't sentimental. He didn't keep mementos or trophies. "Did you find out her name?"

His assistant squirmed from the censure of his icy tone. "Jones," he said hurriedly. "Ashley Jones."

Sebastian went still as he held the pen in midair. He stared at the heavy paper, the words a blur, as memories of Ashley Jones crashed through him. He remembered her soft brown hair cascading down her bare shoulders. Her wild energy and her earthy laugh. His body clenched, excitement pulsing through his veins, as he thought about her sun-kissed skin and wide pink mouth.

That woman had haunted his dreams for the past month. He had tried to purge Ashley from his mind, distracting himself with work and women, but he couldn't forget her uninhibited response. Or her haughty rejection.

Sebastian remembered that morning vividly. She had still been naked in bed when she had told him she wasn't interested in anything more than a one-night stand. She had shared more than her body that night, but now he wasn't good enough to breathe her rarefied air. Her lips had been reddened from his kisses, but she wouldn't deign to look him in the eye.

Ashley had no idea that he was the most sought-after

bachelor in Miami. A billionaire with incredible influence. Women of power, wealth and royalty chased after him. He had shed the stench of the ghetto years ago and now belonged to the glittery world of high society. But she had dismissed him as if she was a princess that belonged in an ivory-white tower and he still belonged in the filthy streets. Who did she think she was? Ashley had never lifted a finger for the lifestyle she enjoyed, while he continued to fight for the empire he'd created with his bare hands.

"I think she's the daughter of that tennis legend," his assistant continued in a scandalized whisper. "You know, the murder-suicide. It was big news a few years ago."

Donald Jones. Sebastian's nostrils flared as he forced back the rising hot anger. He knew all about the tennis player and his family. He had made a point of learning everything about Ashley.

There had been a few surprises when he had met her, but his first impression had been correct. She was a spoiled heiress who lived in paradise. She didn't know the meaning of scraping by, suffering or surviving. For a woman like Ashley Jones, the world catered to her.

Until now. Sebastian narrowed his eyes as an idea formed. Anticipation beat hard in his chest as he considered the possibilities. He knew why she was here. She wanted to find out how he'd got her precious island and how she could get it back.

His mouth twisted as he imagined his revenge. She wouldn't be so quick to dismiss him now that he had something she wanted. Now was his chance to watch her bow down and lose that superior tone. Sebastian wanted to turn the tables and strip this woman of her pride and status. Take her to bed for one night, indulge in the exquisite pleasure that would make the most cynical lover believe in destiny, and then discard her.

"Please send her in," Sebastian said coldly as the call of the hunt roared in his blood, "and then you may leave for the day."

Ashley sat on the edge of the pearl-white leather chair as she watched the sun set over the Miami skyline. She felt a pang of homesickness as she saw how the tall buildings pierced the coral and dusky pink streaks in the sky. She felt uncomfortable surrounded by steel and glass, noise and people. She missed sitting alone in her favorite spot in the cove of her island and watching the sun dip past the endless turquoise ocean.

She may never see it again. Fear squeezed her heart, and her fingers pinched her white clutch purse. Bile churned in her stomach as she remembered the eviction letter. She still felt the same agonizing horror when she had discovered a Sebastian Cruz had bought her loan and now owned her family island because she'd missed two payments.

Ashley pressed her lips together and prayed that she could meet Mr. Cruz and come to an understanding. Get her island back immediately. What was she going to do if she couldn't get the man to see reason?

She couldn't think this way. Ashley exhaled slowly, wishing the panic that banded her chest would dissolve.

Defeat was not an option. This was her last chance, but she was going to find a way to get back her family home.

Ashley glanced around the waiting room, noticing that it was quieter now that most of the office workers had gone for the day. It didn't make the space any less intimidating. She almost hadn't stepped into the building when she noticed the towering height and the aggressive sleek lines. It had taken more courage than she'd care to admit to stay seated on the chair throughout the day, feeling small and invisible, as she watched the employees attack the day with ruthless energy.

Her head jerked when she heard purposeful footsteps echo against the polished black floor. The tall man in the designer suit and prestigious school tie she'd spoken with earlier approached her. "Miss Jones? Mr. Cruz can see you now."

Ashley nodded as her throat tightened with anxiety. Her hands went suddenly cold as she rose from the seat. She felt uncoordinated, her legs stiff and her borrowed heels heavy, as she followed the man in the suit.

You can fix this, she reminded herself fiercely as she nervously smoothed her hand over her hair. It had taken ages to coax her wild mane into a tight bun and she felt as if the waves were threatening to break free.

As she tried to keep up with the man who was undoubtedly an assistant, she tried not to notice the imposing features of the stark and colorless corridor. She didn't know how this Sebastian Cruz had got Inez Key, but she knew it had to be a mistake. She couldn't imagine why someone with this amount of wealth would want a run-down island.

Ashley glanced at the assistant. She was tempted to ask about Sebastian Cruz, but she sensed the man wouldn't reveal much. She regretted not researching the man who owned Cruz Conglomerate. If the executive suite indicated anything, she suspected Sebastian Cruz was an older, formal gentleman who valued propriety and status.

Ashley tugged at the vintage white dress that had once belonged to her mother. She was glad she'd made the choice to wear it. It was outdated and restricting but she knew she looked sweet and demure.

Now, if only she could remember to speak like a lady. Ashley paused at the grand black doors to Mr. Cruz's office. Everything went into slow motion as she watched the assistant knock and open the door. *Just watch your mouth.* Ashley swiped the tip of her tongue along her dry lips. She knew more than anyone how one reckless word could ruin everything....

Ashley barely heard the assistant's introduction over the sound of her heart pounding in her ears. She sensed the magnitude of the room but controlled the impulse of looking around. She placed a polite smile on her lips, stretched out her hand and froze when she saw Sebastian Cruz.

"You!" she blurted out as she instinctively snatched her hand back. Standing before her was the one man she'd hoped she'd never meet again. *This* was Sebastian Cruz? The man had turned her world upside down a month ago, had torn down all of her defenses and introduced her to a world of pleasure and promise.

Ashley gasped for her next breath as her body went rigid, primed to flee. What was going on? This could not be Sebastian Cruz. It was Sebastian *Esteban*. The name was burned into her mind forever. A woman never forgot her first lover.

But this man didn't look anything like the mysterious guest who had arrived for a weekend getaway on Inez Key a month ago. The faded jeans and knowing smile were replaced with a severe suit and a stern mouth. Her gaze traveled from his short black hair to his large brown eyes and the hard thrust of his chin. He was attractive but forbidding. Menacing.

Sebastian's raw power was barely concealed underneath the tailored lines of his black suit. His lean and muscular build hinted that he was sleek, swift and that he moved with stealth. This man could fight hard and dirty.

He smiled and a sense of unease trickled down Ashley's spine. This time his smile didn't make her heart give a slow tumble. His sharp white teeth made her think of a cold-blooded animal tearing apart his quarry.

Feeling a little shaky, Ashley took a step back. Sebastian was stunning, but her memories had muted the brutal power and raw masculinity he possessed.

"Ashley," he said silkily and gestured at the chair in front of his desk. He didn't look surprised to see her. "Please sit down."

"What are you doing here?" she asked as conflicting

emotions swirled ferociously inside her. She felt dizzy. Vulnerable. She wanted to sit down and curl into a protective ball but she couldn't give the man any advantage. "I don't understand. He called you Mr. Cruz."

"That is my name," he said as he sat down behind his desk.

"Since when?" She winced when her voice rose. Ashley tried desperately to hold back. "You introduced yourself to me as Sebastian Esteban."

"That is part of my name. Esteban is my mother's family name." His dark eyes were intent as he watched her closely. As if that name should mean something to her. "I am Sebastian Esteban Cruz."

That was his excuse? She stared at him, waiting for more. Instead, he sat in his chair that was as big as a throne and watched her with an air of impatience. He wasn't going to apologize for anything.

"Why did you lie to me? Is that part of your routine?" A woman only had to look at Sebastian Cruz and know he was a heartbreaker. She thought she could remain unscathed by limiting their encounter to a one-night stand. She had been wrong.

But she hadn't been thinking during that sensual weekend, she thought as regret pricked at her. Instead, she had followed a primal call and fallen into Sebastian's bed.

She had known better. Expected more from herself. After being raised by a philandering father, Ashley had recognized the signs of Sebastian's tried-and-true routine. She should have remembered the devastation that immediately followed the promise of paradise.

"When a wealthy person is interested in buying property, it's in their best interest not to reveal who they are," he said unrepentantly. "Otherwise the sale price goes up."

"Inez Key wasn't for sale," she said hoarsely as the anger whipped through her. Now she understood why he'd chosen to visit her island. He had intended to steal her family home from the beginning!

"So you kept saying." He gave a dismissive shrug. "I had approached you through several of my representatives, but I kept getting the same answer. The offered price was extremely generous. I made a personal visit in the hopes that I could convince you to sell."

She had thought it was strange that a man like Sebastian had arrived at her island for rest and relaxation. He was the kind of man who thrived on challenges and conquering uncharted territory. "Instead, you stole it from me," she whispered as her stomach churned. "This is all making sense."

"I didn't steal it," he corrected her. "You missed the deadline to repay the loan. Inez Key is mine."

Ashley didn't like the triumph she heard in his voice. She clenched her purse tighter as she choked back the fury. "That loan is none of your business! It was a private agreement between Raymond Casillas and me."

"And I bought the loan from Casillas. You shouldn't have put up your island as collateral." He mockingly clucked his tongue and shook his head at her poor judgment.

"It not like I had a lot of choices," she pointed out fiercely. How dare this man question her decision? Her father's finances had been a shambles when he died. Sebastian had no idea what she'd had to do, what she'd had to sacrifice, to keep Inez Key. "It was the only thing I have of value."

He tilted his head and captured her gaze. "Was it?" he asked softly.

Ashley stiffened as she sensed the danger lurking beneath that question. How much did this man know? She needed to take control of this meeting. Her legs shook and she felt jittery, but she forced herself to remain standing. "Inez Key suffered a lot of damage during the hurricane, and the insurance wouldn't pay for all of it."

He shrugged. "I don't care how you got into debt."

She wanted to claw at his bored expression. Ashley curled her fingers into her palms as she felt her temper flare dangerously. "I didn't make an agreement with you," she said roughly. "I had a payment plan with Raymond."

"Which you couldn't pay," he said. "You took a gamble and you lost."

Ashley gritted her teeth. It was true and she couldn't deny it. She had taken many risks when she'd accepted the loan. She'd had difficulty finding the money to repay, but she couldn't let it end here. She had to get Inez Key back.

"Raymond understood why I was having trouble making the payments," she said, her voice shaking as emotions ran wild inside her. "He was giving me more time since he had been best friends with my father."

"I'm sure he was the epitome of understanding and compassion. But it was smart of you to keep it out of the banking system." He wagged his finger at her. "I would have found out about it earlier."

Did he think this was funny? That this was a game? Her future was at stake here. "And then you wouldn't have had to sleep with me to get that kind of information," she retorted.

Sebastian's gaze slowly traveled down her tense body, resting briefly on her gentle curves. "That isn't why I took you to bed."

Her skin burned. She couldn't stop the fragmented memories flooding her mind. She remembered his hot masculine scent and the taste of his golden skin. Her dress felt tight as she recalled the sharp hiss between his teeth and the bite of pain when his strong fingers had tangled in her hair.

Ashley abruptly looked away. She had a tendency to remember that night at the most inconvenient moments. Her heart was pounding against her chest and her body was flushed. "You didn't have seduction in mind the moment you stepped on Inez Key," she mumbled. "I find that highly unlikely."

"I didn't know that you would indulge in pillow talk after sex," he drawled as he leaned back in his chair and steepled his long fingers together. "I certainly didn't expect you to reveal your agreement with Casillas. That was a bonus and it was impossible for me not to use that information for my benefit."

Ashley stared at Sebastian as her chest twisted painfully. How could he be so callous about that intimate moment? Didn't he realize that she never confided in anyone? But she had felt close and safe enough to tell him her worries. She had been interested in his opinion and valued his advice. It was only in the light of day that she realized she had been lulled into a false sense of security.

She somehow knew that rare slip of the tongue would come back and haunt her. He had used that moment of weakness to his advantage. "I will not allow you to take this island from me!"

Sebastian was unmoved by her heated declaration. "It's too late."

"Why are you being so unreasonable?" Her voice echoed in her ears. She lowered her hands firmly against her sides and tried again. "Why can't you give me a second chance?"

He seemed genuinely surprised by her question. As if she was more naive than he had given her credit. "Why should I? Have you done anything that would suggest you deserve a second chance?"

She saw the way his eyes darkened. There was something about his choice of words. Suspicion slithered and coiled around her weary mind as she crossed her arms. "Is this because I kicked you out of bed the next morning?"

Ashley wanted to bite her tongue the moment she spoke without thinking. She knew she had to be careful with her words. She cringed as she heard his husky chuckle.

Sebastian's smile was a slash of white against his dark skin. "Don't flatter yourself."

She knew she had caught him off guard when she'd

refused his offer to continue the relationship. Sebastian would never know how much the idea had both delighted and scared her. If he had seen her resolve weaken, he would have gone in for the kill. Her answer came across cold and unfeeling and she knew the rejection had stung.

To think she had felt bad about it! She had spent hours reviewing that moment and wishing she had refused more gracefully. And more than once she wished she had the courage to have accepted his offer.

But she realized that even after one glorious night, she was in danger of becoming the kind of woman she hated. A sexual creature. A woman who was driven by her emotions and needs. She had pulled away to protect herself.

"I can't help but think this is all personal," she said, glaring at him.

He arched a dark eyebrow. "How is that possible when we had not met until I arrived on Inez Key?" he murmured.

Ashley felt as if she was missing something. She knew they'd never met. One would never forget the briefest encounter with Sebastian Cruz. "You lied to me about your name, you had a hidden agenda and you seduced me. I was right to follow my instincts and get rid of you."

"And I'm right to follow my instincts and remove you from the island immediately," Sebastian said, clicking his computer keyboard as if the discussion was over.

Immediately? Panic gripped her chest. Before she'd walked in here she'd had two weeks to leave the island.

She was making this worse. "Inez Key is all I have," she said in a rush. "Without it, I have no home, no money..."

He didn't glance away from the computer screen. "That is not my concern."

She marched over to his desk and braced her hands on the edge. She would demand his attention if she had to reach over and grab him by the throat. "How can you be so cruel?" she asked in a low growl.

He lifted his gaze and held hers. "Cruel? You don't know the meaning."

She leaned forward. "I can't lose Inez Key. That is my home and my livelihood."

"Livelihood?" He scoffed at the word. "You haven't worked a day in your life. You rent out your home to wealthy people for the occasional weekend."

She let that criticism slide. She may not have a traditional job, but that didn't mean she didn't work hard to hold on to everything that was dear to her. "They pay good money for privacy. You did. What makes you think others won't?"

He reached for his pen and uncapped it. "There aren't enough rich celebrities looking for privacy to pay back your loan."

"I haven't been doing it long enough," she insisted. She needed to buy a little time. "Raymond understood that."

Sebastian shook his head. "Raymond Casillas wanted you to dig a deeper hole. He knew you were never going to be able to pay back the loan. Why do you think he offered in the first place?"

Ashley straightened and took a step away from the desk. "I don't know," she muttered. She didn't want to talk about it. Her skin felt prickly as the nausea swept through her.

"He hoped you would pay back in another way. And I think you knew that. Which is why you had requested a contract. Under most circumstances, it would have been a smart move."

"A lot of good it did me," she said under her breath. That contract now put her right in the hands of the ruthless Sebastian Cruz.

"You didn't want there to be any misunderstanding. You would offer Inez Key as your collateral, not your body." Sebastian paused. "Or your virginity."

She flushed bright red and refused to meet his gaze. "You knew?" Ashley whispered. She had done everything to conceal her inexperience. Out of pride, out of protection. She couldn't allow Sebastian to know how much advantage he had in that moment. But how did he know? How did she give herself away?

He set down the pen. "You should have told me." His tone was almost soft. Kind.

Ashley took another step back. She felt exposed. She wished she could walk right out of the office, but her unfamiliar heels felt like shackles. "I had already told you too much. And how did you know that Raymond wanted…" She swallowed roughly as her voice trailed away.

"Casillas has a reputation for liking innocent girls," he said with distaste as he leaned back in his chair. "And once he found out that you and I had been together, he was no longer interested in helping you out."

She closed her eyes as mortification weighed heavily on her shoulders. Sebastian had discussed their private moment with Raymond? He was just like her womanizing father and his raucous drinking buddies. A wave of disappointment crashed through her. She had expected better of Sebastian. "You're disgusting," she whispered.

"I do what is necessary to win."

He was a worthy opponent. She didn't care if his indiscretion helped her escape Raymond. He was still a dangerous enemy and she needed to remember that. "This isn't over. I will see you in court," she declared as she headed for the door.

"Good luck with that," he called out after her. "You can't afford legal advice and any good lawyer will tell you that you don't have a case."

"Don't underestimate me." She tossed the warning over her shoulder.

"How badly do you want Inez Key?" he asked lazily as she grabbed the door handle.

She dipped her head as she considered the question. How could she explain? Inez Key was more than her home. It was the only thing left of her family yet it was also a constant and unwelcome reminder. It was her sanctuary but it was also her dungeon. She was both caretaker and captive. She was determined to live there until she exorcised her demons. "Probably as much as you did."

His chuckle sent a shiver down her spine. "You shouldn't have told me that."

She turned around and narrowed her eyes. He looked so calm and in control as he lounged in his chair and watched her with barely concealed amusement. "What do you want, Cruz?"

His smile sent a shiver down her spine. "You."

CHAPTER TWO

SEBASTIAN SAW ASHLEY flinch from his answer. He knew she wasn't surprised by his admission. He saw the flare of interest in her eyes and the flush in her cheeks before she tried to shield her reaction. She was trying to hold back her response, but her body was betraying her. She couldn't hide the hectic pulse beating at the base of her neck. Ashley still wanted him, but she wasn't going to admit it.

"You've made it very obvious," Ashley said in a withering tone.

"I'm not ashamed of it." He didn't consider his desire for Ashley a weakness. It was more of a problem, a distraction and a growing obsession. She, on the other hand, was ashamed by the attraction they shared. She acted as if it went against everything she believed in.

"I'm not for sale," she declared.

The corner of his mouth slanted up. "You said the same about Inez Key and look at how that worked out."

Her jaw clenched. "I'm serious, Cruz," she said in a growl.

If she'd been serious, she would have tossed back his

indecent proposal. Used a few choice words and punctuated her indignation with a slap. Instead, she held the door handle in a death grip. She was wavering. Horrified but enthralled. If he played this right he could have Ashley back in his bed for more than a night.

"I'm sure we can work out an arrangement," he said smoothly as the excitement burned inside him. He had ached for her for weeks and the sensation intensified now that he knew the wait was almost over.

"You are no better than Raymond," she said in a hiss.

Sebastian smirked. Her comment just proved how innocent and unworldly she really was. Hadn't she realized by now that he was much, much worse?

"On the contrary, Casillas had set a trap. I'm being extremely honest about what I want." And he wanted Ashley more than anything. It didn't make sense. She wasn't like the other women in his life. She was untamed and inexperienced. Trouble. An inconvenience.

He should cut her loose. After all, he was lying about what he was willing to offer in exchange. He wasn't letting her back on that island. He wasn't going to break a promise just so he could please this spoiled little princess. But he was intrigued to see what her price would be.

"Honest?" she asked, the word exploding from her pink lips. "How can you say that when you introduced yourself under a different name with the intent of seducing the island from me?"

He rose from his seat and approached her. This time she was too angry to be cautious. She didn't catch the scent of danger. Her brown eyes glittered and she thrust out her chin.

Sebastian wondered why she attempted to hide behind the shapeless white dress. Her beauty was too bold, her personality too brash, to be restrained. His palms itched to pull her hair free and watch it tumble past her shoulders. He wanted to smear the pale makeup from her face and reveal the island girl he knew.

"You're the one who isn't being honest," Sebastian said as he stood before her, noticing how her chest rose and fell with agitation. "You knew what Casillas was really after and you didn't disabuse him of that idea because you needed the money."

"I tried the banks but—"

"Casillas makes your skin crawl. Don't you think he knew that? Did you realize that made you even more desirable to him?" Sebastian asked. "You tried to play the game and got in too deep."

Ashley raised an eyebrow. "Did *you* consider that I fell into bed with you because I wanted to get rid of my virginity? That I needed to so I could escape Raymond?"

Sebastian jerked his head back. He had *not* considered that. The possibility ate away at him like acid. He was not going to be used by a pampered princess.

Sebastian gripped her chin with his fingers and held her still. He felt the fight beneath her smooth, silky skin. "Did you?" he asked in a low, angry tone that would send his employees scurrying for safety.

Her eyes gleamed with reckless defiance. "Not so sure anymore, are you?"

He watched her closely as the unfamiliar emotions squeezed his chest. With her natural beauty and independent spirit, Ashley Jones could have had any man. He didn't know why she'd waited for her first sexual experience, but if she needed to get rid of her virginity, she would have picked an uncomplicated man whom she could control.

He stroked the pad of his thumb against her chin as he held his fiery emotions in check. "I think you slept with me because you couldn't help it," he said in a husky voice. She wanted him even though it meant yielding. Surrendering. "Casillas had nothing to do with it. You forgot all about him when you were with me."

She tried to slap his hand away. "Dream on."

He couldn't help but dream about Ashley and the night they had shared. He remembered every touch and kiss. Every gasp and moan. Ashley hadn't been faking it. "You want me so much that it scares you. And that's why you tried to push me away."

"I pushed you away because I didn't want to continue the fling," she argued. "You served your purpose and I was done. I have no interest in playboys."

He dropped his hand. *Served his purpose*? He knew she said that to hide the fact that he would always be a significant part in her love life, but she was going to pay for those words. "I'm not a playboy."

"Ha!" she said bitterly. "You tried to hide it when you were at Inez Key, but I grew up around womanizers. I know what kind of man you are. You would dangle a woman's home as bait, but we both know you will not give it back."

Sebastian bit back a smile. Ashley Jones thought very highly of herself. Did she really believe he would give up his treasure for another taste of what they'd shared? "I never said I'd give back your home."

She went still and frowned. "I don't understand. You asked me—"

"How much you wanted Inez Key," he clarified as he stepped closer, inhaling her citrusy scent. "The ownership of the island is not up for grabs. I keep what is mine and I will not let it slip through my fingers."

Ashley paled and she leaned against the door. "I've taken care of the island for years," she said in a whisper. "I have given it my love, sweat and tears. I've sacrificed everything for it."

"Why?" There was nothing remarkable about the island. It had no natural resources or historical significance. It was in an undesirable location and he had been the only prospective buyer interested in the island.

"Why?" she repeated dully. "It's my home."

Sebastian saw the guarded look in her eyes and knew she wasn't giving the whole answer. He also knew she wouldn't share it with him. She'd learned her lesson and didn't trust him anymore.

There had been moments during that weekend when Ashley had been unguarded and spontaneous. Now she was wary. He ignored the surprising pang of regret. It was time she learned how the real world worked and he had given her a very valuable lesson. "Your attachment to Inez Key doesn't make any sense."

"What about you?" she countered. "Not that many

people would go to such lengths to steal someone's home."

"I didn't steal it," he said with a hint of impatience. "You couldn't pay back the loan so the island is now mine."

"What are your plans for it?" she asked as if it hurt to think of the changes he was going to make. "I can't imagine you want to live there. I'm sure you have many homes. Inez Key is practically roughing it in comparison."

"Don't worry about it," he said as he reached for the door. It was time to force her into making a decision. "Inez Key is now my concern."

Ashley bit her bottom lip as she stared at the open door. The beat of silence stretched until her shoulders slumped. "Cruz."

"The name is Sebastian," he reminded her. She had said his name repeatedly during that one night. She'd said it with wonder and excitement. With longing and satisfaction. And tonight it would be the last thing she said before she fell asleep.

Sebastian. No, she wouldn't call him that. Sebastian had been a mysterious stranger on the island. His intensity and raw masculinity had unleashed a fierce sexual hunger that she hadn't known was in her. She would never be the same again.

This arrogant man was calculating and intimidating. He was breathtaking and she couldn't take her eyes off him. But he was not the fantasy lover she remembered.

Maybe that was the problem. Had she built up that

one magical night in her head? Everything had been so new. Almost foreign. She wouldn't feel overwhelmed from the wild sensations if she had sex with him again. Yet the memory of sharing a bed with Sebastian still made her weak in the knees.

"If you have no intention of giving me back my home," she asked carefully as her heart pounded against her ribs, "what are you offering?"

"You'll be the caretaker and stay in the cottage behind the main house."

She held back the flash of anger. She had been the mistress of the house. She had free rein of the island. Now he was offering the role as caretaker as if it was a gift? "Not good enough."

He placed his finger against her lips. "Careful, *mi vida*," he said softly as his eyes glittered with warning. "I don't have to let you on the island at all. I don't have to let anyone who is living there stay."

She gasped at his thinly veiled threat. "*No*. This has nothing to do with the other families on the island. They've been there for generations."

"You are going to champion the others?" he mocked. "How adorable."

She thought of the five families that lived on the small island. They had been there for her during her darkest moments. Since then, she had provided for them and protected them. She wasn't going to let them down. "Don't interfere with their lives," she said. "This is between you and me."

"Yes, it is," he drawled as he closed the door. Sebastian rested his hand above her head. He was too close. She felt trapped. Cornered.

It was a struggle to remain still and meet his gaze. "What do you want from me?"

"Two weeks in my bed."

Her skin went hot and her mouth dropped open. "I wouldn't stay in your bed for two more minutes, let alone—"

"Make it three," he said coldly.

Her eyes widened. "You bastard." She bit out the words.

"And now it's four," he said with no emotion. "Do you want to make it five weeks?"

A month with Sebastian? The wall she had painstakingly built around herself had shattered after one night with him. What would happen to her after four weeks in his bed?

Now if only she could silence the dark excitement building inside her, threatening to break free. She didn't like this side of her. She was not going to let this sexual hunger govern her thoughts and decisions. She was nothing like her parents.

"Ashley, one month won't be enough for you," he promised.

She pressed her lips together as she struggled to remain silent. She shouldn't have allowed him to rattle her. Her angry words always had consequences.

"It may not even last that long," he said. "I have a short attention span when it comes to women, but you'll beg me to stay."

That was what she was afraid of. She prided herself

on not being a sexual woman, until she met Sebastian Cruz. One look at him and the dormant sensations had sprung violently to life. Her response to his touch had frightened her. She hadn't recognized herself. This man had wielded a power over her like no other.

She was going to break this spell he'd woven. She'd figure out how he lowered her defenses so easily, and kill the craving she had for Sebastian Cruz. And when this month was over, she would never let a man have this kind of hold on her again.

"I want to make sure I understand this," she said shakily. "I will have a home on the island if I share a bed with you for a month?"

"Correct," he said as his eyes held a devilish gleam.

There had to be a catch. Why would he kick her out of the main house only to give her a smaller one on the island? It was convenient for him to have a caretaker who already knew Inez Key, but did he think this arrangement would continue for as long as he wished? "How do I know that you won't fire me?"

"You'll have a contract just like my other employees," he murmured as his attention focused on her mouth.

Her lips stung with awareness. They felt fuller. Softer. She tried not to nervously lick them. "How long do I have before I give you my decision?"

He moved closer, his mouth above hers. She felt his warm breath waft over her skin. "You have to give it to me now."

Alarm jolted through her veins. "Now? That's not

fair!" What was she saying? Sebastian didn't play fair. He played to win.

"Take it or leave it," he said.

She wanted to look away. Find another option. As much as she wanted to stay on Inez Key, she didn't think she was strong enough to fight the desire she had for Sebastian. But she couldn't walk away from this. "I'll take it," she whispered.

Sebastian captured her mouth with his. His kiss was bold, rough and possessive. She wanted to resist. Was determined to give no response. Yet she parted her lips and leaned into him as he deepened the kiss. Their tongues parried as he pulled her closer. She tasted his lust and it thrilled her. She yielded as he conquered her mouth.

Ashley jerked away. *What was wrong with her?* Her heart was racing and she fought the urge to place her fingers on her tingling lips. She couldn't look at Sebastian. She was confused. Aroused. Her emotions had been ambushed.

How could she have responded so eagerly? For him? Sebastian Cruz represented everything she despised in a man. "I need to leave," she said as she clumsily reached for the door handle. "I have a few things I need to deal with back home."

"You're not going home." Sebastian wrapped his hand around her wrist and pulled her hand away from the door. "You will return to Inez Key on my terms."

She stared at him as his calmly delivered words filtered into her jumbled mind. He wasn't allowing her to go home? How dare he? But then, it wasn't her home anymore. Technically, it was his. "I said I would share a bed with you. There was nothing—"

"You are now my mistress," he said as he raised her hand and pressed his lips against the skittering pulse on her wrist. "You live where I live. Sleep where I sleep."

Mistress? Her knees threatened to give out. She hated that word. Her dad had kept many mistresses. Vulgar women who didn't care who they hurt as long as they got the attention they felt they deserved. "I didn't agree to that."

"I didn't say that I would share my nights with you," he reminded her. "I am sharing a bed. That could happen at any time of day. Or all day."

All day. The wicked excitement pulled low in her belly. No, this was bad. This was really bad. What had she gotten herself into?

"Backing out already?" he said in a purr.

This was her chance. She could extract herself from this agreement and run back to her safe little world. But that world no longer existed. He owned it. Now she had to fight for a little piece of it. Ashley swallowed roughly. "No."

"Good." Sebastian's satisfaction vibrated in his deep voice as he pulled the door open and led her out of his office.

"Where are we going?" she asked, stumbling in her heels as she tried to keep up with him.

"To get you out of that dress."

She went rigid. He wanted to seal the deal *now?* She wasn't ready. Her mind froze yet her nipples tightened in anticipation as her legs went limp.

"I'm calling a stylist," Sebastian announced. "The dress you're wearing hides your body and ages you about two decades."

She didn't care. She didn't like dressing up or bringing attention to her body. Her clothes were meant to fade into the background. "Why do I need another dress?"

"I have an event I must attend and you are coming with me," he said as they reached his private elevator.

An event? No doubt it was glamorous and luxurious. There would be the Miami elite attending. Many of them would be the friends and former lovers of her parents. It was going to be a nightmare. "I don't want to go."

"You don't know much about being a mistress, do you?" he asked as he wrapped his arm around her waist and dragged her against him. "You really don't have a say in the matter."

Ashley was very aware of his hand spanning the small of her back. She felt delicate, almost fragile, next to him. She didn't like it. "Are you aware that there's a difference between mistress and sex slave?"

"Try not to put ideas into my head," he murmured.

The last thing she wanted was to be seen in public on the arm of the most unapologetic playboy. After years of shielding herself from the tabloids that had been fascinated with her parents' escapades, she didn't want the world to see how far she had fallen.

No one would be surprised, though. She was, after all, the daughter of Linda Valdez and Donald Jones. "I thought men hid their mistresses," she complained under her breath, "not showed them off."

"You have a lot to learn, Ashley," he said as his hold tightened on her waist. "I'm looking forward to teaching you everything."

CHAPTER THREE

HOW HAD SHE got to this point? Ashley stared at her reflection in the full-length mirror. Sebastian had brought in a stylist and hairdresser to his penthouse apartment at the top of his office building and they had spent the past few hours getting her ready for the night. Most women would have found it fun and relaxing. She thought it had been pure torture.

Her eyes were wide and her hands were clenched at her sides. The sumptuous walk-in closet faded in the background as she focused on her wild mane of hair. Her gaze traveled from her red lips to her stiletto heels. There was something familiar about the look.

Was this how all of Sebastian's women dressed? She couldn't live up to this sexual promise. This outfit, this look, was for a woman whose only goal was to please a man. Who placed her worth on whom she could attract and how long she could keep the man interested. She had seen plenty of women like that while she was growing up.

Ashley frowned and studied the orange dress a little closer. Why would Sebastian want a woman who didn't make any demands? He didn't seem to be the type who would surround himself with vapid women who didn't challenge his intellect. But then, she didn't know much about his love life.

Love? She snorted at the word. Sex, she mentally corrected herself. His sex life. If she asked him, would he remember all his lovers or were his women indistinguishable, one from the other?

The possibility pricked sharply at her. She didn't want to be grouped with those women. Nameless and forgettable. She couldn't go out looking like this. Like one of his mistresses. The dress wasn't as revealing as she'd feared, but the daring attitude carried more than a promise of sex. It suggested her status and her price.

She abruptly turned her head and a memory collided with the movement she saw in the mirror. She froze. *No, no, no!* Slowly looking back, Ashley stared at her reflection with a mix of panic and horror. Big hair. Little dress. Bold color.

For a moment, she resembled her mother.

Linda Valdez had always worn bright and daring colors. She had wanted Donald Jones to notice her whether she was watching his tennis match from the players' box or whether she was in a room filled with nubile women. When that didn't work, Linda's dresses started to get shorter and more revealing. She had been afraid to change her hairstyle in case it displeased Donald.

Everything her mother had done was to keep Donald's interest. If his eyes strayed on to another woman, Linda would become desperate for his attention. Ashley knew her father never cared about her mother's interests or opinions; his only concern was that Linda was beautiful, sexually available to him, and that everyone knew it. He would dress Linda in cheap and tasteless clothes and publicly discuss their relationship in the crudest language.

Ashley squeezed her eyes shut as she remembered one dress her mother had refused to wear. The bright red dress had been unforgiving. The corset bodice had painfully thrust Linda's breasts out while the tight skirt had puckered and stretched around her bottom.

Her mother had been extraordinarily beautiful, but that unflattering outfit had exaggerated her curves and made her appear almost cartoonish. Yet what Ashley remembered most was, despite the epic argument about the dress, her mother had reluctantly worn it. That dress represented the inequality in her parents' relationship. Ashley remembered clearly how Linda had hunched her shoulders and bent her head in shame when she wore that dress, defeated and humiliated.

Ashley's nails bit into her palms and she choked back the panic. She fought the urge to kick off the delicate heels and rip off the dress. She wanted to get them off before they tainted her.

It was too late. The clothes weren't the problem. Ashley flattened her hand on the mirror and bent her head as she exhaled shakily. For years she had been determined not to follow in her mother's footsteps. She didn't dress up for a man or try to gain his attention. She didn't barter with her looks. And yet, here she was, a rich man's plaything.

The only difference was that her mother had worked

hard to gain Donald Jones's attention. It had taken strategy to become his mistress. She had tried to bump up her status to become a trophy wife with an "unplanned" pregnancy. Unfortunately, Linda Valdez had not been Donald's favorite trophy.

"You are nothing like Mom," Ashley whispered to herself. She made sure of it. Once she thought her mother had been as perfect as a fairy-tale princess and she wanted to be like her. But as Linda got older, and Donald refused to marry her or give her his name, she became more insecure. She felt her beauty fading and knew she was losing the battle with her younger competitors.

Linda Valdez had been beautiful but fragile. Jealous and tempestuous. Ashley had seen the dark side of love and passion even before her mother had killed Donald before turning the gun on herself.

Ashley had been eighteen when that happened. Before that fateful moment she had been wary of men and kept her distance. As she struggled with the aftermath and scandal of the murder-suicide, she knew she would never allow love or sex to influence her life. Ashley had suppressed her passionate nature and hid on Inez Key. She didn't mind being celibate. She had believed sex wasn't worth the tears and heartache.

There were times when the isolation was almost too much to bear. But it was better than what she had witnessed in her parents' relationship. She was ready to spend her life that way until Sebastian showed up on her island.

She had relaxed her guard under his charm and attention. One night with him and her quiet, contained life had spun wildly out of control. Even now, a month later, she found it difficult to hold back. She was too aware of him. Too needy for his touch.

Sebastian had proven her deepest fear. Ashley knew that she was very much her mother's daughter. She was stronger and more disciplined, but she had been wild in Sebastian's arms. The desire had been primal. Almost uncontrollable. She hadn't been the same since. She didn't want to feel the heights of passion because she knew the crash and burn was inevitable. If she wasn't careful, she would succumb to the same torment as her mother.

Sebastian glanced at his watch and strode to the door leading to the walk-in closet. He was not used to waiting for a woman. They followed his schedule and didn't cause any inconvenience. Ashley needed to learn that she was no different. He would not give her any special treatment. "Ashley, I'm not a patient man. It's time to leave."

As much as he would like to stay in and reacquaint himself with Ashley's curves, this was one party he couldn't miss. Wouldn't. The opening of his newest club would bring in hundreds of thousands for charity. His old neighborhood needed that money. And yet, even now, he was tempted to strip off his gray suit, knock down the door and reclaim Ashley. He went hard as he imagined sinking into her welcoming body.

"Ashley?" he snapped.

"Have fun without me," she said through the door.

Sebastian closed his eyes and inhaled sharply. He should have known that she would pout and sulk. Heiresses. It didn't matter if they lived in stilettos or sandals. Each of them knew how to throw a tantrum.

"You're coming with me," he said in a low voice. "That's the agreement."

"Actually, I didn't agree to it," she said, her voice loud and clear. "I said I'd share your bed. I didn't say anything about dressing up like a whore and being put on display to stroke your ego."

Whore? Sebastian shook his head. The dress and shoes were bought at one of the most exclusive boutiques in South Beach. He had paid the hairstylist and makeup artist an exorbitant fee to give Ashley a natural look.

Even if Ashley rolled out of bed and only wore a wrinkled sheet, she couldn't look like a whore. There was something in the way she carried herself. She acted like a queen. Like she was too good for the rest of the world. Too good for him.

"Fine," Sebastian said as he walked away from the door. He could find another woman in a matter of minutes. Someone who was so grateful to be on his arm that she wouldn't challenge him every step of the way. "You don't want Inez Key that much. Understandable. It really isn't much of an island."

"Wait," she called out.

Sebastian hesitated. He didn't wait for anyone. That was one benefit he discovered after making his first million. The powerful people who used to ignore and instantly dismiss him would now wait endlessly for a minute of his time. Why should he treat Ashley any differently?

And yet he was compelled to turn around. Because he wanted Ashley. No other woman would do. She had already invaded his dreams and captured his imagination. When Ashley wrenched the door open and stood defiantly in the threshold, his breath caught in his throat.

Her long brown hair fell past her shoulders in thick waves. He bunched his hands as he remembered how soft and heavy it felt. His gaze drifted down to her face. Only the scowl marred her exquisite beauty.

He couldn't stop staring. The thin leather dress was perfect for Ashley. The casual design made him think of the oversize T-shirts she favored, yet the burnt-orange color reminded him of the sunset they'd shared on Inez Key.

"Perfect," he said gruffly.

She skimmed her hands uncertainly against the metallic embellishments that gave the simple dress an edge. "Did you choose this?"

Sebastian shook his head. "I told the stylist what I expected." He'd wanted something that had symbolized the weekend they'd shared in Inez Key. He didn't know that the dress would cling to her curves and accentuate her sun-kissed skin. His gaze gravitated to her long, toned legs. He remembered how they felt wrapped tightly around his waist. Sebastian swallowed roughly as his mouth felt dry.

"It's too short." She tugged at the hem that barely skimmed the top of her thighs. "Too revealing. Too—"

"Sexy as hell," he said in a growl.

Ashley's breath lodged painfully in her lungs as she watched Sebastian advance. She took a step back and bumped against the door frame. The man moved quietly, like a jungle cat ready to pounce, and she stood before him like helpless prey. Her heart was already beating hard when she saw him. Now it wanted to explode out of her chest.

Ashley wasn't sure how she was going to get out of this situation. She wasn't sure if she *wanted* to. She liked how he looked at her. Liked this tension that coiled around them, excluding everything else. She felt beautiful, powerful and vibrantly alive. Only Sebastian made her feel this way.

But how many other women had felt like this with Sebastian? Her pulse skipped hard as the question bloomed in her mind. Just as he was about to reach her, Ashley held up her hand to stop him. She hoped he didn't see how her fingers trembled. "Not so fast."

"Don't worry, *mi vida*," he said, his voice husky and seductive. "It will be slow and steady."

"That's not what I meant." She felt the heat flood her face as she imagined Sebastian exploring her body, taking his time while she begged for completion. Begged for more. "First, some ground rules."

He raised an eyebrow. "You can't be serious."

Were mistresses not allowed to negotiate? She found that hard to believe. What they had was a business deal. "Do not tell anyone about this arrangement," Ashley demanded as she crossed her arms, forming a barrier. She knew how men bragged. She remembered hearing her father discuss his conquests to any man who'd listen. Each story got bolder and raunchier as the men tried to one-up each other. "This is a private matter."

Sebastian watched her carefully. She couldn't tell if he was offended by her request or if he didn't know why it was worth mentioning. "I don't discuss my private life," he confided in a low voice. "And I won't let anyone talk about you."

Ashley blinked. She wasn't expecting that answer or the sincerity in his dark eyes. Sebastian Cruz was a good liar. He knew what she wanted to hear. If she didn't know that he would say or do anything to get his way, she'd almost believe him.

"Anything else?" he drawled as he moved closer, towering over her.

Ashley felt the pulse fluttering at the base of her throat. His scent, his heat, excited her. But she had one demand that wasn't negotiable. If he denied her this, she would walk out immediately. "You will have to use protection."

He reached out and brushed his knuckle along the line of her jaw. She shivered with anticipation at the gentle touch. "I always do."

"Always?" she taunted. Womanizers didn't think much about the future. They focused on instant gratification. It was the women who had to protect themselves and deal with the consequences alone.

"Always," he repeated as his fingertips grazed her throat and shoulder. "I take care of my lovers."

Sure. That had to be the real reason. It had nothing

to do with giving up control. "And you wouldn't want a gold digger to get pregnant and live off your money."

Sebastian's eyes flashed with agreement. "Any more rules?"

Ashley nervously licked her lips with the tip of her tongue. She wanted to create a list of rules, but her mind was blank. "No…"

"Good." Sebastian wrapped his fingers around her wrists. His hold was firm and commanding. She gasped when he held her hands high above her head. He leaned into her and Ashley hated how her body yielded to him. Her soft breasts were thrust against his hard chest and her pelvis cradled his erection. Sebastian surrounded her.

His powerful thigh wedged between her shaky legs. "Now, for my ground rules."

Ashley swallowed hard. She should have expected he would have rules of his own. She was ready to refuse them all, but she was secretly intrigued. She wanted to know what he demanded from a woman.

"First," he said as he pressed his mouth against her cheekbone, "you are available to me twenty-four hours a day."

"You don't ask for much, do you?" she asked sarcastically as the excitement clawed up her chest.

"And you have no claim on me," Sebastian said as he kissed his way down the curve of her throat. She couldn't refrain from arching her neck and encouraging more. "When I want you, I will call for you."

Now, *that* she had expected from Sebastian. He would decide when and where. Any affair would meet his schedule and the woman would have to learn how to adapt.

"Maybe you don't understand," Ashley said, closing her eyes as his hot breath warmed her skin. "I'm not the kind of woman who sits around and waits."

"You will be with me." His mouth hovered against her wildly beating pulse point at the base of her throat. He circled it with the tip of his tongue, silently showing that he knew how he made her feel. "It will be worth the wait."

She took in a ragged gulp of air. "You talk big—"

He cupped her cheeks with his large hands and kissed her. She was ready to counterattack, but he disarmed her immediately. His lips were demanding as he drew her tongue inside his mouth. She was out of control, mindlessly following his lead as the desire bled inside her.

When he withdrew, Ashley saw the stain of lipstick on his firm mouth and the way his eyes glittered knowingly. "I know how much you want this. Want *me*."

She was embarrassed at her response. Humiliated that he stopped the kiss. She felt scorched. Boneless. Ashley remembered feeling like this. Sebastian knew exactly how to touch her. She wanted more and yet she wanted it to stop. She needed to take control but at the same time she wanted to throw caution to the wind and see where she landed.

"Anything else?" she asked hoarsely.

His hand grazed her breast and he drew lazy circles around her hard nipple with his fingertip. "I expect total obedience from my women."

She flinched. She wasn't sure which part of his rule bothered her. The fact that she was lumped into a group known as "his women"? Or the obedience part? She wasn't going to let this man—or any man—master her. She wasn't a plaything. "Following the rules has never been my strength," she said.

"You'll learn. All you need is the right motivation." Sebastian smiled as he trailed his fingertips down her rib cage. His touch was as light as a feather and yet her skin tingled with awareness.

"I can't promise you obedience," she said between pants. "In fact, I won't."

Her words made him smile. "I can make you promise anything."

She wanted to give a bitter laugh. Slap his hand away. Tell him he was only fooling himself. But deep down she knew Sebastian could have that power, and she didn't want to test it. "You are very sure of yourself."

He didn't reply. Instead, he splayed his hand between her thighs. Sebastian's eyes held an unholy gleam when he realized she wore nothing underneath her dress. He murmured his approval in Spanish as he began to stroke the folds of her sex.

Ashley immediately clamped her legs together but it was too late. Sebastian wasn't going to let that deter him. He gave a husky laugh of triumph as she responded. She looked away as the liquid heat flooded her body.

"Look at me," he said roughly.

Ashley shook her head. She couldn't look in his eyes and show him how she felt. How he made her feel. From his expert touch, it was obvious that he already knew. The humiliation burned and yet she bucked against his hand.

She wouldn't look at him. And yet she couldn't tell him to stop. She didn't want to push him away. She felt the white heat whipping through her, catching fire. Her fear was that he would stop unless she followed his command.

Sebastian growled. "Look at me," he repeated.

She squeezed her eyes shut and shook her head again. A guttural moan escaped from deep in her chest as Sebastian dipped his finger into her clenching core. Ashley felt his hot gaze. She knew he saw everything. He knew what she wanted. What if he held back? Oh, God…what if he didn't stop until she revealed her deepest need and darkest fantasy?

"Ashley." His voice was raw and urgent.

She was compelled to open her eyes. Ashley met his intense gaze just as the climax rippled through her. Her mouth sagged open and her muscles locked as she chased the pleasure. Sebastian saw everything and she couldn't hide. How was he going to use this to his advantage?

He slowly, almost reluctantly, withdrew from her. Ashley ached from the loss and she sagged against the wall. Her body trembled. She wanted to hold on to him, but she wouldn't dare.

"Total obedience," he reminded her quietly.

His words were like a slap. Was this a display of his dominance? Did he want to prove that he could make her do whatever he wished?

Ashley pushed away from him and smoothed her dress with clumsy hands. She would not submit to his will. “No, Cruz,” she said as she fought to stand straight on wobbly legs. “That will never happen.”

“Haven’t you learned by now, Ashley?” he asked as the challenge glinted in his eyes. “I always get what I want.”

CHAPTER FOUR

As Ashley stood in the VIP section of Sebastian's dance club, she couldn't help but feel as if she had fallen into the looking glass. The flashing lights were hypnotic and the dancers moved to the music as if they were in a trance. She had never seen a place like this before. It was fantastical. Otherworldly and a little frightening.

And this was just part of Sebastian's kingdom. The moment they entered, she had felt the ripple of interest and awe. At first she had been uncomfortable being in the spotlight, but as Sebastian spoke to members of the Miami elite, she realized she was invisible to the guests. They lobbied for Sebastian's attention and saw no need to speak to her. She was arm candy. An expensive accessory.

She should feel grateful that no one noticed or cared about her. She recognized a few of her parents' friends, but they didn't seem to remember her. She felt small and powerless in the cavernous club. More than once, Ashley wondered how much of the club reflected Sebastian's personality. It was darkly sensual and seductive. The music pulsated from the floor and she tried to ignore the carnal rhythm, but her heartbeat matched the tempo.

The wild laughter punctuating the air made her flinch. She didn't want to be here, around these people who had enjoyed her parents' downfall. Ashley wished she was back on Inez Key. It was quiet and relaxing. Calm and predictable. That was where she belonged. It had been *her* kingdom.

But there had been a time when she'd needed to get away from her island. Sebastian must have known that. She remembered the unexpected fun she'd had with Sebastian on that weekend when he let her take his boat out for a spin.

The offer had been too tantalizing to resist. She loved being out on the water and had wanted to try his speedboat. At the time, she had thought her acceptance had nothing to do with the promise of having Sebastian's undivided attention.

Ashley had known the boat would slice through the choppy waves and reach incredible speed. She had wanted to go on a fast-and-hard ride, determined to forget Inez Key and her financial problems for a few hours.

She remembered Sebastian's warm smile as he had teased her, suggesting she was trying to tip him out of the boat. Perhaps she had been trying to test his courage. She had to find out if his restraint had just been a guise. Ashley had wanted to know how long it would take before he grabbed the wheel.

He never did. Sebastian had been lazily sprawled on the chair next to her, arms outstretched, his dark glasses perched on his bold nose. Sexual heat had bubbled underneath their banter, but she had enjoyed his companionship.

Sebastian had been relaxed and unconcerned while she made hairpin turns and the boat flew over the waves, but he had been alert. He had noticed every move she made, offering the occasional direction only when she hesitated.

Ashley had to wonder if any of that rapport had been real or part of the seduction. Had he done that to lower her guard or had he enjoyed those moments, too? Looking around this nightclub, she sensed the simple joy of a sunny afternoon would have been lost on him.

She glanced up, her heart lurching to a stop as she watched gorgeous couples dance with unbridled enthusiasm on the mezzanine. Their movements were bold and suggestive. Her skin flushed and she shifted uncomfortably. She was already painfully aware of Sebastian and primed for his touch. She didn't need anything else to encourage her imagination.

Her grip tightened on her small clutch purse and she fought the urge to retreat. The club was mysterious and spellbinding. Dangerous. Much like it's owner. If she lowered her guard, the music would pull her in. The atmosphere would seduce her into releasing her inhibitions. That could ruin her. Take her to a point of no return.

Ashley studied the DJ booth and the small VIP areas that circled the dance floor. She recognized a few movie stars and professional athletes lounging on the big white couches with other celebrities and models. All of the party girls were glamorous creatures with wild hair and generous curves.

"And how is your mother doing?"

Ashley turned sharply as she caught the question. A trio of beautiful women were standing in front of Sebastian. She didn't know which one asked the question. They all looked similar with their smooth hair, flawless makeup and colorful dresses that wrapped around them like skimpy bath towels.

"She's recuperating well," Sebastian replied before he smoothly changed the subject. Within moments he had the group of women giggling and fawning all over him.

Ashley wondered if she was the only one who noticed the way his features softened at the mention of his mother. Or the flash of worry in his eyes before he banked it. She wished she hadn't seen it. She didn't want to know anything about him. The less she knew about his private life, the better.

What they shared was a business agreement and she needed to keep an emotional distance. She was having a short-term sexual relationship with Sebastian and she wasn't required to love, respect or even *like* the man.

So what if he had been the most fascinating and exciting man when they first met? Sebastian had been playing a role. Or had he? She thought she had seen glimpses of the real Sebastian during the quieter moments on Inez Key. It was as if the island life had pulled away the harsh mask and revealed his romantic nature.

That was not his true character, she reminded herself fiercely as disappointment rested heavily in her chest.

She wasn't going to be like her mother, who clung to her benefactor's rare thoughtful gestures and created a fairy-tale love story out of it. There was nothing Sebastian could do to make her think he was anything other than a cold-hearted and ruthless womanizer.

"Sebastian!"

Ashley lifted her head when she heard a booming male voice over the music. She saw a large, muscular man approach Sebastian with his arms outstretched. The stranger was about the same age as Sebastian but was built like a giant. The curvy blonde woman at his side looked tiny in comparison.

"Omar," Sebastian greeted. Ashley was startled by Sebastian's wide smile and the way his face lit up before he embraced his friend.

She was more surprised that Sebastian *had* friends. Sebastian could be charming and a scintillating conversationalist, but for some reason, she assumed he was a loner. An outsider.

"And who is this?" Omar asked, gesturing at Ashley while Sebastian gave the other woman a kiss on the cheek.

Ashley felt a twinge of fear. Omar was obviously a good friend. Would Sebastian lie to spare her embarrassment? Why would he do that? Yes, he'd made her a promise, but his friend was going to be more important than a temporary mistress.

She didn't trust Sebastian. She had to get in front of this before he showed just how little power she had in this arrangement. Ashley thrust out her hand to Omar. "I'm Ashley."

Sebastian wrapped a proprietary arm around her waist as his friend shook her hand. "Omar and I grew up in the same neighborhood before he became a football star."

Ashley nodded as she tried to fit this new information in with what she knew about Sebastian. She didn't expect him to value friendships from his old world. She had seen a few self-made men who had discarded old friends while in pursuit of making strategic alliances. Sebastian wasn't as ruthless or driven as she thought.

"And this is my wife, Crystal," Omar introduced the blonde.

"It's a pleasure to meet you," Ashley said as she greeted Omar's wife. The woman was beautiful, but Ashley recognized the subtle signs of multiple cosmetic surgeries. Most of the women she knew while growing up had the same unlined forehead, puffy lips and enhanced breasts.

"I like your dress," Crystal said as the two men started speaking to each other in Spanish.

"Thank you," Ashley said as she pulled at the short hem. She was still uncomfortable in it, but it wasn't as revealing as Crystal's. Most of the women in the club wore dresses that were staying on their bodies with little more than double-sided tape and a prayer.

Crystal gave a cursory glance over her outfit as if she was adding up the price. "Who are you wearing?"

Who? Oh, right. She remembered this part of the social world that she used to belong to. It was all about getting the designer bag or dress that no one else had.

She had once been like that until her world came crashing down. "I forgot to ask about the designer."

Crystal shook her head as if she couldn't believe Ashley would forget such an important detail. "So how did you two meet?"

Ashley glanced at Sebastian, but he was involved in an animated conversation with his friend. She hadn't come up with a cover story but she knew she had to be very careful. It was best to keep it as close to the truth as possible. "I met him a month ago. We immediately hit it off."

"I'm surprised," Crystal said as she studied Ashley, as if she was cataloging all of her flaws and shortcomings. "You're not really his type."

"What is his type?" Ashley asked reluctantly, not entirely sure if she wanted the answer.

Crystal gave a laugh of disbelief. "You don't know?"

She shrugged. "I didn't know who Sebastian truly was until it was too late."

"How is that possible? He's in the news all the time. From the financial page to the gossip column. Have you been living under a rock?"

"More like a deserted island."

Crystal frowned as if she wasn't sure Ashley's comments was a joke or the truth. "Well, I would say Sebastian's women are more…"

"Blonde?" Ashley supplied wearily. "Curvaceous? Vacuous?"

"Accomplished," Crystal corrected her.

Ashley's muscles stiffened. That hurt. She wasn't proud of where she was in her life. She had fallen in status and wealth. Her world had become smaller and she was no match for Sebastian. But she had achieved more than she thought was possible. She had taken care of the families on Inez Key. She maintained her island home with nothing more than ingenuity and hard work. Her most important accomplishment had been becoming a woman who was nothing like her mother.

Ashley was proud that she hadn't broken under the heavy burden placed on her five years ago, but she wasn't going to share that. Not with Crystal or anyone at the nightclub. They would belittle it. Dismiss it. Sneer at her. She remembered this world. All the guests cared about was being noticed. They would never understand that her greatest achievement was creating a peaceful life hidden from the spotlight.

"Accomplished? You mean famous," Ashley corrected.

Crystal shrugged. "They are the best in their fields or famous for their philanthropy and humanitarian efforts. He's dated CEOs and pro athletes. Politicians and princesses."

"I guess he doesn't feel threatened by a woman's achievements," she said with a fixed smile. If this was true, what was he doing with her? She had struggled in school and dropped out of college in her first semester. She had no skills or special talents. No ambitions other than to build the strong and happy family life she'd never had.

"Don't get me wrong," Crystal continued, as if her words hadn't pierced Ashley's thin guard, "he's had his share of supermodels and movie stars. He's just not interested in a woman whose goal is to be a wife or a girlfriend."

What about a mistress? Not that she strived for that job. She had been blackmailed into bed because she had no power or influential friends. Ashley bit the tip of her tongue in case she blurted out her thoughts.

Crystal tilted her head. "I feel like I've seen you before."

Ashley stiffened. She remembered comments like that. It only took a few moments before they connected her with one of her father's scandals. "I haven't been in Miami for years."

"Have you been in the news lately? I have to admit, I'm a bit of a news junkie," Crystal said as she pressed her bejeweled hand over her impressive cleavage. "TV, newspapers, blogs, tabloids. I get my news anywhere and everywhere."

"No, I haven't done anything newsworthy."

"Crystal, they are playing our song," Omar said as he wrapped his large hand over his wife's wrist. "It's time to hit the dance floor."

Sebastian watched Ashley as her frown deepened. She hadn't spoken much. She had stood at his side, but he knew she wasn't paying attention to her surroundings.

Was she was thinking about tonight? How she would lose control in his arms? She had no idea that he also couldn't stop thinking about the magical night that lay ahead. Or that he would make sure she lost control before he did.

He didn't know how much longer his restraint would

last. Having her close to him, touching him, was a test. He was careful not to stroke her skin or allow his hand to linger on the curve of her hip. Once he started, he wouldn't stop.

He tightened his hold on her waist. "Smile, Ashley."

Ashley gave a start and then glared at him. "I am smiling."

"No, you're not." He dipped his head and pressed his mouth against her ear. She shivered with awareness and his body clenched in response. "But I know one way I can put a smile on your face."

She yanked her head back and bared her teeth. "I'm smiling, I'm smiling. See?"

"Can you look less bloodthirsty and more adoring?"

"Why? The only people who looked at me were Omar and Crystal." She tugged at her short hem again. "Don't get me wrong, Cruz. I'm grateful that I'm unrecognizable. I can only assume I look like all your other mistresses."

He'd never had a mistress, but she didn't need to know that. He didn't want her to get any ideas that she was different or special. He'd had many lovers, but he'd never had to pay for the exclusive rights of a woman.

"And how much longer do we have to stay here?" she asked.

"Eager for bed, *mi vida*?" He certainly was. He hadn't felt this desperate since he was a teenager. It was difficult to circulate among the crowd when he wanted to drag Ashley to his bedroom.

She clenched her jaw. "No, I'm tired of acting like I know what's going on. Your guests talk about people

I don't know and places I haven't been. I wasn't aware that you were raising money for a charity until you talked that socialite into giving double. Where is the money going?"

"To my old neighborhood," he said tersely. He briefly closed his eyes as he tried to banish the memory of graffiti-stained walls and the stench of rotted garbage.

She sighed. "Can you be a little more specific?"

"You wouldn't recognize the address. It's the ghetto," he said with a hint of defiance and anger. He should have had the idyllic childhood that Ashley had enjoyed. While her life had been luxurious and carefree, his days had been difficult and unsafe. He'd had to fend for himself and his family and there were many early days when he had failed.

He'd left the ghetto years ago, but he had honed his survival instincts in his old neighborhood. Stay alert, know how to fight and shut down any potential threat before it gained power. Those rules helped him in the streets and in building his empire.

Her eyelashes flickered. "You're right. I don't know where that is, but only because I don't get out much. And the money is for…?"

"The medical clinic," he said slowly as he watched her expression. She showed no pity or fear. No disdain about his background. Just polite interest. Considering her sheltered and privileged life, Sebastian wondered if she understood living in the ghetto was like a prison term.

He grabbed her hand, ignoring how it fit perfectly in his, and led her out of the VIP section. "Let's dance."

He couldn't wait anymore. He needed to feel her curves flush against his body.

Ashley froze and dug her heels in. "I don't dance."

Sebastian stopped and turned around. "You don't dance. You don't drink. You don't party." He didn't believe any of it. He knew many heiresses and socialites. They lived to be seen at the right places with the right people. "What do you do?"

Ashley shrugged and looked away. "Nothing that would interest you."

It shouldn't interest him. He didn't care what women did when they weren't with him. Sebastian didn't want to know about their jobs, hobbies or passions. Yet he was intensely curious about Ashley. "You don't date."

She looked at him cautiously from the corner of her eye. "I never said that."

She didn't have to. "I was your first," he reminded her. And for some reason that was important to him. Was it because she was his first virgin? He didn't like the possessive streak that heated his blood and made him want to keep her close.

"I've been busy," she declared as she tried to slip from his grasp.

"Busy doing what?" he asked as he pulled her closer. How did she fill her day? "You live in a tropical paradise. You don't have a job or obligations. Most people would kill for that kind of life."

"Is that what you think?" She abruptly stopped and pressed her lips together. "Okay, sure. My life is perfect. And that's why I will go to great lengths to keep it."

Sebastian narrowed his eyes as he watched Ashley's guarded expression. What was she hiding? He was about to go in for the kill when he felt a feminine hand on his sleeve.

"Sebastian?"

He recognized the cultured voice before he turned around and saw the cool blonde standing next to him. He dropped his hold on Ashley as he greeted his former flame with a kiss on the cheek. "Hello, Melanie," he said.

"And who is this?" she asked with false brightness.

Sebastian swallowed back a sigh. This always seemed to happen when an ex-lover met the current one. He found the territorial attitude tiresome. "Melanie, this is Ashley Jones. Ashley, this is Dr. Melanie Guerra. She works at the medical clinic."

"And I'm also your predecessor," Melanie said bitterly as she shook Ashley's hand. "I believe you stole him from me."

"Would you like him back?" Ashley asked hopefully.

Melanie was momentarily surprised before she gave a shrill of laughter. Sebastian wrapped his hand around Ashley's arm and shot her a warning look. He wasn't sure what Ashley was going to do next. It was a rare feeling.

"No, thanks," Melanie said as she gave Ashley a thorough look. "Our fling was very brief and he dumped me after he came back from some island off the Florida coast. I got a bouquet of flowers, a bracelet from Tiffany and no explanation. Now I understand why."

Ashley went rigid under Sebastian's grasp. To his surprise, Ashley didn't respond to Melanie's statement.

Her expression was blank, but he sensed her slow burn of anger.

"She's not really an upgrade, is she, Sebastian?" Melanie said. She smiled, knowing she had dropped a bomb, and strolled away with her head held high.

"I apologize for her, Ashley," he said roughly. "Melanie isn't known for her tact or manners."

"I'm sure that wasn't what drew you to her in the first place," Ashley replied, her eyes flashing with anger. "You were dating her when you slept with me. Are you with someone now?"

"I'm with you." He didn't want anyone else. No woman compared to her and he didn't know why.

"Is there anyone else?" she asked insistently as she tugged away from his grasp.

"What if there was?" he asked. She had no claim, no power over him, and he would remind her of that every moment of this agreement. "What would you do about it? What *could* you do about it?"

She thrust her chin out with pride. "I'd leave."

He scoffed at her declaration. "No, you wouldn't." She wouldn't walk away from him. She'd entered this agreement because she wanted to explore the pleasure they shared.

"Inez Key means everything to me, but—"

"It has nothing to do with the island," he said. He wasn't going to let her hide behind that reason. "You got a taste of what it's like between us and you crave it."

She crossed her arms and glared at him. "No, I don't."

"It's okay, *mi vida,*" he said in a confidential tone. "I crave it, too."

"Of course you do. You're insatiable," she argued. "It doesn't matter who you are sleeping with as long as you have a woman in your bed. You're like all men who are ruled by lust and—"

"I'm not an animal," he replied as the anger roughed his voice. "I don't sleep with every woman who flirts with me. I can control my baser instincts. You, I'm not so sure about."

She gasped and took a step back. He saw the surprise and guilt flicker in her dark brown eyes. "What are you talking about?" she asked, her eyes wide.

"You can't wait to go to bed with me," he said with a satisfied smile as the desire swirled inside him. When they finally got to be alone, he knew she was going to go wild. The anticipation kicked harder in his veins.

"I can't wait to get this agreement over with, if that's what you're talking about," she said. "And you didn't answer my question. Are you with another woman right now?"

Ashley was tenacious. "You have no right to ask me that question."

She tossed back her hair and raised an eyebrow. "Because I'm your mistress?"

"Exactly." He splayed his arms out with exasperation. "You really don't have an understanding on how this arrangement works."

"And you don't seem to understand how I function," she retorted. "If you're in a relationship with someone,

I'm going to leave. Play any mind games with me and you will regret it."

He knew she was bluffing, but her voice held a hardened edge. As if she was talking from a past experience. "You'll lose the island."

Ashley leaned forward. "And you won't get another night with me," she said with false sweetness. "Those cravings you have will just get stronger and there will be nothing you can do about it."

Their gazes clashed and held. It was time to teach Ashley a lesson. She suspected just how much he wanted her and was testing her power over him. He wasn't going to let her get away with it.

He heard a feminine squeal of delight next to him. "Sebastian!"

Sebastian reluctantly turned as a woman wrapped her arms around his shoulders and clung to him. He barely recognized the model who had flirted with him a few weeks ago and he couldn't remember her name. She was an exotic creature, but she didn't capture his imagination like Ashley.

"It's been forever since I've seen you," the model declared before she brazenly kissed him on the mouth.

Knowing that Ashley was watching, Sebastian didn't pull away. He wasn't going to allow Ashley to make any demands on him.

Ashley hunched her shoulders as the bile-green jealousy rolled through her. The conflicting emotions were ripping her in shreds. She wanted to pull the other woman away and yet she felt the need to hurt Sebastian the way he was hurting her.

She looked away, unable to see Sebastian in the arms of another woman. She hated this feeling. The ferocity scared her. She didn't know if she could contain it. Ashley jerkily turned away. She refused to live this way for even a moment. She wouldn't tolerate this, even if it meant losing her family home forever.

Ashley pushed her way through the dance floor. She was dragged in and then thrust from side to side as she bumped against dancers. She gritted her teeth and placed a shaky hand on her churning stomach. She had to get out of here.

Forcing herself not to look back, Ashley wasn't even going to think about where she could go next. She didn't have money for a taxi or a hotel room. It didn't matter. She just needed to get away.

She stepped out of the club and took a deep breath, inhaling the hot and humid air. A crowd of people was waiting to get into the club and the flashing lights from the sea of paparazzi cameras blinded her. She felt lightheaded as the emotions battled inside her. Her legs wobbled just as she felt Sebastian's hand wrap around her waist.

"Make me run after you again," he whispered against her ear, "and you will not like the consequences."

"That wasn't my plan," she said quietly. "And you will not like the consequences if you make me angry again."

"I believe the term is jealous," Sebastian said as he escorted her to his black limousine.

"I'm not jealous." Jealousy would mean that her emotions were involved. That it wasn't just sex between them. "I simply don't share."

"Neither do I," he warned.

"Where to, Mr. Cruz?" the chauffeur in the dark suit asked as he opened the door for them to enter the car.

"Home," Sebastian said.

Ashley shook her head. "I'm not getting in there with you." She sensed the chauffeur's surprise, but she didn't look at him. She knew it was a bold statement, when Sebastian could easily pick her up and toss her in the backseat. Considering the dark mood he was in, he might choose the trunk.

His hand flexed on her waist. "I'm not in the mood for a scene."

She felt the attention of the crowd and the flashing lights from the cameras were going fast and furious. She didn't want an audience, but she had to tell Sebastian exactly how she felt. "I told you that I don't play games," she said in a low voice, hoping no one could hear their conversation. "If you are going to spend the next month trying to make me jealous, we are going to end it here."

There was a long beat of tense silence before Sebastian spoke. "You're right. I shouldn't have done that and I'm not proud of it," he said begrudgingly. "I was trying to prove a point and it backfired."

Ashley didn't move or look at him. She knew this was as close as she was going to get to an apology but she needed more. He wasn't going to give it to her. It was best to end this now.

"It won't happen again," he said. "I promise."

She glanced up. She hadn't expected that from Sebastian. She stared into his eyes and saw the sincerity and regret. She didn't know if she should trust it. He could be lying. This could be a game to him. The man was a seducer. A womanizer.

But she wanted to believe him. And that's what scared her. She was willing to believe he would honor his promise when there was no proof that he would.

It was because she wanted to stay, she realized dazedly. Her body yearned for his touch and she knew she would regret it if she left. Sebastian had been correct; this agreement wasn't just about Inez Key. She wanted another chance to experience the exquisite and intense pleasure one more time.

Ashley gave a sharp nod and saw the sexual hunger flare in Sebastian's eyes. Excitement gripped her as she stepped into the limousine. She found it hard to breathe as her heart pounded in her ears. She was ready for whatever the night may bring.

But she would not surrender.

CHAPTER FIVE

ASHLEY SAT NEXT to Sebastian as the limousine slowly drove through the busy streets of Miami. The bright, colorful lights streamed through the dark windows. She stared at the tinted divider that separated them from the driver. She knew the chauffeur couldn't see or hear them. No one could. They were alone in a luxurious cocoon and the wait was agony.

The air crackled between them. The silence clawed at her. This was no longer lust. This was chemistry. Ashley knew Sebastian felt this dark magic between them.

She turned her head and greedily looked at Sebastian. She noticed every harsh angle in his face and the powerful lines of his gray suit. Her heart stopped for one painful moment when she saw his face tighten with desire.

"Ashley," Sebastian said huskily.

She rubbed her bare legs together and shivered when he said her name. It was a plea and a warning. He didn't want to wait any longer. Couldn't.

"Cruz," she said breathlessly. She blushed as she fought the overwhelming need to touch Sebastian and hold on to him. She took a sharp intake of breath and inhaled his clean, masculine scent. She felt the heat invade her body. She wanted to get closer and burrow her face into his skin.

"Call me Sebastian," he reminded her. He spoke softly, but she saw the glint in his eyes. He was the hunter and she was the prey. Ashley went very still, every instinct telling her he was about to pounce.

Instead, he reached for her hand. She felt a tremor in him as he raised her fingers to his mouth. A sense of power flooded her body. She was an average woman, young and with very little experience, but she could make the great Sebastian Cruz tremble.

"I want you right now." Sebastian brushed his mouth against her knuckles and her skin tingled from his touch. "But I know you're not ready. You need something more private before you lose control. Feel safe before you say exactly what you want."

He knew. He knew exactly how she felt. In his bed, she would go wild. It would be just the two of them. No interruption. No confined spaces. But here…in this limousine, on the crowded streets, she would be careful. She would be constantly aware of her surroundings.

Sebastian cupped her jaw with his hands. She felt surprisingly delicate under his large fingers. "You don't need to hold back with me."

"I'm not," she lied. She was cautious with everyone. She usually didn't act unless she knew the outcome. She didn't speak until she considered the consequences.

"I'll take care of you, *mi vida,*" he said in a low, clear voice.

Her heart gave a twist. She wanted to believe him. She wanted to believe that he cared more than this moment, more than the thrill of the hunt. That he cared about her. She would like to think he was the kind of man who viewed sex as something more than a sport.

But that wasn't a fairy tale she could afford to believe. "Do you tell that to all your women?" She tried to say it lightly, but she couldn't hide the cynical edge in her voice.

"I'm telling it to you," he said as he covered her mouth with his.

He kissed her and she immediately melted into him. She had dreamed about this moment every night since he had left Inez Key. She didn't realize how much she had yearned for his touch until now. But it wasn't enough. She needed more.

Sebastian's kiss was slow and tender. That wasn't what she wanted. She wanted to feel the heat and the passion from their first night. Ashley kissed Sebastian with abandon.

She poured everything she felt into the kiss and it was like touching a lit match to a firecracker. Something inside him broke free and Ashley tasted the wildness in his kiss. It excited her and she deepened the kiss, craving more.

"If you don't want this," he said roughly against her lips, "tell me now. This is your last chance to walk away."

Ashley was surprised that Sebastian was giving her an escape. Thanks to their agreement, he no longer had to seduce or romance her. She thought he would grab and take—and some part of her wished he would take the decision away from her. Then she couldn't blame herself for wanting this or enjoying his touch.

She wouldn't completely shatter here, in the back of a limo. No matter what he did, she wouldn't lose her inhibitions. Not when she felt as if they could get caught any moment.

Sebastian, however, didn't seem to be aware of their surroundings. Or he simply didn't care. This time, she could seduce him while he got lost in the sensations.

She was in full control and she was almost dizzy with the power. She knew she could ask for anything and he would give it to her. But she wanted something more. Ashley wanted—needed—Sebastian to surrender. She needed to see that he would do anything, give up control, just for the taste of her.

But how did one seduce a seducer? Could a man like Sebastian be seduced if he knew all the techniques and tricks? She knew she had to be daring. No fear. No hesitation.

Ashley deepened the kiss. She yanked off his tie and hastily unbuttoned his shirt. She stopped midway and flattened her hands against his warm skin. Sebastian moaned against her mouth as her fingertips tugged the dusting of dark curls on his chest.

She wanted more and shoved his jacket off and pulled his shirt down his arms. Tearing her mouth away from his, she kissed a trail down his chin and neck. She felt the choppy beat of his pulse and smiled as it matched hers.

Sebastian bunched her dress in his hands. She couldn't

strip bare for him. Not now. Not here. She stopped him, her hands firm against his. "Not yet," she mumbled against his chest.

"Are you telling me what to do?" he teased.

By the end of the night, he wouldn't notice that he was following her directions. He wouldn't care that she was in charge. Sebastian would only notice how she made him go wild. He would find out just how much power she had over him.

"I'm telling you to be patient," she corrected him as she grabbed his belt and pulled him closer. "Good things happen to those who wait."

"I have never found that to be true," he drawled.

She held his gaze steadily. "Trust me." The agreement didn't make them equals, but she needed his trust as much as she needed his touch.

Ashley was pleased when Sebastian reluctantly pulled his hands away from her dress and continued caressing her legs. Her fingers shook as they skimmed along his waist. Without taking her eyes off him, she slowly unbuckled his belt and pressed her hand against his erection. Her breath fizzled in her lungs when she realized how large and powerful he was. Her memory had not exaggerated.

"I'm not that patient," he warned as she rubbed her palm against him.

"Good to know." Her seduction was working. She had admired the restraint and patience he had displayed on Inez Key. It set him apart from the playboys she knew. Ashley knew he wasn't reckless or impulsive, but now she knew he had a limit.

But knowing his limit didn't make him any less dangerous. And right now *she* was feeling dangerous. She wasn't ready to stop this. She didn't think she could if she wanted to.

Ashley slowly unzipped his trousers and shoved them past his hips and down his legs. His hooded eyes glittered as he was sprawled half-naked before her. She couldn't stop staring at his masculine beauty.

"Now you." His voice was thick with desire as he reached for her.

She held up her hands. "Not yet." Ashley wasn't ready to give up the power that was rolling through her. She wanted to set the pace or he would take over. This would be the most brazen move she'd ever made.

She met his gaze as she wrapped her fingers around his thick penis. Sebastian hissed as she stroked him. She watched with fascination as he responded to her quickening pace. She felt his power underneath her skin and she wanted more of it.

Ashley knelt down in front of Sebastian and took him in her mouth. His deep moan echoed in the interior of the car as he clenched his hands into her hair. She loved the taste of him, loved driving him wild. She enjoyed the bite of pain as he twisted her hair in his fists and she welcomed his thrusts.

Just when she thought she was going to take him over the edge, Sebastian pulled away. She murmured her protest when he lifted her. She wasn't going to let him take this away from her. Not now, not when she found the courage to take charge.

Ashley pushed Sebastian back in the seat and

climbed on top of him. She straddled his hips and met his hot gaze. He didn't look smug or arrogant anymore. He looked wild, almost savage.

She felt beautiful. Confident. She had the man who had invaded her dreams and taken over every waking moment underneath her. He was at her mercy.

"Wait," he said in a growl as he reached for his wallet and retrieved a condom. As he tossed his wallet aside and slid on the condom with quick, efficient moves, Ashley realized he was nowhere near to losing control. He had the sense to remember protection and it had slipped her mind. Was she fooling herself, believing she was in charge?

Ashley placed her palms on his broad shoulders just as he clenched his hands on her hips and guided her down. The heat washed over her. She tossed back her head and moaned as he filled her.

The sensations were almost too intense. She rocked her hips as the pleasure rippled through her. Sebastian leaned forward and captured her breast with his mouth. She begged for more, her words broken and jumbled, as the heat flared deep in her pelvis.

He cupped her bottom and squeezed as he murmured his encouragement in Spanish. She didn't catch all the words. She rocked harder, chasing the pleasure that she didn't quite understand. Couldn't quite curb. But she wasn't scared because she knew Sebastian would take care of her. He wouldn't let her go too close to the fire and burn.

Sebastian grabbed her hips and controlled the rhythm. She could barely catch her breath. She saw the muscle bunching in his clenched jaw. She saw the lust glittering in his dark eyes. He was desperate to hold on to the remnants of his control. He wanted to be the last to let go.

Ashley wasn't going to let that happen. She was in charge. She would make him beg for release and she would decide if she would give it to him.

Sebastian slid his hand to where they were joined. He pressed his fingertip on her clitoris and Ashley stilled. She arched back and groaned as the climax ripped through her body. Her mind went blank as she surrendered to the white heat.

"Sebastian!" His name ripped from her throat. Ashley slumped against him, her muscles weak and pulsating, as she heard his short cry of release.

So this is how it feels to be a rich man's plaything, Ashley thought as she lay in bed hours later, naked and spent. Sebastian was curled next to her, his arm wrapped around her waist. Even in his sleep, he made his claim known.

She was now a mistress. A sigh staggered from Ashley's throat as she looked at the moon through the windows. The one thing she swore she'd never become.

Ashley knew she should be filled with shame and self-hatred. She should feel as if a piece of her soul had been stolen. Instead, she felt protected. Taken care of. Cherished.

Was this how her mother felt when she had been a mistress? Was this why Linda designed her life around

Donald? Why she suddenly came alive every time he stepped into the room?

No, her mother had it much worse, Ashley realized. Linda made the mistake of falling in love with her benefactor.

Ashley turned and looked at Sebastian while he slept. She wouldn't make that mistake. She may desire Sebastian, she may even be infatuated with him, but she would not fall in love. If she did that, she'd never recover.

Hours later Ashley dived into the crystal-blue infinity pool that was on the rooftop of Sebastian's penthouse apartment. The water felt cold and refreshing against her skin. The pool was designed for lazy afternoons under the hot sun, but Ashley swam down the length as hard and as fast as she could.

She loved the water. Whenever she was upset or worried, she found peace watching the waves or swimming laps. But today, nothing could calm her.

Ashley tried to exhaust herself as she thought about what had happened in the limousine. And the wild, fierce sex they'd had when Sebastian carried her to bed. And this morning…

She felt her skin flush. Reaching the edge of the pool, Ashley did a turn and kept swimming. She was becoming a sexual creature and there were no signs that she could pull back. She needed to return to Inez Key before she got to the point of no return.

Ashley paused when she heard a splash. She stopped

swimming and started to tread water. Looking around, she saw Sebastian swimming toward her.

Her stomach tightened as she watched his clean, powerful strokes. She couldn't deny his strength and masculinity. Ashley couldn't stop staring. She was tempted to jump out of the pool before she wrapped her body around his.

Instead, she remained treading water, refusing to give an inch, watching him approach with a mix of dread and excitement. When he surfaced, she immediately thought that he was too close. She saw the amused gleam in his dark eyes.

"I thought you were at work," she said. She had been grateful for the time alone. She was used to solitude and thought the time away from Sebastian would help break this sexual hold he had over her. No such luck. She only had to look at him and she was right back where she started. Her pulse kicked with excitement as she savored the heat sizzling through her veins.

"I came back because I wanted to see you," he replied as his gaze settled on her skimpy bikini top.

Knowing that she had the ability to distract him from work gave her more joy than it should. He probably tossed these meaningless comments to every woman in his sight. "I found this swimsuit in the cabana," she said as she slicked back her wet hair. "There were quite a few of them."

"They are there for guests," he said, moving even closer. "They are not from my ex-lovers, if that's what you're thinking."

Her insecurity was pathetically obvious. She hated

what she was becoming. "If you say so." She realized he had moved in even closer. Ashley couldn't take it anymore and slowly moved to the corner of the pool.

"Where are you going?" With one smooth move, Sebastian cornered her. She felt the edge of the pool against her back and Sebastian's strong legs bumping against hers.

Her hands grazed his defined chest as she tried to tread. "My God, you are insatiable."

Sebastian rested his hands on the pool ledge, trapping her. "You were the one who woke me up this morning. Not that I minded…"

She didn't want to think about that. How she acted before she thought. She couldn't even use the excuse that she had been dreaming. That would make Sebastian more arrogant than he already was.

Ashley treaded hard and fast with her legs but she was getting tangled with Sebastian's. She was very aware of his body. His solid chest and golden-brown skin. The strong column of his throat and his sensual mouth.

Sebastian bent his head and kissed her. She arched her back as his hand slid down the curve of her breast. Ashley moaned as he rubbed his thumb against her hard nipple.

"I have a favor to ask," she said breathlessly.

"I can't wait to hear it." He dipped his head and whispered in her ear, "You don't have to be shy with me."

"I need to visit Inez Key," she said in a rush.

"No." His quiet, authoritative tone bothered her almost as much as his words.

She reared back her head. "What do you mean, no? Aren't you the least bit curious of why I need to go?"

He shrugged. "You have no authority on or responsibility to the island. It's mine."

"Shouldn't I at least get bonus points for asking?" She realized what she'd said and shook her head. Why was she asking for permission? If she wanted to go, she would. Thanks to a very informative phone conversation with Clea, Ashley knew Sebastian had added security on Inez Key. But she knew all the best hiding spots.

Sebastian's mouth formed into a grim line. "Don't even think about it."

"You don't know what I'm thinking," she said as she hoisted herself out of the pool.

"I'll arrest you for trespassing."

All right, he did know what she was thinking. Was her face that expressive? Or was she just predictable? "You'll have to catch me first," Ashley said as she strolled away. She refused to show how much she believed he would follow through on his threat.

"You won't get far," Sebastian said as he watched her from the pool.

Yes, she would. Ashley grabbed her towel and walked as regally as she could back to the penthouse. She was painfully aware of Sebastian watching her. Her skin felt hot and tight and her hips seemed fuller as they swayed with each step. She waited until she was out of sight before she wrapped her towel tightly around her body and ran down the steps as if she was being pursued.

CHAPTER SIX

A WEEK LATER, Ashley strolled from one guest to another at Sebastian's glamorous cocktail party. They were on the rooftop of the Cruz hotel in Jamaica. The breeze carried the scent of the ocean and the tropical-fruit appetizers the waiters offered.

Ashley wasn't sure why she'd quietly assumed the role as hostess. She could say that she was bored or that she rebelled from Sebastian's attempts to keep her away from the party. The truth was she wanted to show him that she was more than just decoration. She had some skills that weren't marketable but still valued in certain circles.

If Sebastian suspected that she would sabotage him, she hoped he realized he had no cause for concern. She knew how to act, what to provide and how to dress. Ashley's skin was bare of jewels, but her simple white dress made her stand out from the dark suits and frilly and colorful dresses.

More important, she made sure everyone felt comfortable and welcome. She knew this party changed the way Sebastian saw her. She saw the admiration and pride in his eyes.

"I thought you didn't like parties," Sebastian said as she made her way to him.

"When did I say that?" Ashley asked. She tilted her head as she tried to remember. "No, I said I didn't party. No late nights. No club hopping. Nothing like that."

Sebastian didn't try to hide his skepticism. "Not even in college? You had only been there for one semester."

"And you think I got kicked out of school?" What made him think that? She had done some dumb things when she was a teenager, but she wasn't a troublemaker. "No, I was struggling at school. I always had trouble with my grades. I dropped out after my parents died. I didn't see the point in staying."

She'd never wanted to go to school. Her parents forced her for their selfish reasons, but she had to admit that college offered her a respite from the tension at home.

"If you were such a poor student, how did you get into college?"

"My father pulled some strings and gave a big donation to the school," she admitted with the twist of her lips.

Sebastian raised his eyebrows. "Must have been nice to have rich parents," he said coldly. "They opened a lot of doors and gave you many opportunities."

"That wasn't why they did it," Ashley said as she tightly gripped the stem of her champagne flute tightly. "They wanted me out of the way. But I know what you're saying. I was given a lot. I had the resources to make something of myself. And where did I wind up? Broke, homeless and a rich man's sexual plaything."

Sebastian's eyes narrowed. "You twist my words."

She knew what he was saying. Really saying. That he could have conquered the world by now with that kind of financial support. "You may have had to crawl out of the ghetto but I'm sure someone helped you," Ashley said roughly. "Teachers, neighbors, relatives. Maybe the kindness of strangers."

"Then you would be wrong."

Ashley felt her heart pinch. Sebastian had had a grueling and lonely journey to the top. She couldn't imagine the strength and sacrifice it took to get to where he was. The more she learned about him, the more she admired and respected him. It made it difficult keeping her distance from Sebastian.

"And what about now?" she asked, deciding to take a different tack. "I'm sure that you would do exactly what my father did. If one of your sisters needed to get into a school, get a job or even a place to live, you would throw all of your money and influence to get it for her."

Something flickered in his eyes, but his face showed no expression. She watched Sebastian take a healthy gulp of champagne. "Yes, I would."

"And she would accept that help," Ashley predicted. "That doesn't make her spoiled."

"Of course not. I expect my sisters to come to me whenever they need help."

"But I'm a spoiled brat because I lived off my parents' money?" she asked. "You think I haven't worked a day in my life. That I'm just hanging around, working on my tan, until I land a rich husband."

"Are you trying to tell me that you aren't an heiress who enjoyed the good life," he asked.

"I once enjoyed being a socialite when I didn't have to worry about money or the future," she admitted. The amount of money she had wasted in those years still made her sick to her stomach. "But that disappeared the moment my mother pulled a gun on my father. My friends used their connection with me to sell the most salacious and untrue stories about my family. My father's money was gone and I inherited a mess. It has been a struggle for five years to keep what I had left."

"You could have gotten a job," he drawled.

She should have expected that she would receive no sympathy from Sebastian. "I couldn't leave Inez Key. Everyone thinks I've been living in paradise. No one wants to look past the island and notice that I've been living hand to mouth for years. Any money I had went to taxes or to the islanders who relied on me."

"If your home has been such a headache, why are you so desperate to go back?"

Ashley pressed her lips together. She had been trying to prove a point, but Sebastian only noticed the one thing she had been trying to hide. "You wouldn't understand," she muttered.

"Try me."

She looked away as she struggled with the urge to tell him everything. Why did she start this? Why was it so important for Sebastian to see her as something more than a pampered heiress? His opinion shouldn't matter so much.

"Inez Key is the only place where I feel safe." She

knew she'd told him that before but she wasn't willing to explain why. That she wasn't destructive or cruel when she was on the island. That she didn't have the ability to destroy people's lives and families if she disconnected with the world.

Sebastian's face darkened. "Do you feel unsafe now?" he asked hoarsely as his eyes glittered. "Here, with me?"

She didn't feel unsafe. She was scared. Worried of how addicted she was to Sebastian's touch. Afraid of the emotions whipping through her. Frightened of what she was becoming. A sexual woman. Emotional. Falling in love.

"You've enjoyed yourself the past couple of weeks," Sebastian stated. "And why not? Private planes, designer clothes and state-of-the-art spa services. We've been to the Bahamas, the Cayman Islands and now Jamaica. You've stayed at the most luxurious resorts that would put Inez Key to shame."

And he thought it was all because of the money he spent? Let him think that. If he knew she enjoyed his company, his attention and his touch, it would give him far too much power over her.

She had been amazed that Sebastian had taken time out of his busy schedule to show her the sights. He had taken her everyplace she had underlined in her travel guide, but he had also taken her to his favorite spots. She had cherished those moments as they offered her a deeper understanding about Sebastian Cruz.

"Is that why you dragged me along on your business

trip?" she asked coolly. "So I would see what the world outside Inez Key had to offer?"

"You don't seem to mind. Your every need has been catered to."

She had made the most of what he had to offer. It reminded her of what she used to take for granted. No wonder he thought she was a spoiled socialite. Little did he know that she'd had a makeover and subjected herself to the most painful spa services for his approval.

It was only later when she realized that she was following her mother's pattern. She could tell herself that she chose bright colors because it reflected her mood. That the mane of hair was easier to deal with and the short dresses were needed in the tropical heat. It wasn't true. It was all to please Sebastian.

Not that it mattered. He didn't seem to notice her haircut or her smooth skin. The lingerie she wore was for his pleasure as much as it was for hers, but he managed to get it off her before he gave it an appreciative look.

"And your needs are catered to especially in bed," he murmured.

Ashley blushed. She wasn't quiet about what she wanted in bed. The nights they shared had been mind-blowing. She had never expected that it would become more magical. She clung to Sebastian all night, eager and greedy for his touch.

"I have no complaints," she replied stiffly. She wondered how amazing it would be if Sebastian had any emotion behind every caress and kiss. Her knees weakened at the thought.

"Nor do I," he whispered as he leaned forward. "You are a very generous lover."

Her face felt incredibly hot from his compliment and the noise from the cocktail party seemed louder. She never refused Sebastian and it had nothing to do with her role as his mistress. She was always ready for him at the most inconvenient times. Even now her breasts felt heavy, her nipples tight, as her skin tingled for his caress.

But she didn't have that power over him. Sebastian wanted her but only on his terms. His timetable.

"If you will excuse me," she said as she forced herself to step away. They were not equals and they never would be. "I'm not being a good hostess. I should circulate with your guests."

Impatience gleamed in his eyes. "Running away again, *mi vida?*"

She didn't answer and she walked away. Ashley felt his gaze on her. She knew she couldn't hide from Sebastian Cruz. He saw everything.

Sebastian fought the impulse to grab Ashley and pull her closer. To find a dark corner and reacquaint himself with her scent and taste. Instead, he restrained himself as he watched the haughty tilt of her head as she glided through the crowd.

Ashley may think she was an island girl but she was meant for the glittery world of high society. She had nothing in common with the guests, but she worked the room with effortless grace. The businessmen were dazzled by her friendly smile and their wives gravitated to her sunny personality.

"Who's the girl?"

Sebastian's hand tightened on his champagne glass when he heard the gravelly voice. He turned to see Oscar Salazar, one of his fiercest rivals.

"Salazar." He gave the man a brief handshake. "I didn't see you come in."

"Your attention was elsewhere. I can see why." A streak of red highlighted Salazar's blunt cheekbones as he stared at Ashley. "You always had good taste in property."

"Don't let her hear you say that," Sebastian warned. Not that he was going to allow Salazar that close to Ashley. He was territorial, but he knew better than to show it around Salazar. The man liked to compete. The more Sebastian wanted something, the more determined Salazar was in wrestling it free from him.

The possessive feeling was so strong that Sebastian almost vibrated with it. He couldn't remember the last time he'd felt this way. The women in his bed had always been interchangeable and temporary. If any of them tried to make him jealous, Sebastian didn't hesitate to cut them loose. He never second-guessed or regretted his actions. He knew he could replace his lover with someone who was willing to follow his rules.

But it was different with Ashley. The woman didn't understand the word *obey*. She was exasperating, difficult and never boring. Why did he allow her to act that way? Was it because she was his mistress? Was it because he was her first? Or did it have anything to do with sex?

He wanted to share his day with Ashley. It didn't matter if they were exploring the waterfalls of Jamaica, falling asleep in each other's arms or enjoying a cup of coffee in a busy sidewalk café. He yearned for her. So much that he found himself calling her when he was at the office just to hear her voice.

"Who did you say she was?" Salazar asked as his gaze narrowed on Ashley's slender body.

Sebastian gritted his teeth. He had to play this carefully. "Her name is Ashley."

"She looks familiar."

He doubted Salazar socialized with Donald Jones. He was too young and had only made his fortune a few years ago. "You probably saw her in Miami," Sebastian said. He tossed back the champagne but didn't taste it.

Salazar dragged his gaze away from Ashley. "She's different from your other women."

And that automatically made her an intriguing challenge. The ultimate prize. The man understood what made Sebastian tick. "I don't have a type."

Salazar smiled. "This one looks more innocent. Untamed."

Sebastian curled his hand into a fist. "You don't know anything about her." *And you're not going to.*

"But I know you," Salazar said. "You'll tire of her very soon."

No, he wouldn't. He wanted more than a month with Ashley. Craved for something more. "And you'll swoop in and catch her?"

Salazar shrugged. "I wouldn't normally take your hand-me-downs…"

Sebastian wanted to punch his rival. No one talked about Ashley that way. *No one.* Instead, Sebastian stepped in front of Salazar and stared him down. "Stay away from Ashley," he said in growl.

Salazar looked very pleased that he'd riled him. "Worried that you don't have that much of a hold on her?" he taunted.

He *was* worried about that. The only way he got Ashley back in his bed was through blackmail. He wasn't proud of it. She wanted him but not enough to make the first move or accept his original offer.

"She's mine," Sebastian warned in a low voice. Most people would scatter from the threat in his tone, but Oscar Salazar's smile only widened.

"Not for long." Salazar returned his gaze on Ashley. "I could steal her away if I wanted to."

"No, you couldn't." Sebastian's heart pounded against his ribs as the need to defend his territory coursed through his veins. "You have nothing she wants. No extra incentive."

"Incentive?" Salazar's eyes glowed as he pondered the new information. "She has a price?"

"One you couldn't afford," Sebastian snapped.

"I'm sure I could get a bargain," he murmured.

"You've been warned, Salazar." He didn't like this side of him, but he couldn't stop it. He was ready to unleash all of his power and weapons on Salazar. If he had fangs, he would have bared them. "Go anywhere near her and you're dead."

"Understood." Salazar took a sip of his champagne and casually strolled away. Sebastian wanted to follow, but one of his Jamaican business partners chose that moment to approach.

Sebastian ruthlessly pushed aside any thought of Salazar. His blood roared in his ears and his hands shook with the need to land his fist into Salazar's jaw. He had nothing to worry about. He didn't trust the man, but he knew Ashley wouldn't be interested in Salazar's questionable charms.

Yet he kept an eye on Ashley during the cocktail party. Sebastian was always aware of where she stood. Even when he was in a deep conversation with his executive assistant, Sebastian heard Ashley's earthy laugh from across the room.

He wasn't sure what made him look up a few minutes later and actively seek her out in the party. His mother would have called it a premonition. Sebastian knew it had more to do with the fact that he was attuned to her.

He found her next to the door on the rooftop. The ocean breeze tugged at her white dress and her long brown hair. His voice trailed off as he noticed that Ashley stood ramrod straight. Her tension was palpable. Her polite smile was slipping and he saw the caution in her eyes.

It took him a moment to realize Oscar Salazar had his back to the party and was talking to her. A red haze filled Sebastian's vision as the anger flared inside him. He strode through the crowd, determined to keep Salazar away. He didn't notice the guests as he bumped shoulders and cut through small groups. A few guests saw the murderous rage in his expression and immediately got out of the line of fire.

He didn't know what Salazar was saying to Ashley, but it didn't matter. Ashley was *his*. Body and soul.

He saw Ashley's face whiten. The color leached from her sun-kissed skin as if she was going to be sick. She turned her head and Sebastian knew she was searching for him. Their gazes clashed. Her brown eyes shimmered with hurt. Pain. Betrayal.

Ashley flinched and jerked her attention back at Salazar. Ashley's mouth parted in shock a moment before she slung her champagne in Salazar's face. She dropped the flute on the ground and marched away before Salazar could react.

Sebastian wanted to chase after his woman. Comfort and protect her. But first he had to take care of Salazar. He turned and glared at Salazar's proud face. That man needed to learn that if he slighted Ashley, the wrath of hell was upon him.

Ashley brushed away the last tear as she gathered up her T-shirt and jeans and dumped them in the smallest suitcase she could find. Her hands shook as she zipped up the case. How could Sebastian do this to her?

Why was she so surprised? She meant nothing to him. She was just the mistress. A very temporary one. Hadn't she seen enough on how men treated their mistresses? Why did she think Sebastian would have been any different?

Ashley jumped when she heard the door of their bedroom swing open and bang against the wall. She refused to look at Sebastian. She knew he filled the doorway with his hands clutching the frame. He was barring her exit and she felt his anger pouring through him.

"What happened between you and Salazar?" he asked with lethal softness.

"Bastard," she muttered as she lifted the suitcase off the bed.

"He's been called much worse, but what did he say to you?" Sebastian asked impatiently. "I couldn't get a word out of him."

"No, you are the bastard," Ashley said as she thrust a finger at him. He looked like a dark angel. He had discarded his jacket and tie, but that didn't diminish his raw masculinity. There was something angry and volatile about him. Dangerous and powerful. "I trusted you. I thought we had an agreement."

"We do," he said as he stepped into the room. "You are my mistress for a month."

"Which you told Oscar Salazar." Her voice shook as she remembered the way that man had looked at her. As if he wanted to sample the goods before he made a bid.

"I didn't say you were my mistress." Sebastian's voice was as stinging as the flick of a whip. "I warned him off."

Then how did Oscar know? She didn't act like a mistress. She didn't dress like one, either. The only way he would have known was if Sebastian said something. "You broke your promise and you broke our agreement. I'm leaving."

"Like hell you are." Sebastian rushed forward. He

grabbed the case and tossed it on the floor. "You're not going anywhere until I say so."

She'd never seen Sebastian like this. His movements were rough and clumsy. His sophisticated veneer was slipping. It was as if he was upset that she was leaving. But that was ridiculous. Sebastian Cruz didn't care enough to panic.

Ashley thrust out her chin and met his gaze. "You can't tell me what to do. I'm not your mistress anymore."

A muscle bunched in his jaw. "Then you will never see Inez Key again."

"Fine," she retorted. She pressed her lips together as the horror snaked through her. She wanted to take those words back.

His eyes widened with surprise. He was silent for a moment, his breathing hard, as a strange urgency pulsed around them. "Fine? You are ready to walk away from the home you fought to hold on to?" he asked as he stepped closer. "The home you took care of and made sacrifices for? The one where you lowered yourself and slept with me so you could stay on the island?"

"This isn't about Inez Key. It's about you," she replied. "You don't care about what is important to me and you certainly don't care about my feelings."

He rocked back on his feet as he looked at her with such intensity that she felt she was going to burst. "How are you going to get back?" he asked. "You have no money."

Ashley closed her eyes as the pain ricocheted inside her. He didn't deny her accusation. He didn't care about her feelings. "I don't know," she whispered. "I'll hock this dress. I'll swim all the way home. Maybe I'll trade my body for favors. That's what everyone thinks I do anyway."

He snatched her wrist. She felt the tremor in his hand. "Don't even joke about it."

"Why not, Sebastian?" She tried to yank her arm away from him but he tightened his hold. "You made me a joke. You made me a mistress."

"And you accepted," he said. "You had other choices. You could have walked away but you didn't."

"You dangled my home as bait," she cried out.

"Like you said, Inez Key had nothing to do with it," he reminded her coldly. "You wanted to be with me but you were afraid to go after it. And now you're upset because you like being a mistress."

Her gasp echoed in the room as she went still. "No, I don't," she said in a scandalized whisper. "Take that back."

"I stand corrected." Sebastian let go of her wrist. "You like being *my* mistress."

She wanted to slap him. Push him away. But it was true. She liked sharing his bed and enjoyed seeing the desire in his eyes when she walked into the room. She treasured their private moments and was proud to be at his side in public. She ached for his touch and she was greedy for his undivided attention. She would accept whatever role he chose for her if it meant she could share a part of his life.

And he knew it. He knew that she would take the

measly crumbs that he offered. He knew he had that much power over her. "Get out of my way."

He crossed his arms and braced his feet. Any concern he felt a moment ago had disappeared. Sebastian was calm and in charge again. "Make me."

And now he was going to prove how she had no power over him. Ashley curled her hands into fists and dug her nails into her palms as she tried to hold back the rioting emotions. "I'm warning you, Sebastian. I'm about to lose control."

Sebastian wasn't worried. "I can handle it. Give me your best shot."

"Oh, my God." She thrust her hands in her wavy hair. "You *want* me out of control? Are you insane?"

"I want you to stop hiding. Stop running away."

That was all she wanted to do. Run. Hide. Regain control of her temper before she broke into a million pieces. "You have no say in what I do."

"I'm sorry about Salazar," he said grimly. "I warned him off but I revealed more than I should."

"Did you tell him I had a price?" she asked wildly. "That he could talk me down from my asking price because I was damaged goods? That I should accept his offer because you would kick me out of your bed soon?"

"I'm going to kill him," Sebastian said through clenched teeth.

"You'll have to get in line," she declared as she strode to the door. "I knew I shouldn't have trusted you, Sebastian. I respected your wishes but you didn't respect mine."

Sebastian was at the threshold before she could get there and slammed the door shut. "You are not leaving."

She reached for the doorknob. "I see no reason to stay."

"What about this?" he asked as his hands covered her shoulders.

It was the only warning she had before Sebastian turned her around and covered his mouth with hers. His kiss crushed her lips. Ashley pressed her hands against his chest, determined to push him away. He ignored her attempts as he settled her against the door.

Excitement burned through her. She shouldn't want this. Shouldn't encourage it. Yet she did want it, had waited for this moment. Ashley wanted to feel his hands shake with barely restrained emotion. She wanted the last of his control to snap and show exactly what was going through his mind.

Sebastian shoved her lace panties down her hips before he lifted her up. She wrapped her legs around his waist when he yanked her dress up her thighs. As he deepened the kiss, Ashley tore at his shirt, wanting to strip it from his body.

Sebastian groaned against her swollen lips. "Tell me you don't want this."

She wished she could. She wished she didn't come alive under his touch or that she was always waiting, yearning, for his kiss. Ashley bucked her hips, silently demanding more.

Sebastian whispered something in Spanish as he shucked his trousers off. She couldn't tell if it was a prayer or a curse. She clung to his shoulders, yielding to his fierce kisses, unable to deny him anything. Desire and anger coiled deep in her belly, hot and tight. It was a potent combination. A dangerous mix.

Ashley tensed when she felt the crown of his penis pressing against her. She hated herself for wanting this. Hated that she made it so easy for him. She tilted her hips as he drove into her welcoming heat.

She turned her head and moaned as he filled her. Ashley held on to Sebastian tightly as he thrust deep. His rhythm was ferocious and wild. She couldn't get enough. The sounds of their uneven breaths and the creaking door were harsh to her ears. The scent of hot, aroused male electrified the air. She clutched to his fine cotton shirt as she rocked her hips against him.

"Walk away and you'll never feel like this again," he declared gruffly as he burrowed his head against the base of her throat. His teeth nipped her skin as if he was leaving his brand.

Ashley knew he was right. Only Sebastian had this power over her. The sexual hunger clawed inside her. It was unbearable, pressing against her, demanding to break free.

"You will always be mine."

Ashley's sobs caught in her throat as the violent climax ripped through her. She sagged against him as he continued to thrust. She couldn't fight the truth anymore. When he discarded her and moved on to another woman, she would still long for his touch.

She surrendered to the knowledge that she would always be his.

* * *

Sebastian woke up to the sound of his cell phone. He reached for the bedside table, his hands fumbling, but he couldn't find it. Blinking his eyes open, he immediately noticed two things: it was daylight and Ashley wasn't curled against him.

The silence in the hotel suite indicated that he was alone. Ashley was probably sulking. Angry that he'd proved his claim on her once and for all. He rolled out of bed and stalked naked to where he had shed his clothes the night before. He grabbed his cell phone from the pile of clothes and saw that his assistant was calling him.

"What is it?" he asked abruptly.

"I just found out that Ashley left Jamaica."

He hunched his shoulders as the news slammed against him. He'd made his claim and it had scared her off. She'd waited until he'd fallen asleep before she'd sneaked out of his bed. "How?" His voice was raspy and low.

"I heard a rumor," his assistant said nervously. "I don't have verification at the moment."

Sebastian closed his eyes as he got a bad feeling. He knew Ashley was angry with him, but she wouldn't betray him. Not like this. "Where is she?"

"With Oscar Salazar," his assistant whispered. "She's on his private plane back to Miami."

CHAPTER SEVEN

THE SUN STREAKED across the morning sky as Ashley saw a glimpse of Inez Key. The wind was cold and all she wore was a T-shirt, jeans and boat shoes. She didn't care. Her bottom lip quivered and the emotions crashed through her. She was home.

Home. She studied the antebellum mansion as she considered the word. It didn't feel like home anymore. Was it because it was time for her to move on or because she knew Sebastian owned it?

She knew she didn't belong here. Not because she was trespassing, and not because she'd ruined any chance of staying on as caretaker. There was no way Sebastian would allow her back now that she'd broken her promise.

But she didn't use Inez Key as just a home. It had been her hideaway. She had stayed here after her parents' murder-suicide because it was a safe place. She could evade prying eyes and evade living life.

Ashley knew she had been a lot like her mother and that scared her. She had an all-or-nothing attitude like Linda Valdez. Passionate about her causes, extremely loyal to her friends, and a hot temper that took years for her to control. Ashley knew how to hold on to a grudge and her friend's enemies were her enemies. It was only a matter of time before she followed in her mother's footsteps. To love completely and unwisely. To destroy and self-destruct.

Ashley thought she had escaped from that future when she hid away on Inez Key. It was paradise and yet solitary confinement. Her wild temper disappeared and her passions quieted. She was still fiercely loyal, but she wasn't consumed by love. She thought she'd broken the cycle and become the woman she wanted to be. But one night with Sebastian and Ashley realized she had only been fooling herself.

Ashley closed her eyes as the bleakness swirled inside her. She didn't want to think about that. Not now. First, she needed to step onto the beach and let the sand trickle between her toes. Then she needed to lie down and let the quiet wash over her. She would watch the view of the Atlantic Ocean and find the familiar landmarks. It could take hours before she felt whole and strong again. Days. But it would happen and then she would figure out what to do next.

Ashley struggled with exhaustion as she stepped out of the water taxi and paid the captain. It took effort to smile and give her thanks. She walked along the wooden dock, but she didn't feel like her old self. Everything felt new and different. She was different and she would never recapture the old Ashley Jones again.

She heard the boat speed away, but she didn't look back. The changes on the island had her attention. She noticed the repairs on the house and the fresh coat of paint. The wild vegetation was tamed. Inez Key was slowly returning to its former glory.

Unlike her. She was breaking down. Breaking apart. Even though she was finally back on Inez Key, she had to keep it together. She sensed that this island could no longer contain her.

Ashley walked to the front door of the main house and tried to open it. To her surprise, it was locked. She frowned and jiggled the doorknob. That was odd. Inez Key was a quiet and safe place with just a few homes and buildings. No one locked their doors. She couldn't remember the last time she'd used the key or where she had left it.

"Ashley, is that you?" Clea asked as she walked from around the house. She gave a squeal and ran to Ashley, welcoming her with a big hug. "What are you doing back?"

"I was going to get my things and leave," Ashley said as she gestured to the door. "But the main house is locked."

"I know, isn't that strange? Who locks their doors?" Clea asked. She planted her fists on her hips and shook her head. "I haven't been in there since they started renovating."

"A lot has changed." She gave a nod at the tropical flowers and plants near the white columns. At first glance the landscaping looked natural, but she knew it had been meticulously planned. How did Sebastian manage all of the changes when the island had only recently been in possession? "I wasn't gone that long."

"The new owners have been busy," Clea said as she guided Ashley away from the front door. "And there are a lot of new security features. It won't be long before the guards find you."

"They haven't torn anything down," Ashley murmured as she gave the main house one last look.

"It's more like adding and updating," Clea said. "I'm glad to see they have respect for the history of the island, but I think the way of life on Inez Key won't be the same."

The gentle rhythm of the island life would change if there were bodyguards and security features. "Have you heard from the new owners?"

"We received letters from Cruz Conglomerate," the housekeeper said as they walked along a dusty path. "I thought it was going to be an eviction letter like yours, but they promised nothing has changed for us."

At least Sebastian didn't break that promise. She had suspected it was a threat to keep her in line, but she couldn't be sure. "What else did the letter say? Anything about turning the island into a resort or a hotel?" Or worse, razing it and destroying it inch by inch. Ashley shuddered at the thought.

She didn't think Sebastian would do that, but she obviously couldn't predict his every move. She suspected he wanted Inez Key for an exclusive getaway. He had undoubtedly posed as a paying guest to see if buying the island was worth his time.

And after spending a few weeks with the man, she noticed his interests focused on travel and leisure. She had stayed at some extraordinary hotels and exclusive resorts. All of them were part of his global business. Her home was definitely going to be part of that. The crowning jewel of his empire.

"No, I haven't heard what they plan to do with Inez Key," Clea said without a hint of concern. "We're expecting to see the new owner next month after the renovations are complete."

"You've already met the new owner," Ashley said bitterly. She hated how her voice caught in her throat. "You know him as Sebastian Esteban."

Clea halted and stared at Ashley. "That man took your island from you? The man you fell in love with?"

She shifted her lower jaw as she fought back the spurt of anger. "I did not fall in love with Sebastian Cruz."

"Honey, I saw how you were with him," Clea argued with a knowing smile. "You were in full bloom every time he looked at you."

Ashley closed her eyes as her skin heated. She couldn't be in love with Sebastian. She had more pride than that! The man had kicked her out of her home, made her his mistress and ruined her life.

But she couldn't hide from the truth anymore. She had been enthralled by Sebastian Cruz. It was more than the sizzling sexual hunger. Ashley didn't want to admire his hard-earned accomplishments or value his opinions. She tried not to help him or smile at his humor. She hid the longing for Sebastian's company and the way her heart leaped every time he entered the room.

None of it worked. No matter how hard she had tried, she had fallen for a man who had no respect for her. He only wanted her for sex.

It was official. She had inherited the same self-destructive tendencies as her mother.

"I'll get over it," Ashley muttered.

Clea patted Ashley's arm. "What are you going to do to get the island back?"

The question caught her by surprise. She had given up that plan weeks ago. "Nothing. I've done everything in my power." And discovered she was no match for Sebastian. "The most I could get out of Sebastian was the caretaker position, but I managed to mess that up."

"Caretaker? The owner of the island becoming a hired hand? I don't think so! Just as well you didn't get that job," Clea said with the cluck of her tongue. "You'll think of something. In the meantime, stay with Louis and me. Just for a couple of days."

The offer was tempting but Ashley hesitated. "I don't want to get you in trouble. He made it very clear I had to have his permission to stay on Inez Key. If he knew I was staying with you…"

Clea curled her arm around Ashley's. "Don't worry about him," she said in a conspiring tone. "He'll never know you were here."

Where was she? Icy anger swirled inside Sebastian as he strode across the beach on Inez Key the next evening. He curled his shoulders as the cold ocean breeze pulled at his jeans and hoodie. He didn't notice the colorful birds flitting from one flower to the next. The sound of rolling waves faded in the background. There was only one thing on his mind: finding Ashley.

He couldn't believe she would have pulled a stunt

like that. It was bad enough she had left his bed in the middle of the night, but to escape with Salazar? His anger flared white-hot. She was going to pay for that.

Didn't she know that he would follow her? Or was that the plan all along? Was Ashley determined to prove her sexual power? Her hold on him had been obvious on their last night in Jamaica.

He had chased her back to Miami and invaded Salazar's kingdom only to discover she wasn't there. Salazar had had great fun at his expense. Sebastian's anger had been a slow burn until the other man made one too many innuendos. The guy was no longer laughing and Sebastian hoped he'd left a scar. It would be a daily reminder to Salazar not to come near his woman.

Sebastian hated the fact that he had been compelled to chase Ashley. She made this decision. She chose to give up her last chance to stay on this island.

But he couldn't turn back now. When he first heard she'd left, he had been numb. It took a split second for the fury to crack through his frozen shell and drive him into action. The need to follow had been instinctive and strong. He seized upon it, not caring what his colleagues thought.

He had no strategy. He wasn't looking ahead. That wasn't how he operated, but Sebastian was working on pure rage. His anger had festered as he spent hours searching for her in Miami.

Sebastian let the anger swell inside him, ready to burst through his skin. Ashley Jones was a spoiled princess and he was going to teach her a lesson.

But where was she?

She had to be here. Sebastian ignored the panic squeezing his chest. If she wasn't in Inez Key, he had no idea where she would be.

Sebastian stopped and looked around. The island was quiet and sleepy, but it did nothing to cool his temper. He heard the rustle of palm trees and the incessant chirping of birds. Inez Key looked idyllic, but that was an illusion. Who knew such a small piece of land would cause him so much grief?

He looked over his shoulder and glared at the black roof of the main house. It may have been a dream home for some, but an image of the antebellum mansion had been in his nightmares since his childhood. He didn't see the gracious beauty but instead the cold emptiness. It was better suited as a museum than a family home. If he could, he would burn it down.

He would destroy the whole island if he had the chance, Sebastian thought grimly. He wanted to erase this particular ocean view. Get rid of the briny scent that still triggered bad memories. Wipe away the sunset that had been the backdrop of the night he had lost his innocent childhood.

No, he would keep the sunsets, Sebastian decided as he glanced at the cloudless sky. For the past month he had associated Ashley with sunsets. The orange-and-pink streaks were no longer ominous but instead held promise. He remembered every detail of the night Ashley had sat next to him on the veranda as they had watched the sun set.

Her warmth and soft femininity had cast a spell on him. He'd had trouble following their desultory conversation; Sebastian knew Ashley had been nervous that evening. It was as if she had known they would wind up in bed together. He had felt as if he could hear her heart pound against her ribs as a flush had crept into her cheeks.

Excitement had coiled around his chest when the stars blanketed the night sky. The thick and heavy air between them had crackled. She had teased his senses and a dangerous thrill had zipped through his veins.

Wild sensations had sparked inside him, pressing just under his skin when he had kissed her. That moment had been magical. Sebastian had meant to gently explore her lips, but the passion between them had exploded into something hot and urgent.

He'd keep the sunset, Sebastian decided. And the island, too. It was, after all, where he had first met Ashley. He didn't want to erase those moments he had shared with her, so the house must stay as well. It wouldn't be that great a hardship. Since he had stayed in the mansion with Ashley, Inez Key no longer had power over him.

He walked swiftly along the beach, following a bend that led to a cove. Sebastian paused and looked around, wondering where Ashley would hide. It would be somewhere that made her feel safe and protected. That could be anywhere on this small island. He had heard so many stories about Inez Key. As a kid who was raised on the dangerous streets, he had thought they were fairy tales.

His heart clenched when he saw Ashley curled in a tight ball next to a large piece of driftwood. Her damp jeans were caked with sand and she was almost dwarfed in her sweatshirt. Her hair was pulled up into a messy ponytail, but what he noticed the most was her tear-streaked face.

The anger slowly weakened as he stared at her. Ashley was suffering and he was to blame. When he first started this journey, he wanted to take away her safe little world. He got what he wanted and now he felt like a monster.

Sebastian had to fix this and get Ashley back. He needed her. Somehow he had been aware of it from the moment they met. He always knew this woman would be his redemption and his downfall. She would tame him and at the same time drive him wild.

He knew the moment Ashley saw him. Her body went rigid and she jumped up. Even from a distance, he could see Ashley was considering her options to pounce or make a run for it.

She wouldn't get far, he decided. He was ready to chase her, the thrill of the hunt in his blood. Ashley must have known that hiding was futile. Her shoulders sagged in defeat but she held her ground.

"What are you doing here?" she asked as she looked around the cove. "I didn't hear your speedboat."

"Which is why I took a different boat," he said as he walked toward her. He had known the only way he would find her was using the element of surprise. "Don't worry. I dismissed the security, so you don't have to hide."

Her eyes narrowed with suspicion and that annoyed him. Did she really think he'd lie about that? About everything? Did she think he lied with such fluency that he was incapable of speaking the truth?

"How'd you know I would be here?" she asked. "Did your security guards call you?"

"No, you managed to get past them. But then, you know all of the hiding places. It had been a lucky guess," he said as he stood in front of her. He wanted to grab her arms and shake her for making him worry. For making him chase her from country to country. And yet, he wanted to hold her close and not let her go.

"And it just happened to be your first guess?" Ashley clenched her jaw. "Am I that predictable?"

"It wasn't my first guess. I hunted down Salazar." He shoved his fists in the pockets of his hoodie. "He enjoyed that."

If he had hoped Ashley would show a hint of discomfort or remorse, he would have been greatly disappointed. "Good," she taunted. "Why should I be the only one embarrassed?"

"I'm very territorial and you know that," His low voice held an edge. "That's why you went off with him. It was a bad move."

"Is that what you think?" She raised her eyebrows with disbelief. "I don't base every decision on you. I had to get out of there and I took the first flight I could find. Salazar offered. Normally I would keep my distance from someone like him, but I was desperate."

"How desperate?" Sebastian asked. Ashley wasn't the kind of woman who would sleep with any interested man, but he knew how she responded when she was desperate and cornered. "How did you repay him for the favor?"

"What are you suggesting?" she snapped. "Do you think that I would sleep with him? Of course you do. After all, I'm sleeping with you for a chance to stay on this island."

"I don't think you had sex with Salazar," Sebastian said. Ashley was wild and sexy with him and *only* him. He had seen how she recoiled from Salazar's touch. She may have played on Salazar's twisted desires to get a ride home, but Ashley wouldn't touch another man. "I do, however, believe you went with him to hurt me."

She covered her face with her hands. "You're right. I did. I'm ashamed of what I did. I swore I would never act that way, and what happened? I allowed my emotions to take over. Oh, God. I'm just like her."

Her? Sebastian frowned. Who was Ashley comparing herself to?

"It doesn't matter how much I tried to..." She took a deep breath and lowered her hands. She squared back her shoulders and struggled to meet his gaze. "I'm sorry, Sebastian. I felt I had to leave but I didn't need to go with Salazar. There were other options. Better options. I can tell myself that I was desperate to get back here, but the truth is I wanted to swing back at you."

She'd succeeded. It was as if Ashley knew exactly where to strike. He must have lowered his guard or revealed how he felt when they were in bed. He was addicted to Ashley. He couldn't stop thinking about her, couldn't refrain from touching her. She was his weakness and she exploited it. Just as he knew Inez Key was her weak spot.

"Why is this place so important to you?" he asked. "Why are you willing to fight for just a piece of it?" He watched as she swallowed roughly. For a moment he didn't think she would answer.

"It's where I grew up," she said unevenly, as if she had to pull out the words. "It was a special place for me and my mother."

"That's it?" He sensed there was more. This island had a pull on Ashley that she couldn't break. What would cause that?

"No, it's more than that," she admitted. "Whenever the tabloids found out about my dad, my mom would bring me here. There was no TV, no internet and no paparazzi. We could stay here and heal."

"You're lucky you had this place," he said harshly. "I would have killed for this island when I was a child."

"I'm not so sure." She held her arms close to her body. "Sometimes I felt like my mom used this place to hide from reality. The lack of distractions should have given her some clarity. Instead, it became a cocoon that blocked out all the facts. It gave my dad a chance to hide the worst of his sins. He would beg for forgiveness, swear it was all lies, and we would head back to the mainland until the cycle started all over again."

Inez Key wasn't quite the haven he thought it was for Ashley. It was connected to good memories and bad. It was part of her childhood and the loss of her innocence.

"And there is no need to escort me off the premises.

I'm going." Ashley announced. She bent down to brush the sand off her jeans.

"You'll leave with me and return to Miami."

"Our deal is off," she said as she straightened and dusted off her hands. "From the moment you broke your promise."

"Which one?" he muttered.

She narrowed her eyes. "I'm confused. What are you saying?"

"About last night…" He took a deep breath. This was going to be difficult but it couldn't be ignored. "We didn't use protection."

Ashley went pale as she stared at him. She didn't say a word. He wasn't sure how she was going to handle the news. From the way she interacted with the young islanders, he knew she liked children. Sebastian could easily imagine that she would be a fierce and protective mother. But that didn't mean she liked the idea of having *his* children.

"I apologize," Sebastian said as he raked his hand through his hair. "I don't know what happened. I always remember to use protection."

His claim seemed to wake her up. "Of course you do," she said in a withering tone.

"I'm serious." He watched her stalk past him. "I don't take any unnecessary risks."

"I'm sure you believe that," she said over her shoulder.

"But you don't." He had been careful about protection every time. It hadn't been easy. He almost forgot on more than one occasion, so caught up in the moment that nothing else seemed to matter. It had never been like that with any other woman.

But why didn't she take his word for it? Why was she that determined to see the worst in him? "It doesn't matter what you believe," he decided. "It was my responsibility and I failed you."

Ashley turned around. "Sebastian, I don't need you to take care of me. I can take care of myself. I've been doing that since I can remember."

"There's no chance of you being on the Pill?" he asked hopefully.

Ashley glared at him. "What do you think? You were my first." Her voice rose with every word. "I never had a need until I met you and I wasn't planning a repeat performance."

"We've been together for weeks and you still haven't considered protecting yourself from pregnancy. Why is that? You know, there are a lot of women who live well because they had a rich man's baby." He didn't think Ashley was one of those women, but he also knew his judgment was impaired when she was around.

Ashley rubbed her hands over her face and blew out an exasperated puff of air. "I have no interest in getting pregnant, no interest in having your baby, and I no longer have any interest in this conversation."

He ignored the sting from her words. "You have to admit that this is a concern." He needed to be more careful next time. He needed her to trust him so that there *would* be a next time.

She looked away and stared at the water. As if seeing the ocean would calm her and give her a sense of peace. "Is this how you respond whenever you have a pregnancy scare?" she asked.

He clenched his teeth. "I've never had one because I always use protection."

She pressed her lips together. "I find it hard to believe that a man with your—" she paused "—legendary sex life has not had any paternity suits, payoffs or baby drama."

"Believe it," he said in a growl.

"Every time I think I'm wrong about you, I am slapped with the truth. You remind me a lot of my father. He was something of a playboy." Her lip curled in a sneer when she said the word. "He was supposed to be a tennis legend, but he's known more for his sexual escapades and paternity suits."

"I am not a playboy," he insisted. He hated the word. It diminished everything that he had achieved. "And I'm nothing like your father."

"Right. Right." She raised her hand to stop him. "Because you're smarter. You use protection. Sometimes."

"Ashley, I give you my word." He grabbed her arm and held her still, but she looked the other way. "If you become pregnant, I will take care of you and the baby."

She whipped her head around and stared at him. "You would? Why?"

He was offended by her surprise. "You and the child would be my responsibility."

She tilted her head as she studied him with open suspicion. "What do you mean by taking care?"

"I would take care of you financially and I would be involved in the child's life." He would want a lot more, but he would wait to discuss it if there was a child. There was no reason to tell Ashley every sacrifice he would make for his family.

"Really?" She pulled away from his grasp. "You wouldn't ask for a termination or take legal action against me and swear I'm lying about the paternity?"

"What kind of man do you think I am? No, don't answer that." He was already feeling volatile and he knew he wasn't going to like what Ashley had to say.

"It's what my father did," she said with disgust. "It's what most men do."

"You don't know much about men. Or me." Sebastian took a step forward until they were almost touching. He noticed Ashley didn't back down. Most people would. "I take care of my family. That would include you and the baby."

She frowned and studied his face. "This doesn't make any sense."

"Let me make it clear to you," he said through gritted teeth. "If you are pregnant with my child, I will give him my last name. I will let everyone know that he is mine and that I take care of what is mine. I will protect and provide for him."

She stared at him as if in a daze.

"And if I need to marry his mother," he forced the words out, "I will do so."

Her mouth dropped open. "Are you serious?"

"But don't take that as a marriage proposal," he warned. "The only reason I would marry any woman is if she was carrying my child."

CHAPTER EIGHT

"COME ON, ASHLEY, we'll discuss this later. We need to leave," Sebastian said as he stuffed his hands in his hoodie pocket. He was never comfortable with the topic of marriage. The idea of sacrificing his freedom usually made him break into a cold sweat. Right now, he felt the hope and longing swirl inside him as he imagined Ashley's belly swollen with his child.

"Already?" she said with a sigh.

He heard the longing in her voice and hated how it affected him. Sebastian wanted to make her happy. He wanted to give her everything she wanted and be the reason there was a smile on her face. He glanced at his watch. "You can show me around the island before we leave."

Ashley's eyes lit up, but she gave him a suspicious look. "Really?" she asked uncertainly. As if she knew he was trying to make up for the argument they'd just had.

"Show me everything about Inez Key," he said. He knew a lot about this island, but he wanted to see it through her eyes.

Ashley grabbed his hand. "First, I'll show where the best place is to scuba dive. Oh, and surf. Did I tell you about the time I got stung by an eagle ray? It was an extremely painful experience, but not as much as when I broke my ankle when I fell from climbing a palm tree. I'll have to show you which ones are best to climb."

"I can't wait," Sebastian said with a small smile. He was curious to know what Ashley was like as a child and wanted to hear every story and anecdote.

They had explored the island for an hour, hand in hand, as Ashley pointed out her favorite spots. Some were connected to happy memories while others were breathtaking views.

"Do you know how the island got the name Inez Key?" Sebastian asked as he walked beside Ashley.

"It's called a key because it's a small island on coral," she explained.

"And Inez?"

"I assume the first settler on this island named it after a loved one." She stared at the main house as she slowed her pace. Her tour was almost done and then she would have to leave Inez Key.

"Assume?" he asked sharply.

"Okay, I'm not an expert on everything about this island. You should ask Clea. Her family has been on this island for generations," Ashley said as her smile dipped. Once she thought her descendants would live here for generations. She had imagined having a big family and the island being their safe haven. "Now that you mention it, I'm surprised my father didn't change the name. Make it Jones Key or something like that. Are you going to change the name?"

"Never."

His gruff response surprised her. "Why not? The name doesn't have any meaning to you."

Sebastian's hand flexed against hers. "How long have you lived here?" he asked.

"This wasn't our primary residence," she replied as she focused her attention on the main house. "I spent my summers on this island. My mother brought me here when she needed a getaway."

"So it wasn't used very often," he murmured. "It was almost forgotten."

"I'm sure it wasn't always like that. It's been in my family's care since before I was born. My father got it—"

"Got it?"

Ashley bit her tongue. Funny how he caught her choice of words. The man noticed everything. She had to be more careful. "My father's story about this island changed constantly," she admitted.

"What did you hear?" he asked as he slipped his hand away from hers.

She felt the tension emanating from Sebastian and hesitated. She didn't like revealing her family history. It offered people a chance to question her heritage and judge her. "It's difficult to extract the truth from the legend. Some say my father won it in a poker game. Others suggested it was a gift from a woman. I once heard a politician bought it for him in exchange for silence."

"What do you think happened?"

I think he stole it. She didn't know how her father had got the island, but she knew what kind of man he was. He cheated on and off the tennis court, but that wasn't her only clue. She remembered the sly look in his eyes when he spoke of Inez Key. She knew something bad happened and she had been too hesitant to dig deeper.

Ashley forced herself to give a casual shrug as she marched to the main house. "It's hard to say."

"I'm sure you have a theory." Sebastian watched her carefully.

"Not really," she said in a rush as they stood by the columns in the back of the main house. "Well, that's it of Inez Key."

"Don't you have more stories to tell?"

Ashley returned his smile. She had talked endlessly about her childhood adventures on Inez Key, but Sebastian hadn't seemed bored. He had been genuinely interested. "That's for another day," she promised.

"Thank you for sharing your stories," he said gently. "And for showing me your island."

She suddenly felt shy, as if she had shared a secret part of her. Ashley felt the warmth rush through her. "What's your favorite part of Inez Key?"

"The cove," he said. "It's the perfect hideout. No wonder the sea turtles nest there."

Ashley frowned. She didn't remember telling him about the nests that are laid during springtime. "How did you know we have sea turtles?"

Sebastian paused. "Uh, I think Clea said something about it."

"We usually get the loggerhead turtle to nest on our

island. Two months later, all of these hatchlings find their way to the water. It's an amazing sight."

"I'm sure it is," he murmured.

"I think the sea turtles pick this place because there aren't that many predators. The island is a good hideaway for people, too. The paparazzi never bothers us." Not even when her father was caught up in one scandal after another. She didn't know if it was because it was hard to find the remote island or because no journalist found it worthwhile to follow the betrayed mother and child.

Sebastian saw the shadows in her eyes. Was she recalling a bad memory from her childhood or was she reluctant to leave. "It's time to go, *mi vida*."

Ashley bit her lip. "Can't we stay just for the night?"

"Impossible." He didn't want Ashley to stay any longer. It was Cruz property now and the last thing he needed was the previous owner hanging around causing trouble. "I need to be at my mother's tomorrow morning."

"I'm sure she didn't extend the invitation to me," she said. "I can stay here until you return."

Sebastian hated that idea. He didn't want to spend another night away from Ashley. He hadn't been able to sleep and he ached all night to have her in his arms. The idea of finding a replacement hadn't even occurred to him. He only wanted Ashley.

"You forget our agreement," he said silkily. "You are supposed to be with me every day for a month. You missed a few days when you skipped out on me in Jamaica. That's going to cost you."

"Cost me?" Her face paled as she looked around her beloved Inez Key. "What do you mean?"

"You have not been with me for a consecutive thirty days," he explained. He smiled as he realized this gave him the chance to keep Ashley at his side for a little bit longer. "I'm adding those missing days at the end of your month."

Her lips parted in surprise. "That was not agreed upon."

He didn't care. He had torn through Miami looking for this woman and he wasn't ready to give her up. "Would you rather we start over and make this day one?"

Something hot and wild flared in her eyes. Ashley dipped her head as she dug her foot in the sand. "I thought you'd be bored staying with one woman for a month."

Sebastian frowned. That had been true, but not with Ashley. Now he was trying to find ways to keep her in his bed.

"Wait a second." Ashley lifted her head and stared at him with something close to horror. "Does this mean I'm meeting your mother? No. No way."

"I don't have much of a choice. Anyway, she's expecting you."

Ashley closed her eyes and slowly shook her head. "Do you usually introduce your mistress to your mother?" she asked huskily.

"I've never had a mistress," he admitted.

Ashley opened her eyes and stared at him.

Sebastian scowled. He hadn't planned to tell her that,

but for some reason it was suddenly important for her to understand that he wasn't that kind of man. Yet now he felt exposed under her gaze. As if he'd revealed too much of himself. "Don't think that makes you special."

Ashley glared at him. "Why should I? You had pushed me in a corner so efficiently. It was only natural to assume you blackmailed women in your bed on a regular basis."

He stepped closer. "You wanted to be in my bed," he declared. "I only had to give you an extra incentive."

She gave a haughty tilt to her chin. "Think that if it makes you feel better."

He curled a finger under her chin and brushed his thumb against her wide pink mouth. "You will need to curb your tongue before you meet my family," he warned her softly.

She tried to nip his thumb with her teeth, but he had anticipated that response. He removed his hand before she could catch him.

"I can't make any promises," she said and paused. "Did you say I'm meeting your family? I thought it was just your mother."

"My sisters will be there. That means their husbands, fiancés and children will also be around."

"Why? Is there a special occasion?"

"No, my family has these get-togethers all the time." And he worked hard to be there for his family. He didn't just write a check for his relatives—he was present for every important moment of their lives.

"Is there anything I should know about your family?" she asked.

"Do not introduce yourself as my mistress," he ordered.

She clucked her tongue. "Do you think I wear that label as a badge of honor?"

"You made it clear in Jamaica that you are my woman." He reached for her hand and laced his fingers with hers. "I didn't have to make a claim. You wore that status with pride."

"That was before you introduced me as your mistress," she said as the anger tightened her soft features. "I thought we actually made a good team until you warned off Salazar. Then you had to mark your territory. So how am I supposed to define this relationship?"

He was not going to introduce Ashley as his lover or girlfriend. That gave her privileges she didn't deserve. The reason he made Ashley his mistress was to knock down the status she never worked hard to earn. "You won't need to."

"Are you serious?" She tugged at his hand but he didn't let go. "Didn't you tell me you had sisters?"

"Yes, four of them."

"And how often have you brought a woman home to meet the family?" she asked brightly.

He exhaled sharply. "I haven't."

"You are in for an inquisition." Ashley smiled broadly as she imagined the treatment he would receive.

Or she was dreaming up ways to make his life miserable. He could send Ashley back to his penthouse apartment while he went to visit his family, but he didn't like that idea. He wanted Ashley there with him, but it was a risk. "Cause any trouble and you will regret it."

She flattened her hand against her chest. "Me? I won't have to say a word. I'll just cling to your arm and bat my lashes like a good little mistress."

"Ashley," he warned.

"At least tell me why we need to visit your family. Isn't your mother recuperating?"

He gave her an assessing glance. "How do you know about that?"

"What? Was it a secret? You said something about it at the opening of your club. I've often heard you talk to your mother on the phone."

Sebastian's eyes narrowed. "I didn't realize you knew Spanish." How much had she heard in his conversations? Did she also catch the endearments he whispered when they were in bed? He had to be more careful.

"I'm not fluent," she said. "I don't know anything about your mother's condition."

"She's recovering from heart surgery," he explained. "There had been a point when we didn't think she was going to make it. My mother made a dying request and we called the priest."

Ashley squeezed his hand in silent sympathy. "I won't do anything to upset her. I promise."

"Thank you." Sebastian realized how he was gripping her hand as if it was a lifeline. He reluctantly let go. "I don't want you to discuss our relationship with anyone in my family. Don't mention Inez Key. In fact, don't give any personal information."

"Should I pick an assumed name?" she asked wryly.

"Ashley Jones should be fine." It was a common name. His family wouldn't make the connection.

"Okay," she said with a shrug. "If that's what you want."

Her quick agreement made him suspicious. "What are you up to?"

"Nothing. I'll just keep the conversation all about you." She rubbed her hands with exaggerated glee. "I can't wait to learn all your secrets."

Dread seized his lungs until he remembered that there was an unspoken agreement with his family on some topics that were forbidden to discuss. "Good luck with that," he said with icy calm. "I don't have any."

Ashley made a face. "Everyone has secrets."

"You don't anymore," he said. "I uncovered them all when I took you to bed."

"You are so hung up on being my first," she muttered. Ashley looked flustered and shy. "If I knew that my virginity would have been so important to you…"

Sebastian stepped in front of her, blocking her from turning away. "What would you have done?" he asked. She had not been above using her virginity with Raymond Casillas to get what she wanted. "Keep away from me until I begged? Waited for a wedding ring on your finger?"

"No!" she said, staring at him with wide eyes. "I would have told you."

Would it have been that simple? Could their first night have been about two people giving in to a fiery attraction? "Why didn't you?"

"I didn't want you to know how inexperienced I was," she confessed as a ruddy color streaked her high cheekbones. "It would have given you the upper hand."

He always had the advantage even with the most experienced women. Although there had been some nights with Ashley when he wasn't sure who was seducing whom. She had gradually begun to realize the depths of his excitement when she made the first move. She was beginning to tap into the sexual power she held over him. He should hide his responses, or at least take over when she became too daring, but he didn't want to.

"You had nothing to worry about, *mi vida*. You're a very sensual woman." He noticed how his compliment horrified her. "I'm surprised you abstained for as long as you did. Why did you wait?"

"Lack of opportunity?" she hazarded a guess.

She was not telling him the truth. Not the whole truth. "That's not it at all," he said gently. "Men would subject themselves to Herculean tasks if it meant a chance for one night with you."

"Every man but you," she muttered. "You just had to snap your fingers and I was there."

"Why did you wait?" he repeated. What he really wanted to ask was, *Why did you choose me?*

"If you saw the house I was raised in you would understand." She crossed her arms and looked at the ocean, unable to meet his eyes. "My mother was a mistress. A sexual plaything for my father. My father was a womanizer. He was worse than his friends. The things I saw…heard. I didn't want to be a part of that."

Sebastian felt a sharp arrow of guilt. Shame. He was beginning to think he had made a mistake when he'd claimed Ashley as his mistress. He thought she didn't like the drop in status. Instead, he had made her the one thing she swore she would never be.

"And yet you slept with me." It didn't add up. Did she sleep with him so she could stop Raymond Casillas from calling in her debt? "According to you, I'm just like your father."

"I thought you were," she said quietly before she walked away. "I'm not so sure anymore."

The next evening, Ashley was on a luxurious patio that overlooked a private beach as she watched the sunset with Sebastian's mother. A group of children were playing in the sand. Music drifted from the open windows of the Cruz mansion and Ashley heard Sebastian's sisters bicker while they prepared the dinner table.

"Why is this the first I've heard of you?" Patricia Cruz asked as she intently studied Ashley.

Ashley hid her smile. She had a feeling that Sebastian took from his mother's side in temperament. "I don't know what to tell you, Mrs. Cruz. Perhaps you should ask Sebastian."

She gave a throaty chuckle. "He's not very forthcoming."

Neither was his mother. The older woman wasn't a tiny and weathered woman who favored housedresses and heavy shawls. This woman was tall and regal. Her elegant gray shift dress highlighted her short silver hair and tanned skin.

Patricia Esteban Cruz was polite but wary. She had expected Sebastian's family and home to be just as guarded. When Ashley had seen the iron gates open to the Cruz's beachfront mansion, panic had curled around her chest. She had looked out the window and saw a forest of palm trees flanking the long driveway.

Ashley had tried not to gasp when she spotted the villa at the end of the winding lane. The home was unlike anything she had seen. She had expected the Cruz mansion to be a dramatic and modern house. A fortress. But this was gracious and traditional with its terra-cotta rooftops and soft white exterior. Ashley was used to high society but this was another level. It was a reminder of Sebastian's power and influence.

"His sisters, however, are very warm and open," Ashley said. They had easily welcomed her. Sebastian's siblings were boisterous and inquisitive, but they had made Ashley feel as if she belonged.

And they had no reservations talking about Sebastian. At first it had been a trickle of information and it quickly became a flood of memories. The anecdotes and stories all described Sebastian as curious, volatile and too smart for his own good. He had been a lot of trouble, but everyone spoke about him with pride, love and exasperation.

"Yes, they didn't have as hard of a time as Sebastian," she said with a heavy sigh. "When my husband died, Sebastian became the head of the family. He was only a boy. Not even fifteen."

There was a fine tremor in the woman's fingers and Ashley noticed the gray pallor underneath the woman's skin. It was clear Patricia was still fragile from her surgery. "Sebastian doesn't talk about that time in his life. Or his father."

"He lives with the constant reminder," the older woman said. "He looks just like his father. My husband was very much a traditional man. Proud and artistic."

"Your husband was an artist?" Ashley asked.

She nodded. "He was a painter. Watercolors. He wasn't famous, but he was very respected in the art world. Some of his landscapes can be found here in my home." Patricia's eyes grew sad. "He stopped painting when we moved to the ghetto. He was working two jobs and feeding a growing family."

This was why Sebastian scoffed at the way she made a living. She may repair and maintain Inez Key, but she never had to do hard labor. She didn't know the strain of having a family depend on her.

"Which of your children inherited your husband's artistic talent?" From what she could tell, all of the Cruz daughters were brilliant, successful and creative.

"Mmm, that would be Sebastian."

"Really?" Sebastian thrived in the cutthroat business world. She hadn't seen any indication that he had an artistic side.

"You should have seen the work he did at school," Patricia said with a hint of pride. "His teachers encouraged him to find classes outside of school. If only we had the money. But Sebastian told he me didn't have the inclination to pursue it."

Ashley imagined Sebastian saying that with a dismissive wave of his hand. But she wondered if Sebastian didn't choose the arts because he had to be sensible. He would have known it would have been a financial strain for the family and he acted disinterested to protect his mother's feelings.

"Well, if there's one thing I've noticed about Sebastian," Ashley said brightly, "he can do anything he puts his mind to. If he had wanted to be an artist, he would have been."

"And what is it that you do, Ashley?" Sebastian's mother asked. "You're twenty-three? I'm sure you have found your passion by now."

Ashley knew it was another attempt to learn about her past. She wasn't willing to share, and not just because of Sebastian's request. It was unlikely that she would meet Patricia Esteban Cruz again, but she didn't want to be judged by her parentage.

"I'm still trying to figure that out," Ashley carefully replied. "What did you want to be when you were twenty-three?"

"Home." Patricia had a faraway look in her eyes. "I wanted to be home, safe and sound with my babies while my husband was happily painting pictures of sunsets and nighthawks."

Nighthawks? Ashley frowned. Those birds were indigenous to the keys. She hadn't realized they were up here on the mainland.

Ashley turned sharply when she heard the piercing squeal of a child's laughter. She saw Sebastian, sexy and casual in a T-shirt and jeans, at the edge of the beach. The water lapped at his bare feet as he held one of his nephews in his strong hands.

"More, Tio Sebastian! More!" the little boy shrieked as Sebastian tossed him high in the air before catching him. One of his nieces clung to Sebastian's legs with her thumb firmly planted in her mouth. Ashley noticed the toddler had attached herself to her tio Sebastian the moment they had arrived.

"Ah, my grandchildren are precious to me, but they wear me out," Patricia confessed as she watched the trio on the beach. "Sebastian is so patient with them. Gives each of his nieces and nephews extra attention. If only he was so patient with his sisters."

"He's very good with children." She remembered how gentle he had been with Clea's granddaughters on Inez Key. Ashley had been concerned Sebastian would be like most of her paying guests who didn't want to hear or see children on the island. She recalled how he had found them playing on the beach one day and when he had approached them, Ashley's first thought had been to protect them. Ashley thought the girls would have been scared or intimidated by Sebastian. But he had surprised her when he had crouched down in front of the curious children and got down to their level.

A smile tugged on Ashley's mouth as she remembered that hot and humid morning. The scene had been so incongruous with Sebastian's dark head next to Lizet and Matil, who wore silly hats to protect them from the sun. He had given the girls his full attention, speaking in a low voice as he praised their efforts in building a sand castle.

The children immediately adored him, with Lizet shyly offering her battered pink bucket while Matil danced excitedly around them. Ashley had quietly watched as Sebastian had played with the children.

She had been amazed by the gentleness and patience he had displayed.

"He would make a good father," Patricia declared.

Ashley wanted to reject that idea. Sebastian was a playboy. A good father would be sweet and tender. A family man. He wouldn't be someone like her father who would destroy a family in his pursuit to have sex with many women.

But Sebastian wasn't like Donald Jones, Ashley realized with a start. Sebastian cared about his family. Family was his haven, not his burden. He honored his commitments and was willing to put his family's needs before his. And he would protect his loved ones instead of overpowering them.

Ashley knew she would be included if she was carrying his baby. She closed her eyes and imagined Sebastian holding her close as his fingers splayed against her swollen stomach. His touch would be gentle and possessive. He would not allow anything to happen to them as a family. As a couple.

"Do you think differently?" Patricia asked, jarring Ashley from her musings. "Do you think Sebastian would make a bad father?"

"He would be the father any child would hope for," Ashley said slowly as she thought about how Sebastian embodied everything she hoped for in a man, a husband, and yet he was also everything she feared. "But I don't think he has the inclination to become one."

"That's what I'm worried about. Sebastian had to look after his sisters at such a young age. He may not want to do it again. But that man should have a wife. Children of his own."

"Carry on the Cruz name?" Ashley added as she absently rubbed her flat stomach. She wanted Sebastian's child. More than one. She wanted to create a large family filled with sons and daughters that had the same dark hair, stubbornness and strength as their father. Most of all, she wanted to see those children bring out Sebastian's fierce paternal side.

"Exactly." Patricia smacked her armrest with her hand like a judge would bang a gavel. "He should marry."

Don't look at me. Ashley gritted her teeth before the words tumbled off her tongue. Men didn't marry their mistresses. She had it on good authority. Her mother had tried every trick for twenty years to make Donald her husband.

Donald and Linda may have shared a past and a child, but they never shared a family name. Donald had given his surname to Ashley, but she had never understood why. Why had she been considered good enough for the Jones name and not her mother?

But Sebastian was different, Ashley thought as she watched him set down his nephew and hoist his small niece into his arms. He would marry her if she was carrying his child. She longed for a traditional family but not like this. If she was pregnant with his baby, she would have some tough decisions to make. She had been tolerated in her father's home, part of a package deal. Ashley wasn't going to go through that again.

* * *

Later that night, Sebastian stepped out of the bathroom and into the guest bedroom. The steam from his shower curled around him as he slung a towel low around his waist. His heart beat against his ribs as he anticipated having Ashley all to himself.

He stopped in the middle of the room when he noticed Ashley wasn't in the large bed waiting for him. She wasn't in the sitting area or at the desk. Sebastian turned and saw Ashley standing at the long open window, the gauzy curtains billowing against her.

Desire slammed through him as he noticed how the silk slip skimmed against her gentle curves. The dark pink accentuated her sun-kissed skin and the short hem barely reached her thighs. He was tempted to pull the delicate shoulder straps until they broke and watch the silk tumble to the floor.

It took him a moment to notice that Ashley was waving at someone outside. "Who are you waving to?" he asked gruffly. As much as he enjoyed the sight, he was prepared to cloak her with something heavy. He should be the only one who saw her like this.

"Your sister Ana Sofia and her husband," she responded without looking at him. "Apparently, they take a moonlight stroll along the beach every night."

"I'm sure that's real romantic when it's pouring down rain." He refused to hear the catch in her throat. "You and Ana Sofia were thick as thieves tonight."

She turned away from the window and he saw her smile. "She wanted to tell me all of the mean things you did to her while you were growing up. I have to say, none of it surprised me."

"I had to be strict with her," he said as he approached her. "I'm her big brother and our father had died."

She nodded. "I understand, but you're lucky you had your sisters."

"It didn't feel so lucky," he muttered.

"Well, I was an only child. I would have loved a sister or two."

He noticed Ashley had watched how his family interacted with a mix of amusement and bewilderment. "They were in full force today. You didn't find them overwhelming?"

"It took some time to get used to it," she admitted. "Your sisters got a little vocal at the dinner table."

"That?" He rested his hand against the wall and he leaned into her. "That was nothing."

She gave him a look of disbelief. "You were arguing about a vase that broke almost twenty years ago."

"I was blamed for that because I was supposed to be looking after my sisters." He hadn't been surprised that Ashley didn't side with him during the argument. Did she still see him as the opposition? The enemy? "Ana Sofia was the one who actually broke it."

"Twenty years ago," she reminded him. "You can certainly hold a grudge."

"You have no idea." He gritted his teeth and took a step back. Sebastian wasn't going to reveal just how much a grudge motivated him. Dominated his thoughts. "I'm sure this happened in your house, too. Who were you able to blame when you broke something? The family dog?"

"It never happened, but I don't think my parents would have noticed. Quite a few breakables were thrown against the wall during an argument in my house," she said matter-of-factly. "And I can't count how much damage occurred during one of my father's famous house parties."

Was this why Ashley didn't drink or party? Why she didn't enjoy dancing and preferred her solitude? He wouldn't blame her. Ashley's home life was more of a war zone than a wonderland. "How did you escape? Did you spend a lot of time at a friend's house?"

"Not really. Once their parents found out that I was a mistress's love child I wasn't invited over. Something about being a bad influence." She grimaced as if she had tasted something unpleasant. "Love child. It sounds like I was born out of love, but I wasn't. I hate that label."

And she hated the label of mistress. He didn't know that it would hurt her so much. He didn't know she had been an outcast because of the stigma. He had made a power play without considering Ashley's past. But how could he fix it now?

Ashley raked her hand over her hair and rolled back her shoulders. Sebastian had seen that movement before. He knew this was a sign that she was finished with the conversation.

"I've been meaning to ask," she said as she walked away. "Did your father paint this watercolor?"

His gaze flew to the framed picture that hung on the wall. He'd forgotten about the picture of the sunset. "Yes."

"It's very good," she said as she walked to the bedside table and gave the picture a closer look. "It reminds me a lot of the sunsets I see on Inez Key. It kind of makes me homesick."

The longing in her quiet tone scored at him. He wasn't going to fall for this guilt trip. He had to be strict with Ashley or she would soon discover that he was willing to give her almost anything she wanted.

"Is this another attempt to go back to the island?" he asked as he followed her.

She jerked her head in surprise and turned to face him. "No. I'm a mistress for a month and I have to be at your beck and call for a little over two weeks. I can wait."

The pang of guilt intensified. He should honor his word and allow her to become the caretaker for Inez Key. But he didn't want her on the island. She didn't belong there. Ashley Jones belonged in his bed and at his side.

"What if we renegotiated?" he asked.

Ashley frowned and she studied his expression, as if trying to determine whether he was reneging. "What are you talking about?"

"The time frame remains the same but we drop the mistress part," he suggested as he reached for her. "Forget the rules I set in place."

She pressed her hand against his bare chest. Her fingers curled in the damp mat of his dark hair. "What's the catch?"

"No catch," he said as he moved closer.

"Is this renegotiation because you don't want your mistress in your family home," she asked, "or because you can't tolerate the idea that your mistress might be having your baby?"

"You know, I should have walked away when you broke your promise," he said. "You were supposed to be available to me at all times, but you went off with Salazar for a few days."

Ashley gave an exasperated sigh. "You make that sound much more scandalous that it was. And may I remind you that you broke both of my rules?"

"Do you want to drop the mistress label or not?" he asked roughly as he gathered her tightly until her body was flush with his.

She swiped her tongue along her bottom lip. "What would I be known as instead?" she whispered.

"Mine."

He saw the flare of heat in her dark eyes. She dipped her head and looked away. "I'm serious."

"As Ashley." *My Ashley. My woman. Mi vida. Mine.* And the next man who tried to take her away from him would deeply regret it.

Ashley frowned and lifted her head to meet his gaze. "Do you still expect total obedience?"

"If it hasn't happened yet, it's not going to," he said as he pressed his mouth against the fluttering pulse point at the base of her throat. He liked how trusting and wild she was in his arms. That was all he needed.

"I can make my own decisions on which events to attend with you?" Ashley asked, her breath hitching as he shoved the delicate strap down her shoulder. "And what I'm going to wear?"

Sebastian cupped her breast with his large hand. He

felt her tight nipple against his palm. "Yes," he said almost in a daze.

"And tonight I could get my own bedroom?"

He stilled as something close to fear forked through him. "No," he said with a growl. He should have known that if he gave her an inch, she'd take a mile. The only hold he had left on Ashley was the sexual chemistry they shared. She couldn't hide her emotions, her needs, when they were in bed. He wasn't going to allow any distance between them.

"Why not?" she teased. "Is it really that important to you? I—"

"You are not kicking me out of your bed again. You don't want sex tonight? Fine," he snapped. "But we're sharing the same bed. Always."

"It's a deal," she said with a seductive smile. "And Sebastian?"

"What?" His tone was harsh as the relief poured through him.

"I want you tonight," she said as she reached for the towel wrapped around his waist. "All night and every night."

"I've noticed," he drawled as his heart pounded in his ears. Sebastian lifted Ashley and she wrapped her legs around his waist. He had wondered when she was going to admit that she couldn't keep her hands off him. He knew she wouldn't have made the confession as a mistress.

This impetuous renegotiation was going to give him everything he wanted.

CHAPTER NINE

THE ELEGANT SOUTH BEACH restaurant offered a spectacular view and an award-winning menu, but Sebastian barely noticed. He didn't care that he had a mountain of work waiting for him at the office or that some of the most powerful people in Miami were sitting nearby, hoping to catch his eye. Nothing mattered except the exquisite brunette at his side.

Sebastian leaned back in his chair and smiled as he heard Ashley's earthy laugh. It made him tingle as if a spray of fireworks lit under his skin. Ashley's laugh was one of his most favorite sounds. It was right up there with her moan of pleasure and the way her breath hitched in her throat when he knew just how to touch her.

He watched Ashley as his friend Omar told her about one of their ill-conceived childhood antics. Omar embellished the story, making it sound as if he'd saved Sebastian from a gruesome death instead of the daily violence they had faced. His friend's wife shook her head as she listened to the story with a mix of horror and amusement.

Sebastian wished he could freeze this moment. It was rare for him to feel content. Satisfied. Hopeful. He didn't allow himself a lot of downtime. He couldn't remember the last time he'd spent the evening with his friends. Sebastian didn't feel the need to relax and have a drink. He was always pursuing the next challenge, creating the next strategy.

All that changed once he had Ashley at his side. His body tightened with lust as he studied her. She wore her hair piled high on her head. He was tempted to reach over, pull the pins and watch the heavy waves fall past her bare shoulders. He suspected she chose the style to tease him all evening.

Her dress was another matter. Short, strapless and scarlet, Ashley had worn it to please him. She knew how to showcase her curves and she was aware that his favorite color was red. The bold cleavage made him grit his teeth, but he was secretly touched that she dressed with him in mind.

He was glad she chose to be at his side tonight and every night. Not as his mistress, but as… As what? His lover? His girlfriend? Possibly the mother of his child? He was reluctant to give her that kind of power or accept her claim in his life. He wasn't sure what Ashley was, but she was important to him.

But their month was almost up. If she wasn't pregnant, he had to let her go. Unless he followed through and allowed her to become the caretaker of Inez Key. It wasn't an ideal choice since he wasn't going to live on the island. But he planned to visit frequently….

Ashley tilted her head back and laughed. "I can just

picture it," she said between gasps as she flattened her hands against her chest. "You two were trouble."

"Wait a second!" Crystal's eyes lit up as she pointed her finger at Ashley. "Now I know why you look familiar."

Sebastian saw Ashley stiffen. He wanted to silence Omar's wife. Protect Ashley. It was unfair for Ashley. She had lowered her guard only to be confronted with her family history.

"You are the daughter of that tennis legend," Crystal exclaimed.

"Yes, I am," Ashley confirmed quietly as she reached for her water glass. "How did you know?"

"Like I said, I am a news junkie," Crystal said proudly. "There was something about the way the light hit your face. You look exactly like your mother."

"Thank you," Ashley said. Was it only Sebastian who noticed the pain that flashed in her eyes? Linda Valdez had been a beautiful woman, but Ashley didn't like being compared to her mother.

"Who are you talking about?" Omar asked his wife.

"Ashley's father was Donald Jones. The tennis star," Crystal explained.

Sebastian admired Ashley's calm. He knew what she was thinking. That his friends were going to see her differently because she was a love child and her mother was a mistress. Because her parents died in a murder-suicide.

She would soon learn that his friends—his true friends—didn't judge. After surviving the ghetto and witnessing the darker side of humanity, nothing shocked them.

"Donald…Jones?" Omar repeated slowly and gave Sebastian a quick glance.

Damn. Sebastian's gut twisted with alarm. He'd forgotten that Omar knew how his past was intertwined with Donald Jones. Sebastian gave the slightest shake of his head and Omar immediately went quiet. He hoped Ashley didn't notice the silent exchange.

"Oh, I'm sure I have mascara streaming down my face," Ashley murmured as she pressed her fingertips underneath her eyes. She grabbed for her purse and stood up. "I'll have to fix my makeup."

Sebastian quietly rose from the table. He knew Ashley wanted to hide. Just for a moment so she could firmly fix the cool mask she displayed to the public. The one that made people think she lived a quiet and uneventful life on a private island.

"I'll come with you," Crystal offered as she scrambled out of her seat.

Ashley didn't say anything, but Sebastian noticed the tension in her polite smile. He wanted to intervene and protect her from the intrusive questions Crystal would undoubtedly ask. He couldn't. His guarded response would create more questions.

He reached for her and pressed his lips against her temple. He felt Ashley lean against him briefly before she stepped away. He wanted to block Crystal, but Ashley was experienced in facing this kind of attention with grace.

He sat down once the women left the table and immediately faced Omar's disapproving glare. "Donald

Jones?" his friend asked angrily. "It can't be a coincidence."

He wasn't going to insult his friend with a lie. "It's not."

Omar rubbed his forehead and exhaled sharply. "What have you done, Sebastian?"

He jutted out his chin. "I settled an old score. Karma was taking too long."

"I thought you put all this behind you," Omar said. He looked around to make sure no one could hear the conversation. "You've become richer and more powerful than Jones."

That didn't mean he'd won. "It doesn't erase what he did."

Omar shook his head. "I don't get it. Why now? Why, after all this time?"

There had been a time when Sebastian had been consumed by the injustice. It ate away at him, making him feel weak and empty. He had been an angry boy. He had been a kid who'd lost his innocence too soon and his childhood the moment he had been thrown into a cruel world. He wanted to get what was stolen from him and pushed himself every day to the brink of exhaustion to become rich and powerful.

He had suffered setbacks and bad luck, but by the time he had made his first million, Sebastian wasn't thinking about Donald Jones. His goal had been to protect his family from losing everything. They would never be at the mercy of the Donald Joneses of the world.

But then his mother had heart surgery, and everything changed. He realized he was still the angry little boy who couldn't allow the injustice to go untouched.

"When we thought my mother was dying, she had only one request." Sebastian remembered his mother lying on the hospital bed, pale and fragile. She had struggled to speak and he knew this favor meant everything to her, even after all these years. "How could I deny her?"

"I know your mother," Omar said with a frown. "She didn't ask for revenge."

"What I'm doing is righting some wrongs," Sebastian argued. "Finding justice."

"Then I have to ask you this." Omar rested his arms on the table and leaned forward. "What threats did you make to Ashley? What did you take from her? And what will she have left when all this is done?"

"You don't have to worry about Ashley. Spoiled heiresses always land on their feet." Sebastian winced. He shouldn't have called her that. Ashley had once lived in a world of excess and privilege, but if she were really a pampered princess, she wouldn't have survived on her own for this long.

"She's no spoiled heiress," Omar insisted. "Believe me, I'm married to one. Ashley is innocent. She's going to be collateral damage. Just like you were."

Sebastian glared at his friend. Ashley wasn't getting the same treatment that he had received. She lived in luxury and under his protection. "Omar, you don't know what you're talking about."

"I hope not," Omar's eyes were dull with disappointment. "Because I never thought I'd see the day when you became just like Donald Jones."

"I am nothing like that man," he hissed.

"Time will tell," Omar murmured. "Sooner than you think."

It was hours later when Ashley returned to the penthouse apartment with Sebastian. Despite Crystal's inquisitive nature and the painful memories that were dredged up with her pointed questions, Ashley had been determined to end the night on a lighthearted note. She didn't want anyone to know how much her family's action still hurt after all these years.

Sebastian excused himself and went to his office to return a few phone calls. She knew he would be there for a while and she was grateful to have a moment alone. Kicking off her heels, Ashley headed to the swimming pool.

She was too tired to swim. The cold water wasn't going to take away the chill that had seeped into her bones. Ashley paced around the pool as she tried to purge her memories.

"Ashley?" Sebastian's voice cut through her troubled thoughts. "What are you doing here?"

She shrugged. "Just thinking. Don't you have some calls to return?"

"That was hours ago," he said as he strolled toward her.

"Oh." She stopped and stared at the Miami skyline. She had no idea that much time and passed.

"What did Crystal say when you two were alone? Did she upset you?"

Ashley shook her head. "Crystal kept asking the same questions everyone else does. It's nothing I can't handle."

"Her questions stirred up something?"

"I still can't forgive what my parents did to each other," she muttered. "Most of all, I can't forgive myself."

Sebastian frowned. "Why do you need forgiveness?"

Ashley crossed her arms tightly against her. She wanted to remain quiet, but the confession pressed upon her chest. "When I was eighteen I'd had enough of my father's infidelities. I couldn't stand the fact that my mother was unable to see what was going on right under her nose."

"What did you do?" Sebastian asked.

"I told my mother the unvarnished truth." She closed her eyes and remembered her mother's expression. It had been a gradual transformation from disbelief to shock. The pain had etched into her mother's face and Ashley didn't think it would ever disappear. "I had been harsh and I didn't spare her feelings. I was the one who told my mother about his long-standing affair with her best friend."

Sebastian showed no reaction. He wasn't scandalized by her parents' choices or her actions. Most people were and couldn't wait to hear all the dirty details. Instead, he said, "That had to have been the most difficult moment in your life."

"No," she admitted for the first time. "It had been a

relief. I felt we could have a new start. I wanted to end the drama and the fear. I never felt safe while I was growing up. I never knew when another fight would happen."

She wasn't sure why she was telling Sebastian this. Ashley had never shared this secret. She had destroyed her family and no matter how much she stayed on Inez Key and barred herself from the world, she would never find redemption.

But Ashley didn't feel the need to hide this from Sebastian. If anything, she was compelled to share it with him. Her instincts told her that he would understand.

"I didn't care that I betrayed my father," Ashley said, rubbing her hands over her cold arms. "I felt like he had betrayed us a long time ago."

"I take it that your father found out."

"Yes, he shipped me off to college. I should have been grateful to get out of that toxic environment, but instead I retaliated." She had been hurt and out of control. She didn't think she had done anything wrong and her father should have been the one who was punished. "I should have stopped, but instead I told my mother about his other…transgressions. The ones that the tabloids hadn't uncovered. My mother responded by shutting me out of her life."

"Both your parents punished you for telling the truth."

"A month later they were dead," she said as the old grief hit her like a big wave. "Instead of protecting my family, I destroyed it. I caused so much pain."

"You didn't know that would be the end result."

"I knew it wouldn't end quietly. That wasn't their style." She walked past Sebastian, no longer able to face him. She had to get away and find somewhere she could grieve and suffer alone. "People always want to know what triggered the murder-suicide. No one has figured out that I'm the one who set everything into motion."

"Ashley?" he called after her.

She reluctantly turned around, prepared to see the condemnation and disgust in Sebastian's eyes. "What?"

"Whatever happened to the best friend?" he asked. She realized he had already figured out but was looking for confirmation. "The one who had an affair with your father?"

Only he would ask her that. He knew how her mind worked. It should scare her, but she felt he empathized. He knew she wasn't as innocent as she appeared. What he didn't know was that it was the last time she'd confronted and took action instead of running away and hiding.

"I wanted vengeance," she said. "It was wrong of me. I should have let it go, but I couldn't let her get away unscathed. She had pretended to be a loyal friend, but I made sure everyone discovered her true nature. She lost everything that was important to her—her status, her social connections and her husband."

"We're not so different," Sebastian said quietly. "I would have done the same."

Ashley silently walked to Sebastian and rested her head against his shoulder. She sighed as he wrapped his arms around her. She wasn't sure if it had been smart to reveal her darkest secret to Sebastian. He had used her confessions in the past. He had broken his promises.

If he wanted to destroy her completely, nothing could stop him from using this information.

The next morning Sebastian covertly watched Ashley at the breakfast table. Her tousled hair fell over her face like a veil and she wore his bathrobe that overwhelmed her feminine frame. She grasped her mug with both hands and stared into the coffee as if it held all the answers of life.

He knew she loved her morning coffee to the point that it was a sacred ritual, but this was ridiculous. She was hiding from him. Distancing herself.

And Ashley was too quiet for his liking. In the past he would assume the lack of conversation meant she was plotting his demise. Today he suspected she was uncomfortable about sharing her secret with him.

He was offended but he also knew she had a right to feel this way. He didn't have a great track record when it came to Ashley Jones. When she told him about the loan with Raymond Casillas, he had used that information for his benefit. He had also used her sexual attraction to make her his mistress. A broken promise or two, and the possibility that he accidentally got her pregnant....

Sebastian swallowed back an oath. She was probably counting down the minutes until this agreement ended. He needed to show Ashley that he could take care of her in and out of bed. He had to honor his agreement and have her stay on Inez Key.

But would she still want to be with him? Or was she

already distancing herself because there were only a few more days of their arrangement? Was it too late to prove to Ashley that he could be the man she wanted?

Sebastian hated this uncertainty. Most women were content with his attention and his lifestyle. That wasn't enough to hold on to Ashley. For a moment he wished she were pregnant with his child. He had a blistering need to create a lasting connection with this woman.

There was one place he could start. "I have to go on another trip today," Sebastian announced. "I want you to come with me."

Ashley pushed back her hair. "Where are you going this time?"

"Inez Key."

Ashley jerked with surprise. Her fingers shook as she set the coffee mug down with a thud. "You want *me* to go to Inez Key? Why?"

Because he wanted to make her happy. Give her everything she wanted. Find some kind of compromise that could even assuage the guilt that pressed against his chest. "The renovations are almost complete," he said as if that explained everything.

"That was fast," she said with a frown. "How did you manage that?"

"You can accomplish anything when you have money." And he had thrown a great deal of money on the project. Everything had to be perfect in the main house. The grounds had to be exactly as they were twenty-five years ago. Nothing else would do.

"Why do you want me along?"

"You're going to be the caretaker of the island," he said as he took the last sip of his coffee.

Ashley dipped her head. "About that..."

His hand stilled as he listened to her hesitant tone. He thought she would be pleased. Excited to remain on the island. Grateful for the chance to stay.

"I have to decline the offer."

"Why?" She had stayed with him for a month to gain the right to be on the island. Now she was throwing back his offer. "Isn't that what you wanted all along?"

"I needed the island five years ago. It was my haven." Ashley glanced up and met his gaze. "But I'm a different person now and I can't put my life on hold anymore. It's time for me to move on. I can't do that if I'm at Inez Key."

Sebastian struggled with the temptation to argue. He wanted to convince her that the island was the best place for her to stay, but deep down he knew it wasn't true. It was the best thing for *him* if she stayed. She would remain on an isolated island with no single men and always available to him. He liked that idea far too much.

"What are you going to do instead?" he asked gruffly.

Ashley looked away. "I don't know. I'll think of something."

She didn't seem excited about this change in her life. She simply accepted it. But if she didn't want Inez Key anymore, he had no hold on her. Unless he asked her to live with him.

Sebastian's heart pounded hard against his chest. He wanted to extend the invitation, but he wasn't sure what her answer would be. She had rejected him before, and that was before she discovered how he'd double-crossed her. Ashley knew what kind of man he was and she would not willingly choose to share her life with him.

"You should still visit Inez Key with me," he decided. "It would be a good time to collect your things and say goodbye to your friends."

"You're right," Ashley said softly. "I should have one last look and then move on."

Ashley didn't like staying in the antebellum mansion at night. There were too many memories and too many shadows to face in the lonely and quiet house. But tonight was different. The islanders had decorated the beach with torches and flower garlands for her. They danced to the beat of a makeshift drum, sang old pirate songs and drank rum.

The gathering felt more of a coming-of-age celebration than a going-away party. She felt the love and understanding from everyone. She was going to miss them, but she knew they would be thinking of her as she started this new journey.

"Thanks for inviting me to Inez Key," Ashley said to Sebastian as she curled against him while they took the winding staircase to the master suite. "I'm glad I came."

"The islanders are really going to miss you."

"Try not to sound so surprised," she said with an exasperated smile. "Everyone on Inez Key has been like family to me. Clea treated me as an honorary daughter. I'm not sure what she thinks of you." Ashley's smile dipped as she remembered how the older woman had stared intently at Sebastian for most of the party.

"She's angry with me because I'm the reason you're leaving," Sebastian said as he opened the door to the master suite. "She may always see me as the enemy."

Ashley stepped out of Sebastian's arms as she stepped into the master bedroom. She blinked when she noticed the change. The heavy furniture and the four-poster bed that once dominated the room had been replaced. The colorful and modern furniture changed the feel of the room. Erased the oppressive feeling she had whenever she had stepped inside.

"I forgot," Sebastian muttered. "This room had too many memories."

"No, it's okay. I'm right where I want to be." She cupped Sebastian's face with her hands and kissed him. This might be the last chance she had to touch him and lay with him. After her month was up, she no longer had a claim to him.

She broke the kiss and reached for his hand before she silently walked to the bed. She crawled onto the sumptuous bedding and reached for him.

Sebastian didn't seem to be in any rush. He cradled her face and brushed his mouth against hers. His gentleness made Ashley's breath catch in her throat.

He continued to kiss her slowly. Sebastian pressed his mouth against her forehead and her cheeks. His lips grazed the line of her jaw and the curve of her ear. It was as if he was committing her features to memory.

"This is how I would have made love to you the first time," he said as he dragged the thin shoulder straps of her dress down her arms. "If I had known you were a virgin."

"Our first night was special. Perfect," she insisted as she tilted her head back and arched her neck, silently encouraging him to continue. "I don't need a do-over."

"I scared you off," he reminded her as he kissed a trail down her throat.

"I scared myself," she corrected breathlessly as her pulse skipped a beat. "It was too much, too intense. I'd never felt that way before."

"You wanted to hide," he said as he reverently peeled her flirty sundress from her body. "That's why you had rejected my offer."

"It was stupid of me," she admitted as she dragged the buttons free from his shirt. She leaned forward and pressed her mouth against the warm, golden-brown skin she had just revealed. "I didn't mean to come across as a coldhearted bitch."

"What if I made that offer now?" Sebastian's tone was casual, but she sensed he was not asking lightly. "How would you respond?"

Her heart lurched. "That depends," she said huskily. "What is the offer?"

Sebastian shrugged off his shirt and lowered her onto the mattress. He stood before her, proud and male. "Come back to Miami with me."

For how long? And in what role? The questions burned on her tongue but she remained silent. Would she be his occasional hostess or his arm candy? Would she be his hostess or his baby mama?

Ashley wanted to accept his offer immediately and

not look too closely. Refuse to negotiate and dismiss any reservations. She loved him with a ferocity that bordered on obsession. She now understood why her mother had risked everything to be with the man that she loved. The only difference was that Ashley had chosen a good man. A man who would treat her with respect and adoration.

"Well?" Sebastian asked impatiently.

Ashley bit her lip. She wasn't sure whether he was suggesting this because he thought she was pregnant. He had asked her every morning and it didn't help that her period was late. Was he making a strategic move or was this invitation from the heart?

She stretched slowly against the mattress and watched Sebastian's features tighten with lust. "No incentives this time, Sebastian?" she teased.

"I don't have anything you need," he said as he hooked his large fingers underneath the trim of her panties and slowly dragged the scrap of silk down her trembling legs.

She swiped her tongue along her bottom lip. "Don't be too sure about that."

"Tell me what you want," he encouraged softly. "Ask for anything and I will give it to you."

She wanted his love. Ashley knew she should look away before her eyes revealed the truth, but she was ensnared by his hot gaze. She wanted more than his attention or his heart. She wanted everything Sebastian Cruz had to offer. She wished to be part of his life, his future and his very soul.

"You." Her voice croaked as the emotions gripped her chest. "I want you and don't hold anything back."

"And you shall have it," Sebastian said as he crawled onto the bed and hovered above her. His strong arms on either side of her head as his hands pinned her wavy hair. She couldn't move if she'd wanted to.

Sebastian crushed her lips with his mouth before he licked and kissed his way down her chest. He captured her tight nipple with his teeth and teased her with his tongue until the sensations rippled under her skin.

Ashley twisted underneath him as he caressed and laved his tongue against her flat stomach. She bunched the bedsheets in her fists. Her legs shook with anticipation when he cupped her sex with a possessive hand.

Sebastian held her gaze as he stroked the folds of her sex. Her skin grew flush and her breathing deserted her as he rocked her hips. He placed his mouth against the heart of her. Ashley moaned as her core clenched. She went wild under his tongue as he savored the taste of her.

Her climax was swift and brutal. Ashley went limp as her heart raced. She heard Sebastian remove his clothes and she slowly opened her eyes. Sebastian stood at the side of the bed, gloriously naked as he rolled on a condom.

He didn't say anything as he parted her legs with forceful hands before he settled between her thighs. She watched the primitive emotions flickering across his harsh face as he surged into her.

Ashley's gasp mingled with Sebastian's low groan. She rolled her hips as he began to thrust. It was a slow and steady rhythm that was designed to make her lose her mind.

Her flesh gripped him tightly as he surged in deeper. Ashley wanted more. Wanted this to last forever. She wanted Sebastian forever.

"I love you." The words tumbled out of her mouth in an agonized whisper.

Sebastian went still. Ashley closed her eyes and turned her head away. She hadn't planned to reveal her final secret to him.

Sebastian drove into her. His rhythm grew faster. Harder. She didn't dare look at him. Did he feel triumphant or annoyed? Was he amused or irritated by her spontaneous words?

The bed shook with each demanding thrust. It was as if he was branding her with his touch and making the most intimate claim. Another climax—harder and hotter—took her by surprise. She cried out just as Sebastian found his release.

He collapsed on top of her and she welcomed the weight of his sweat-slick body. There was no doubt anymore, she decided as she gulped in air. She belonged to Sebastian Cruz forever.

CHAPTER TEN

THE NEXT MORNING Ashley stood by the double doors that led to the balcony. It was a perfect day at Inez Key; hot with very little humidity. The ocean was calm and a vivid blue. The tropical flowers were opening under the brilliant sun.

But her troubled thoughts didn't allow her to enjoy the view. Ashley glanced at the bed behind her. The sheets were rumpled and the pillows had been thrown on the floor at some time during the night. Yet this morning she had woken up alone.

Sebastian was avoiding her because she had told him she was in love with him. Ashley bit her lip as she recalled that moment. What had gotten into her? She was good at hiding her feelings, but she'd lowered her guard last night. She had been compelled to share how she felt.

And Sebastian didn't say anything in return. In fact, he didn't say anything at all.

Ashley rubbed her forehead and leaned against the door frame. It didn't matter. She had said it in the heat of the moment. He wasn't going to take her words seriously.

She saw a movement on the beach and leaned forward. Sebastian was walking on the dock as he spoke on his cell phone. She couldn't hear his conversation but she knew from the smile and the way he dipped his head that he was speaking to his mother.

Sebastian Cruz was an arrogant and powerful playboy, but he was also a family man. She admired how he took care of his family. She thought that kind of man was only found on unrealistic television shows. But she also noticed how Sebastian treated his mother and sisters.

Unlike the playboys she knew, Sebastian respected women. No matter how exasperated he was with his sisters, Sebastian saw them as successful women who brought a valuable contribution to their fields, community and to the family. He listened to his mother's opinions and sought out her advice. He was ready to help the women in his family if they asked, but he never saw them as useless, porcelain dolls.

Ashley watched from her vantage point, knowing he couldn't see her on the shaded balcony. She could study him and memorize his hard angles and wide shoulders. The man was raw male and sexuality even in his wrinkled cotton shirt and low-slung jeans. It was a shame she wasn't carrying his child.

She'd discovered that this morning, and instead of feeling relieved, Ashley had struggled with her disappointment. She hadn't realized how much she'd wanted Sebastian's baby until that moment. Now there was nothing to keep him at her side.

Ashley saw Sebastian disconnect his call as he

walked to the front door. She couldn't see him but she heard him greet Clea.

"Good morning, Mr. Sebastian," the housekeeper said. Her tone was friendly as usual, but Ashley recognized a bubbling excitement underneath the words. "I've been meaning to ask you, but I haven't had a chance to speak to you alone."

"What do you want to know?" Sebastian's voice was low and rough.

"Did you use to live in this house? I would say about twenty-five years ago?"

Ashley jerked back as her heart stopped. What was Clea saying? That the Cruz family had once owned Inez Key? That was ridiculous, surely.

"Yes," Sebastian said with eerie calm, "this used to be my home until Donald Jones stole it from my family."

Ashley's skin went hot and then cold as the bile churned in her stomach. Her father had taken this island from the Cruz family. Ruined them. And for what? He'd had no interest in Inez Key.

"And you stole it back," Clea said dazedly.

The housekeeper's words echoed in her head. Ashley leaned against the wall as her shaky legs threatened to buckle. That was why Sebastian had been so interested in this island. Why he'd refused to accept Inez Key wasn't for sale.

A collage of images slammed through her mind. Sebastian standing at the dock like a conquering leader. The watercolors Sebastian's father had painted. The shadows in his eyes when he looked at the main house.

He'd set out to seduce and steal Inez Key from her

because her father had stolen it first. It was an eye for an eye.

Ashley inhaled sharply as the fury and pain whipped through her. She tried to breathe, but her chest was constricted. This was why he didn't respond to her declaration of love. Because he had no feelings for her. She was just a pawn in his game of revenge.

How had she got it so wrong?

She had made herself believe that Sebastian was nothing like the men she knew. That he could love and respect a woman. That he was a good man. A man she could trust and share her life with. Because she believed her happiness and safety was his priority. That he wanted what was best for her.

She had ignored her first instinct. Was it his incredible good looks or his overwhelming sexuality that had distracted her? He used her without compunction. She had been a pawn he could easily sacrifice. She had believed what she wanted to believe.

Ashley closed her eyes and turned her head. She wanted to block out the world around her. Pretend that this wasn't happening. Run and never look back.

But there was a simple truth she couldn't ignore: She was no better than her mother.

Linda Valdez wasn't the only woman in this family who made stupid decisions over the men they loved. Donald Jones had not been worthy of her mother's time or tears, but Linda didn't want to see it. Her mother had built a fantasy world, a place where she had finally felt loved and special.

Ashley slowly opened her eyes. She had done the same.

Ashley couldn't speak. It took all of her strength to stand still when her instincts urged her to escape before she lashed out. The walls were closing in on her. The anger—the howling pain—bubbled underneath the surface, threatening to break free. It was going to be ugly and violent.

No, she wouldn't let it. She was not going down the same path as her mother. Ashley curled her hands into fists and dug her nails in her palms. She welcomed the bite, but it didn't take the edge off her fury. Now, more than ever, she needed to be in control.

She had to get out of here. Her legs were unsteady as she walked across the room. She wanted to double over from the pain but kept walking until she found the bag she had packed in the closet.

Her legs felt heavy and she just wanted to fall into a heap and curl in a protective ball. She blinked as her eyes burned with unshed tears. *Don't cry now*, Ashley thought. *Cry when no one can see you or use your weakness against you. Cry when you're alone.*

Alone. She was all alone with no support system. No home. There was no comfort or peace in her life. Sebastian had taken it all away.

Ashley exhaled slowly, but the pain radiated in her body. She knew she had been different from the other women in his life. She questioned how she'd gained his attention, how she'd attracted him, but hadn't wanted to inspect it too closely. She had been too afraid to poke at her good luck in case it fell apart.

Ashley bent to the waist as the agony ripped through her. It had all been an illusion. All of it.

Even the sex. She leaned against her bedroom door as the nausea swept through her. Especially the sex. He had made her feel special and desirable. Powerful and sexy. Sebastian had introduced her to pleasure. Passion. She thought he had felt the same.

Her body burned with humiliation. She wanted the floor to open up and swallow her whole. Ashley quickly grabbed her bag, knowing she only had a few moments to escape.

She was crossing the floor of the master suite when she heard Sebastian's footsteps down the hall. She barely had time to brace herself when the door swung open.

Her heart gave a brutal leap when Sebastian stood in front of her. She felt so small and insignificant next to him, like a peasant standing before an all-powerful emperor.

"Why didn't you tell me?" she asked in a hiss.

Sebastian noticed her stricken expression and the bag clutched in her hand. He glanced at the doors that led to the balcony and immediately assessed the situation. A shadow crossed his harsh features. He closed the door behind him and leaned against it. He didn't speak as he crossed his arms and watched her.

She felt trapped, weak, and had a fierce need to hide it by striking first. She was never more aware of his intimidating height and powerful build than right at this moment. The button-down shirt and faded jeans didn't hide the fact that he was solid muscle. There was no way she could move him.

"You look upset," he drawled.

Did he still think this was a game? Had he no remorse? "What is Inez Key to you?"

He paused. "It was my childhood home."

"And you felt the need to steal it from me? It was my childhood home as well."

"I didn't steal Inez Key," he pointed out calmly, but she saw the anger flash in his eyes. "Your father did."

"What exactly are you accusing him of?" she asked hoarsely. She knew Donald Jones probably did something underhanded. It was how he approached life.

"He won our home in a poker game," Sebastian said. "But he had cheated."

That sounded like dear old Donald, but maybe this was the one time when her father's reputation automatically made him the culprit. "You don't know that. You have no proof."

Sebastian's eyes narrowed. "He bragged about it years later. His friend Casillas confirmed the story."

Ashley wanted to be ill. "Why did he want the island? It doesn't make sense. My father didn't care about property. He rarely used this island."

The anger whipped around Sebastian. "He wanted something else and tried to use the island as a bargaining chip."

"What?" Ashley couldn't shake off the dread. "What did he really want?"

"My mother." His voice was cold and harsh. "Jones said he wouldn't take the island if he could take my mother to bed instead."

The words drew blood like the lash of a whip. She could easily imagine her father trying to make a deal like that. She'd seen him try many times. And he occasionally succeeded. "Is that why you slept with me?" she asked.

"No," he said in a raspy voice. "I took you to bed because I wanted you and I couldn't stop myself."

She wasn't going to believe that. Not anymore. He had already proven that she had no power over him. He didn't stop himself because he wanted to continue playing the game.

"Don't lie to me," she warned. "It was an eye for an eye. My father tried to blackmail your mother into bed. You did the same to me. Only you were successful." Because apparently she had a price.

"My father wasn't going to let Jones touch my mother. She was his wife. The mother of his children. He should have killed that man for suggesting it."

"And I was a spoiled heiress living the life you should have had," she whispered. She gripped her bag until her knuckles turned white. She wanted to get out. She needed to escape before she said too much or crossed the line.

"Put down the bag," Sebastian ordered. "You're not going anywhere."

"I believed every word you said," she said and scoffed at her ignorance. "You said you would look after me if I got pregnant. I actually thought you meant it."

"I still mean it." Sebastian froze and his gaze quickly traveled down the length of her body.

"Don't worry, Sebastian. I'm not pregnant. Or was that part of the plan too?"

He took a step toward her. "I would never do that to an innocent child."

Ashley backed away. She didn't trust herself around Sebastian. She'd already made a few assumptions and poor choices. He had the ability to make her forget her best intentions with one simple touch. Worse, he knew it.

"But you would do it to me because I couldn't possibly be innocent. I'm Donald Jones's daughter, right? I must be punished."

"Let me explain," Sebastian said as he reached for her.

"No! Don't you touch me. You no longer have that right."

He held up his hands. "Listen to me. When we thought my mother was dying, she made a request. If she survived the surgery, she wanted to live out her remaining years on Inez Key."

Ashley remembered Patricia's faraway look when she'd talked about her home. She was remembering Inez Key. It had been lovingly re-created in the watercolors her husband had painted. It was the paradise she had lost.

"Oh, well, that makes all the difference," Ashley said with heavy sarcasm. "Your mother wanted the island. That excuses the fact that you seduced me and stole my home."

"I'm not making any excuses," he said as he watched her reach the door.

"No, you don't think you need to. You were only getting justice, right?"

"What he did—"

"My father stole the island from you. You stole it from me," she said as she swung open the doors and fled down the stairs. She heard Sebastian's footsteps behind her. "My father wanted to humiliate your parents by blackmailing Patricia into bed. You blackmailed me and tried to humiliate me by making me a mistress. My father's action drove you into poverty. Your actions leave me homeless and broke. Have I missed anything?"

"I had no plans for revenge," Sebastian said as he followed her. "My goal was to buy Inez Key and make it my mother's home."

"Oh, you didn't *plan* to repeat history," she said as she marched to the front door. "You *accidentally* fell into the same pattern that my father followed. What a relief! You don't know how *happy* it makes me feel that you are exactly like Donald Jones."

Sebastian glared at her. "I didn't start this twisted game. I finished it."

"Congratulations, Sebastian. You won." She almost choked on the words as she opened the door and crossed the threshold before she slammed the door shut. "I hope it was worth it."

Ashley didn't notice the aggressive lines of steel and glass as she strode into the Cruz Conglomerate headquarters. The impressive lobby and stunning artwork no longer intimidated her. The anger coursing through her body silenced the noise and the crowds of people surrounding her. She didn't care about anything other than saying a few choice words to Sebastian.

She crushed the buff envelope in her hand as she waited impatiently at the reception desk. She wasn't looking forward to seeing Sebastian. It had been a month since she'd left Inez Key and she didn't feel ready.

She still loved the rat bastard. She shook her head in self-disgust. It was a sign that she was definitely her mother's daughter.

Her first instinct had been to ignore the letter he sent. But how could she? She had felt numb for the last few weeks until she had seen his name on the envelope. She had been pathetically pleased that he knew where she lived. That he was still aware of her.

That ended when she read the letter. Her body shook with anger and hurt, confusion and despair. Every dark emotion whipped through her body until she leaned on the wall and slid to the floor.

This was why she'd cut him out of her life. She couldn't go through this pain. She wasn't going to let her unrequited love tear her apart.

The elegant receptionist hung up the phone and gave her a curious look. "Mr. Cruz will see you right away, Miss Jones."

Ashley nodded as the surprise jolted her system. The last time she was here she had been ignored and forgotten. Now she was given immediate access to Sebastian? She hadn't been prepared for that. Ashley glanced at the exit and took a deep breath. She wasn't going to hide from him. Not anymore.

She was here. Ashley was here to see him. Sebastian stood in the center of his office and buttoned his jacket.

His fingers shook and he bunched his hands into fists. This was an opportunity he couldn't squander. His future, his happiness, was riding on the next few minutes.

The door opened and Ashley rushed inside. "What the hell is this?" she asked as she held up the envelope.

He barely noticed his assistant closing the door and leaving them alone. Sebastian greedily stared at Ashley. This time she didn't feel the need to dress up. He was glad. She looked stunning in her black T-shirt, cutoff shorts and sandals. Her hair was a wild mane and her skin carried the scent of sunshine.

He frowned as he saw that Ashley was vibrating with anger. "That is payment for Inez Key," he said. He thought he had explained everything in the letter.

"Why would you give this to me?" Ashley asked, shaking the envelope close to his face. "You got the island because I couldn't pay back the loan."

"I want to pay you my highest offer because I made a mistake. I went after this island even though it wasn't for sale. My actions were legal but unforgiveable," he admitted through gritted teeth.

"And you think throwing money around is going to make it all go away?" she asked, tossing the envelope onto the floor. "Typical. You rich and powerful men are all the same."

Ashley may look sweet and innocent, but she knew just how to hurt him. "Stop comparing me to your father."

She raised her eyebrows. "Oh, is that what this is all about? You're uncomfortable with the idea that you are just like Donald Jones? Refuse to believe it even though you think like him. You act like him. You destroy lives like him. The only difference is that you out–Donald Jones the original."

"The difference is that I regret what I did. It's tearing me up inside, knowing that you hate me. That your opinion of me is so low." He cursed in Spanish and thrust his hand in his hair. *That you loved me once but I destroyed those feelings.*

"And so you send me a check because you feel responsible? Because you think if you throw enough money at me you think I'll forgive you?" Her voice rose. "Don't get me wrong, Sebastian. I could use the money. I'm flat broke and I don't know if I can make rent next month. But I won't take a penny from you. You think this will absolve what you did? It won't."

"I know that. I can't erase what I did." Sebastian would never forget the hurt in Ashley's eyes when she realized his original plan. He wanted to be a hero in her eyes. He wanted her to look at him in wonder and admiration the way she used to. "The only thing I can do is repair the damage and make amends."

"It's too late."

"I refuse to believe that," he said as the hope died a little inside him. "I want what we had and I am willing to do whatever is necessary to make it happen. Tell me what you need from me. What can I do to regain your trust?"

She glanced up and met his gaze. "There is nothing you can do."

Sebastian felt as if his last chance was disintegrating in his hands. He didn't know what to do and the panic clawed at him. If she gave him a mission, he could earn her trust. But she didn't want anything from him.

"Stay with me," he urged. His request was pathetically simple. He couldn't dazzle her with his wealth and connections. "Give me a chance."

She shook her head. "You don't have to make this offer. I'm not pregnant."

"That's not what I'm asking." Sebastian tasted fear. This reunion wasn't going the way he had envisioned. He was losing her. If she didn't want to be with him, he had nothing to use as leverage. She wasn't interested in his money or power. Those were disadvantages in her eyes. All he could give her was himself. It wasn't enough, but it was a start.

"I need you," he said quietly. "You left this giant hole in my life. I can't sleep. I can't concentrate. All I do is think of you."

Ashley looked away. "You'll get over it."

"I don't want to," he said harshly. "I knew you would be my downfall the moment we met. I didn't care. Nothing mattered but you."

"Getting the island back mattered," she said as the tears shimmered in her eyes. "You used me and betrayed my trust. You planned to cut me out with nothing because that is what my father did to your family. I was just part of your revenge. You would have tossed me to the wolves if you hadn't been attracted to me."

"That's not true! I love you, Ashley."

"Stop playing games with me," Ashley said in a broken whisper. She took a step back and he grabbed her hand. He wasn't going to let her go again.

"You don't have to forgive me at this moment." It hurt that she didn't believe him, but he was willing to work hard at regaining her love and her trust. "Just be with me and I'll prove my love to you every day."

She looked down at their joined hands. Sebastian took it as a good sign that she didn't let go. "I want to but I can't go through this again," she whispered.

He knew how much it cost her to say those words. She risked so much. Maybe even more than when she had declared her love. She still may have feelings for him, that she was willing for another chance. "I want to be the man you need. I want you to believe in me. In us."

The tears started to fall down her cheeks. "I want that, too."

"Stay with me, Ashley," he urged her as his heart pounded fiercely. "I will give you everything you need. Everything you want."

"Stay as what?" she asked as she stepped closer and pressed her hand against his chest. "Your lover? Your mistress?"

"I'm going to make you my wife very soon."

Ashley tugged his tie. "You have to ask first."

"I will," he promised as he covered her mouth with his. "And I'll keep asking until you say yes."

Five years later

Ashley heard the incessant chirping of the nighthawks as she stepped out onto the patio. It had been weeks since she and Sebastian had visited Inez Key. Every time she stepped on the wooden dock, she was struck by how much the island had changed and how much it remained the same.

Sebastian had painstakingly restored the main house, adding a few touches to accommodate his mother's age and mobility. The antebellum house was no longer stark and silent. It was always filled with the shrieking laughter of children and the waft of spices in the big kitchen as everyone had a hand in cooking for the large family dinners.

But this dinner was different, Ashley decided as she caught Sebastian's eye and slowly walked to him. The sky was streaked with orange and red and the birthday candles flickered on the cake she held.

The guests at the long table clapped and cheered when they saw her. She smiled when they began to sing "Happy Birthday." She walked barefoot as the ocean breeze pulled at her casual sundress.

Everyone on Inez Key was there to celebrate. The main house was festooned with streamers, bunting and balloons. The bright colors and loud music reflected the festive spirit of the day. The islanders and the Cruz family mingled at the party that had started early in the day and showed no signs of fading.

Ashley glanced at her mother-in-law. She knew it had been a long and emotional day for Patricia. The older woman, dressed in a vibrant red, was dabbing her eyes with one hand while holding Ashley's infant daughter with the other. Patricia continued to fulfill the wish she'd made almost thirty years ago. She was home surrounded by her family.

Ashley carefully set the cake down in front of Sebastian as he held their boisterous three-year-old twin boys in each arm. She felt his heated gaze on her as the guests sang the last verse.

"Happy birthday, Sebastian," she murmured as she scooped up one of the boys who tried to lunge for the cake. "Make a wish."

"I have everything I want, *mi vida.*"

"Ask for anything," she encouraged her husband, "and I'll make it happen."

Ashley saw the devilish tilt of his mouth as the desire flared in his eyes. Anticipation licked through her veins as she watched Sebastian blow out the candles.

As the guests clapped, Ashley saw Sebastian's satisfied smile at the blown-out candles. The curiosity got the better of her. "What did you ask for?"

"If I tell you, it won't come true," he teased. "But this is going to be one birthday wish I'll never forget."

* * * * *

THE FAR SIDE OF PARADISE

ROBYN DONALD

CHAPTER ONE

STONE-FACED, Cade Peredur listened again to the tape of his foster-brother's final call—a frantic, beseeching torrent of words recorded just before Peter Cooper killed himself.

'Cade, where are you? Where the *hell* are you—oh, with Lady Louisa, I suppose. Damn it, Cade, I need you more than any woman could—why aren't you home? *Why can't you be there for me?'*

A short pause, broken only by his breathing, jagged and irregular, and then, 'Cade, I've been such a fool—such an idiot.'

Not a muscle of Cade's face moved at the sound of choked weeping.

At last Peter said in a thick, despairing voice, 'Taryn was my last—my *only*—hope. It hurts—so bloody much, Cade, so much…' Another wrenching pause and then, in a voice Cade had never heard before, Peter said, 'There's nothing left for me now. She laughed when I asked… *laughed…*'

The silence stretched for so long that when he'd first heard it Cade had been sure the call was over.

But eventually his brother whispered, 'It's no good, Cade. I'm sorry, but it's no good any more. I can't—I just can't live with this. She's gone, and she's not coming back. Tell the parents I'm sorry to be such a useless son to them, but at least they'll still have you. You're the sort of man they wanted me to be, and God knows I tried, but I've always known I didn't have what it takes. Get married, Cade, and give them some grandchildren to adore. They'll need them now…'

He stopped abruptly. Then he said unevenly, 'Try not to despise me, Cade. I love you. Goodbye.'

Cade switched off the tape and walked across the luxurious room to look unseeingly across the London cityscape, fighting to control the rush of blind rage threatening to consume him. The call had come eight hours before he'd arrived home and by the time he'd got to Peter's apartment his brother was dead.

Peter had worshipped him, emulated and envied him, then finally grown away from him, but Cade had always been intensely protective of his younger brother.

Hands clenching, he turned and walked into his office, stopping at his desk. The photograph on it had been taken at his foster-parents' fortieth wedding anniversary a few months before Peter's death—Isabel and Harold Cooper all smiles for the camera, Peter's grin revealing a hint of feverish excitement.

As always, Cade was the odd one out—taller than the other two men, his features harsher and his expression unreadable.

His brother's suicide shattered that secure, tight family unit. A fortnight after the funeral, Harold Cooper had died from a heart attack, and while Isabel was still trying to come to terms with the wreckage of her life she'd stepped out into the path of a car. Onlookers said she'd moved as though in a daze.

She'd wanted to die too, but not before she'd begged Cade to find out what had driven her son to suicide.

He'd held her hand while she'd whispered painfully, 'If…if I knew why…it wouldn't be so bad. I just want to *know*, Cade, before I die.'

'You're not going to die,' he said harshly. 'I'll find out what happened.'

Her lashes had fluttered up again, revealing a spark of animation in her gaze. 'Promise?'

To encourage that hope, that flicker of determination, he'd have promised anything. 'I will. But you have to keep going for me.'

She'd managed a pale smile. 'It's a deal.'

That had been the turning point; valiantly she'd gathered her reserves and struggled back to cope with everything life had thrown at her. It had taken months of rehabilitation, and she was now adjusting to living the rest of her life in a wheelchair.

The letter Peter had left for his parents lay in its envelope on Cade's desk. He flicked it open and read it again. Unlike the telephone call, it was free of overt grief. Peter had told his parents he loved them, that he was sorry to cause them pain, but his life was no longer worth living.

No mention of the woman who'd reduced him to this depth of despair. He'd never introduced her to his family, only spoken of her once or twice in a casual, throwaway fashion. The last time he'd gone home—to celebrate his first big commission as a sculptor, a work for a public park in a market town—he hadn't referred to her.

So why that anguished, cryptic mention in his final call?

Cade turned away, his hard, arrogantly contoured face set. What part had Taryn Angove played in Peter's death?

Had something she'd said, something she'd done,

precipitated his final, fatal decision? It seemed possible, although she'd left for her home country of New Zealand eight hours before Peter's suicide.

Cade had always known that revenge was a fool's game; he'd seen the hunger for it eat into the intellect, destroy the soul.

Justice, however, was a different matter.

Progress had been infuriatingly slow. He knew now her return to New Zealand had been organised well before Peter's death. He knew she and Peter had been good friends for almost two years, almost certainly lovers.

He knew Peter's bank account should have been flush with a large advance to buy materials for his commission. Indeed, the money had arrived—and immediately a substantial sum had been taken out and paid directly to Taryn Angove. But the rest of the money had been siphoned off in large weekly cash payments, so that when Peter had died there had only been a few hundred pounds left.

If—and it was only an *if*, Cade reminded himself—Taryn Angove had somehow got her hands on it all, that could be why Peter had killed himself. Unfortunately, so far there was nothing, apart from that initial payment, to connect her with its absence.

But now, thanks to dedicated work by his security people, he knew where she was in New Zealand.

Cade looked across at the suitcase he'd just finished packing. His arrangements were all made and his actions from now on would depend on the woman he was hunting.

All day it had been still, the horizon a hazy brush-stroke where simmering sky met burnished sea, the forest-clad hills around the bay drowsing in the fierce glare of a sub-tropical sun. Cade narrowed his eyes against the intense light to watch seabirds made dumb by the heat fight silent battles over their catch.

Even the tiny waves on the shore were noiseless; all he could hear was the thrum of thousands of cicadas vibrating through the forest-covered hills behind the bay—the prevailing summer sound in this long northern peninsula of New Zealand.

The sibilant hum was penetrated by the imperative summons of his cell phone. Only his personal assistant had that number, so somewhere in his vast holdings something had gone wrong.

From halfway around the world his PA said, 'A few matters pertaining to this meeting in Fala'isi.'

'What about it?' Because of his business interests in the Pacific Basin, Cade had been asked to attend a gathering of high-powered Pacific dignitaries to discuss the future of the region.

Dealing with that took a few minutes. His voice a little tentative, Roger, his PA, said, 'Lady Louisa called.'

Arrogant black brows almost meeting across the blade of his nose, Cade said, 'And she wanted…?'

'Your address. She was not happy when I wouldn't give it to her. She said it was urgent and important.'

'Thanks.' Cade didn't discuss his private life easily, but he did say, 'We are no longer together.'

A pause, then, 'You might need to work on convincing her of that.'

His voice hard and cold, Cade said, 'Ignore her.'

'Very well.'

Cade's mouth curved in a sardonic smile. Louisa wouldn't follow him to New Zealand—it was completely out of her orbit. His *ex*-lover craved luxury and fashion and the heady stimulation of admiration. This remote paradise couldn't satisfy her need for the envy of others.

'Ah…not to put too fine a point on it, but she sounded stressed.' Roger paused. 'Actually, desperate.'

Her father had probably refused to pay a bill. Cade shrugged broad shoulders. 'Not your problem.' Or his. 'How is your daughter?'

His PA hesitated before saying in a completely different tone, 'We hear the results of the first lot of tests tomorrow.'

What the hell did you say to a man whose child could be suffering a terminal illness? 'If you need leave or any help at all, it's yours.'

'I know. Thanks—for everything.'

'No need for thanks—just let me know what I can do.'

'Thanks. I will. Keep in touch.'

Cade closed down the cell phone, his eyes flinty. Against the fact that a three-year-old could be dying, Louisa was a very minor consideration. A sensuous, satisfying lover until she'd decided Cade—influential, moving in the 'right' circles and exceedingly rich—would make the ideal first husband, she'd been careless enough to let him overhear as she discussed her plans on the telephone.

It had needed only a few questions in the right ears for Cade to discover she'd run through most of the fortune inherited from her grandfather. With no chance of support from a father whose income had been decimated by financial crisis, marriage was the obvious solution.

Like Louisa, Cade didn't believe in the sort of love poets wrote about. However, although experience had made him cynical, he intended to marry some day, and when he did it would be to a woman who'd value him for more than the size of his assets. He'd choose carefully, and it would last.

Cade's expression hardened. If Louisa was desperate enough to follow him, he'd make sure she understood that he was not and never would be a suitable husband—first, last or intermediate—for her.

After eyeing the hammock in the dark shade of one of the huge trees bordering the beach, he succumbed to an unusual restlessness that drove him down onto the hot amber sand. He stared out to sea for a long moment before turning. Only then did a drift of movement in the cloudless sky catch his attention.

Frowning, he stared at it. At first nothing more substantial than a subtle darkening of the blue, the haze swiftly thickened into a veil, an ominous stain across the sky.

In the grip of its severest drought in living memory, the province of Northland was under a total fire ban. The manager of the farm he'd rented the holiday house from had impressed on him that any smoke anywhere had to mean danger.

Muttering a word he wouldn't have said in polite company, Cade headed towards the house, long legs covering the ground at speed. He grabbed his car keys and cell phone, punching in a number as he headed towards the bedroom.

'I can see smoke in the sky,' he said curtly when the farm manager answered. 'South, and close—in the next bay, I'd say, and building fast.'

The farm manager swore vigorously, then said, 'Bloody free campers probably, careless with a camp-fire. OK, I'll ring the brigade and round up a posse from here. With any luck, we'll be able to put it out before it takes hold.'

Cade eyed the growing smoke cloud. 'I'll go over and see what I can do.'

'Man, be careful. There's a tap in the bay, but the creek's probably dry. If you've got a bucket there, grab it.' Possibly recalling that the man renting the farm's beach house was an influential tycoon, he added, 'And don't try to be a hero.'

Cade's swift grin vanished as he closed the cell phone. The smoke suddenly billowed, forming a cloud. Until then there had been no movement in the air, but of course the instant some idiot lit a fire the wind picked up.

The faster he got there, the better. He hauled on a long-sleeved shirt and trousers with swift, economical movements, then wasted precious moments looking for a non-existent bucket before giving up.

Not, he thought grimly as he got into the car, that a bucket would be much help, but it would have given him an illusory feeling of control.

He drove too fast along the track to the boundary gate; unlocking it wasted a few more valuable seconds so he left it open to give the manager and his men easy access. Lean hands tense on the wheel, he swung the four-wheel drive onto a narrow public road that led to the next bay.

It took too long to manoeuvre his vehicle around the tight corners through thick coastal scrub that would go up like a torch the moment a spark got into it. When the car emerged into searing sunlight a glance revealed no tents on the grassy foreshore or beneath the huge trees—nothing, in fact, but an elderly car parked in the deep shade cast by one of those trees.

And a woman in a skimpy bikini far too close to an area of blazing grass.

What the hell did she think she was doing?

Putting his foot down, Cade got there as fast as he could. He turned the vehicle, ready for a quick get-away, and was out of the car and running towards the woman before he realised she was directing a hose at the flames.

Tall and long-legged and young, she had a body guaranteed to set a man's hormones buzzing in anticipation. Smoke-smeared and glistening with sweat, she exuded unselfconscious sensuality.

At that moment she turned, pushing back a mane of copper-coloured hair that had been fanned across her face by the hot wind from the flames.

A flame flared up only a few inches from her feet and she jumped back, water from the hose splashing gleaming legs that went on forever.

The woman was crazy! Couldn't she see she wasn't achieving anything except putting herself in danger?

Cade covered the ground between them in a few seconds, watching the woman's expression turn to undisguised relief.

She thrust the hose into his hands and commanded brusquely, 'Keep directing it anywhere the flames try to get away. If they make it to those bullrushes the whole place will go up. I'll wet my towel and have a go at it from the other side.'

'Get dressed first,' he suggested, turning the pathetic dribble of water onto the flames.

She gave him a startled look, then nodded briskly. 'Good thinking.'

Taken aback and amused by her air of command, Cade watched her race across to her car to haul on a pair of inadequate shorts and a T-shirt and jam her feet into elderly sandshoes. Only then did she sprint down to the waves to wet her towel.

A sudden flare almost at his feet switched Cade's attention, but as he sprayed water onto it he wondered why on earth he was bothering. It was a losing battle; a wet towel would be as useless as the meagre trickle from the hose. Yet clearly the woman had no intention of giving up and doing the sensible thing—getting out of there before the fire made retreat impossible.

Cade admired courage in anyone, even reckless, blind courage. She might have lit the fire, but she was determined to put it out.

When she came running up from the shoreline she thrust the heavy, sodden towel into his hands. 'I'll take the hose—you're stronger than me so you'll be more efficient with this. Just be careful.'

The next few minutes were frantic. And hopeless. Working together, they fought grimly to hold back the flames but, inch by menacing inch, the bright line crept closer to the stand of bullrushes, pushing first one way and then, when frustrated, finding another path through the long, dry grass.

'Get back,' Cade shouted when flames suddenly flared perilously close to those lithe bare legs. Two long strides got him close enough to put all his power into beating it out.

'Thanks.' Her voice sounded hoarse, but she didn't move, directing that inadequate spurt of water with a stubborn determination that impressed him all over again.

She looked down at the towel, which was beginning to scorch. 'Go down and wet the towel again.'

'You go.' Cade thrust the towel into her hands and grabbed the hose from her.

Sensibly, she didn't waste time in protest, turning immediately to run across the sand.

His foster-mother's influence was embedded so deeply he couldn't evade it, Cade thought wryly, stamping out a tuft of grass that was still smouldering. Women were to be protected—even when they made it obvious they didn't want it.

He glanced up the hill. No sign of the fire brigade yet. If they didn't appear damned soon he'd grab the woman and, if he had to, drag her away. It would be too late once the bullrushes caught; they'd be in deadly danger of dying from smoke inhalation even if they took refuge in the sea.

Panting, she ran up from the beach and almost flung the dripping towel at him. Her face was drawn and smoke had stained the creamy skin, but she looked utterly determined. Clearly, giving up was not an option.

Cade said abruptly, 'The brigade should be here soon,' and hoped he was right.

His arms rose and fell in a regular rhythm but, even as he beat out sparks along the edge of the fire, he accepted their efforts were making very little headway. No way could they stop the relentless line of fire racing through the grass towards a stand of rushes so dry their tall heads made perfect fuel.

If they caught, he and the woman would have to run, but not to the cars. The beach would be their only refuge.

Once the fire got into the coastal scrub it would take an aerial bombardment or heavy rain to put it out. The cloudless sky mocked the idea of rain, and a helicopter with a monsoon bucket would take time to organise.

And if the wind kept building, the blaze would threaten not only the beach house he'd rented, but the houses and barns around the homestead further up the coast. Cade hoped the farm manager had warned everybody there to be on the alert.

A muted roar lifted his head. Relief surged through him as the posse from the station came down the hill on one of the farm trucks, almost immediately followed by two fire engines and a trail of other vehicles.

'Oh, thank God,' his companion croaked, a statement he silently echoed.

Taryn had never been so pleased to see anyone in her life. Smoothly, efficiently the firemen raced from their vehicles, the chief shouting, 'Get out of the way—down onto the beach, both of you.'

She grabbed a bottle of water from her car and headed across the sand. Without taking off her shoes, she waded out until the water came up to her knees, and only then began to drink, letting the water trickle down a painfully dry throat.

Heat beat against her, so fierce she pulled off her T-shirt, dropped it into the sea and used it to wipe herself down. The temporary coolness was blissful. She sighed, then gulped a little more water.

The stranger who'd helped her strode out to where she stood. 'Are you all right?' he demanded.

He was so tall she had to lift her face to meet his eyes. Swallowing, she said hoarsely, 'Yes. Thank you very much for your help.'

'Go easy on that water. If you drink it too fast it could make you sick.'

Taryn knew the accent. English, clipped and authoritative, delivered in a deep, cool voice with more than a hint of censure, it reminded her so much of Peter she had to blink back tears.

Not that Peter had ever used that tone with her.

The stranger was watching her as though expecting her to faint, or do something equally stupid. Narrowed against the glare of the sun on the sea, his disconcerting eyes were a cold steel-blue and, although Taryn knew she'd never seen him before, he looked disturbingly familiar.

An actor, perhaps?

She lowered the bottle. 'I'm taking it slowly.' Stifling a cough, she kept her eyes fixed on the helmeted men as they efficiently set about containing the flames. 'Talk about arriving in the nick of time!'

'I wouldn't have thought the village was big enough to warrant a fire station.'

A note in his voice lifted tiny invisible hairs on the back of her neck. He was very good-looking, all angles and strong bones and lean distinction. Not exactly handsome; that was too neutral a description for a man whose arrogantly chiselled features were stamped with formidable self-assurance. His aura of cool containment was based on something much more intimidating than good bones. An odd sensation warmed the pit of Taryn's stomach when she met his gaze.

Unnerved by that flinty survey, she looked away, taunted by a wisp of memory that faded even as she tried to grasp it.

'They're a volunteer group.' She took refuge in the mundane and held out her bottle of water. 'Would you like some?' Adding with a wry smile, 'I've wiped the top and as far as I know I have no diseases you need worry about.'

'I'm sure you haven't,' he drawled, not taking the

bottle. 'Thanks, but I've already had a drink—I brought my own.'

Stick to social pleasantries, she told herself, rattled by a note in his voice that came very close to mockery. 'Thank you so much for helping—I didn't have a hope of stopping it on my own.'

'Didn't it occur to you that lighting a fire in the middle of a drought could be dangerous?'

No, not mockery—condemnation.

Controlling an intemperate urge to defend herself, Taryn responded evenly, 'I didn't light it. I came down for a swim but before I got that far I noticed someone had had a fire on the beach above high tide mark to cook *tuatua*—shellfish. They didn't bother to put it out properly with sea water so I hosed it down, but a spark must have lodged somewhere up in the grass.'

'I see.'

Nothing could be gained from his tone or his expression. Stiffening, she said coldly, 'As soon as I saw smoke I rang the emergency number.'

'Ah, so that's why they arrived so quickly.'

Screwing up her eyes in an effort to pierce the pall of smoke, she said, 'It looks as though they're winning, thank heavens.'

Heat curled in the pit of her stomach when her gaze met his, aloof and speculative. Something in his expression reminded her she'd been clad only in her bikini when he'd arrived. And that the shorts he'd ordered her to get into revealed altogether too much of her legs.

Shocked by the odd, primitive little shiver that tightened her skin and set her nerves humming, she looked away.

He asked, 'Are you a local?'

'Not really.' She'd lived in the small village a mile away during her adolescence.

'So you're on holiday?'

Casual talk between two strangers abruptly hurled together...

Taking too deep a breath of the smoky air, she coughed again. 'No.'

'What do you do?' He spoke idly, still watching the activity on the grass behind the beach.

'I'm a librarian,' she responded, her tone even.

The brows that lifted in faint surprise were as black as his strictly controlled hair. In an abrupt change of subject, he said, 'Should you be swimming on your own?'

Taryn parried that steel-blue survey. 'This is a very safe bay. I don't take stupid risks.'

How did this man—this *judgmental* man, Taryn decided—manage to look sceptical without moving a muscle?

In a bland voice, he said, 'Fighting the fire looked risky enough to me. All it needed was a slight change of wind and you'd have had to run like hell to get to the beach safely. And you probably wouldn't have saved your car.'

That possibility had occurred to Taryn, but she'd been more afraid the fire would set the coastline alight. 'I can run,' she said coolly.

His gaze drifted down the length of her legs. 'Yes, I imagine you can. But how fast?'

His tone invested the words with a subliminal implication that summoned a swift, embarrassing heat to her skin.

That nagging sense of familiarity tugged at her again. *Who was he?*

Well, there was one way to find out. Without allowing herself second thoughts, she said coolly, 'When it's necessary, quite fast,' and held out her hand. 'It's time I introduced myself—I'm Taryn Angove.'

CHAPTER TWO

CADE'S heart pounded a sudden tattoo, every nerve in his body springing into instant taut alertness. This young Amazon was *Taryn Angove*?

OK, so courage didn't necessarily go with attributes like compassion and empathy, but she was nothing like the women Peter usually fell for. They'd all been startlingly similar—slight and chic, with an intimate knowledge of fashion magazines and the latest gossip, they'd pouted deliciously and parroted the latest catchphrases.

Cade couldn't imagine any of them trying to put out a fire, or throwing commands at him.

Mind racing, he took in the implications.

Did she know who he was?

If she did, she'd suspect that although this meeting was a coincidence, his presence in New Zealand wasn't. So she'd be wary…

Chances were, though, that Peter wouldn't have spoken of him. An unpleasant situation some years before, when Peter's then lover had made a determined play for Cade, meant that Peter rarely introduced his girlfriends to his family. He'd once admitted that although he referred to Cade occasionally, it was only ever as his brother.

Cade knew the value of hunches; he'd learned which ones to follow and which to ignore. One was warning him right now to keep quiet about the connection.

'Cade Peredur,' he said smoothly, and shook Taryn Angove's outstretched hand. 'How do you do?'

He could see why Peter had fallen for her. In spite of the smoke stains, she was very attractive—beautiful, in fact, with fine features and creamy skin set off by coppery hair.

Not to mention a lush, sinfully kissable mouth…

Ruthlessly, Cade disciplined an unexpected kick of lust. Nowhere near as easily affected as his brother had been by a lovely face and lissom body, it exasperated him that Taryn Angove had a definite and very primal impact on him.

Which he had to suppress.

His investigation team hadn't been able to turn up a single person who wasn't shocked and astonished by his brother's death. The police had been unable to add anything beyond the fact that there had definitely been no foul play.

Peter had taken Taryn Angove to the theatre the previous night. She'd stayed with him that night and then he'd delivered her to Heathrow for the flight home. He'd cancelled an appointment with friends the following evening, but he'd spoken by telephone to them and he'd seemed perfectly normal.

Yet only a few hours later he'd killed himself.

From New Zealand, Taryn been asked to do a video interview with the police, but it revealed nothing; she hadn't mentioned anything that might have upset him, so they didn't consider her a person of interest. Although sympathetic, for them there was no doubt that Peter had committed suicide, and so there was nothing to investigate.

So she was the only person who might be able to help Cade find out why Peter had done it.

And there was the question of what had happened to the money…

Looking down into the wide green-gold eyes lifted to his, noting their subtle darkening and the faint flush visible even under a patina of smoke, Cade decided a change of tactics could be in order.

He'd come here determined to use whatever weapons might be necessary to find out what she knew. He'd try appealing to her better instincts—if she had any—and, if that failed, then intimidation might work. Or paying her off.

Now he'd met her, he wondered whether such weapons would be necessary. Taryn seemed nothing like he had expected. In order to choose the best method of persuading her to talk, he'd have to find out what made Taryn Angove tick.

Which meant he needed to get to know her.

Ignoring the electricity his touch zapped across her nerve-ends, Taryn concentrated on his grip—firm but not aggressive and completely confident.

Just her luck to be sweaty and smoky, with stringy hair clinging to her probably scarlet face. How did he manage to look so…so much in control?

Not that it mattered. Too late, she remembered who he was—periodically, she'd seen photographs of him in the press and appreciated his sexy, angular impact. He was a big player in financial circles and appeared occasionally in the gossip magazines a flatmate in London used to devour.

In them, he was usually squiring a beautiful titled woman with very expensive taste in clothes.

When he released her hand she said calmly, 'Thanks so much for coming to help when you saw the smoke.'

Broad shoulders lifted again dismissively. 'It was a matter of self-interest.' At her enquiring look he enlarged, 'I'm holidaying in the next bay.'

Had he bought Hukere Station? She dismissed the idea immediately. High-flyers like Cade Peredur didn't invest in remote agricultural areas in New Zealand's subtropical north; they went to the South Island's glorious mountains. Anyway, he didn't look the sort to want a cattle station; from what she remembered, his interests lay in the cutthroat arena of finance and world-shaking deals. And sophisticated English aristocrats.

In that cool, slightly indifferent tone he told her, 'I saw smoke in the air so I came to see what I could do.'

Taryn looked past him and said with a shiver, 'I'm so glad you did. I wish the idiots who lit that fire could see what their carelessness has led to. The thought of all these pohutukawa trees going up in flames is horrifying. Some of them are over five hundred years old. In fact, Maori legend says that the big one along at the end of the beach was used to tie up the first canoe that ever landed here.'

His gaze followed her pointing finger. 'It looks old enough, certainly.'

Taryn shrugged mentally at his lack of enthusiasm. He was English, and on holiday—why should he share her love for the ancient trees? It was enough that he'd come to help.

'It will take a lot of time before this place gets back to its previous loveliness,' she said. 'It's such a shame.

It's the only good swimming beach close to Aramuhu township, but no one will want to come here until the grass grows again.' Her nose wrinkled. 'It looks horrible and it smells beastly, and everything—and everyone—would get covered in soot.'

Cade accepted the opportunity she'd offered—whether deliberately or not, he couldn't tell. 'If you'd like to swim, why don't you try the beach I'm staying at?' He nodded towards the headland that separated the two bays.

Startled and a little wary, she looked up. Caught in an ironic blue-grey focus, she felt her pulse rate surge and automatically ignored it. 'That's very kind of you,' she said without committing herself.

'It seems only fair.'

For the first time he smiled, sending languorous heat curling through Taryn. 'Fair?' she asked, only just stopping herself from stuttering.

'You might well have saved the beach house from going up in flames—and me with it,' he replied, noting that the farm manager was on his way towards them with the fire chief.

Noted too, with something close to irritation, the swift appreciative glances both men gave Taryn Angove.

Not that he could blame them. Those shorts showed off her glorious legs, and her bikini top accentuated her more obvious assets; only a dead man would ignore them.

The thought no sooner formed in his mind than he realised how bleakly appropriate it was. A man as dead as Peter…

'Hi, Jeff.' The smile Taryn gave the farm manager was friendly and open, but the one she bestowed on the grey-haired fire chief sparkled with mischief. 'Mr Sanderson.'

The fire chief gave a brief grin. 'Why am I not surprised to find you trying to put out a fire with nothing more than a garden hose?' he asked in a not quite fatherly tone before turning to Cade.

The farm manager introduced them and, as they shook hands, Cade said, 'It didn't take you long to get things under control.'

Hugh Sanderson nodded. 'Easy enough when you've got the men and the equipment. However, I'll leave a gang here to keep an eye on it. Just as well you both kept at it—probably saved a lot of destruction. Do you know how it started?'

'Ms Angove's theory seems logical,' Cade told him. 'All I saw was smoke in the sky.'

She flashed a green-gold, glinting glance at him as she explained what she thought had happened.

'Yeah, that would be it.' The fire chief indicated the sign that announced a total fire ban. 'Some idiots think a fire on the beach doesn't count. Thanks for keeping it away from the bullrushes—although I damn near had a heart attack when I saw you two trying to put it out.' He transferred his gaze to Taryn. 'No more heroine stuff on my patch, all right? If that fire had got into the rushes you'd have been in serious trouble, both of you. You OK?'

'Fine, thanks.' Her radiant smile made light of smoke stains and sweat.

The older man grinned. 'You never were one for keeping out of mischief. Patsy was just saying the other day she hadn't seen you for a while. Come and have a cup of tea with us when you're in town next.'

Cade waited until they'd gone before asking thoughtfully, 'What sort of mischief did you indulge in?'

She flushed a little, but laughed before explaining, 'When we first came to Aramuhu I was twelve, and I'd spent the previous eleven years living with my parents on a yacht in the Pacific. Fruit grows wild in the islands and I was used to just picking something off the nearest tree whenever I was hungry. At Aramuhu we lived for a few months next door to Mr and Mrs Sanderson and one day I took a cherimoya from his orchard.'

'Cherimoya?'

'It's bigger than an apple, sort of heart-shaped with bumpy green skin. Cousin to a custard apple.' Her voice sank into a sensual purr. 'They have the most delicious taste in the world. My mother marched me over to apologise and offer to work to pay for it. Mr Sanderson decided I could weed the garden for an hour, but once I'd done that he gave me a bag of them to take home. Even when we moved to a new house he made sure we were supplied with ripe ones in season and he still likes to tease me about it.'

Cade wondered if that husky tone was reserved for fruit, or if she murmured like that when she made love. His body tightened—and then tightened again for an entirely different reason at another thought.

No doubt Peter had also found that sleepy, sexy note both erotic and beguiling…

In an ironic tone that banished the reminiscent softness from her expression he said, 'Ah, small town life.'

'Where everyone knows your business,' she agreed with a swift, challenging smile. She focused her gaze behind him and he looked over one shoulder to see a racy red car hurtling boisterously down the road.

When he turned back she was frowning, a frown that disappeared when she asked, 'Did you grow up in a big city, Mr Peredur?'

'I was born in one, yes.' When taken away from his mother, he'd been living in the stinking backstreet of a slum. 'I'm going back to the beach house now. The invitation to swim is still open.'

And waited, concealing his keen interest in her answer.

She hesitated, then said lightly, 'I'm sticky and hot and I'd love a swim, thank you. I'll follow you in my car.'

'Right.'

Taryn watched him stride towards his Range Rover, long legs carrying him across the sandy ground in lithe, easy paces.

In a word—*dominant.* He compelled interest and attention by sheer force of character.

The swift fizz of sensation in the pit of her stomach startled her, but what made her increase speed towards her own car was the arrival of the one driven by a journalist for the local newspaper, an old schoolfellow who'd made it more than obvious that he was angling for a relationship.

Although she'd tried as tactfully as she could to show him she wasn't interested, Jason didn't seem to understand.

She fought back an odd clutch of apprehension beneath her ribs when she saw the possessive gleam of his smile as he swung out of the car, camera at the ready.

'Hi, Taryn—stay like that and I'll put you on the front page.'

'I've done nothing—showcase the men who put out the fire,' she returned. From the corner of her eye she noticed that Cade Peredur had opened the door of his vehicle, but not got in; he was watching them across its roof.

'Babe, they don't look anywhere near as good as you do.' Jason gave a sly grin and lifted the camera.

'No.' She spoke more sharply than she intended.

He looked wounded. 'Oh, come on, Taryn, don't be coy—we'd sell a hell of a lot more issues with you in those shorts on the front page instead of old Sanderson in his helmet. How about coming out with me tonight? I've been invited to a soirée at the Hanovers' place and they won't mind if I bring along a gorgeous girl.'

'No, thank you,' she said, keeping her voice even and light.

'Going to wash your hair, are you? Look,' he said, his voice hardening, 'what is it with you? Think you're too good to go out with an old mate now, do you? I'm not trying to get into your pants, I—'

He stopped abruptly as a deep voice cut in. 'All right, Taryn?'

'Fine, thank you,' she said quickly, adding rather foolishly, 'Jason and I went to school together.'

'Hey,' Jason exclaimed, ever the opportunist, 'you're Cade Peredur, aren't you? Mr Peredur, I'm Jason Beckett from the *Mid-North Press*. Can I ask you a few questions about the fire?'

'The person to tell you about it is the fire chief,' Cade said evenly. He looked down at Taryn. 'You go ahead—I'll follow.'

'OK,' she said, fighting a violent mixture of emotions.

Cade watched her walk across to her car and get in, then looked down at the reporter. Yet another man smitten by Taryn Angove's beauty; he should feel a certain amount of sympathy for the good-looking kid even if he was unpleasantly brash.

Instead, he wanted to tell him to keep his grubby hands and even grubbier statements to himself, and stay away from her if he valued his hide.

Shrugging, Beckett said, 'Well, that's women for you, I guess.' He produced an ingratiating smile. 'Are you planning to buy Hukere Station, Mr Peredur? I've heard rumours of development, a farm park…'

'I'm on holiday, nothing more,' Cade said evenly, nodded, and strode back to his vehicle.

In her car, Taryn took a deep breath and switched on the engine. The hot air inside the vehicle brought a moment of giddiness, but at least it wasn't too smoky. Grimacing, she looked down at her legs, stained and sticky with a vile mixture of sea water, perspiration and smoke. The swim she'd been promising herself all week had never seemed so desirable, but she should have said, *No thanks, Mr Peredur*, and headed back to the small studio unit that was her temporary home.

So why hadn't she? She turned the key and waited patiently for the engine to fire.

Partly because she'd wanted to get away from Jason. But more because she was curious—and that forbidden tug of response excited her as much as it alarmed her.

Her mouth curled into a wry smile as she eased the car up the hill. It would take a woman made of iron to look at Cade Peredur and not feel *something*. As well as innate strength and authority, he possessed a brain that had taken him to his present position. Add more than a dash of ruthlessness to that potent mix, and the fact that he looked really, really good…

Yes, definitely a top-of-the-list male.

But not a man any sensible woman would fall in love with.

Not that *that* was going to happen.

Bitter experience had taught her that although she could feel attraction, when it came to following through on it she was a total failure.

In a word, she was frigid.

Without volition, her thoughts touched on Peter, the jumble of shock and sorrow and bewilderment assailing her as it always did when she recalled his proposal—so unexpected, so shatteringly followed by his death. Guilt lay permanently in wait, making her wonder yet again whether her response had driven him to take that final, lethal step.

If only she'd been a little less incredulous—if she hadn't laughed—would he have made a different decision?

If she'd stayed in England as he'd wanted her to, instead of coming home, would she have been able to help him get over her refusal?

All those *if*s, and no answers…

The car skidded slightly. Feeling sick, she dragged her mind back to driving. Although the station road was well maintained, it still required concentration.

At Anchor Bay she pulled up and switched off the engine. Cade Peredur's big Range Rover stopped beside hers and he got out, appraising eyes coolly intent as he surveyed her.

Tall as she was, a little more height would be a distinct asset when it came to dealing with this man. Taryn tried to dissipate another tingle of sensation by collecting her bag. As she walked towards Cade she felt embarrassingly self-conscious. She glanced away, gaze skimming a huge flame tree to one side of the bay, and caught sight of the house.

It was a relief to be able to say something impersonal. 'Oh, the bach is still here,' she exclaimed. She'd half-expected some opulent seaside mansion, suitable for very rich holidaymakers, against the bush-covered slope that backed the lawn.

'Bach?'

'The local term for a small, basic cottage, usually by a beach or a lake.'

Cade said, 'Obviously you know the place.'

'When I was at school, the previous owners allowed the school to hold its camps here—it's a very safe beach. The bach was just a ruin then. Possums used to nest in the ceiling, and I've no doubt there were rats under the floor.' She looked around reminiscently. 'Over there, under that pohutukawa, when I was thirteen I was offered a cigarette by a boy I was madly trying to impress.'

'And did you accept it?'

She gave him a mock-scandalised glance. 'Are you kidding? My parents are doctors! I stopped trying to impress him right then.'

He smiled. 'Good for you. Would you like to see what's been done to the house?'

It was difficult to match the abandoned shell she recalled to the house now. It had been almost completely reconstructed, its stone outer walls repaired and the timber ceilings stripped and oiled so that they gleamed.

'It looks great,' Taryn said, gazing around the long living room.

Although it must have cost a mint to renovate, it didn't look glossy or smartly out of place. Comfortable and beachy and cool, it had shelves containing a large collection of books and some seriously good pictures hung on the walls. Somehow it suited Cade Peredur.

He said, 'There's a changing room and a shower in the cabana over by the flame tree. You can leave your bag and your clothes there—I'll join you in a few minutes and bring you down a towel.'

She summoned a bright smile. 'Thank you. And then I can prove to you how competent I am in the water.'

Cade's answering smile didn't soften his face. In fact, Taryn thought as she walked across the coarse warm grass to the beach hut, the curve of his firmly chiselled mouth had made his striking, hard-edged face seem both cynical and forbidding.

Safely in the small building, she wondered if anything ever did soften those arrogant features. When he kissed…?

She tried to imagine being kissed by Cade Peredur. Heat sizzled through her at the thought, but she couldn't see his face softening into a look of…well, *love* was out of the question, but what about lust?

The word *soften* just didn't fit the man. In his world it took an intimidating blend of brains, courage and formidable will to reach the top of the tree. When he kissed a woman it would be as a conqueror…

Hastily, she stripped off her clothes, pulling a face as she discarded them. They smelt disgusting—a mixture of smoke and sweat. They looked horrible too, both shorts and T-shirt smeared with ashy smudges and black marks. Even her bikini stank of the fire.

So, probably, did her hair and her skin.

Blissfully, she washed it all off in the sea's warm caress. A few minutes after she waded into the water, she caught movement on the beach from the corner of her eye and inched her head around so she could watch Cade Peredur stride across the sand.

Her heart jumped, startling her. Formidably and blatantly male, he seemed like some potent, elemental figure from the dawn of time—sunlit bronze skin and a perfect male body showing off sleek muscles that proclaimed strength and energy.

Some of which she could do with right now. Deep in the pit of her stomach, that hidden part of her contracted and sent another hot wave of sensation through her.

Lust, she thought, trying to douse it with a prosaic and practical attitude.

Although she'd never experienced anything so powerful before, this keen urgency that alerted every cell, tightening her skin and making her heart race, was merely run-of-the-mill physical attraction.

And if she tried to act on it, she knew exactly and in humiliating detail what would happen next; it would vanish, leaving her cold and shaking with that familiar fear. But even those mortifying memories couldn't banish the shimmers of sensation that pulsed through her, stimulating and undisciplined.

She turned away when Cade dropped his towel and made a fluid racing dive off the rocks at the side of the bay. An unexpected wave caught her—unexpected because she was too busy drooling over the man, she thought furiously as she inhaled water. Spluttering, she spat out a mouthful of salt water and coughed a couple of times to clear her lungs, opening her eyes to see her host heading towards her, strong arms cutting through the waves.

Oh, how...how inane! She'd probably just convinced him she wasn't safe in a shower, let alone the sea.

Sure enough, he trod water when he reached her and demanded, 'Are you all right?'

The sun-dazzled sparkles of water clogging her lashes surrounded him with an aura, a dynamic charge of power that paradoxically made her feel both weak and energised at the same time.

'Fine,' she returned, only a little hoarse from the dousing. Her heart was thudding as though she'd swum several kilometres through raging surf.

Get a grip, she commanded.

The last time she'd felt anything remotely like this she'd been nineteen and amazingly naive. She'd decided it had to be love, and became engaged on the strength of it. What a disaster that had turned out to be!

But there was nothing girlishly callow about her response to this man. Her body throbbed with a dark, potent sexuality unlike anything she'd ever experienced before.

She'd deal with that later. Right now, she had to get herself back onto an even keel.

Somehow she managed to produce a smile and said the first thing that popped into her head. 'Race you to shore.'

Cade's brows shot up as though she'd surprised him, but he recovered instantly. 'You get a handicap.'

'OK,' she agreed.

However, even with the handicap, he beat her comfortably. At least swimming as fast and as hard as she'd ever done worked off some of that wildfire energy.

When she stood up he said, 'You're good.'

'I was brought up almost in the water,' she said, breathing fast. He too, she noted with satisfaction, was breathing more heavily than normal. She added, 'My parents love the sea so much they called me after it.'

'Taryn?'

'No, Taryn is apparently derived from an Irish word meaning *rocky hill*. I had an Irish grandmother. But my second name is Marisa, which is from a Latin word meaning *the sea*.'

He observed dryly, 'It's a very pretty name, but I don't think it would help if you got cramps and there was no one around to help.'

'I've never had even the slightest twinge of cramp,' she said defensively, extremely aware of the way water gleamed along the muscular breadth of his shoulders, highlighting the effortless power beneath the skin. 'Anyway, I know how to deal with it.'

'Those medical parents?'

'And a Pacific upbringing,' she said shortly. 'Want to know how it's done?'

He laughed. 'Like you, I've never had cramp, but just in case—yes, demonstrate.'

When he laughed he was really something, she thought confusedly. Trying to speak prosaically, she said, 'First you change your kick. That often works. If it doesn't, take a deep breath and float face down, then pull your leg up, grab your foot and yank it upwards.'

She demonstrated, glad to be able to hide her face in the water for a few seconds. When she'd finished, she stood up and said, 'That almost always does the trick, I'm told.'

But he wasn't going to let her off so easily. Bumblebees zoomed through her bloodstream when he scanned her face with hooded blue-grey eyes. 'And if it doesn't?'

'Assume the same position and massage the offending muscle,' she told him succinctly, taking a surreptitious step back before her brain scrambled completely, overcome by all that bronzed skin, sleeked by water and backed by muscles and hard male authority.

He laughed again, teeth very white in his tanned face. 'Fine, I'll accept that you can deal with cramp. Are you on shift work to be able to take the day off?'

The abrupt change of subject startled her. 'I'm not working right now.'

His brows met over the distinguished blade of his nose. 'Really?'

Was there a hint of disparagement in his tone? Taryn bristled. Parrying a keen, questioning look, she said with cool reserve, 'I've been overseas, and when I came back I took a job selling souvenirs to tourists. It's getting close to the end of summer and tourists are slackening off, so I'm no longer needed.'

'Is there plenty of work around here?' His voice was casual. 'The village looked to be pretty small.'

Aramuhu was small, and there were very few jobs. But her future was none of his business. 'I'm sure I'll find something,' she said dismissively.

He smiled. 'I'm sure you will.'

Something in his tone caught her attention. Their gazes met, clashed, and the glint of awareness in his eyes summoned an intense, elemental response from her.

Taryn forced herself to ignore the shiver scudding down her spine, the tingle of anticipation.

Her breath stopped in her throat and she had to fight an odd belief that those few seconds of silent combat were altering the very fabric of her life, fundamentally changing her so that she'd never be the same again.

This unexpected attraction *was* mutual. Cade felt it too and, if she were willing, he'd probably enjoy a light-hearted, temporary affair.

Taryn didn't do casual affairs—didn't do *any* sort of affair. She'd had more than enough of the stark embarrassment when men realised that, although she could shiver with desire, when it came to actually making love she froze.

Her impetuous youthful engagement had caused such fierce disillusionment she'd been left emotionally bruised, so wary she'd never allowed herself to feel anything more than friendship for the men she'd met. Over the years she'd developed effective methods of brushing off unwanted approaches, yet this time temptation whispered seductively through her.

She'd stay well away from him—not give herself any chance of weakening. Turning away, she dived back into the welcoming water.

CHAPTER THREE

CADE didn't follow her. Taryn told herself she should be pleased. She'd be prepared to bet her next year's income—always providing she had one, she thought uneasily—that on his home turf he'd be hip-deep in swooning women. He had to be in his early thirties and he wasn't married. Most men with his financial and personal assets would enjoy playing the field.

As she hauled herself up onto the rocks she decided acidly that when he did make up his mind to marry he'd probably choose a glamorous model or actress. After five years or so he'd divorce her and marry a nice girl from his own strata of society—whatever that was—who'd give him the required couple of children. And in his fifties he'd divorce the second wife and marry a trophy one thirty years younger.

And she wouldn't want to be any of those wives.

That thought made her grin ironically before she slid back into the water.

Half an hour later she'd showered and reluctantly got back into her smelly shirt and shorts, emerging from the luxurious cabana to meet Cade, his muscled elegance defined by clothes that made her feel like a ragamuffin.

Only for an instant. The appreciative gaze that skimmed her bare legs did considerable damage to her composure. How on earth could he convey leashed interest with one swift glance—a glance that set her treacherous blood fizzing?

Possibly she'd misread his attitude, because his voice was coolly impersonal when he asked, 'Would you like a drink?'

'No, thank you,' she said at once, squelching a pang of regret. 'I smell of smoke and I really want to get out of these clothes.'

And could have bitten her tongue out. Would he think she'd made an unsubtle proposition? If he said something about a Freudian slip she'd have to bite back an indignant reply in case he guessed what she'd been thinking.

But he was too sophisticated to take her up on her clumsy choice of words. Not a muscle in his face moved when he said, 'Then some other time, perhaps.'

'That would be nice.' Taryn thought in self-derision that platitudes were so useful for filling in awkward moments.

Then Cade's smile hit her like a blow to her solar plexus. It turned her thoughts into chaotic, disconnected responses—all of which indicated, *He is utterly gorgeous...*

And he knew the effect that smile had on the opposite sex too.

Calmly, he said, 'If you want to swim, come and do it here. Nobody is going to want to swim in the next bay for a while.'

'I... That's very kind of you,' she said automatically. Yet another platitude.

Of course she wouldn't accept. Yet some traitorous part of her couldn't help wondering if this surprising invitation was the first step in—what?

Nothing, she thought sturdily, but heat scorched her cheeks and she hastily bent to pick up the bag containing her togs.

'So that's agreed,' he said calmly.

Taryn had never met another man with his uncompromising aura of authority and controlled, potent sensuality. She preferred her male companions to be interesting and unthreatening.

Like Peter.

That memory drove the colour from her skin. She produced a meaningless smile and said, 'Actually, it isn't, but it's very kind of you to offer, and I'll probably take you up on it.'

She got into the car, frowned as the engine took a sluggish couple of moments to power, waved with one hand and drove off.

Cade watched the elderly vehicle, its persistent rattle deepening his frown. It certainly didn't look as though she had all Peter's money; if she did, she'd have been able to buy a brand-new car. The amount he knew for certain she'd received wasn't enough for that.

Perhaps she was canny enough to save it.

Unfortunately, he didn't know enough about her to make any reasonable judgement.

But that, he decided, could be dealt with. If she needed a job, he could provide her with one for long enough to find out whether she was a money-grubbing opportunist…

Taryn stopped at the top of the hill to look down into the next desolate bay. One fire engine remained there and a couple of the firemen were checking the perimeters of the burn but, although wisps of smoke still drifted up, the fire had clearly been controlled.

No little red car, either, she noted. Her frown

deepened. Jason was becoming rather too pressing, a nuisance.

But not dangerous.

Unlike the man she'd just left.

Dangerous? She gave a snort and muttered, 'He's a *businessman*, for heaven's sake.'

Tycoons Taryn had seen on television or in the news were sleek, well dressed and well manicured. The thought of them being dangerous anywhere but in the boardroom was laughable.

So what made her foolish mind fix on that word to describe Cade Peredur?

Instinct, she guessed,

And Cade had certainly *looked* dangerous when he was scotching those greedy tongues of flame. He'd used her wet towel like a weapon, flailing it with an economy of movement that showed great strength as well as determination.

Also, there had been something in his manner when he approached Jason that had indicated a formidable male threat—one Jason had recognised.

OK, Cade was dangerous, as any strong man could be. But he was in complete control of all that strength. And none of it was directed at her.

So she didn't have to worry or feel intimidated.

Images of his powerful body filled her mind. Water-slicked and gleaming, every long muscle lovingly delineated, he'd stolen her breath away.

Yes, her decision to see no more of him had been the right one. She glanced down, frowning at the sight of the tight fist pressed against her heart, and let her hand drop, spreading out the fingers before shaking them so they relaxed.

Plenty of women must have felt the same surging

chemistry when they set eyes on Cade Peredur. Some of them would have ended up in his bed.

'Lots, probably,' she said aloud to a fantail flirting its tail from a nearby bush as it kept its beady black eyes fixed on her.

Smiling, she confided, 'Men like Cade Peredur—men who positively *seethe* with masculine confidence—always know they've got what it takes to make a woman happy in bed.'

Unless she was inherently cold…

But not one of his lovers had managed to make their liaison permanent.

And when—*if*—she ever fell in love properly, with a man who'd understand her fear of sex and help her overcome it—she wanted permanence, a lifelong alliance like that between her parents. She wanted trust and equality and a family, laughter and commitment and security…

None of which immediately brought Cade to mind.

'So forget about this love business,' she told the fantail. 'Because I don't think the sort of man I want exists in this world.'

And she'd keep away from any more chance meetings with Cade Peredur. Next time she was struck by the urge to go to the beach she'd slake it with a shower. She wouldn't have to keep it up for long; he had to have things to do and places to go—empires to run, worlds to conquer, women to overwhelm—so he'd soon leave New Zealand.

And, once he was gone, her life would return to normal. No chills, no cheap thrills when those hard blue eyes met hers, no shivering awareness of his sheer physical impact…

For several moments more she stood looking down

at the blackened landscape, frowning at the ugly stain across the grass and the rank smell of incinerated vegetation.

Then she stiffened her spine and got into the car and drove back to the sleepout she rented in an orchard a few kilometres from the village. Basic but comfortable, it boasted a miniature kitchen and a slightly larger bathroom, and the wide terrace outside made up for the lack of space within.

Clean once more, and in fresh clothes, she picked up an apple from the bowl on the bench and dropped into the lounger to demolish the fruit, carefully not thinking of Cade Peredur.

She needed to find work. She'd quite enjoyed selling souvenirs to tourists, but the summer wave of visitors through the village had receded, leaving her behind.

Jobless and drifting…

Ever since Peter had killed himself, an aching emptiness made her question the value of her existence.

'Time to stop it,' she said out loud, and made a sudden resolution.

Drifting was for slackers, for losers.

It was more than time to find some direction to her life. Before she'd gone to the United Kingdom, she'd enjoyed her work in one of Auckland's largest libraries. In London she'd worked in a coffee shop run by a New Zealand friend until she met Peter. They'd clicked straight away and he'd introduced her to his friends—a very earnest, intense artistic circle who'd treated her as a kind of mascot.

Peter had even found her a new job; she'd been in her element cataloguing the immense library collected over fifty years by the deceased uncle of one of his acquaintances.

Although she and Peter had become close, there had been no sexual spark between them, so his proposal had come as a shock. She'd thought he was joking and burst out laughing.

Only he hadn't been. And then she'd had to refuse him as gently as she could.

His death had horrified her. She should, she thought wearily, have realised it wasn't artistic temperament that caused his bouts of depression, always followed by tearing high spirits. She had wondered if something was wrong, but it had never occurred to her that *she* might be the cause.

Assailed by questions for which she'd never know the answers, and bitter remorse at not handling the situation better, she'd come back to Aramuhu, the only place she'd ever really called home.

But there was nothing here for her, no answers. So now what? The future stretched before her, featureless and uninviting.

'I need to make a plan,' she said aloud, resisting an impulse to give up. Unlike her parents, she was not a born rover. Yes, she wanted some purpose in her life, and she'd like to settle somewhere like Aramuhu, with a steady job in a nice library.

Unfortunately, the village was too small to be able to afford a salaried librarian. Like the fire brigade, the busy little library was run by volunteers.

OK, so if she were Cade Peredur, how would she go about making a worthwhile life?

A list of all the things she had to offer would be a good start. 'So what's stopping you from doing that?' she asked the empty room, and got out of the chair.

The following morning she surveyed the list with a frown. It looked reasonably impressive—she hoped.

Much more impressive than the bank statement she'd just opened. It told her she had enough money to last for two weeks. Something perilously close to panic pooled icily beneath her ribs.

Ignoring it, she sat down and wrote at the bottom of her list: *Stay here?*

That had to be her first decision. Living was cheap in Aramuhu—but the sleepout was used for kiwi fruit pickers in season, so it was temporary. She could stay there for another couple of months, perhaps.

She could go to her parents in Vanuatu, but she had no medical skills, and they didn't need a librarian or even a secretary. Besides, it would only ever be a stopgap.

Frowning, she added a final few words: *If so, disengage from Jason.* Not that he seriously worried her, but she was beginning to feel uneasy at his refusal to take no for an answer.

An abrupt summons from the telephone startled her.

Not Jason, please.

'Yes?' she said cautiously.

And recognised the voice instantly when he said, 'Cade Peredur here.'

How did he know her number? Her stomach tightened when he went on without pausing, 'Do you have decent computer skills?'

Startled, she glanced at her ancient laptop. 'They're not bad.'

'I've just been called to a business meeting at very short notice, and I need someone to assemble and collate information for me from the Internet and possibly transcribe notes. Would you be interested?'

That crisp, deep voice showed no indication of any

interest in her but the purely businesslike. 'Well, yes,' she said cautiously.

'You are still looking for work?'

'Yes, but…' Taryn gathered her scattering wits and took a deep breath as that forbidden word *dangerous* appeared in red letters across her brain. Common sense demanded she say no, and mean it.

'What's the problem?' he enquired.

Pushed, she responded tersely, 'None, I suppose, if I discount the fact that we met for the first time yesterday, and I don't know very much about you at all.'

There was silence, as though she'd accused him of some deviant behaviour, before he said, 'I can probably come up with a reference. Who would you like to give it?'

Flippantly, she returned, 'How about the Prime Minister?'

'United Kingdom or New Zealand?'

Funny man.

Or seriously influential. 'Oh, don't bother,' she retorted. 'Where is this business meeting?'

'Fala'isi.'

An island basking in the tropical sun… Firmly, she pushed back memories of halcyon days. 'I didn't realise it involved travel.'

'Have you a current passport?'

'Yes, but—'

'It's only a short flight from Auckland.'

Fala'isi was a small island nation known for its good governance, safety and lack of corruption. However, she said, 'There are good temping agencies in Auckland—'

'It's a long weekend,' he said evenly. 'I've tried, and everyone's away on holiday.'

Of course, it was Anniversary weekend. Torn, Taryn wavered.

Into the silence, Cade said with cool, crisp detachment, 'I can assure you I have no designs, wicked or otherwise, on you, your body or your well-being. I've been called in to advise at an informal meeting of political and influential figures from around the Pacific Rim. It will last a week. My personal assistant in London is unable to help—he has family problems. I need someone who can type well, find information on a wide variety of subjects, check its accuracy and collate it in time for me to be armed for each session. Someone who's discreet. You'll be busy, but there should be enough time for you to swim and otherwise enjoy yourself. Obviously, you'll be well compensated for your time.'

The lick of irritation underlying his words angered her, but was oddly reassuring. It sounded as though she were merely the easiest solution to an unexpected difficulty. And in Fala'isi it was highly unlikely she'd come up against any situation she couldn't deal with.

However, it was the thought of her bank balance that made the decision. She needed the money. And she wasn't likely to lose either her head or her heart in a week.

'All right, I'll do it,' she said quickly, before she could change her mind. 'But I'll need an address and contact details.'

She'd give them to her landlady. Just in case…

Three hours later Taryn was sitting in a sleekly luxurious jet feeling as though she'd been tossed without ceremony onto a merry-go-round. Cade had taken over, efficiently organising their departure.

The first shock had been the helicopter ride to the

international airport at Auckland. The second arrived hot on its heels when, after swift formalities, Cade escorted her to this plane. The third came when she realised that not only was it private but they were the only passengers.

Feeling ridiculously as though she'd been kidnapped, she obeyed the pilot's instructions and strapped herself in, and they were soon streaking northwards over an ocean as serene as its name. Taryn knew how swiftly the Pacific Ocean could turn violent, but today it was rippling watered silk, agleam all the way to the horizon beneath a sky just as blue and benign.

Not that she could concentrate on it; a few moments ago Cade had finished concisely briefing her on what she'd be expected to do in Fala'isi.

She said warily, 'I assume you won't want me attending the social occasions.' He'd spoken of cruises, dinners, a cocktail party…

His brows lifted. 'I don't expect you to work for the entire time. If you don't want to attend any of the social occasions that's not a problem. You grew up in the tropics—have you ever been to Fala'isi?'

'No.' She paused, then said lightly, 'But, from what I remember, tropical islands in the Pacific have coconut palms and coconut crabs, and most of them are surrounded by lagoons of the most amazing blue on the planet. There's glorious singing, and whole families somehow manage to perch on little motor scooters.'

'Your parents were brave taking a young child so far from civilisation.'

There was no condemnation in his tone but she had to control a spurt of defensiveness. Her parents didn't need defending. 'They're experienced sailors. And they were desperately needed—still are. There are very few doctors in the outlying islands. My parents are kept busy.'

'So they settled in Aramuhu for your schooling?'

'Yes,' she said briefly.

'Where are they now?' Cade asked, his blue-grey eyes intent.

'Back in the islands,' she told him, wondering a second too late if she should have hedged, let him believe they were within reach. 'In a bigger, more easily sailed yacht that's also a mobile clinic.'

A clinic that the unexpected and very generous donation from Peter had helped to fund. When he'd received the advance for his sculpture, he'd transferred the money into her account.

Horrified, she'd wanted to return it, only to have him grin and say, 'Let me do this, darling girl—it's probably the only time I'm ever going to do anything altruistic. You bring out the best in me.'

He'd had to talk hard to persuade her, but in the end she'd accepted it. He'd been pleased when she'd shown him a photograph of the yacht…

Hastily, she glanced away to hide the tears that stung her eyes.

'Do you see them often?' Cade asked.

'No.' Something in his expression made her say crisply, 'I suppose that sounds as though I don't get on with them but I do—and I admire them tremendously for what they're doing. I think I told you I'd been overseas for two years, having a ball in London and working there to finance trips to the Continent.' She added with a smile, 'Known to all young Kiwis as the big OE—overseas experience. It's a rite of passage.'

Cade leaned back in the seat and took a swift glance at her profile. 'When did your parents go back to the

Pacific islands on their mission of mercy?' he asked, keeping his voice detached.

'Once I'd settled at university,' she said cheerfully. 'And now I've revealed some of my story, how about yours?'

Ironically amused, he met coolly challenging green-gold eyes, their size and colour emphasised by dark lashes and brows. No way was he going to tell her of his early childhood; he'd padlocked those memories and thrown away the key years ago.

Cade wondered if she realised just how much she'd revealed. *Admire* didn't mean the same as love. It sounded as though her parents had seen her through school and then more or less abandoned her.

And he was beginning to believe she didn't know that he and Peter had been brothers. If she did, she'd have been a little more wary when she'd spoken of her time in London.

He said economically, 'My life? Very standard. Good parents, good education, a university scholarship, first job in the City, then striking out on my own.'

'And then success,' she supplied with a smile.

Cade caught the hint of satire in the curve of her mouth.

Yes, she was challenging him, and not just sexually, although he was extremely aware of her in the seat beside him. His body stirred at the recollection of the silky texture of her skin and the smooth curves her bikini had displayed.

'That too,' he said non-committally. 'Does success interest you?'

She considered the question, her forehead wrinkling. To his surprise, he realised he was waiting for her answer with some expectation. Which was reasonable;

he'd hired her to remove her from her comfort zone so he could find out what sort of person she really was.

Of course, he wouldn't allow himself to be distracted—he didn't do distraction. Not even when it came as superbly packaged as Taryn Angove.

'It interests everyone, surely,' she said at last. 'But it depends on how you define it. My parents are hugely successful because they're doing exactly what they want to do, which is helping people—making a difference to their lives. Sometimes *saving* their lives.'

'So that's your definition? Success means following your passion?'

She gave him a startled look, then laughed, a sound without much humour. 'Seems to be.'

Something more than idle curiosity persuaded him to ask, 'Do you have a passion?'

He saw her withdrawal, but she answered with a rueful smile, 'Not one I've discovered yet. What's your definition of success?'

That had changed over the years, from his initial instinctive need to survive a neglectful, drug-addicted mother. He had no intention of divulging his motivations to anyone, let alone Taryn, who'd made out a list that ended in *disengage from Jason.*

The list had been on the table, as though she'd dropped it there when he'd arrived to pick her up a few hours ago. She'd gone into her bedroom to bring out her pack, and deliberately and without guilt he'd read down the items. He needed all the ammunition he could muster to remind him that her reaction to Peter's proposal had so shattered his brother he'd killed himself.

When had she added that last significant note? After they'd met yesterday?

Jason presumably had been her lover; the journalist

had certainly bristled with a territorial air when he'd been talking to her.

So she hadn't mourned Peter for long.

CHAPTER FOUR

THAT thought grated so much Cade turned his head and looked out at the sea below.

One thing the years with an erratic mother had taught him was to read people. As soon as he'd met Taryn he'd noted the subtle signs of her response to him. What he hadn't anticipated was his own reaction to her—a quick, fierce hunger he was having difficulty controlling.

But what worried him was an unexpected and alarmingly unwelcome inclination to believe every word she said. Cade was cynical rather than suspicious, but his life and career had taught him not to trust anyone until he knew them.

And that, he reminded himself, was why Taryn was sitting beside him—in order for him to gather information about her.

He said, 'I suppose my definition of my own success is to do whatever I do well. And to keep faith with the people who rely on me.'

She waited as though expecting more, then nodded, her expression thoughtful. 'Sounds good.'

And meant very little, she thought a touch sardonically. If she'd hoped to get something other than platitudes from him, she'd just learned he wasn't going to open up to her.

After all, he was now her employer. There were protocols to be observed, a suitably respectful distance to be kept. Possibly, in a subtle English way, he was indicating she'd better forget the informal, unconventional circumstances in which they'd met.

Glancing up, she met hooded steel-blue eyes, unsparing and probing. Sensation sizzled through her and she said the first thing that came to mind. 'I hope I can do the job.'

In an indifferent voice, he said, 'Having second thoughts, Taryn?'

When she shook her head he went on, 'Fala'isi is a civilised place, and all I expect from you is a week of quite straightforward work.' His voice hardened. 'Because you are beautiful there will be people who misunderstand our relationship, but I'm sure you're sophisticated enough to deal with that.'

Heat burned across her cheekbones. Cade's tone had been casually dismissive, as though in his world beauty was taken for granted.

He was far too perceptive. She'd barely recognised the caution in herself, a warning based on nothing more than her own response to him. Time to show him she could be completely professional.

'Of course I can,' she said. She added, 'And I don't suspect you of ulterior motives.'

He nodded. 'Good.' And began to talk of their destination, of the two cultures that had been so successfully integrated by the family that ruled Fala'isi, and of the vibrant economy that made the island state one of the powers in the Pacific.

Taryn listened and commented; from her parents she knew enough about island politics to appreciate the sharp intelligence of his remarks, the astute judgement and skilful manipulation of information. Not that he revealed much of his feelings; he probably felt they were none of her concern.

And he was entirely right; this inchoate desire to understand him was neither comfortable nor sensible.

But he did say, 'It's more than possible that somebody might try to pump you for information about me.'

'They'll fail,' she said promptly, 'because I don't know anything about you.'

He raised his eyebrows. 'You didn't research me on the Internet?'

'Yes, of course.' As far as she'd been able. She'd downloaded a couple of pictures of him with stunning women, and read several articles about his business tactics, but she'd found nothing personal about him. 'Just as anyone else could.'

He showed his teeth in a mirthless smile. 'I'm sure I don't need to tell you to be discreet.'

'No,' she said shortly.

'Good.' He looked up as the cabin attendant came through.

Taryn welcomed the interruption. She was probably imagining the unspoken undercurrents that swirled beneath the mundane words he'd spoken. Yes, he'd called her beautiful—but in a tone of voice that gave no indication what effect she had on him.

She wrenched her mind away from such a subversive thought. OK, so she was acutely conscious of Cade—and she now knew he liked what he saw when those hard, crystalline eyes roved her face, but she understood how little that superficial appreciation meant.

What would her parents think of the man beside her, at present intent on a sheaf of notes?

Her gaze traced the arrogant lines and angles of his

profile, the olive skin and arrogantly perfect line of mouth and chin…

Physically, he was magnificent. And after searching the Internet the previous evening she knew he was renowned for his ferociously brilliant mind and what one commentator called his *iron-bound integrity.* Another had commented on his almost *devilish good luck.*

What were his parents like? She'd found a reference to his *climb from the stifling mediocrity of middle-class England* but nothing else personal.

Unless you counted the photographs of him with exquisite women. At the thought of those women—bejewelled, superbly groomed, confident—a foolish pang of envy darkened her mood.

He looked up and for a moment their eyes locked. Her confusion turned into a flash of fire at the base of her spine, in the pit of her stomach.

It was quickly dampened by his drawled question. 'Something bothering you?'

'No,' she said swiftly and not, he suspected, entirely truthfully.

He was convinced of it when she added, 'I was wondering if you have a Mediterranean heritage.'

Cade shrugged negligently. 'Not that I'm aware of.'

He didn't know who his birth father was—it could have been anyone. His real father, the one who'd loved him and disciplined him and shown him how to be a man, was ruddy of complexion and blue-eyed, but Harold Cooper had handed on far more important things than superficial physical features.

Cade had no illusions as to what his life would have been if he hadn't been fostered by the Coopers.

He'd have grown up on the streets and probably ended up in jail, possibly dying young like his wretched mother before him. Instead, he'd been loved and cared for, given rules to live by, taught everything he needed to make a success of his life.

Even when his new parents had had their miracle—the child they'd been told would never eventuate—their love for Cade had never faltered. Peter had been a joy to them all, a beloved small brother for Cade to protect and help.

He owed the Coopers everything but the fact of being born—and he was prepared to do anything to give his mother the closure she craved.

Why had Peter chosen to end his life? It had to be something to do with Taryn.

Cade was accustomed to finding answers, and he needed this answer more than any other. His mother feared that Peter had died because he hadn't felt valued by his parents.

The Coopers had certainly been worried about Peter's choice of career, but he had real artistic talent and, once they'd realised he was determined to make his own path, they'd stopped suggesting he choose something steady and reliable.

One way or another, Cade would get to the truth. It shouldn't take him long to discover Taryn's weaknesses and use them to find out what he needed to know.

He glanced across; she'd picked up a magazine and was skimming the pages, stopping now and then to read more carefully. She was beautiful in a healthy, girl-next-door kind of way, her clear green-gold eyes seeming to hide no secrets; her attitude was candid and direct. Cade could see nothing in her to suggest she'd mock a man's offer of love.

Yet she must have cut Peter's confidence to shreds for him to choose death rather than face life without her.

Into Cade's mind came that final note on the list she'd made out: *disengage from Jason.*

Had she *disengaged* from Peter too, then gone on to view the world with that same innocent gaze?

It would be interesting, he thought grimly, to see Taryn's reaction when she found out the accommodation waiting for them on Fala'isi. She knew he was rich; she'd sensed he was attracted to her.

How would she accept sharing the same luxurious beachfront lodgings with him?

Would she see it as an opportunity? With cold self-derision, he fought the kick of desire in his groin and forced his attention back to the papers in his hand.

Taryn looked around the room, furnished in tropical style with lush green plants cooling the flower-scented air. One wall was highlighted by a magnificent *tapa* cloth in shades of tan and cream, black and cinnamon, and in a corner a serene, smoothly sculpted figure of a frigate bird in flight seemed to hover above its pedestal.

Peter would have loved it…

The knot of apprehension in her stomach loosened when Cade said, 'Choose whichever bedroom you'd like.'

Helpfully, the porter said, 'That room over there has a very beautiful view of the lagoon, madam, and the one on the other side of the *fale* has a lovely intimate view of the pool and the terrace garden.'

She looked at Cade.

Shrugging, he said in a tone that edged on curtness, 'I don't mind where I sleep.'

Taryn responded equally crisply, 'In that case, I'll take the one with the pool view.'

The porter, tall and magisterial, smiled his approval as he scooped her very downmarket pack from the trolley and headed towards the bedroom.

Shoulders held stiffly, Taryn followed him. She'd not expected to be whisked by luxury launch from the airport on the main island of Fala'isi to a fairy tale atoll twenty minutes offshore, nor to be ushered into a beachfront bungalow she was expected to share with Cade Peredur.

That was when she'd faltered, only to feel foolish when Cade said, 'There are two bedrooms.'

'Each with its own bathroom, madam,' the porter had supplied in a reassuring voice that made her even more self-conscious.

OK, so for a moment—but only a moment—she *had* wondered if she'd walked into a situation she didn't even want to think about. But there was no need for the glint of satirical amusement in Cade's hard eyes. She was not an overwrought idiot, seeing danger where there was none!

After a quick survey of the room she'd chosen, she smiled at the porter when he set her pack tenderly onto the luggage rack.

'Thank you, this is perfect,' she said.

'The lagoon is excellent to swim in, madam,' the porter told her before ushering her into the bathroom, where he demonstrated the switches that lowered the blinds and showed her how to work the multitude of jets in the shower.

The bathroom was circular, its walls built of rock topped by a glass ceiling that allowed a view of palm fronds against a sky of such intense blue it made her blink.

The porter noted the direction of her gaze. 'The rocks

are from the main island—from a lava flow of ancient times.'

His warmth and innate dignity brought back childhood memories and lifted her heart. If it weren't for her unusual response to the man in the next room, she'd relish this return to the tropics.

But without Cade Peredur she wouldn't be here.

She did her best to repress an excitement she hadn't allowed herself to feel for years—since the debacle of her engagement to Antony. Since then, any time she'd felt an emotional rapport, she'd reminded herself that men wanted more than affection. For them—for most people—love included passion.

She'd been utterly convinced she loved Antony, and just as certain that the stirrings of sexual attraction would progress to desire.

Her mouth twisting into a painful grimace, she turned and walked back into the bedroom, thanking the porter as he left.

She'd been so wrong. Making love with Antony had been a disaster. Try as hard as she could, she'd been unable to respond. In the end, her frigidity had caused their love to wither and die in pain and bitter acrimony.

Which was why she'd been so relieved when Peter had shown no signs of wanting anything more than friendship...

And dwelling on a past she couldn't change was fruitless and energy-sapping.

Although this exclusive, secluded retreat had probably been built with extremely wealthy honeymooners in mind, this was a business situation. If she kept that in mind and stayed utterly, coolly professional, she'd enjoy her stay in Fala'isi.

She allowed herself a single wistful glance at the aquamarine pool before unpacking her meagre allowance of clothes and indulging in a quick refreshing shower. For a few seconds she dithered, trying to decide on the most suitable garment.

Which was silly. As part of the office furniture, no one would notice what she wore. Firming her mouth, she slipped on a pair of cool, floaty trousers and a soft green shirt, combed her hair into a smooth cap and tied it back, then re-applied her only lipstick and after a deep breath walked back into the big, airy living room.

Her treacherous heart bumped at the sight of Cade, tall and dark in casual clothes, standing on the terrace. He turned before she'd taken more than a couple of steps into the room and watched her come through the huge glass doors to join him.

That cool scrutiny set every nerve twanging with eager, anticipatory, thoroughly scary awareness.

'Everything all right?' he asked.

'Absolutely.' She tore her gaze away to examine the surroundings. 'Whoever set this place up certainly homed into the romantic ambience of the South Seas.'

Palms shaded the bamboo furniture, luxuriously upholstered in white. Impressive boulders—probably also relics of the fiery creation of the main island—skilfully contrasted with vast earthenware pots holding lushly foliaged shrubs and, a few steps away, thick white rope provided the hand-rail in the shimmering pool. Bold, brilliant flowers danced in the sun, their colours clashing with a sensuous bravura Taryn envied.

'The Chapmans—the family who rule Fala'isi—are famous for their acumen and their commitment to excellence,' Cade said coolly. 'They know what people expect from a place like this.'

'They're also noted for steering Fala'isi so well the islanders now have the highest standard of living in the Pacific Islands. And that,' Taryn finished, 'is much more important.'

He gave another of those piercing looks, as though she'd startled him, and then to her surprise he nodded. 'I agree.'

So he wasn't as cynical and arrogant as she'd suspected.

He resumed, 'We'll eat lunch here, and then I have some facts I'd like you to check and validate while I attend a preliminary meeting. It shouldn't take much more than an hour, so once you've finished I suggest you do some exploring, swim if you want to.'

'On my own?' she couldn't help saying.

His short laugh acknowledged the hit. 'It would be extremely bad for business to allow anyone to drown here.'

'Does that mean there's always someone keeping watch?'

'Discreetly,' he said, a sardonic note sharpening the word. He surveyed her face and said with the perception she was beginning to expect from him, 'You don't like that.'

'Not particularly.'

He didn't say *Get used to it*, but that was probably what he was thinking. Thankful she didn't live in his world, she added, 'But that won't stop me swimming.'

And wished she'd stayed silent when she recognised a note of defiance in her tone.

'Somehow I didn't expect it to. You seem to live life on your own terms.'

For some reason, his comment startled her. 'Doesn't everyone?'

'You're remarkably innocent if you believe that,' he said cynically. 'Most people meekly follow society's dictates all their life. They buy what they're told to buy, live where they're told to live, in some societies even marry whoever they're told to marry. You appear to be a free spirit.'

'I don't think there's any such thing as true freedom,' she said slowly, then stopped.

She did not want to open herself up to Cade Peredur. It would be safer to establish boundaries, a definite distance between them, because instinct told her that even this sort of fragile, getting-to-know-you exploration could be dangerous.

There's that word again…

She laughed and finished brightly, 'And I've never thought of myself as a free spirit. It sounds great fun.'

And braced herself for another sceptical Peredur scrutiny.

Instead, he picked up a sheaf of papers. 'Around five I might have notes for you to transcribe—not many, as this afternoon's meeting is a procedural one. At seven we'll head off to pre-dinner drinks, and dinner will be at eight.'

Startled, she stared at him. 'What do you mean—*we*? You told me I wouldn't be expected to go to any of the social occasions.'

'That was because I hadn't realised most of the men were bringing their wives and significant others.' He stemmed her impetuous protest with an upheld hand. 'Don't bother pointing out that you're neither. I've just been down that road with Fleur Chapman, the wife of the man who's convened this conference. She wouldn't hear of you being left out.'

Colour stung her cheekbones. Of course he would

have objected; social occasions were not in this job description. 'I'm here as your researcher, not to attend parties.'

He responded just as crisply, 'Mrs Chapman has heard of your parents' work, and can see no reason why you shouldn't attend. In fact, she was appalled to think of you staying hidden in the *fale* like a shameful secret, as she put it.'

Dismayed, Taryn stared at him. He—and Mrs Chapman—had cut the ground from under her feet, and she suspected he knew it. Possibly he resented being forced to take her with him.

No more than she did, but the Chapman family had ruled Fala'isi for a couple of centuries; not only were they extremely rich, they were a powerful force in the Pacific where their descent from the ancient chiefly family of Fala'isi gave them huge prestige.

If the Chapmans were interested in her parents' work, she thought suddenly, there was a chance they might be prepared to help. With so many worthwhile calls on charity spending, her mother and father scrabbled for enough money to keep their clinics going.

This was possibly something she could do for her parents.

But she made one further effort. 'I haven't brought any suitable clothes.'

Dispassionately, Cade said, 'Naturally I'll organise that.' Overriding her instant horrified objection, he went on, 'The manageress of the boutique here will be along about three to discuss what you'll need.'

'I can't let you pay for my clothes,' she blurted.

One straight black brow lifted. 'You can't stop me,' he observed with cool amusement. 'Whether or not you wear them is entirely up to you.'

The prospect of appearing in public with him—in clothes he had paid for—sent prickles of apprehension across her skin. There would be sideways glances and assumptions, some of them almost certainly salacious, and the sort of gossip she despised.

Apparently he could read her mind, because he startled her anew by saying in a hard voice, 'If anyone—anyone at all—says anything untoward, I'll deal with it.'

Of course he wasn't being protective, she thought, alarmed by the swift rush of warmth his words caused. She quelled it by telling herself that he wouldn't want them to be connected in any way.

Office girl and tycoon? Not with the lovely Lady Someone in his life.

Stoutly, she responded, 'I'm quite capable of looking after myself, thank you.'

Anyway, she doubted if anyone would mistake her for Cade's latest lover; no matter what she wore, she couldn't achieve that elegant, exclusive, expensive look.

'I've noticed,' he said dryly, 'but in this case you won't need to.'

When she looked up he was smiling. Her heart flipped, honing her awareness into something so keen and compelling she felt it in her bones. Tension pulled through her, strong as a steel hawser, and it took all her will not to take a step towards him.

She managed to resist, but couldn't conquer the reckless impulse to smile back at him, although her voice was uneven when she said, 'How often does someone tell you you're a very dictatorial man?'

Involuntarily, Cade responded to her smile; it was pure challenge backed by a hint of invitation, and he guessed she was trying to force a reaction from him, judge for herself why he'd brought her here.

It took an exercise of will to clear the urgent hunger that fogged his brain.

OK, he wanted her—but, much more than that, he wanted what she knew. Instead of confronting her directly about Peter's death, he'd decided on a more subtle approach—one that did *not* involve acting on this elemental attraction, as unwanted as it was powerful.

However, he couldn't stop himself from saying, 'Calling me dictatorial makes me sound like some blood-thirsty despot intent on holding on to power by any means, no matter how cruel. How often does someone tell you you're beautiful and ask you why you're still unattached?'

Her eyes widened, then were veiled by thick, dark lashes. 'Rarely,' she said curtly. 'And usually it's as a sleazy pick-up line from a man I wouldn't be seen dead with.'

'Touché.' OK, so he'd been blunt, but what the hell had caused the frozen shock he'd seen for a millisecond before her expression had closed him out?

Something shattering. Peter's suicide? Possibly.

Damn, he thought, as sounds from outside heralded the arrival of waiters with lunch. *Damn and double damn.* Their inopportune arrival might have cut off a chance to introduce the subject.

He was going to have to, sooner or later, yet he found himself intensely disinclined to raise the matter. And that was a worry.

'Ah, here's lunch,' he said, his voice as clipped and curt as he could make it.

It was impossible to tell what she was thinking, but she responded calmly, 'Good, I'm hungry. And I'm really looking forward to diving into the lagoon. It's too long since I swam in really warm water.'

Into his head flashed a tantalising image of her in her bikini, all slender limbs and silken skin, a gleaming, golden nymph from one of the raunchier legends.

Angered by the violent involuntary response from his body, Cade headed for his own room, but stopped at the door to say over his shoulder, 'When you do swim, make sure you use sunscreen.'

'Yes, sir,' she responded smartly. 'New Zealand spends summer under a huge hole in the ozone layer, and wearing hats and slapping on sunscreen at frequent intervals has become part of our national character.'

Cade had to hide a smile. Over lunch, served on the terrace, he asked her about her childhood and, although she spoke readily enough about that, she was surprisingly reticent about other aspects of her life. He already knew she'd been engaged once, but when he'd provided her with an opportunity to mention it, she hadn't.

Which proved nothing, he thought, irritated by a potent mixture of feelings—the sensual hunger somehow magnified by a growing protectiveness. Clearly she didn't feel her parents had abandoned her. In fact, she'd snapped at the bait he'd dangled in front of her by mentioning that Fleur Chapman might be able to help them in their mission of mercy.

So the fact that they'd more or less left her to her own devices once she'd left secondary school didn't seem to concern her. He felt an odd sympathy, remembering his own parents' sacrifices—the money saved for a trip to France, the gap year they'd insisted on financing…

During the afternoon meeting he found it surprisingly hard to concentrate; his mind kept slipping back to the smooth fall of Taryn's hair, turned by the sun into a flood of burnished copper, the way her crisp voice was softened by an intriguing husky undertone, her open pleasure in the food.

And that, he thought grimly as he headed back to their *fale*, was something new; no other woman had come between him and work. He'd liked his lovers, enjoyed spending time with them—even Louisa, before she'd decided to change the rules of their relationship. But his previous women had only occupied a small niche in his life.

Taryn Angove was different. How different? He searched for a word to describe her, and could only come up with fresh—*fresh* and apparently frank, intensely seductive.

Had Peter too thought she was different?

Cade welcomed the acid bite of that thought; it dragged his mind back to focus. He couldn't afford to let his hormones overpower his brain cells.

A call on his cell phone interrupted him; he stopped beneath a large spreading tree with brazen scarlet flowers and spoke to the private detective who'd been investigating Taryn.

When the call was over he pocketed the cell phone and punched one hand into the palm of his other. Beneath his breath, he said explosively, 'Why the hell did you have to do it, Peter? Why didn't you just laugh straight back in her face and find a woman who could love you? Why take the coward's way out?'

The bitter words shocked him into silence. He lifted his gaze to the sea, but saw Taryn walking across the sand towards the *fale*, the *pareu* slung across her hips emphasising their seductive sway. Water turned her hair into gleaming copper and gilded her skin so that she seemed to walk in a golden, shimmering aura. She was even more alluring than the images his brain had been conjuring all afternoon.

Heated desire gripped him so fiercely he had to turn away. It would be no hardship to seduce her, he thought grimly, no hardship at all.

Yet he could not. Dared not. Never before had hunger fogged his brain, whispering a temptation he wanted to yield to.

CHAPTER FIVE

CADE dragged his gaze away from Taryn, trying to clear his mind by fixing his attention on the hibiscus bush a few feet away. The fiercely magenta heart of each flower glowed in a silken gold ruff, hues so intense he was reminded of the time he'd visited an official mint and watched molten gold being poured.

Taryn had a quick, astute brain and plenty of character, so she was unlikely to be drifting without purpose. Yet since she'd got back from England her only job had been selling souvenirs to summer tourists, and she certainly didn't seem to be in a hurry to find more work.

He found himself strongly resisting what should have been the obvious reason. If she had most of Peter's advance in her bank account, she wouldn't need to worry about working for some years.

Everything pointed to her being the one who'd accepted—or stolen—the money from his brother. There was no proof, yet no other person had been close enough to Peter to make it seem likely he'd have given them money. If he'd showered her with it, only to have his proposal turned down with mockery and laughter, then that could have been a reason for Peter's tragic decision.

And she hadn't mentioned Peter. Or shown any signs of grief.

An innate sense of justice forced him to admit he didn't expect her to break into sobs every half hour. That wouldn't be her style.

Nor his, yet he grieved deeply for his brother.

So, was she as good as he was at hiding her feelings—or did she have none? His eyes narrowing, he watched her stop at the outdoor shower set under a big poinciana tree. She tossed the length of fabric around her hips over a shrub, turned on the tap and lifted her face to let the water flow over her.

The bikini was decorous enough but, moulded against the clean curves of her body by the veil of water, she might as well have been naked.

Was this a deliberate pose, letting him see what she had on offer?

Lust tugged urgently at him, swamping his cold calculation with a hot, angry hunger. Abruptly, he turned away, overcome with self-disgust. He couldn't let himself become too fixated on her. He'd always been in charge of his physical reactions; it was humiliating to want a woman who might be everything he despised.

He had to persuade her to open up so he could better judge whether to trust her version of what had happened. He needed to see for himself what she'd felt—if anything—for his brother.

Mouth set in a firm line, he headed down the shell path to the *fale*.

Taryn almost hummed with pleasure beneath the shower, but water was likely to be precious on a coral atoll, so she turned off the tap and wrapped her *pareu* around her again to mop up.

She was so glad to be back in the tropics. Stroking through the silken waters of the lagoon, she'd felt a surge of something very close to renewal. Oh, the warm sea against her skin, the sand shimmering white against the green bushes beneath the coconut palms—they all had something to do with it but, although the sun beat down with a languorous intensity only known in the tropics, her raised spirits were caused by something deeper than delight at being back, a feeling much stronger, much more intimate than a sensory lift, welcome though that was.

It was strangely like a rebirth, an understanding that life could be worthwhile again.

And it had *nothing*—not a thing—to do with being here with Cade, whose controlled dynamism was a force to be reckoned with. Perhaps she'd finally accepted that she'd never know why Peter had changed so abruptly from a best friend to a would-be husband…

Or whether her shocked refusal had led to his suicide.

Her bitter remorse at her stunned response would always be with her. But from somewhere she'd found a renewed sensation of confidence, of control of her own destiny.

Once she got back to New Zealand she'd find a job—move to Auckland if it was necessary—and start this next stage of her life.

There was no sign of Cade when she reached their accommodation. Squelching a stupid disappointment she walked through the glass doors into her bedroom, bare feet warm against the cool smooth tiles on the floor.

Perhaps she could put her skills as a librarian to use in some tropical area?

She smiled ironically. If she managed to find such a position she wouldn't be living in a place like this, subtly groomed and organised to give rich, demanding clients the illusion of paradise.

Strange that here, in a spot dedicated to a romantic idea of leisure and sensuous relaxation, she should feel a resurgence of the energy she'd lost when Peter died.

She was dressed and combing her wet hair back from her face when movement caught her eye. Swivelling, she realised that Cade had walked to the edge of the terrace and was bending to pick a hibiscus flower.

For some peculiar reason, her heart lurched at the sight of his long fingers stroking the ruffled, satiny petals—only to freeze a moment later when a casual, dismissive flick of his fingers sent the exquisite bloom onto the ground.

It shouldn't have affected her so strongly. Yet she almost gasped with shock, and took an instinctive step sideways to hide from sight.

After a few seconds she told herself she was being ridiculous. She forced herself to breathe again and glanced sideways into an empty garden. Her heartbeat settling into its usual steady rhythm, she scolded herself for being so foolishly sensitive. Nothing had happened. He'd merely picked a flower and tossed it away.

Later, when she emerged from her room, Cade was standing just outside the glass doors with his back to her. He had to have excellent hearing because, although she moved quietly, he turned the moment she came into the big, cool living room.

Their eyes met, and another little chill ran the length of her spine until he smiled. 'Enjoy your swim?' he asked.

'It was lovely,' she said, oddly disconcerted. Had he seen her walk up from the beach? She repressed a sensuous little shiver. She'd been perfectly decent with her *pareu* draped around her—and he was probably bored by the sight of women parading around in bikinis.

'How did you find the computer set-up?'

She blinked, then hastily reassembled her wits. 'Oh, excellent. No problems.'

He nodded. Now, he thought stringently—give her that opportunity now. Yet it took all his notorious drive to say casually, 'Your computer skills would have come in handy when you were in London.'

Taryn smiled. 'Not at first. I worked in a coffee shop, until a friend found me a job cataloguing a library, which was perfect. I could dash over the Channel or around the country whenever I wanted, providing I got the work done.'

'A very good friend,' Cade observed. 'One who knew you well.'

'Yes, a good friend indeed,' she said tonelessly.

Cade sent a keen glance, but could read nothing from her smooth face. He let the silence drag on but all she did was nod.

Cade held out a sheaf of notes. 'I'd like you to get these down now.'

Heart thudding, Taryn took the notes and escaped into her room. It was a relief to sit down at the desk and concentrate on the swift, bold handwriting, and an even greater relief when he left to meet someone.

When she'd finished getting his clear, concise notes into the computer and backed them up, she closed things down and stood up. Cade had just returned and the sun was heading towards the horizon. It would seem to fall more quickly as it got closer to the clear, straight line where sea met sky, and there might be a mysterious green flash the instant it slipped over the horizon. She'd seen it a couple of times, and looked forward to seeing it again.

She picked up the printed copy and walked into the

sitting room. Cade got up from the sofa where he'd been reading the work she'd collated after lunch.

After a quick perusal of the copy, he said, 'This is exactly what I need, thank you.' He glanced at his watch. 'You have half an hour to get into whatever you're wearing to cocktails and dinner.'

When she frowned, he said smoothly, 'I assume you've chosen something suitable to wear.'

Under the boutique manager's interested survey she'd chosen something, but whether it was suitable or not time would tell. Impulsively, she said, 'It still seems too much like gatecrashing for me to feel comfortable about going.'

'We've already had this conversation. You've been personally invited.' His mouth curled up at the corners. 'Of course, if you met someone on the beach you'd like to further your acquaintance with—'

'No,' she interrupted, startled.

'Then what's your problem?'

Taryn hesitated. Impossible to tell him that for some reason she hated the thought of being tagged as just another of his women, a holiday convenience.

But his cool, speculative gaze demanded an answer. Gathering her wits, she snapped, 'I'm your researcher, not arm candy.'

His smile stopped any further words, a smile that, allied to such a powerful presence, made him a walking, breathing, potently dangerous adrenalin rush.

'Candy is sweet. Your tongue is far too sharp for you to be considered anything like that.' He took her hand. 'If you don't get going we'll be late.'

It was like brushing against an electric fence, she thought wildly. Breathing was impossible. Dumbfounded by the wildfire intensity of her reaction to his touch, she let him turn her towards her room.

'Off you go,' he said calmly, and started her off with a movement so gentle it could hardly be called a push.

Taryn's body responded automatically and she got halfway to her room before her dazzled brain came to life. How dared he? Frowning, she swung around and, in her most forthright voice, said, 'I'm not a child to be told to go to my room. And please don't ever push me like that again.'

His brows climbed. 'I'm sorry,' he said unexpectedly, adding abruptly, 'And you don't need to be afraid of me. I don't hurt women.'

The words burst out before she could stop them. 'I'm not afraid of you!'

Cool it! She was overreacting, giving too much away, allowing him to see how strongly he affected her. After a jagged breath, she said crossly, 'I just hate it when people stop a perfectly good rant by apologising.'

That spellbinding smile made a brief reappearance. 'I take your point, but you haven't time for a really good rant right now. Later, you can let go all you like.'

An equivocal note in his voice dried her throat. She could read nothing in the starkly handsome face, and surely he wasn't hinting…

He resumed, 'You flinched when I touched you.'

Wishing she'd ignored it, she said, 'Not because I was afraid. I just wasn't expecting it. And, although I'm delighted you don't hurt women, how are you with children and animals?'

He subjected her to a look she could barely parry. Silkily, he said, 'Superb.' She was choking back laughter when he added, 'And, to reassure you, from now on I'll only touch you after asking permission.'

His smile, and the glinting look that accompanied it, stopped her breath again. He *was* flirting with her!

Common sense warned her she was way out of her league—but there was no reason to let him know that.

Rallying, she said, 'So you'll say, "Taryn, I want to push you out of the way of that shark. Is that all right?" And then wait for my answer?'

'If that happens, I might force myself to ignore this conversation,' he said smoothly.

A note in his voice produced a swift wave of heat across her cheekbones. This was dangerous stuff. Put an end to it right now, she commanded herself.

But how?

OK, she'd pretend to take him seriously, as though his eyes weren't gleaming with amusement and her blood wasn't pumping a suspicious and inconvenient excitement through her veins.

In her most prosaic tone, she said, 'Well, that's all right then.' She glanced at her watch as if checking the time. 'And if I'm to be ready on time I'd better get going.'

And managed to force her suddenly heavy legs to move away from him. *Cold shower* was her first thought once she reached the sanctuary of her room.

Icy water would have been good, but she had to content herself with a brisk splash in the lukewarm water available. However, by the time she'd knotted a sleek *pareu* that fell from her bare shoulders to her ankles in a smooth column of gold, her pulse had calmed down—almost.

After a careful examination in the mirror, she gave a short nod of satisfaction. The inexpensive *pareu* looked almost as good as the designer clothes the shop manageress had brought to show her. Her own slim gold sandals made no concession to her height; she could wear ten-centimetre heels and still be shorter then Cade.

Exactly twenty-five minutes after she'd left, she walked back into the sitting room, to meet a narrow-eyed glance from Cade that sent her pulse rate soaring again. In tropical evening clothes, he was *stunning*, she decided faintly, trying to control the overheated reactions ricocheting through her.

His quizzical expression made her realise she was staring a little too openly. Without censoring the thought, she said, 'I hope this is suitable.'

'I'm not an expert on women's clothes,' he said, his level voice mocking her turmoil, 'but no man in the place is going to think it other than perfect.'

She pulled a face. 'It's not the men I'm worried about.'

Hard mouth easing into an oblique smile, he said, 'The women will be envious. You look fine.' A little impatiently, he finished, 'Let's go.'

Nerves tightened in the pit of her stomach as they walked down a shell path beneath the coconut palms to the venue for the cocktail party, a wide terrace open to the sea and the sunset.

Taryn's swift glance told her that every other woman there was clad in designer resort wear, the sort of clothes featured in very upmarket magazines as ideal for the captain's cocktail party.

And, judging by the massed array of jewels sparkling in the light of the westering sun, she was the only employee. Worse, a man who turned to watch them walk in smiled sardonically and said something in a low voice to his companion, an elegant blonde who moved so she could see them both clearly.

Taryn gave them a coolly dismissive glance, tensing when Cade slid a firm hand beneath her elbow.

'Ignore them,' he said in a low, inflexible voice, looking over her at the couple.

Taryn didn't see his expression, but the glance he sent towards them must have been truly intimidating. Their rapid about-face almost amused her, and helped to ease her chagrin.

He commanded, 'Relax.'

Ignoring the rush of heat to her cheeks, she blurted the first thing that came to mind. 'You were going to ask before you touched me again.'

'I did make an exception for sharks,' he said soberly.

She spluttered, then laughed, and he released her. Feeling an abrupt chill, almost as though she'd been abandoned, she took a quick look around, turning as a handsome couple came up to them, their hosts Luke and Fleur Chapman.

After introducing them, Cade said, 'Luke's family are rather like feudal overlords here.' Then he added, 'But you know this, of course. As well as their strong New Zealand connection, your parents keep you up-to-date with Pacific affairs.'

Taryn said cheerfully, 'Ever since a Kiwi married Luke's father we've considered the Chapmans of Fala'isi to be honorary New Zealanders.' She gave a comradely grin to Fleur Chapman. 'And of course our newspapers and every women's magazine had a field day when another Kiwi married Luke.'

Both their hosts laughed, but Fleur said thankfully, 'They seem to have lost interest in us now we've settled into being a boringly married couple.'

The glance she exchanged with her husband made

Taryn catch her breath and feel a sudden pang of something too close to envy. Nothing *boring* in that marriage, she thought.

What would it be like to have such complete trust in the person you loved?

Fleur turned back to Taryn. 'And we've heard of the wonderful work your parents do. Later, when we have time, we must talk more about it.'

Their warmth and friendliness set the tone of the evening. Her tension evaporated, and with Cade at her side she felt oddly protected—and that, she realised, was both ridiculous and more than a little ominous.

About the last thing she needed was a man's protection; she'd been looking after herself quite adequately since she left secondary school.

As she smiled and chatted with people she'd previously seen only on the news, she observed their reactions to Cade. Intrigued, she saw that respect for his formidable achievements was very much to the fore, mixed with a certain wariness.

If anyone else was speculating on the relationship between Cade and her, it didn't show. Most of the women noted her clothes, and an observant few even recognised her *pareu* to be a cheap beach wrap from the boutique.

Only one mentioned it, a charming middle-aged Frenchwoman who said, 'My dear, how clever of you! You put us all to shame with sheer powerful simplicity!'

The unexpected compliment brought a flush to Taryn's skin, making Madame Murat laugh as she turned to Cade. 'I hope you appreciate her.'

Cade's eyes narrowed slightly, but he favoured her with a smile. 'I do indeed,' he said blandly.

Which left Taryn wondering why she felt as though she'd been observing to some covert skirmish.

'I think our hostess is indicating it's time for dinner,' Cade observed.

Obediently, she turned, only to stop in mid-step. 'Oh,' she breathed. 'Oh, *look*.'

With the suddenness of the tropics, the sun vanished below the horizon in a glory of gold and crimson, allowing the darkness that swept across the sea to make landing in a breath of warm air. Torches around the terrace flared into life, their flames wavering gently in the gardenia-scented breeze, and from the distant reef came the muted thunder of eternal waves meeting the solid coral bulwark that protected the lagoon.

'Sometimes there's a green flash,' she said quietly, eyes still fixed on the horizon.

For the first time since Peter's death, Taryn felt a pang of joy, a moment of such pure piercing delight she shivered.

'Are you cold?' Cade murmured. 'Do you need a wrap?'

Taryn couldn't tell him what had happened. Not only was the exaltation too intimate, but in a subversive way Cade's presence had contributed to it, making him important to her in a way beyond the solely physical.

And that was scary. Magnetic and disturbing, yet underpinned by a solidity she found enormously sustaining, Cade was getting too close.

'I'm not cold,' she told him with a return to her usual crispness, 'but somehow I got the idea that the cocktail party and the dinner were two separate events. I'd planned to collect a wrap from the *fale* to wear to dinner.'

'My mistake,' he said blandly. He nodded at a waiter,

who came across immediately. Cade said, 'Describe the wrap.'

'It's draped over the end of my bed,' she said, touched by his thoughtfulness. 'A darker gold than this—bronze, really—with a little bit of beadwork around the sleeves.' And when the man had moved off she said, 'Thank you.'

He nodded, but didn't answer as they walked through a door onto another terrace. A long table was arranged exquisitely, candle flames gleaming against silver and crystal and lingering on pale frangipani flowers and greenery.

Foolish resentment gripped Taryn at the sideways glances Cade was receiving from a very beautiful woman in a slinky black sheath that played up her fragile blonde beauty.

Grow up, she told herself. This was ridiculous; she had absolutely no claim on him. OK, so she felt good. That showed she was getting over the shock of Peter's death. Beyond standing beside her at a sensitive moment, Cade had nothing to do with it.

Nothing at all.

CHAPTER SIX

WHEN Cade took her arm again, Taryn was rather proud of the way she managed to restrain her wildfire response to that casual touch. Too proud, because he sensed it. Fortunately, he put it down to nervousness.

'Relax,' he advised crisply. 'These are just people—good, bad or dull. Often all three at different times.' Without pausing, he went on, 'I asked Fleur to seat us side by side so that you wouldn't have two total strangers to talk to.'

In other words, he thought she was a total social novice. Well, when it came to occasions of this rarefied nature, she *was*, she thought ruefully.

He guessed her reaction. 'Normally, I'm sure you're able to hold your own,' he told her.

'How do you do that?' she asked impulsively.

He knew what she meant. *How do you read my mind?*

After a long considering look that curled her toes, he smiled. 'You have a very expressive face.'

Whereas he'd elevated a poker face to an art form.

Before she could answer, he went on, 'I thought you might be jet-lagged.'

'I don't think so, thank you.' Then she tensed again as his lashes drooped. Her breath locked in her throat.

She swallowed and added a little too late, 'But it was kind of you.'

His hooded gaze matched his sardonic tone. 'I try.'

The odd little exchange left her with stretched nerves. Fortunately, the waiter arrived with her wrap and handed it to Cade, who held it out for her. She slid her arms into it and wondered if the brush of his fingers against her bare skin was deliberate or an accident.

Whatever, it sent sensuous little thrills through her as she sat down.

She turned to greet her neighbour, a pleasant middle-aged man from Indonesia. Cade's other dinner partner was the blonde woman with the come-hither gaze and, to Taryn's secret—and embarrassing—irritation, she made an immediate play for the attention he seemed quite happy to give her.

Cattily, Taryn decided that if the woman had anything on beneath the clinging black sheath it would have to be made of gossamer. Her moment of delight evaporated and the evening stretched before her like a punishment.

Several hours later, she heaved a silent sigh of relief when the evening came to an end. Goodbyes and thanks were said and, perhaps emboldened by excellent champagne, the woman in the clinging sheath flung her arms around Cade's neck and kissed him. Although he didn't reject her, he turned his cheek so that her lips barely skimmed it and then, in a gesture that seemed to be steadying, held her away from him.

Not a bit embarrassed, she gazed into his eyes and said huskily, 'I'll look forward to talking to you about that proposition tomorrow.'

Taryn struggled to control her shock and the concentrated venom that cut through her. Jealousy was a despicable emotion—one she had no right to feel.

Nevertheless, she had to tighten her lips to keep back an acid comment when she and Cade were walking away.

Coconuts lined the white shell path, their fronds whispering softly above them in the slow, warm breeze. Taryn struggled to ignore the drowsy, scented ambience that had so seduced the original European explorers they'd thought the Pacific islands the next best place to paradise.

Desperate to break a silence that seemed too charged, she said, 'I once read that human life in the islands would have been impossible without coconuts.'

'When you say *the islands*, you mean the Pacific Islands?' Cade queried.

'Well, yes.' Good, a nice safe subject to settle the seething turmoil inside her.

Somehow, seeing another woman kiss Cade had let loose something primitive and urgent in her—a female possessiveness that sliced through the restraint she'd deliberately imposed on herself after the violent end of her engagement.

It needed to be controlled—and fast. After swallowing to ease her dry throat, she said sedately, 'It's convenient shorthand for New Zealanders when we refer to the Polynesian islands.'

'So are coconut palms native to this region?'

Judging by his cool, dry tone, Cade wasn't aware of her feelings. Thank heavens.

'Possibly.' Yes, her voice sounded good—level, a little schoolmistressy. 'No one seems to know where they originated because they populated the tropics on this side of the world well before any humans arrived here. The nuts can germinate and grow after floating for years and thousands of miles.'

When he didn't reply, she looked up in time to see something dark and fast hurtling down towards her. She gave a choked cry and ducked, stumbling as a vigorous push on her shoulder sent her lurching sideways into the slender trunk of the nearest palm.

She grabbed it and clung. Cade too had avoided whatever it was and as she sagged he pulled her upright, supporting her in a hard, close embrace.

Heart thumping, stunned by the speed of his response, she asked in a muted, raw voice, 'I think…was it a fruit bat?'

He was silent for a few tense seconds. 'It certainly didn't hit the ground, so it was flying.'

'That's what it would be, then.' Her tone wobbled—affected by a wild onrush of adrenalin, she thought feverishly.

And by Cade's warmth, the disturbing masculine power that locked her in his arms…

No!

Yet she didn't move. 'I'd forgotten about them,' she babbled. 'They don't attack, of course—they just scare the wits out of people who aren't used to them.'

She had to fight the flagrant temptation to bury her face in his shoulder and soak up some of the formidable strength and composure from his lean, powerfully muscled body.

Lean, powerfully muscled—and *aroused* body…

As if reacting to the heat that burned through her, he relaxed his grip a little and looked down.

Taryn's mouth dried and her pulse echoed in her head, drowning out any coherent thought. Sensation ran riot along insistent, pleading nerves.

Mutely, she met the probing lance of his scrutiny, her lashes drooping as the shifting glamour of moonlight played across the angles and planes of his face, so rigid it resembled a mask.

Except for that glittering gaze fixed on her lips.

As though the words were torn from him, Cade said roughly, 'Damn. This is too soon.'

Taryn froze, every instinct shrieking that this was a bad, foolish, hair-raisingly terrifying statement.

Every instinct save one—the primal, irresistible conviction that if Cade didn't kiss her she'd regret it for ever.

Her lips parted. 'Yes,' she said in a husky, faraway voice. 'Too soon.'

'And you're afraid of me.'

She dragged in a deep breath. Oh, no, not afraid of Cade.

Afraid—*terrified*—of being shown once more that she was cold, too cold to satisfy a man…

But she didn't feel cold. This had never happened before—this wild excitement that shimmered through her like a green flash at sunset, rare and exquisite, offering some hidden glory she might perhaps reach…

She stared up into narrowed eyes, saw the hard line of his mouth and knew he was going to step back, let her return to her chilly, isolated world. Somehow, without intending to, Cade had breached her defences, challenged that self-imposed loneliness, making her want—no, *long*—to rejoin the real world, where people touched and desired and kissed and made love without barriers.

'No,' she blurted, desperate to convince him. 'Not of you—of myself.'

Frowning, Cade demanded, 'Why?'

She had to tell him, but her voice was low and shamed and bitter when she admitted, 'I'm frigid.'

His brows shot up in an astonishment that strangely warmed her. 'Frigid? I don't believe it. Tonight, I saw you literally stopped in your tracks by a sunset. No one who responds so ardently to sensory experiences could possibly be frigid.'

When he bent his head she stiffened, but he said in a quiet voice, 'Relax. I would never hurt you, and I'm not going to leap on you and drag you into the bushes.'

The image of controlled, disciplined Cade losing his cool so completely summoned a spontaneous gurgle of laughter.

He smiled, and traced the outline of her lips with a hand that shook a little. The shame and fear holding her rigid dissipated a fraction, soothed by the sensuous shiver of delight that almost tentative touch aroused.

His voice deep and quiet, he said, 'There are very few frigid women, didn't you know? It's usually a term imposed by clumsy, carelessly inconsiderate men. Who slapped you with that label?'

When she hesitated, he said swiftly, 'If it's too painful—'

'No,' she said wonderingly, because for the first time ever she thought she might be able to talk about it. In his arms, his heart beating solidly against her, she felt a strong sense of security, almost—incredible though that seemed to her bewildered mind—of peace.

Nevertheless, she had to swallow before she could go on. 'It's just that I was engaged but I wasn't able to respond. It upset my fiancé and in the end it mattered too much.'

She stopped. She didn't tell him—had never been

able to tell anyone—of the shattering scene that had ended the engagement.

'So, if you truly are frigid, why are you snuggling against me so comfortably?'

Taryn said huskily, 'I don't know.'

'Do you feel completely safe?'

'Yes,' she said instantly.

'So if I kiss you, you're not going to be scared, because it's only going to be a kiss?'

Her whole body clenched as a wave of yearning swept through her—poignant, powerfully erotic and so intense she shivered with it. 'I'm not afraid,' she said, adding a little bitterly, 'Well, I suppose I am, but it's only of freezing you off.'

He lifted her chin. Eyes holding hers, he said above the wild fluttering of her heart, 'Well, let's see if that happens.'

And his mouth came down on hers.

Somehow, she had expected an unsubtle, dominant passion, so she was startled at first by his gentle exploration. Yet another part of her welcomed it and her mouth softened under his, her body responding with a languorous lack of resistance, a melting that was bone-deep, cell-deep—*heart*-deep.

As if he'd been waiting for that, he lifted his head. 'All right?'

The taut words told her he was holding himself under intense restraint, every powerful muscle in his big body controlled by a ruthless will.

Taryn could have been scared. Instead, a wave of relief and delight overwhelmed her and she turned her head and said against the hard line of his jaw, 'It's—saying that is getting to be a habit with you. I'm absolutely all right.'

He laughed, deep and quiet, and this time the kiss was everything she'd hoped, a carnal expression of hunger, dangerously stimulating, that sent unexpected shivers rocketing through her in a firestorm of reckless excitement.

He raised his head and slid his hands down to her hips, easing her closer. When he resumed the kiss, her breasts yielded to the solid wall of his chest. He was all muscle, all uncompromising strength, summoning from an unknown source in her an intense, aching anticipation that promised so much.

This time when he lifted his head Taryn's knees buckled and she couldn't hold back a low, sighing purr. Cade held her a little away and surveyed her with such a penetrating stare that she closed her eyes to shield herself.

Instantly, his arms loosened, leaving her chilled and bereft, her breasts aching with unfulfilled desire, her body throbbing with frustration.

He asked, 'Did I hurt—?'

'No,' she broke in, and her tender lips sketched a weak smile. 'Of course you didn't—I'd have punched you in the solar plexus if you had.'

An odd half smile curled his mouth. 'You could have tried,' he said, dropping his arms. 'But I suspect that's enough experimentation for now.'

Disappointment clouded her thoughts. For a moment her mind flashed back to the fragile blonde in her clinging black sheath. 'I'm not a frail little flower, easily bruised,' she said tersely.

Why were they talking when they could be repeating those moments of shattering pleasure?

She parried his unreadable survey with a lift of her

brows, only to suffer an odd hitch to her heartbeat when his mouth curled into a smile.

'Far from it,' he said and stepped back, away from her. 'And I think we've proved pretty conclusively that you're not frigid, don't you?'

Taryn banished a forlorn shiver. What had she expected? That he'd sweep her off her feet and prove in the best—the *only* way—that Antony had been completely wrong, and she was more than capable of feeling and responding to passion?

Seduce her, in other words. A hot wave of embarrassment made her turn away. There would have been precious little seduction to it—she'd gone up like a bushfire in his arms.

Cade was a sophisticated man. He'd been far more thoughtful than she'd guessed he could be, but a few *experimental* kisses from her weren't going to mean anything to him. And he was making sure she understood it too.

So it was up to her to seem just as worldly, just as relaxed about her newly discovered sexuality as he clearly was with his. 'I…yes,' she muttered. 'Thank you.'

He'd stayed totally in control, whereas the second he touched her she wouldn't have cared if they'd been in the centre of some huge sports stadium as the sole show for tens of thousands of spectators.

With whole banks of spotlights and television cameras focused on them, she enlarged, hot with humiliation.

Kissing Cade had been mind-blowing—and stupid. Out of the frying pan into the fire…

Her grandmother's domestic saying seemed the perfect way to describe her situation. Desperate to get away, she started to walk off.

Without moving, he asked, 'Did you leave something behind?'

Taryn stopped, cheeks burning, when she realised she'd set off in the wrong direction. If he was smiling she'd…

Well, she didn't know what she'd do, but it would be drastic. Pride stiffened her shoulders and straightened her spine as she turned to face him.

He wasn't smiling.

No emotion showed on the arrogant face—no warmth, nothing but a mild curiosity that chilled her through to her bones.

Just keep it light, casual, everyday. After all, she'd kissed quite a few men in her time.

It took most of her courage and all her will to set off in the right direction and say cheerfully, 'No, and I'm blaming you entirely for scrambling my brains. If you want any respectable work from me, I don't think we should allow that to happen again.'

His expression didn't change as he fell into step with her, but his tone was cynical. 'For some reason, I don't think of respectability when I look at you.'

Taryn had to bite her lip to stop herself from asking what he did think of. He might be the sexiest man she'd ever met, and he certainly kissed like any woman's erotic dream, but he was her employer, for heaven's sake.

Worse than that, she admitted with stringent—and strangely reluctant—honesty, she was far too intrigued by him. Letting Cade's addictive kisses get to her could only lead to heartbreak.

If his lovely blonde neighbour at dinner had shown her anything, it was that there would always be women around him, only too eager to fall into his arms and his bed.

'Well, I am respectable. And we have a professional relationship,' she said stiffly.

'We did.' He paused, and when she remained silent he added, 'I suspect it might just have been converted into something entirely different.'

His cool amusement grated. 'No,' she said firmly.

She'd had little experience when it came to emotional adventures, and she'd never known anything like the response that still seethed through her like the effect of some erotic spell.

Well, she'd just shown she could be as foolish as any eighteen-year-old, but she didn't do sensual escapades.

So, if he still wanted to play games, she'd—what?

The sensible reaction would be to run as if hellhounds were after her.

'No?' he asked almost negligently.

'You've been very kind and understanding, and I am grateful.' She paused, unable to summon any sensible, calm, sophisticated words. In the end, she decided on a partial truth. 'But, although you helped me discover something about myself I didn't know, I don't expect anything more from you than a resumption of our working relationship.'

Cade glanced down. She wasn't looking at him; against the silver shimmer of the lagoon through the palm trunks her profile was elegant, sensuous—and as determined as the chin that supported it.

Oddly enough, he believed she'd been convinced she was frigid. He'd deduced something of it even before she'd told him; her reactions to his touch had warned him of some emotional trauma. Suppressing an uncivilised desire to track down and punish the man who'd done such a number on her, he wondered if this was why she'd refused Peter.

No, she'd *laughed*... That implied a certain crudity—or cruelty.

She'd rejected Peter in a manner that had left him so completely disillusioned he'd been unable to live with the humiliation.

So was now the time to tell her who he was?

Not yet, Cade decided. There was more to Taryn than he'd thought, and he'd only got just below the surface.

Why was she back-pedalling? She must realise she had no need to whet his appetite; he was still fighting to control a ferocious surge of hunger. In his arms she'd been eager and passionate, her willingness summoning sensations more extreme than anything he'd felt since his untamed adolescence.

But she had every right to remind him of their professional relationship. And he had every right to tempt her into revealing herself more. He stamped down on the stray thought that his desire might be gaining the upper hand.

'Fair enough,' he said, finishing, 'Although I should warn you that I'm particularly fond of exceeding expectations.'

And waited for her reaction.

CHAPTER SEVEN

TARYN gave him a swift, startled glance, faltered on a half step, recovered lithely and looked away but, beneath the shimmering gold *pareu*, her breasts lifted as though she'd taken a deep breath. The languorous perfume of some tropical flower floated with voluptuous impact through the warm air as they turned off the main path towards their accommodation.

Was she resisting an impulse to take the bait? Cade waited, but when she stayed silent continued with a touch of humour, 'However, as we're back to being professional, here's what's happening tomorrow.'

He gave her the programme, finishing with, 'And the day ends with a dinner cruise on the harbour.'

At her nod, he said blandly, 'To which you are, of course, invited.'

'I've given up protesting,' she said, irony colouring the words.

Cade permitted himself a narrow smile as he opened the door. 'And of course you'll be perfectly safe with all those people around.'

'I'm perfectly safe anyway,' she returned a little sharply, and said a rapid, 'Goodnight,' before striding gracefully towards the door of her room.

The fine material of her *pareu* stroked sinuously

across the elegant contours of the body beneath it, and he found himself wondering how she would look when it came off…

He waited until she reached for the handle before saying, 'I've always believed that the best strategy was standing and fighting, but retreat is probably the right tactic for you now. Sleep well.'

She turned her head and sent him a long, unwavering look before saying, 'I shall,' and walking through the door, closing it quietly but with a definite click behind her.

Safe behind it, Taryn dragged air into famished lungs and headed for the bathroom, churning with such a complex mixture of emotions she felt as though someone had pushed her head first into a washing machine.

A shower refreshed her marginally, but sleep proved elusive.

Every time she closed her eyes she relived those searing kisses, so midnight found her wide awake, staring at the drifts of netting that festooned the bed.

Was Cade looking for an affair? Just thinking about that made her heart jump nervously and stirred her senses into humming awareness.

If so, she'd refuse him. He'd accept that—and, even if he didn't, she didn't need to worry about her safety, because he wasn't the sort of man to force her.

Repressing a shudder at old memories, she wondered why she was so sure.

For one thing, the blonde woman in her skimpy black shift would be only too eager to indulge him if all he wanted was a quick fling. And, judging by various covert glances Taryn had intercepted, several other women at dinner wouldn't mind being seduced by his muscled elegance and magnetic impact.

But what convinced her was his restraint, his complete self-discipline when he'd kissed her. She'd dissolved into a puddle of sensation, and he'd known it, but he'd not tried to persuade her into bed.

Her physical safety was not an issue.

So how about her emotions? Was she falling in love?

Restlessness forced her out from the tumbled sheets. She pushed back a swathe of filmy mosquito netting and walked across to the window, staring out at a tropical fantasy in silver and black, the moon's path across the lagoon as bright as the stars in the Milky Way.

No, this passionate madness had very little to do with love. Love needed time; it had taken her several months to realise she loved Antony.

She let the curtain drop and went back to bed. That love, however sincere, hadn't been enough, and she'd been sufficiently scarred to believe she lacked passion. She'd accepted Antony's disillusioned statements as truths.

Possibly that was why she hadn't seen anything more than cheerful camaraderie in Peter's attitude to her.

Bitterly, uselessly, she rued her mistaken impression that he'd been joking when he'd asked her to marry him. She was still haunted by her last sight of him—smiling as she'd waved goodbye and turned into the Departures area of the airport.

A few hours later he was dead. Why? The often-asked question hammered pitilessly at her.

Why hadn't he confided in her? They'd been friends—*good* friends—and she might have been able to help.

Oh, who was she kidding? Peter hadn't wanted friendship; he'd wanted love. If she'd given in to his pleading she'd have been replaying the wretchedness of her engagement, because she hadn't desired him—not as she desired Cade...

Cade's presence had pushed memories of Peter to the back of her mind. He was vital, compelling in a way that completely overshadowed Peter. Guilt lay like a heavy weight on her mind, in her heart—an emotion she'd never appease.

She sighed, turning to push the sheet back from her sticky body. The netting swayed in the flower-scented breeze. She felt heavy and hungry, aching with a need so potent she felt it in every cell.

Cade—tall and dark, and almost forbidding in his uncompromising masculinity, yet capable of consideration. Cade, who possibly wanted an affair.

Cade, who made her body sing like nothing she'd ever experienced before...

A stray thought drifted by, silken with forbidden temptation. What if she embarked on an affair with him?

She didn't dare risk it.

And why, when she'd loved Antony, had his passion never stirred her as Cade's kisses did? Dreamily, she recalled how it felt to be locked in Cade's arms, shivering with eager delight.

When sleep finally claimed her it was long after midnight. The next thing she knew was a voice saying incisively, 'Taryn, wake up!'

She opened her eyes, blinked at a steel-blue gaze and bolted upright. 'Wha—?'

'You've overslept,' Cade said curtly, and turned and left the room.

Stunned, still lost in the dream she'd been enjoying, Taryn stared around her.

Why hadn't her alarm gone off?

Leaning over, she pushed back the hair from her face so she could check, only to bite back a shocked word and twist off the bed.

She hadn't heard the alarm because last night she'd forgotten to set it.

And she'd forgotten to set it because she'd been too dazzled by Cade's kisses to think straight.

So much for professionalism!

Not only that, she'd kicked off her bedclothes. She was sprawled on top of the sheet in a pair of boxer shorts and a skimpy singlet top that had ridden sideways, revealing almost every inch of skin from her waist to her shoulders.

All of which Cade would have been able to see through the fine drift of mosquito netting.

Hot with delayed embarrassment, she dived across the room, performed her ablutions, changed into a businesslike shirt and skirt and walked out into the living room with her chin at an angle and every nerve taut.

Cade was standing at the table checking out a sheaf of papers.

'Sorry,' she said rapidly.

He lifted his head and gave her a long, cool look. Last night's kisses—and whether he'd just seen more of her than was *respectable*—clearly meant nothing to him.

All thought was blotted out by a stark, fierce surge of hunger when he crossed the room towards her. Desperately clinging to her splintering composure, she tried to ignore the powerful, masculine grace of his movements and the erratic beat of her heart.

'Jet lag reveals itself in different ways,' he said laconically. 'Here's what I want you to do after you've had breakfast.'

She forced herself to concentrate, only to be startled

when he finished by saying, 'Drink plenty of water today and try a nap after lunch. It might help.' He looked at his watch. 'I have to go. I'll be back around midday.'

Taryn took a deep breath, letting it out on an explosive sigh once she was safely alone.

'Breakfast,' she said to the silent room, then started at a knock on the door. Fortunately, it heralded a delicious concoction of tropical fruit with good toast to back it up.

And excellent coffee… Mentally thanking that long-ago Arabian—or had he been Ethiopian?—goatherd who'd noticed how frisky his goats became after grazing on coffee berries, she ate breakfast before setting to work.

Although she still felt a little slack and listless, by the time the sun was at its highest she'd finished nearly everything Cade had set out for her.

When he arrived back in the *fale* he glanced at her work. 'Thank you. This is just what I need. I'm having a working lunch but you can eat here or in the restaurant, whichever you prefer.'

'Here,' she said.

Cade's nod was short, almost dismissive. 'And take that nap.'

Clearly he regretted those feverish kisses as much as she did.

Perhaps for him they hadn't been feverish. Had he been taken aback—even dismayed—by the intensity of her response?

Even if he hadn't, his aloofness was understandable; basically, he was indicating that although he'd forgotten himself enough to kiss her, he regretted it and she wasn't to presume on it.

Kiss in haste, repent at leisure—a classic case of the

morning after the night before, she thought, smarting with something close to shame.

Ignoring the tight knot in her stomach, she worked through lunch, and afterwards followed instructions to take a short nap, only to wake with heavy limbs and a threatening headache.

A swim in the lagoon revived her considerably. On her way back to the *fale*, she met the Frenchwoman with impeccable style who'd admired her *pareu* the previous evening.

Beside her was a much younger woman, a stunning opera singer. After giving Taryn an indifferent nod, she began to complain of boredom.

Madame Murat listened to her complaints with a smile, before saying, 'It would be my dream to spend the rest of my life in this lovely place.' She looked at Taryn. 'You, my dear, are here to work, are you not?'

'Yes.' Taryn added brightly, 'But working in paradise is no effort.'

The younger woman gave a significant smile. 'No effort at all when you're sharing…' she paused, before adding on a husky laugh '…*accommodation* with a hunk like Cade Peredur. Lucky you.' Another pause, before she asked, 'What's he like—as an employer, I mean, of course.'

'Very professional,' Taryn said woodenly.

'How maddening for you,' the other woman said, odiously sympathetic. She gazed around the shimmering lagoon and pulled a petulant face. 'I didn't realise we were going to be stuck on this tiny little dot of land all the time we were here.'

After a nod to each of them, she walked away. The Frenchwoman said tolerantly, 'Poor girl—she had hopes of a resort holiday, I think, with handsome men to admire her and a chance to display her jewels. Instead, there are only other wives while our men are working.' She glanced past Taryn. 'Ah, here comes your employer. They must have finished talking for the afternoon.'

Startled, Taryn looked up. Sunlight shafted down between the palms in swords of gold, tiger-striping Cade's lean, powerful form as he strode towards them. Her heart fluttered and her body sang into forbidden warmth as the memory of his kisses sparked a rush of tantalising adrenalin. She blinked against suddenly intense colours, so bright that even behind her sunglasses they dazzled.

Unexpectedly, the woman beside her said, 'Wise of you not to move, my dear. Unless you love him and know it is returned, never run towards a man. This one is coming to you as fast as he can.'

Flushing, Taryn said swiftly, 'He's my employer, that's all.'

'So far, and you are wise not to surrender too soon.' Her companion smiled wryly. 'My children say I am very old-fashioned, but I do not approve of modern attitudes. There should be some mystery in a love affair, some greater excitement than finding out how good in bed a man—or woman—is. A meeting of minds as well as of bodies.' Just before Cade came within earshot, she finished, 'And this man—both mind and body—would be a very interesting one to explore.'

She bestowed a frankly appreciative glance on him as he came to a stop before them and in a voice coloured by amusement she said, 'I hope you do not intend to scold your charming secretary for spending time with an old woman.'

The smile he gave her held cynicism, but was warmed by male appreciation for her soignée chic and elegant femininity. 'I don't see any old women around,' he said, 'and the days of wage slavery are long gone. Taryn would soon put me in my place if I tried to keep her immured in work.'

Madame Murat chuckled and steered the conversation into a discussion of the Pacific economy but, when Taryn admitted ruefully to knowing very little about that, adding that she'd been in London for the past couple of years, the older woman changed the subject to her favourite sights there.

None of them, Taryn thought when she was walking back to their suite with Cade, were sophisticated 'in' places; the older woman had concentrated on museums, galleries and parks—the sort of spots a tourist would be likely to visit.

'Do you like Madame Murat?' Cade surprised her by asking.

'Yes.' It came out too abruptly. She was too aware of him, of his intimidating assurance—and gripped by memories of the compelling sensuality of his kisses.

After clearing her throat, she said, 'Very much.'

His smile was narrow. 'She was fishing.'

Startled, she glanced at him. 'You mean—'

She stopped when she met his cool, cynical gaze. Yes, he did mean it. It hurt to think that the charming Frenchwoman might have targeted her.

He shrugged. 'She was laying ground bait. Her husband is very enthusiastic about a scheme I'm positive will fail, and he's almost certainly suggested she find out what you know of my plans.'

'I don't know anything of your plans,' she said shortly, angry with him for some obscure reason. 'And, even if I did, I do know how to hold my tongue.'

'I'm sure you do,' he returned smoothly, 'but it's always best to be forewarned. What's the matter?'

'Nothing.' When he sent her an ironically disbelieving glance, she enlarged reluctantly, 'Just that I liked her. It sounds ridiculous and overdramatic, but…it feels like a betrayal.'

Cade's eyes were keen. 'Of course you like her—she's a charming woman and a very intelligent one. She and her husband make a formidable team. She won't hold your discretion against you, and might well be useful to you in the future. As for betrayal—' His shoulders lifted and fell. 'It happens.'

Thoughtfully, Taryn said, 'I don't think I like your world much.'

A black brow lifted. 'My world, your world—what's the difference? Every world has its share of innocents and those who prey on them, of honest people and scoundrels. Unless you understand that, you run risks wherever you are.'

Shocked, she asked directly, 'Don't you trust anyone?'

Cade didn't answer straightaway. When the silence stretched too long, she looked up into an austere, unyielding mask.

He gave another barely noticeable shrug. 'A few. And only when they've proved trustworthy. Do you trust everyone you meet?'

After a moment's pause, she said, 'Of course not. Only a fool would do that.'

'And you're not a fool.'

A note in his voice made her uneasy. 'I try not to be,' she returned, irritated by her defensive tone.

The conversation was too personal—almost as personal as his kisses—and, strangely, she felt he was attacking her, trying to find some hidden weak spot he could use.

Don't be silly, she scoffed. *He's just making sure you can be trusted not to give away secrets...*

He asked, 'Did you manage to get some sleep after lunch?'

Hugely relieved at the change of subject, she said, 'Yes, for a short time.'

'I found your notes. You did a good job.'

She tried to suppress a warm pleasure. 'Thank you. I assume there's more.'

'Yes, although I don't need it until tomorrow afternoon. Have you ever been to the main island?'

'Only yesterday when we arrived,' she said dryly.

'In a couple of days I plan to check out the local fishing industry and I'd like you to come with me.'

Taryn said, 'All right. Do you want me to take notes? I can't do shorthand, but I could take notes by hand, or talk into a recorder—or even use the laptop.'

'I've got a recording device you can use. And I won't force you to trek around fishing factories or dirty, smelly boats,' he told her. 'We'll be meeting with the people who run the show, not the fishermen.'

She gave him a swift, amused look. 'I bet I've been in more dirty, smelly boats than you have.'

Cade liked her frankness—a little too much, he conceded sardonically. It could have been an indication of inner honesty—except that she'd shown a chilling lack of empathy for Peter.

Could that have been because of her crass fiancé? He must have been a total fool, because she certainly wasn't frigid by nature.

Quelling a sharp shock of desire, Cade banished the memory of her incandescent response to his kisses. It could have been faked, of course. Unpleasantly aware of a desire to find excuses for her behaviour to Peter, he had to remember to keep an open mind.

'You've spent a lot of time on such vessels?' he enquired as they approached the gardens that shielded their *fale* from the others on the island.

She grinned. 'My parents and I used to spend the holidays travelling for a charity that sent medical aid to the islands. We sailed mostly on traders—and trust me, although they did their best, those vessels smelt and they were quite often dirty. The tropics can make things difficult for anyone with a cleanliness fetish.'

'You didn't think of following your parents into medicine?' he asked casually.

'Yes, but it didn't work out.'

'Why?'

She shrugged, her breasts beneath the *pareu* moving freely. Cade's groin tightened. Seeing her almost naked in her bed that morning meant he knew exactly what the brightly coloured fabric covered. He had to dismiss an image of his hands removing the thin cotton that covered her, then lingering across the satin-skinned curves he'd revealed.

Without looking at him, Taryn said, 'About halfway through my first year of pre-med study I realised that I simply didn't have the desire or the passion. It was my parents' dream for me, not mine.'

'How did they feel about that?'

Her narrow brows met for a second. 'They weren't happy,' she admitted, her tone cool and matter-of-fact. 'I felt really bad about it, but I couldn't see myself being a good doctor. For me, medicine would have been just a job.'

'Whereas for them it's a vocation?'

Her surprised glance sparked irritation in Cade, an emotion that fought with the swift leap of his blood when she turned her head away and the sun transformed her wet red locks into a coppery-gold aureole.

Clearly she hadn't thought him capable of recognising altruism. For some reason he wasn't prepared to examine, that stung.

'Yes,' she said simply. 'They made big sacrifices for me. Because they wanted to give me a good secondary education, they came back to New Zealand and bought the practice at Aramuhu. As soon as they'd organised me into university, they went back to the islands.'

Cade felt an odd, almost unwilling sympathy. Although philanthropic, her parents seemed to have been as casual about her as his mother had been. Had traipsing around after them on their missions of mercy given her a distaste for a lifetime of service?

It bothered him that he didn't blame her.

Her chin lifted and her green-gold eyes met his with a direct challenge. She said firmly, 'So I studied for librarian qualifications—much more my thing.'

'And you've not regretted it?'

'Not a bit.' In the dark shelter of one of the big raintrees, Taryn sneaked an upward glance. Nothing showed in his expression but casual interest, yet her voice tightened so she had to hurry over her final remark. 'My parents are perfectly happy with the way I've organised my life, and so am I.'

In any other man, she'd have accepted his words as idle chit-chat, the small coin of communication, but she was pretty certain Cade didn't do casual. When he asked a question, he really wanted the answer.

A hot little thrill shivered through her as they walked out into the sun again. His kisses had indicated one sort of awareness, but did this conversation mean he felt more for her than uncomplicated lust?

Startled by a swift, passionate yearning that went deeper than desire, far deeper than anything she'd experienced before, she blinked and pretended to examine the shrubs beside the path.

Those hard eyes saw too much and, although she didn't understand him in any real way, somehow he stirred a secret, unsuspected part of her. She longed to warm herself in the intense primal heat she sensed behind the uncompromising exterior he presented to the world.

Abruptly, she stopped walking. Keeping her face turned away from Cade, she touched a hibiscus flower, letting her fingertips linger on the brilliant satin petals. It took all her self-possession to say in a level voice, 'Only a flower could get away with this combination—vivid orange petals with a heart as bright and dark as a ruby. The colours should clash hideously, but somehow they don't.'

Control restored, she lifted her hand and turned back to him, insides curling when she realised he wasn't looking at the bloom. Instead, his gaze was fixed on her mouth. Sensation ricocheted through her, tantalising and tempting.

Without haste, he said, 'It's all part of the forbidden, fated lure of the tropics, I believe.'

'Forbidden? Fated?' She let the flower go and resumed walking. In her most prosaic tone, she said, 'The European sailors who first explored these islands thought they'd found paradise.'

'Ask Luke Chapman to tell you about the first Chapman who arrived in Fala'isi. His story might change your mind about that.'

'Oh, the Polynesians were warlike, of course,' she admitted, keeping her voice practical. 'But they were hugely hospitable too, and although there were episodes when the two cultures clashed badly—like Captain Cook's death in Hawaii—they weren't common.'

Wanting Cade Peredur was asking for trouble. Better to keep her distance, stay safe behind the barricades, not waste her time and emotional energy on a man who—at the most—would suggest an affair.

Probably one as brief as tropical twilight, and with as little impact on him.

And there was always the possibility that her body was playing tricks on her, luring her on with a promise it couldn't fulfil. In spite of Cade's kisses, if they made love her desire might evaporate as swiftly as it had with Antony. She could do without a repeat of that humiliation.

Mouth firming, she bade her erratic heartbeat to settle down as they reached the *fale*.

'Those first explorers called them the Isles of Aphrodite,' he said, surprising her again. 'Love has to be the most dangerous emotion in the world.'

Her brows shot up. 'Dangerous? I can see that sometimes it might be,' she conceded. 'But fated and forbidden? That's a bit extreme. Plenty of people fall in love and live more or less happily ever after.'

'Plenty don't. And love has caused huge amounts of angst and misery.'

'Like any extreme emotion,' she agreed, heart twisting as she thought of Peter. Trying to ignore the sad memories and guilt, she said quietly, 'But there are different kinds of love. The love of parents for their children, for instance. Without that, the world would be a terrible place.'

Cade's face froze. 'Indeed,' he said evenly.

What had she said that had hit a nerve?

CHAPTER EIGHT

FOR a highly uncomfortable few seconds Cade looked at Taryn from narrowed eyes before asking abruptly, 'So what do you plan to do once you're back in New Zealand?'

'Find a proper job.' She grabbed at her composure and, once they were in the cool sitting room of the *fale*, said daringly, 'I'm thinking of asking you for a reference about my research abilities.'

'I expected as much.' His voice was level and lacking in emotion. And then he drawled, 'However, I'll need a little more experience of your skills before I can give you a reference that would mean anything.'

The words were innocuous enough—quite reasonable, in fact—but a note in his voice set her teeth on edge.

Meeting eyes that were narrowed and intent, she said crisply, 'I don't like the sound of that.'

His brows lifted. 'Why?'

Wishing too late she hadn't opened her mouth, Taryn knew she had to go on. 'Because that almost sounded like the sort of thing a sleazy employer might say to a defenceless employee.'

The half beat of silence tightened her nerves to

screaming point, until he laughed with what seemed like genuine amusement.

'You're far from defenceless,' he said coolly, 'and I rather resent you suggesting I'm sleazy. If you need the reassurance, any reference I write for you will be based entirely on your work, which so far I've found to be excellent.'

'Thank you,' she contented herself with saying.

He asked in that objective voice she was beginning to distrust, 'You're a beautiful woman. Do you have to set boundaries whenever you take a new position?'

'No.' Too brusque, but she wasn't going to elaborate.

However, he said, 'But you have had to before.'

'Do I act as though I expect every employer to try to jump me?'

His look of distaste made her stiffen and brace herself.

He said, 'No, but it's clear that you've developed ways to defend yourself. Unsurprising, really, since your parents deserted you once you left school.'

His tone hadn't altered, which somehow made his statement even more startling. Taryn said indignantly, 'I wasn't deserted! We kept in touch all the time—if I'd needed them, they'd have been there for me. They still are.'

One black brow lifted, something she realised happened whenever he didn't believe her. 'How long is it since you've seen them?'

She paused before admitting, 'A couple of years.'

'It sounds pretty close to being abandoned.'

'No, you don't understand—'

'I understand abandonment.' His voice was coldly deliberate. 'My birth father I never knew. My mother abandoned me at birth to be brought up by my grandmother. When she died, I lived with my mother, but I was eventually taken into care. I lived—happily—with foster parents after that, but recently I've lost my foster-brother.'

Shocked and horrified at what her innocent words had summoned, Taryn said quietly, 'Yes, you obviously do understand abandonment, and I'm very sorry for that, but my parents haven't abandoned me. I'm a big girl now, Cade—Mr Peredur—and quite capable of looking after myself without needing them to shepherd me through life.'

'Oh, call me Cade,' he said negligently. 'We might not have been introduced formally but last night in my arms you called me Cade without hesitation.'

Colour burning through her skin, she said, 'I haven't thanked you for making sure that fruit bat didn't blunder into me.'

He shrugged. 'At the time I thought it was a fallen coconut I was rescuing you from. You've been digging trenches and laying barbed wire along your defences since you woke up this morning. Why? Because we kissed?'

'Of course not.' Immediately she'd spoken, she wondered if she should have told him the exact opposite.

Then he wouldn't have smiled—the cool, easy smile of a conqueror—and lifted his hand. Her eyes widened endlessly in fascinated apprehension, but all he did was push back a lock of sea-damp hair that clung to her cheek. His fingers barely grazed her skin, yet she felt their impact like a caress, silkily sliding through her body to melt every inhibition.

Dropping his hand, he said, 'It's quite simple, Taryn.

If you don't want me to touch you, all you need to do is say so.'

Neither his face nor his tone revealed any emotion beyond a wry amusement.

She resisted the need to lick suddenly dry lips. Cade's touch had paralysed her, banishing everything but a swift, aching pleasure from his nearness. He filled her gaze, blotting out the seductive lure of the tropical afternoon with a potent male magnetism that sapped both her energy and her will.

Again Cade held out his hand but this time, instead of touching her, he waited, his expression cool and challenging. Desire—hot and irresistible—pulsed through her, overwhelming her fears in a honeyed flow she felt in every cell in her body. He was watching her with an intensity that was more seductive than any caress or polished words, as though she were the most important thing in his life.

Slowly, eyes locked with the steel-sheen-blue of his, she fought a losing battle against the impulse to take what he was offering and ignore the common sense that urged her to say no.

Yet she didn't say it. Couldn't say it.

'What is this?' The words stumbled huskily from her, almost meaningless, yet he seemed to know what she wanted from him.

He said, 'You must know—since last night, if not before—that I find you very attractive. And you seem to reciprocate. But, if you're not interested, all you have to do is refuse. However, if I'm right and this—' his mouth twisted '—*attraction* is mutual, then we should decide what to do about it.'

Plain words. Too plain. And he knew damned well that the attraction was mutual! For a moment she suffered a pang of angry rebellion. Why didn't he woo her with passion, with heady kisses?

She knew the reason. Because he wanted her to know that whatever he felt was not love, not even a romance. He'd made it quite clear—he trusted no one. If she succumbed, it would be a business affair with no promises made and no hearts broken, just a clean cut when it was over.

Her only sensible response must be that simple syllable of refusal.

Yet still it wouldn't come.

Would succumbing to his offer be so dangerous…?

Or would it finally free her from fear, from the poisonous aftermath of Antony's violence?

Fighting a honeyed, treacherous temptation, Taryn searched for something sensible to say, words to get her out of the situation before she got too tangled in her rioting emotions.

None came.

She glanced upwards. As usual, she couldn't read anything in the arrogant features. Indignantly, she thought that his enigmatic look would be etched into her memory for ever.

In the end, she said as steadily as she could, 'In other words, why don't we both scratch an itch?'

Cade inspected her from the top of her head to her toes, his cryptic gaze fanning that treacherous desire deep inside her.

But when he spoke his voice held nothing but detachment. 'If that's how you see it, then yes.'

She bristled, made angry by a foolish, obscure pain.

Still in that judicial tone, he continued, 'But for me there's more to it than that. I've met a lot of beautiful women. I don't believe many—if any—would have held that hose and, in spite of knowing she hadn't a hope of doing it, still tried to stop the forest going up in flames.'

And, while she silently digested that, he went on, 'I want you. Not just because you make my pulse leap whenever you come into the room, but because I find you intriguing and I enjoy your company.' His broad shoulders sketched a shrug. 'If you want a declaration of undying love I can't give it to you. I know it exists—I just don't seem to be able to feel it myself. Why are you shaking your head?'

'I'm not asking for that.' Yet she hated the thought of being just another in the parade of women through his life.

He frowned. 'Then what do you want?'

'I don't know.' She hesitated, before adding in a troubled voice, 'To be reassured, I suppose—and I don't even know what I mean by that, but it makes me sound horribly needy and clinging, which I am not.'

'You most emphatically are not,' he agreed dryly. 'Well, what is it to be?'

When she didn't answer, he said in an entirely different voice, 'I could kiss you into agreement.'

Taryn opened her mouth to deny it, then closed her lips over the lying words.

Quietly, he said, 'So which will it be?'

Her thoughts tumbled in delirious free fall. Making love to Cade would be a step into a wildly stimulating unknown. Yet, in spite of being convinced she'd respond to Cade's lovemaking as eagerly as she had to his kisses, at the back of her mind lurked the dark cloud of apprehension that had been her constant companion since her engagement.

Now was a chance—perhaps her only chance—to find out whether she could be what Antony had called *a real woman*—one who enjoyed passion and could give herself in that most fundamental way.

And what harm could possibly come from a short affair when both she and Cade knew the rules?

None at all, that reckless inner part of her urged. Love had no part in this, so she'd be unscathed when the time came for them to part. And if—*if* she could surrender to desire fully and without shame, she'd be free at last of humiliation and able to consider an equal relationship some time in the future.

Slowly, reluctantly, she lifted her eyes and met Cade's gaze, which was narrowed with desire—for *her*—and, as she thrilled with a potent, spontaneous surge of sensuous hunger, she knew her answer.

If she didn't take this opportunity, she'd always regret her cowardice. Whatever happened, even if it ended in tears and heartache, she was desperately in thrall to a need she didn't want to resist.

But her voice wobbled when she said, 'I… Then it's yes.'

Cade fought back a fierce satisfaction—so fierce it startled him. With it came a driving, insistent hunger and something he'd never expected to feel—an intense need he immediately tried to block.

Because it was still too soon. Those enormous green-gold eyes and her soft trembling mouth certainly betrayed desire, but he sensed fear too.

For the first time in his life a headstrong passion had almost overridden his mind and his will. If he took her now he could wreck everything. She needed to be sure of his ability to rouse her, confidence that he wouldn't hurt her before she could come to him without restrictions, without fear or shame.

She needed gentling. Wooing…

He needed to know her better.

He shied away from that thought. And he, he thought grimly, needed to find a way to control this almost desperate sexual drive.

Watching her so he could gauge her reaction, he said with as much resolution as he could muster, 'It's all right, I'm not going to drag you off into a bedroom right now.'

'I didn't think you would,' she returned smartly. 'I'm sure your motto is always business first.'

He permitted himself a narrow, humourless smile—probably looking more like a tiger ready to pounce, he thought with grim humour. 'So why are you still holding yourself as stiffly as a martyr facing the stake?'

'I'm not!' But she was; already she could feel her shoulders start to ache.

And Cade's response didn't relax her at all. 'You need time to get to know me better,' he said.

Taryn paused, her mind racing against the thud of her heartbeats. In the end she nodded. 'Yes, I do,' she admitted, chagrin colouring her voice. 'Everything's happened so fast I feel as though I've been whisked off by a tornado. And you obviously need time too.'

'I know what I want.' He gave another of those twisted smiles, as though he understood the riot of emotions clouding her thoughts. 'It's all right, Taryn. There will come a time when we both know it's right. Until then, we'll carry on as we have been.'

Abruptly, that shaming relief fled, to be replaced by a disappointment so acute she almost changed her mind there and then. But he was right, she thought, clinging to a shred of common sense. She needed time.

He glanced at his watch, then out into the western sky, already lit with the pageantry of a tropical sunset. 'If we're going to be in time for the dinner cruise on the lagoon we'd better get going.'

Business first, of course, she thought as she nodded and hurried into her room, frustrated yet relieved. Her insides quivered. If only she didn't freeze…

Then she thought of what she'd learned about him, and her heart shuddered. She wanted to know so much more than the few spare statements he'd delivered in that chillingly impersonal tone, but the thought of him as a child, at the mercy of a neglectful mother, hurt her in an almost physical way.

No time for that now, she told herself after a harried glance at her watch. What to wear? The gold *pareu* again? Not entirely suitable for sailing—although the vessel that had anchored in the lagoon that morning looked more like a mini-liner than a yacht.

A swift search through her wardrobe made her decide on a gift from her mother. Pacific in style, the loose top of fine, silky cotton echoed the colours of handmade *tapa* cloth. Its soft cream-white fabric, patterned in chocolate-brown, tan and bronze, made her skin glow. With it, she wore sleek tan trousers and a cuff bracelet of tiny golden mother-of-pearl beads.

When she reappeared Cade gave her a swift smouldering look. Her stomach swooped and colour surged along her cheekbones. She had to steady her voice before she could say, 'I hope this is OK.'

He said, 'Infinitely more than merely OK. You look radiant. We'd better get going or I'll succumb to temptation and try to persuade you to skip the damned evening.'

A stripped, corrosive note in his words lit fires deep inside her.

Some hours later, Taryn leaned against the rail of the opulent vessel, which was owned by one of the most powerful businessmen in Australia.

She'd had an interesting evening. She'd been admired, patronised and ignored; she'd been entertained by Madame Murat, who'd revealed a charmingly indiscreet side that made Taryn chuckle; she'd fended off attempts at flirtation by various men and she'd eaten a delicious Pacific buffet meal beside Cade. He'd shown no overt possessiveness, but he'd clearly been keeping an eye on her.

She turned as someone came towards her, stabbed by sharp, unexpected disappointment when she saw not Cade but the son of the yacht owner. Tall and cheerfully laconic, he'd made no secret of his interest.

'Alone?' he said against the babble of talk and laughter from the big entertaining deck. 'Are we boring you?'

'No. I'm admiring the skies.'

He stopped just a little too close beside her. 'They're stunning, but if you want fabulous you should come to the Outback. Nothing beats the stars over the Australian desert. Check them out one day—we've got a cattle station so remote you'd think there was nowhere else on earth. I'd like to take you star-watching there.'

'It sounds amazing,' she told him, keeping her voice non-committal. A flurry of white in the water caught her attention. 'Oh—what was that?'

'What?'

When he turned to see where she was pointing out

she took the opportunity to move along the rail away from him. 'A splash—perhaps dolphins jumping? I presume there must be dolphins here.'

'Might be a whale,' he said, examining the water. He gestured towards a waiter, who came rapidly towards them. 'Binoculars, please,' he said, and turned back to her. 'Sounds as though you're used to dolphins jumping around you when you swim.'

'Not exactly,' she said, 'although pods often turn up off the coast of my part of Northland.'

He smiled down at her. 'What part of Northland? The Bay of Islands?'

'A bit farther north than that,' she said vaguely. He was good-looking and charming in an open, friendly way. Normally, she'd have flirted happily enough with him. But this wasn't normality; nothing had been normal since last night when Cade had kissed her and tilted her world off its axis.

The arrival of the waiter with binoculars eased things. 'Try these,' her companion said, offering them to her.

She squinted into them and suddenly caught a pod of dolphins arching up from the water in a free-wheeling display of gymnastics, graceful and joyous and gleaming in the starshine.

'Oh, lovely,' she breathed, turning to hand over the binoculars, only to discover her companion was now standing behind her, so close she actually turned into him.

'I'll get out of your way,' she said crisply and thrust the binoculars into his hands, ducking sideways.

Cade came striding towards them. Something about him made her stiffen; behind him, a group of people watched, clearly intrigued. Without thinking, she lifted her hand and beckoned, then pointed out to sea where the dolphins played.

'Dolphins,' she said, hoping her smile conveyed nothing more than simple pleasure.

The man beside her took the binoculars away from his eyes. 'They look as though they're moving away.' He looked beyond her, his demeanour subtly altering when he saw Cade approach.

'Hi, mate, take a look at this,' he said, handing him the binoculars. 'We'll go across to them so everyone can see them close up.'

'No, don't do that,' Taryn said swiftly.

Both men looked at her. 'Why?' Cade asked.

'At home we're told not to interfere with them—it disturbs them, especially if they have young with them. If they come across to us of their own accord, that's fine, but deliberately seeking them out isn't.'

Both men looked at each other, then the Australian grinned. 'OK, anything for a pretty lady. I'll get them to break out all the binoculars on board.'

Cade waited until he'd gone before checking out the dolphins.

Eyes narrowing as she watched the sea creatures, Taryn said, 'They look as though they've turned—they are heading this way, aren't they?'

'It seems so.' He lowered the binoculars and looked at her. 'Enjoying yourself?'

'Yes, thank you. It's a fantastic night and the food is delicious, and the people are very pleasant.'

As well as Fleur and Luke Chapman, she'd recognised a couple of business tycoons from New Zealand, one with his wife, a Mediterranean princess. A media baron and his fourth wife were in a huddle with several politicians from countries around the Pacific Rim, and an exquisite rill of laughter came from the opera star as she flirted with her husband.

Which made a change from flirting with Cade, Taryn thought waspishly. She said, 'Everywhere I look, I see faces from the television screen.'

And they all seemed to know each other well; she was the only outsider.

Just then someone else saw the dolphins, now close to the yacht, and called out, and there was a concerted move to the rails.

Taryn said, 'We'll get the best view up in the bows.'

Cade examined her face for a brief second, then nodded. 'Let's go.'

Several people followed them. Taryn tried hard not to wish she could stand alone with Cade in the moonlight watching the glorious creatures ride the bow wave with consummate grace, their curving mouths giving them the appearance of high delight. Silver veils of water garlanded their rounded, muscular backs while they dipped and pirouetted and leapt from the water, gleeful and wild in their unforced joy.

And then, as quickly as they'd come, an unheard command sent them speeding away to an unknown destination. And people who'd been lost in silent wonder broke out into a babble of noise that broke the spell.

Cade said, 'What was that sigh for?'

'Anything beautiful makes me feel sad—in an odd, delighted way,' she said, then laughed. 'They're such magnificent creatures, so wild and free, and they seem to get a huge kick out of wave-riding. You could just *feel* their pleasure, couldn't you?'

He nodded, his eyes searching as he looked down at her. 'I'm glad you saw them.'

Taryn would have enjoyed the rest of the evening

much more if anticipation hadn't been tightening inside her, straining her nerves and clamouring for the evening to end so that she could go back to the *fale* with Cade.

However, once they were alone, he closed the door and turned to her, eyes narrowed and gleaming, his face a mask of intent. She felt a sudden clutch of panic.

'You seemed to have a good time,' he said.

She nodded. 'Did you?'

'No.' His smile was brief and mirthless. 'I kept having to stop myself from striding over and establishing territorial rights every time I saw some man head in your direction.'

Taryn's hiccup of laughter was cut short when he slipped his tie free and dropped it, then shrugged out of his jacket. 'Surely you couldn't have thought that—'

She stopped, watching the way the powerful muscles flexed and coiled beneath his white shirt. Her breath came short between her lips. In a voice she didn't recognise she admitted, 'I understand the feeling.'

He looked at her and said in a completely different tone, 'All night I've been wondering whether that elegant and very suitable garment is as easy to remove as it seems to be. One night I'll find out. And if you want me to keep to our agreement, you'd better get into your room right now.'

Taryn dragged her gaze from his, blinked several times and said in a muted voice, 'Goodnight.'

She heard him laugh as she closed the bedroom door behind her, the low laugh of a man who had his life in order.

The three days that followed were a lesson in sorely tried patience and silent escalating tension. In public Cade treated her with an understated awareness. In private he touched her—her hand, her shoulder, an arm slipped around her waist occasionally.

Taryn knew what he was doing—getting her accustomed to his touch, his nearness, like a nervous filly being broken to the saddle. And the subtle courtship worked; each touch eased her fears, set up a yearning that grew with the hours until she found herself dreaming of him, an erotic dream that woke her into a shivering hunger unlike anything she'd ever known.

Twisting onto her side, she stared past the misty swag of the netting into the warm night, and knew that for her the time of waiting was over.

Her breath eased, but restlessness drove her to switch on the bedside lamp and pick up her watch. Almost midnight—not called the witching hour for nothing, she thought and switched off the light, settling back against the pillows.

Only to toss sleeplessly. Eventually, she got out of bed and opened the screens onto the terrace. The air outside was marginally cooler against her skin.

A blur of movement froze her into stillness.

CHAPTER NINE

IT WAS Cade, gazing out at the night. He turned to watch her as she stood in the doorway. A silver bar of moonlight revealed the strong male contours of his face and the fact that he was still fully clothed.

He didn't speak. Very much aware of her skimpy singlet top and shorts, Taryn swallowed to ease a suddenly dry throat and said abruptly, 'I've had enough time.'

Almost expressionless, a muscle in his jaw twitched as he held out his hand. 'So come to me.'

Taryn looked at him, toughly formidable, his handsome face almost unyielding in its bold angularity. He radiated power and an uncompromising male authority that should have warned her not to push.

Instead, it evoked something close to defiance. He was so clearly accustomed to being in charge, to taking women on his terms, not theirs.

'You come to me,' she returned and, although each word was soft and slightly hesitant, there could be no mistaking the challenge in both words and tone, in her level gaze and the tilt of her chin.

She expected some resistance and was startled when his beautiful mouth curled into an appreciative smile. Noiselessly, he walked across the terrace and, without any further comment, drew her to him, enfolding her as though she was precious to him.

Held against his lean, muscled length, she sighed and relaxed. It was too much like coming home. Lashes fluttering down, she hid her face in his shoulder, every sense languorously accepting and eager.

A finger under her chin lifted her face, gentle but inexorable.

'Look at me,' Cade said, his voice rough and deep.

But she couldn't—didn't dare. Panicking, she thought, *Don't be such an idiot. If looking at him seems too intimate, how are you going to make love with him?*

Shivers raced across her skin when she felt the warmth of his breath on her eyelids, and then the soft brush of his mouth across hers.

His voice was deep and low, pitched so only a lover would hear. 'Open your eyes, Taryn.'

When he repeated the command she slowly lifted her lashes to meet a hooded, glittering gaze that melted her spine.

Instantly, his arms locked around her, crushing her breasts against his broad chest, and the intimate contact of his thighs made her vividly, desperately aware of his arousal.

And her own. Need consumed her, tearing at her with insistent velvet claws. When his mouth came down on hers, she opened her lips to his bold claim and gave him what they both wanted—her surrender, joyous and open and exultant.

Eventually, when she was clinging and helpless with longing, he raised his head. Eyes glittering, he asked, 'Was that so difficult?'

'No,' she said on an outgoing breath and, before she

could change her mind, 'But three days ago I should have told you I don't believe in one-night stands.'

Releasing her, he said calmly, 'Neither do I.'

He trusted very few people and presumably that applied to her too, but there was genuine understanding in his tone. He'd recognised the fears that swayed her—fears and caution that now seemed flimsy and foolish—and didn't think any the less of her for them.

Yet when he took her hand, she hesitated.

'Second thoughts, Taryn?' His voice was aloof.

She reached up and touched his jaw, fingertips thrilling at the slight tactile roughness there. Cade held her hand against his mouth and kissed the fingers that had stroked his skin.

'No,' she whispered. 'No second thoughts. I just need to know you'll respect me in the morning.' A tremulous smile belied the steadiness of her gaze.

Cade's eyes hardened. Tension thrummed between them, fierce and significant.

Until he bent his head and kissed the corner of her mouth. 'Not a whit less than I respect you now,' he said deliberately.

Renewed confidence surged through her. She let him turn her and went with him into her room. Excitement beat through her, quickening as she turned to face him.

'Do you want the light on?' he asked, barely moving his lips.

'No.' She didn't want any other light than that of the moon, a silvery, shadowy glow full of mystery and magic.

Cade's eyes kindled into diamond-bright intensity, burning blue as the heart of a flame. 'You take my breath away,' he said gutturally and pulled off his shirt, dropping it onto the floor.

Taryn's breath stopped in her throat. He was utterly overwhelming, all fluid muscle and bronzed skin and heady male charisma. Acting on instinct, she reached out a tentative hand and skimmed his broad chest, fingertips tingling at the contrast of supple skin and the silken overlay of hair. Her heart pumped loudly in her ears and she sucked in a sharp breath at the raw, leashed strength that emanated from him, balanced by masculine grace and an aura of power.

She muttered, 'And you are…magnificent,' and pulled her little singlet top over her head.

Cade's mouth hardened. For a second she froze, her eyes fixed on his face, but when he kissed her, deeply and sensuously, taking his fill of her, she forgot everything but his mouth on hers and the hands that slid across her back to hold her upright when her knees would no longer carry her weight.

When the kiss was over he scrutinised her face, his glinting eyes narrowing in the taut silence while his hands moved again, one down to her hips, the other lingering to trace the curves of her breasts before finally, just when she thought the tension inside her would have to be released in a groan, he cupped them.

Stunned and charmed, she shivered as he bent his head and kissed an expectant tip.

Desire uncoiled through her so swiftly it shocked her. Nothing, she thought helplessly when he eased her across his arm so that he could take the pink crest of a breast into his mouth—*nothing* in her previous life had prepared her for this charged, voluptuous delight.

At the sensuous tug of his lips, erotic little shudders tightened her skin and she closed her eyes, swamped by the sheer immensity of the sensations sweeping through her.

Dimly, she realised that all her fears had been wasted—whatever had kept her from enjoying sex previously no longer applied. Shivering with a passionate intensity, she was transformed, taken over by a desperate craving for something she didn't recognise, didn't understand. Her back arched in unconscious demand, and Cade lifted his head and subjected her to a darkly probing survey.

Shaken by the hunger surging through her veins, she gasped as he eased her onto the bed. Colour burned through her skin and her lashes fluttered down when he stripped completely.

But once he came down beside her, she turned into him, seeking his strength to appease the hunger burning inside her. His arms tightened around her and he kissed the wildly beating pulse in her throat.

'Open your eyes.' It was a command, not a request.

She tried to steady her voice, force it into something like its normal sensible tone, but the words came out in a husky, languorous whisper. 'It's too much...'

'What is?' And when she didn't answer he bent his head again and his lips closed over the other tightly budding peak.

'Everything,' she croaked, her pulse racing so fast she thought she might faint with the delicious thrill of his caress.

By the time he'd eased her remaining garment from her she no longer remembered that once she'd lain frozen and repelled by just such a caress. His hand moved between her legs and he began to press rhythmically and without haste, setting up a powerful sensuous counterpoint to the exquisite tug of his mouth. Insistent, demanding pleasure built in the pit of her stomach, a driving, powerful ache totally beyond her experience.

'Look at me,' Cade breathed, lifting his head so that Taryn felt his lips brush against her breast with each word.

Molten rills of sensation raced through her—beautiful, devouring, possibly destructive fire, but it was too late to call a halt now.

Not that she would, even if she could. Heat from his body fanned her passionate reaction to the subtle masculine scent that was his alone, and the intoxicating seduction of his skilled caresses had gone straight to her head.

'I think I'm shy,' she muttered, not surprised when he laughed deep in his throat.

Except that a shy woman wouldn't have yielded so quickly, so easily.

She'd wanted Cade from the moment their eyes met, her body surrendering to an elemental hunger her mind had refused to recognise. That hidden, barely registered excitement had tangled logic and caution into knots, sneakily undermining them and persuading her she'd be perfectly safe going to Fala'isi with him.

'Shy?' he murmured, his voice thick. 'A little, perhaps, and tantalisingly elusive, but so intriguingly responsive.'

His fingers slid deeper, towards her acutely sensitive core, and suddenly desire fractured into light that filled every cell in her body with shimmering transcendent sensation, a rapture that took her totally by surprise.

Her lashes flew up. Hugely dilated shocked eyes locking with his, she came apart in his arms, so abandoned to the magic of Cade's lovemaking she had no defence against her wild surrender.

He silenced the gasp that escaped her with a kiss so fierce and sensual she didn't register the flare of satisfaction in his eyes. Her lashes drifted down and she lay cradled against him for several minutes while her heartbeat slowed into normality and the vivid consummation faded into the sweet laziness of sated desire.

Until Cade moved, positioning himself over her. Then, in a reaction she couldn't stop, her body tensed. Bleak despair roiled through her. Willing her muscles to relax, she had to force herself to meet the keen, polished steel of his gaze.

'It's all right,' he said abruptly. 'I won't hurt you.'

'I know.' Hardly breathing, she tried to unlock her muscles.

He bent and took her breast into his mouth again. And somehow, miraculously, passion conquered fear, floating through her in pleasurable ripples that almost immediately coalesced into a mill race of urgent, clamorous anticipation.

Cade lifted his head, narrowly examining her face, then said, 'Yes?'

'Oh, yes,' she breathed.

Blue eyes held her gaze as he eased into her by slow, sensuous increments and began to move almost sinuously, his male strength and power controlled by a will she dimly recognised.

Hunger poured through her in a violent rush, easing his passage with a flood that summoned voluptuous tremors through her. Instantly gauging her response, he thrust more fiercely and she gasped again, hips arching off the bed to meet him, the carnal rhythm projecting her into a world where all she had to cling to was this heady, dazzling sensation and the driving measure of their hearts against each other.

Lost in rapture, almost immediately she crested again in an infinitely more complex, intense culmination that hurtled her through some unmarked boundary on a soaring wave of ecstasy. Just when she was certain she couldn't bear any more pleasure, his breathing became harsh and he flung back his head. Through barely open eyes she saw him reach his fulfilment, his arrogant face a drawn mask of sexual pleasure, every muscle in his body cording in hard tension.

Eventually, while the erotic satiation faded into a dreamy daze, Taryn tried to sort her scattered thoughts. Stupidly, strangely, she longed for some tenderness from him, some acceptance of their mutual ecstasy, but without speaking, he twisted away and settled beside her on his back.

Close, so close, yet not touching. And she needed his touch now, so much she felt the need aching through her.

'All right?' he asked, his voice rough.

Hold me, she almost begged, but a remnant of common sense barred the abject plea. Terrified she might betray herself by letting the words free, she whispered, 'I didn't know it could be like that.'

His mouth crooked in a humourless smile and, without speaking, he turned onto his side and scooped her against him. His chest lifted as he said, 'He must have been a crass fool, that fiancé of yours.'

'Oh, no,' she said quietly. 'He loved me. But we were both so young…and I didn't…couldn't…'

His arms tightened when she stumbled, giving silent support. Oddly enough, it was as though the rapture she'd found with Cade had opened a door she'd slammed shut years ago.

When he asked, 'How young?' she told him.

'Nineteen, and he was twenty-one. Far too young, my parents said, and they were so right, but…at first everything was like a romantic fairy tale. Only once we were engaged he wanted to make love, and he was bewildered—and hurt—when I couldn't…'

She stopped and took a deep breath. Possibly without realising it, Cade was stroking her back and the slight, slow caress was soothing something more than her laboured heartbeat.

In a soft, dragging voice she said, 'I still don't know why I froze every time. He was experienced—I wasn't his first lover. He said I was frigid. And I thought it was true because I was so certain I loved him. But I just couldn't relax…'

Cade said quietly, 'So he found someone new?'

'Oh, no.' She swallowed. 'He tried everything… I think he saw my coldness as a challenge to his masculinity.'

She couldn't go on. Antony had been utterly determined to overcome her frigidity. Sex with him had become an ordeal of new techniques, new attempts at seduction—from watching pornography with her to licking chocolate from her body—in his efforts to discover the magic caress that would miraculously turn her into the willing, eagerly passionate partner he wanted.

His dogged efforts had only made her more tense, eventually creating a rift, one that had rapidly spiralled out of control.

Cade said quietly, 'That doesn't sound like love.'

In a low, shaken voice, she said, 'He got so angry—as though I was doing it deliberately. I didn't know how to handle it—' She stifled a laugh that sounded too much like a sob. 'I wanted to run home to my mummy and daddy like a little girl and have them make things all better for me.'

'But they weren't there for you.'

'They were dealing with an outbreak of dengue fever that was killing people.' Her voice strengthened. 'So of course I didn't tell them.'

'What happened?'

When she shivered his arms tightened around her again. Keeping her face hidden in his shoulder, she mumbled, 'We were fighting a lot…and he…in the end I told him I didn't want him and never would, and he… and he…' She stopped, unable to go on.

'It's all right.' In a tone so devoid of emotion it was more threatening than anger, Cade said, 'Let me guess. He raped you.'

Taryn shuddered. 'Yes,' she whispered, adding swiftly, 'Afterwards he was shattered. He said he still loved me, even though I'd turned him into a monster.'

Every muscle in Cade's big body tightened. 'And you believed that—that self-serving, righteous—' he paused before clearly substituting another word for the one that must have sprung to mind '—*rubbish*?'

'At first I did,' Taryn admitted quietly. 'And even when I realised he had no right—that he was responsible for what he did, I still believed…'

'That you were frigid,' he supplied when she couldn't go on, his voice hard with anger. 'Well, now you know you aren't. Far from being frigid, you're delightfully responsive, all any man could ask for. If he wasn't able to make you respond, it was probably because you sensed the propensity for violence in him. No man has the right to take out his frustration in rape. It's every bit as criminal and brutal as beating a woman.'

Something that had been wound tightly inside her for

years eased, dissipated, left her for ever. She felt oddly empty, yet light and free.

More shaken than she'd ever been, she said, 'I don't know why I told you all this.'

'Feel better?'

She sighed. 'Yes. Thank you.'

Thank you for everything. Thank you for making a woman of me...

'You don't need to thank me,' he said abruptly. 'I've done nothing—you always had the capacity for passion. It was your bad luck you thought you loved someone who didn't know how to arouse it.'

'Stupidity, more like,' she murmured.

He laughed quietly. 'Who isn't stupid at nineteen?'

Comforted, she luxuriated in the heat of his body, the smooth lift and fall of his chest, the sensuous, languid delight of being there with Cade. The world righted, reassembled itself, and she yawned.

'Do you want me to stay?' he asked.

Taryn's acrobatic heart jumped in her breast. It was utterly stupid to feel that this was more important than making love with him; that his question even implied some tenuous commitment...

In a voice she hoped sounded lazily contented, she murmured, 'If you want to.'

His smile sizzled through her. 'At the moment I don't think I can move,' he said and stretched, his big, lithe body flexing before he settled himself back beside her. There was a note of humour in his tone when he finished, 'But if you'd rather sleep alone I'll make the effort. A little later.'

'Mmm.' Another yawn took her by surprise.

'Sleep now,' he said, tucking her against him again.

Taryn had never actually slept with anyone. She and

Antony had always made love in his flat and afterwards she'd gone back to hers, but having Cade beside her felt so natural—so right—she drifted almost immediately into slumber.

Cade waited until her breathing became deep and regular before easing her free of his embrace and turning onto his back, folding his arms behind his head as he stared out into the soft silver-hazed darkness.

Only when she moved away from him did he look at her. Even through the netting, the light of the moon shone strongly enough to pick out the long, elegant line of her sleek body and burnish her skin to a pale ivory quite different from its daylight colour of warm honeyed cream.

His hooded gaze traced the curves of her breasts and waist, the pure line of her profile, the lips his kisses had made tender. Astonishingly, his senses stirred again, startling him.

She'd been a willing and lusty lover, her response deliciously sensual. Yet there had been that intriguing element of…not exactly shyness, more like delighted bewilderment when she'd unravelled in his arms.

Although he was still furious with the man who'd abused her, the realisation that no one else had been able to elicit that shuddering primal response produced a visceral, addictive kick of satisfaction.

Of course, the whole story could be a lie…

His instinctive vehement resistance to this possibility warned him he was on the brink of making a huge mistake—of forgetting the reason Taryn was with him. All he'd intended was to get closer to her, find out what made her tick, why she'd laughed at Peter's proposal—what had made Peter decide his life was no longer worth living if she wasn't in it.

But he'd let himself get sidetracked. Seducing her had not been part of the plan.

Unfortunately, he'd wanted her from the moment he'd seen her. Worse than that, he'd let his hunger eat away at his self-control.

Had that happened to Peter? Was that why he'd killed himself—because she'd bled him dry and then left him?

Cade fought back a cold anger, realising with icy self-derision that he didn't want to picture Taryn in his brother's bed. Shocked to realise his hands had clenched into serviceable fists, he deliberately relaxed every muscle.

He wouldn't let such a stupid adolescent emotion as jealousy crumble his hard-won self-control.

Life had taught him that ignoring inconvenient or unpleasant facts and possibilities invariably led to foolish decisions and bitter consequences.

Why did the thought of Taryn responding to Peter with the same passion and heady desire she'd shown a few short minutes ago make him feel like committing some act of violence?

His mouth tightened. Because he'd allowed her to get to him. Somehow, in spite of everything he knew and suspected about her, he'd let down his guard.

A seabird called from above the palms, a sorrowing screech that lifted the hairs on the back of his neck.

Ignore the damn bird, he thought grimly. Face facts.

Lust meant nothing—any normal man would look at Taryn's beautiful face and lithe body and wonder what she was like in bed. But he'd made love to her knowing—and ignoring—the fact she was the only person who knew what had driven Peter to take his life.

He needed to know the reason, and not just because he'd promised his mother he'd find out. For his own peace of mind.

He suspected Peter had always felt slightly inferior. It hadn't helped that he'd never been able to match Cade physically, or that after their father's frightening bout of cancer when Peter was at school both parents had tended to rely more and more on their elder son.

Certainly his brother's behaviour at university hadn't convinced them he was someone they could rely on. Revelling in the freedom, Peter had wallowed in everything college offered except the opportunity to study.

Cade frowned, remembering how worried their parents had been. Fortunately, his brother's discovery of talent as a sculptor had ended that period of dissipation. To everyone's surprise—possibly even Peter's—his interest had become his passion.

He'd been *good*. He might eventually have been great. To die without ever fulfilling his potential would have been bad enough, but to kill himself because a pretty thief laughed at his offer of love and marriage was a bitter travesty.

Cade took a harsh breath, freezing when Taryn moved beside him. He waited until she settled her long legs and tried not to think of them around his hips, to banish from his mind the way she'd given herself utterly to desire.

To him…

His inglorious satisfaction at that thought both shamed him and brought his body to full alert again.

Staying in her bed had been a stupid, passion-addled decision. As soon as she was sleeping soundly enough he'd leave. Until then, he'd concentrate on the fact that she'd almost certainly spent the money Peter had given her. If she still had any of it, she wouldn't have had to resort to a job in a dead-end village.

Perhaps she'd given it to her parents to finance a clinic or a hospital somewhere?

Angered by this futile attempt to provide an excuse, he stared unseeingly across the room.

Think logically, he commanded. It had to be a possibility; although he might think her parents had a very cavalier attitude towards her, she clearly didn't. She'd been very quick to defend them.

Possibly he could find out if an unexpected amount of money had arrived in her parents' coffers. He'd get someone onto it tomorrow morning.

A slight breeze shimmered through the white mosquito netting. Again Cade glanced across at the woman beside him. As though his gaze penetrated the veils of sleep, she murmured something and turned back to him. A lovely, sensuous enigma, she lay like a child, one hand under her cheek, her face calm except for a tiny half smile that curled her lips. Long coppery hair tangled across her shoulder, half covering her breasts.

Once again, Cade's body stirred into urgent hunger. He swung his legs over the side of the bed and stood up. Lashes fluttering, Taryn gave a little sigh, but her eyes remained closed and almost immediately she sank back into deeper sleep.

Moving with a noiseless tread, Cade scooped up his clothes and headed for the door before he could yield to the temptation to get back into the bed and stroke her into wakefulness, to make love to her again…

No, not to make love.

To have sex with her again, he reminded himself savagely, silently closing her bedroom door behind him.

Back in his own room, he threw his clothes onto a

chair and strode across to the windows, pushing back the shutters to drag warm sea-tangy air into his lungs. It had seemed so simple, so logical to bring her to Fala'isi so he could study her more closely. Instead, he'd got himself into an emotional tangle.

No, not emotional. He was *not* in love with her. He didn't know what love was about, so whatever he was feeling right now was—irrelevant.

CHAPTER TEN

DAZED by memories and dreams, Taryn woke from the best sleep she'd experienced for months and smiled sleepily at the crooning of the doves outside. When she'd first heard them she'd been astonished at such a European sound here, but after only a few days they'd become an intrinsic part of Fala'isi for her.

She'd always remember them—along with last night.

Colour burned up through her skin. She was glad Cade had left before she'd woken, yet some weak part of her mourned his absence.

She flung the sheet back, stretching and wincing a little at the protest from rarely used muscles. Making love with Cade had been a considerably more athletic exercise than she was accustomed to.

He'd known exactly what to do to make her body sing with desire, to waken that urgent, exquisite hunger, then send her soaring into an alternate universe where the only thing that mattered was sensual rapture.

She glanced at her watch, muttering as she leapt off the bed. A quick shower left her no time for memories; she pulled on a cool shift that seemed almost formal in this relaxed atmosphere, but had to summon her boldest face when she finally walked out of her room.

Only to find he wasn't there.

He'd written a note, about as personal as a legal document, telling her he'd be back some time in the afternoon. However, he left her with work to do.

It took her all morning to track down and collate the information he asked for, and when she'd finished she looked along the white coral path for any sign of him.

Nothing. The island drowsed in the bright glow of tropical heat. For once the feathery palm fronds were silent and still against a sky so blue and bold it hurt her eyes. Even the lagoon was too warm when she swam, its silky waters enervating rather than refreshing.

She met him on the shell path just after she'd rinsed off the salt water from her body. Although a *pareu* hid her wet bikini, his gaze kindled and he reached out to touch her shoulder but, to her disappointment, immediately let his hand drop.

'Enjoy your swim?' he asked.

'Very much, thank you.'

Sensation churned through her, exciting yet making her apprehensive. She'd never felt like this before—as though the world was fresh and new and infinitely alluring—and she didn't know how to deal with it. Would he expect her to be blasé and sophisticated?

He broke into her thoughts by saying abruptly, 'I've cancelled the trip to check out the fishing industry.'

After a startled upwards look, she nodded. 'OK.'

His black brows lifted. 'No protests? No insistence that you've been looking forward so much to it?'

She grinned. 'I'm not a liar, unless it's polite white lies. And even then I try to avoid them if I can. I'd find the trip interesting, I'm sure, but business is business. And you're the boss so you get to make the decisions.'

They'd set off walking towards the *fale*, but he

stopped in the brief shade of the palms and demanded, 'Is that how you think of me?'

When Taryn hesitated he said, 'The truth, Taryn.'

'Until yesterday,' she said, hoping he couldn't see that she was hedging.

'Just that?'

She sent him a level glance. 'Do you really want to know, or are you pushing me to prove that I always tell the truth?'

Emotion flashed for a moment in his gaze before his lashes came down. When they lifted again his gaze was steely and relentless. 'Both.'

'I don't like being tested,' Taryn said steadily and set off again, her emotions in turmoil. She didn't know what he wanted from her, but she certainly wasn't going to tell him that last night had changed her in some fundamental way.

If she did, he'd probably send her home.

Making love with him had been like setting off into dangerous, unknown territory with no map, no provisions and no equipment, furnished only with hope. Last night it had seemed simple and right. Today she was more wary. If she wanted to keep her heart free and unscathed, she suspected she should be making plans to get back to New Zealand.

And knew she wouldn't.

Abruptly, she said, 'You already know that I found you very attractive right from the start. But until we changed the rules yesterday I did my best to regard you as my employer.'

'And now?'

He was ruthlessly pushing for something from her, an answer to a question she didn't understand.

Half exasperated, half distressed, she said, 'I have

no claim on you, just as you have none on me. We both know this is a temporary arrangement between us. If you want to forget about it, tell me and we'll call it quits.'

And held her breath, feeling as though her whole future depended on his answer.

Cade said in a voice that brooked no argument, 'I shouldn't have started this out here. We'll talk once we're back in the *fale*.'

In the cool dimness of the living room he glanced at the pile of papers on the table and then, blue eyes hooded, examined her face. 'I want to make sure that the fact that I'm your employer had no bearing on your charming surrender last night.'

'I haven't been to bed with any other of my employers,' she said stiffly, obscurely hurt.

'I didn't intend to insult you,' he said, his voice hard. 'I certainly didn't mean to imply that you slept with all—or any of—your employers. I just wanted to make absolutely sure that you didn't feel pressured into making love.'

Taryn shook her head vigorously. 'No.'

And stopped, because anything more might reveal too much. But couldn't he tell that she'd surrendered wholeheartedly, with everything she had, everything she was?

Once again that flinty gaze probed hers for long heart-stopping seconds, until he seemed to relax and drew her towards him. Almost abstractedly, he murmured, 'You're the only employee I've ever made love to.'

His head came down and he kissed her throat, saying against her skin, 'You taste like the sea, sun-warmed and salty, scented with flowers and the wind.'

Unable to hold back, she turned her face into his and

they kissed, and he found the knot of her *pareu* and it dropped in a wet heap on the floor, leaving her only in her bikini. Cade made a deep noise in his throat and his arms locked around her. Without further resistance, she lifted her face for his kiss, body pressed to body as desire—torrid and compelling—flashed between them.

'And you taste of you,' she said on a sigh when he finally lifted his head.

Taryn expected him to loosen his arms, but he didn't. Resting his cheek on her wet hair, he said, 'Not regretting anything?'

Regret? How could she regret the most wonderful experience of her life so far? Last night had been utterly magical, a revelation to her.

Was being a good lover a talent, something instinctive? How many women had Cade practised with to gain that mastery? Not only had he divined which parts of her were acutely sensitive to his touch, but he'd been slow and subtle and erotically compelling, seducing her until she'd had no thought for anything beyond the enchantment he worked on her willing body and mind.

'Not a thing,' she said huskily.

He smiled dangerously and let her go, but his grip slid down to fasten around her wrists so he could lift her hands to his mouth.

Tiny shivers chased the length of her spine as he kissed each palm. Be careful, some part of her warned. Be very careful. You don't want to lose your heart to him. Remember, he might want you but it's not going to last.

His tone amused, he said, 'Then we're suited in every way,' and kissed her properly again.

Joy fountained through Taryn. Once again, she felt

the swift, piercing surge of desire, brazen as the tropical sun, and this time she had no forebodings, no fear about whether or not she was going to be able to respond. This time she could make love to Cade with complete confidence that the same rapture that had taken her to paradise the night before was waiting for her again.

'You'll get all wet,' she said against his throat.

'Mmm,' he murmured. 'Somehow, keeping dry is not a priority right now.'

'What is?'

He looked into her face with half closed eyes and the fierce smile of a hunter. 'Making it to a bed.'

They got there, but only just, and later, in a dreamy daze as she listened to him breathe beside her, Taryn decided she'd never been so happy before, never felt so completely at one with the world.

She drifted into sleep, but stirred when he got up. Opening her eyes, she smiled mistily at him, that flame of awareness beating high within her again at the sight of him, lean and bronzed and beautifully made, as powerfully built as he was desirable.

He dropped a kiss on her mouth but, before she could reach out and pull him down, he straightened. 'Dinner,' he said succinctly.

'Help, yes!' She swung her legs over the side of the bed and sat up. Tonight they were having dinner with the Chapmans.

Gaze darkening, Cade said, 'Don't move—try not to even breathe—until I get out of the room.'

Thrilled by her effect on him, she obediently froze.

Laughing softly, he left, scooping up his clothes as he went.

I'm in love with him, she thought, suddenly assailed

by a wild mixture of apprehension and delight. *I'm in love with Cade Peredur.*

No, that was just foolish post-coital bliss scrambling her brain. She straightened her shoulders; she was perfectly content with the rules they'd made. Love had nothing to do with this. Eventually, they'd go their separate ways and she'd grieve for a while and miss him like crazy.

She'd gone into their affair with her eyes open and when it ended she'd get on with real life, grateful to Cade for showing her that she was a normal woman who could make love with abandon and joy.

So she'd accept this fantasy interlude for what it was—an enchantment that would end once they left the seductively sensuous lure of the tropics. And, if all went well, she might one day find a man she could both desire and truly love, one who'd love her.

Dinner with the Chapmans was fun; Fleur was an excellent hostess, Luke an interesting man with the same inbuilt authority that marked Cade. Afterwards, they drank coffee and watched the moon rise over the ocean, and Cade mentioned her parents.

'They do magnificent work,' Luke Chapman said. 'I believe they've just acquired a new yacht.'

Taryn nodded. 'A much bigger one. They've had it converted into a sort of mini-hospital and it's working well, but Dad's next project is to find the finance for a shore-based hospital on one of the outlying islands. And, after that, they want to set up a trust that will help local people study as nurses and doctors. He wants to make sure that when he and Mum retire—if they ever do—they leave a working system behind.'

'Big ambitions,' Luke observed.

'And expensive ones,' Cade supplied. 'Where do they find the money to keep going?'

Taryn laughed, then sighed. 'So far it's been mainly donations. Dad's quite shameless when it comes to asking for it.'

'That's a chancy, hand-to-mouth way for a charity—especially a private one—to exist. Setting up the new yacht must have cost them a packet,' Cade said.

'They were lucky—they got a big donation at just the right time.' Sadness struck her at the thought of Peter, who'd been so insistent on donating it.

And, emboldened by the Chapmans' obvious interest, she looked directly at their host. 'They want something along the lines of the health service you have here.'

Which led to further discussion. The Chapmans made no promises but, as she and Cade left, Luke said, 'I'll give you the name of the man who runs our health service. Your father could do worse than get in touch with him.'

Out of earshot, Cade said thoughtfully, 'You're a good daughter.'

Flushing, Taryn replied, 'My parents deserve all the help they can get.'

He said nothing more and she wondered whether he too was thinking of helping her parents. If so, perhaps they might keep in touch…

Don't, she told herself in sudden anguish. Don't hope for anything more. It wasn't going to happen, and wishing for it would only make it harder to recover.

Because now her heart was involved. Oh, she'd tried so hard to ignore it but, as they'd talked over the coffee table, she'd looked across at Cade and *known* she loved him. The knowledge had pierced her like a sword—

transcendent yet shattering. Life without Cade stretched before her, bleak as a desert.

She looked up into a sky so brightly lit by the moon the stars were tiny pinpricks against black velvet. No sign of fruit bats, she thought wistfully.

If it hadn't been for that low-flying one, would Cade have ever kissed her?

Another question she couldn't answer.

Back in the *fale*, Cade glanced at his watch. 'I'm expecting a call from London in a few minutes, so I'll say goodnight now.'

It was like a blow to the heart. She felt her expression freeze and said hastily, 'Oh! Goodnight then.'

He surprised her by kissing her lightly, an arm round her shoulder holding her without passion.

'Sleep well,' he said and left her, walking into his room.

But, once there, he stood indecisively for a few moments, looking around as though he'd never seen the room before.

Every instinct was telling him to get out. He was in too deep and tonight he'd slipped over some invisible boundary, one he hadn't known existed. The whole evening had been—he struggled to find the right word and could only come up with *satisfying*. Satisfying in some deep, unplumbed way that scared the hell out of him.

He was falling and, if he didn't stop the process, he had no idea where he'd land. Damn it, it had been a quiet dinner with a couple he called friends, yet for some reason he'd accessed a level of—again, he searched for a word, finally settling on *contentment*—that still clung to him.

Contentment! He got to his feet and paced the room, angular face dark with frustration. Contentment was for the old, those with no further ambitions to pursue. He had plenty.

Yet, sitting under that voluptuous moon, watching the way its aura cooled Taryn's red hair and turned her skin to satin, listening to the low music of her laughter, he'd found himself thinking that life could hold nothing more for him.

Making love to her had been the most stupid thing he'd ever done.

No, bringing her to Fala'isi was that; their lovemaking had only compounded a problem he'd refused to face. Still didn't want to face.

There was only one thing to do. Before he lost his head and did something irretrievable, he had to tell her who he was, and what he wanted from her.

Surprisingly, Taryn slept well, waking next morning to sunlight and the muted coo of the doves against the slow thunder of the distant waves against the reef. And an aching emptiness because last night Cade had left her alone.

When she emerged, Cade was standing beside the pool, talking into his phone. He glanced up when he heard her, nodded and strode to the other end of the pool, the tension in his powerful back and lean, strong body warning her that something had gone wrong.

The terrace table had been set for breakfast for two, so she poured herself some coffee and spooned passionfruit pulp over golden slices of papaya.

She couldn't hear what Cade was saying, but his tone echoed his body language. He was angry.

When he strode over she asked a little warily, 'Trouble?'

'Problems.' Dismissing them, he sat down opposite

her and examined her face, his expression flinty. 'All right?'

'Of course,' she said automatically. Much more than all right, in fact. Her heart was singing and every cell in her body responded with pleasure to the sight of him. 'Is there anything I can do?'

'No—just a business rival thinking that being on the other side of the world means I'm not keeping my eye on the kitchen. However, there is something I must tell you,' he said shortly. 'Did Peter Cooper ever tell you he had a brother?'

Taryn's spoon clattered into her plate. Searching his face, she swallowed. Nothing showed in the grey-blue eyes but an icy determination. 'Yes,' she answered automatically.

'Did you know I am—was—his brother?'

Taryn had never fainted in her life but, as she felt the colour drain from her skin, she thought dizzily that this was going to be the first time.

He said abruptly, 'Put your head down.' And, when she didn't move, he got to his feet and swivelled her chair around so he could push her head below her heart. The heavy, sick feeling beneath her ribs dissipated but she couldn't think—couldn't even make sense of the words jumbling through her mind.

After a few seconds the dizziness faded and she croaked, 'Let me up—I'm all right.'

'Sure?' He released her, watching her as she straightened.

After one look at his controlled face, she asked inanely, 'How can you be his brother? You don't have the same name.'

He shrugged. 'I went to the Coopers when I was five. Peter was born four years later.'

Taryn blinked, her mind seizing on this because she didn't dare—not yet—ask why he hadn't told her right at the start who he was.

'I see.' Heart twisting at the thought of what he must have endured as a child, she concentrated with fierce determination on the cluster of hibiscus flowers in the centre of the table.

She'd never be able to enjoy their showy vividness again without remembering this moment. *Peter's brother.* Cade was Peter's foster-brother.

Taryn believed in coincidences, but not where Cade was concerned.

Cade made things happen. He must have known that she and Peter had been friends.

Had he deliberately tracked her down? Was his lovemaking a sham? *Why?*

Pain sliced through her, so intense she hugged herself, trying to force the mindless agony away. When she trusted herself to speak again, she asked quietly, 'Why didn't you tell me this when we first met?'

His eyes narrowed into flinty shards. In a tone that almost brought her to her feet, ready to run, he said, 'Because I wanted to find out what sort of woman you were.'

'Why?' Every breath hurt, but she had to know.

He said evenly, 'I wanted to know what the woman who laughed at his proposal was like.'

Taryn almost ducked as though avoiding a blow. White-faced and shaking, she had to force herself to speak. 'How…how did you know that?'

His beautiful mouth tightened—the mouth that had brought her such ecstasy.

'How I know doesn't matter. Are you surprised that I should want to know why he killed himself?'

Dragging in a sharply painful breath, she reached deep into her reserves to find strength—enough strength to force herself up so she faced him, head held high.

'No,' she said quietly. 'Do you think I don't regret laughing? That I don't wish I could go back in time and change how I reacted? I thought he was joking.'

'Men do not *joke* about proposing,' he said between his teeth, making the word sound obscene. 'Why the hell would you think that?'

'Because we didn't have that sort of relationship,' she cried. 'We were friends—good friends—but we'd never even kissed.'

Stone-faced, he asked, 'Never?'

Firming her jaw, she admitted, 'The occasional peck on the check, that's all. Nothing beyond that. In fact, I thought—' She stopped.

'Go on,' he said silkily.

She swallowed. 'I thought he had a lover… There was a woman…' She stopped and forced her brain to leash the tornado of emotions rioting through her. 'Or that he might be gay.'

Cade looked at her, his expression kept under such rigid discipline she had no idea what he was thinking.

'He wasn't. Far from it.' He made a sudden, abrupt gesture, his control splintering. 'So if he never made a move on you, never showed that he wanted you, never indicated he might be in love with you, why the *hell* did he propose?'

'I don't know,' she said wretchedly. 'I really did think he was joking. And I was so taken aback—so startled—I laughed. Until I realised he was serious. I never thought… I *still* find it hard to believe he was in love with me.'

'I'm finding everything you've said hard to believe,'

he said in a level judicial voice. 'I know—knew—my brother better than anyone, and he wouldn't have rashly proposed to a woman he wasn't sure of. Peter wasn't one for wild impulses.'

Taryn opened her mouth, then closed it again.

Harshly, Cade said, 'Tell me what you were going to say.'

When she hesitated, he commanded in a tone that sent a cold shiver scudding down her spine, *'Tell me.'*

'Just that as a brother you might have known him well, but as a man...how much time did you spend with him? He could be impulsive. And before he—'

'Killed himself,' Cade inserted when she couldn't go on.

'Before he died,' she went on bleakly, 'he was ecstatic at scoring that wonderful commission. It meant so much to him. He told me it validated everything he'd done before, and that he'd finally make his family proud of him. He was so happy planning the sculpture, so eager to get on with the work—almost crazy with delight.'

Shocked, she realised she was wringing her hands. She stopped, reasserted control and said without thinking, 'I swear, killing himself was the last thing on his mind.'

'Because he believed you loved him,' Cade said ruthlessly. 'When he proposed, what did you say to him?'

CHAPTER ELEVEN

TARYN flinched when she met Cade's—*Peter's brother's*—hooded, pitiless eyes. 'After I laughed, do you mean?' she asked on a half sob. 'I told him that although I liked him very much and valued him enormously as friend, I wasn't in love with him.'

'And what did he say to those noble sentiments?'

Colour flamed the length of her cheekbones, then faded into an icy chill. 'He said he hoped I'd always remember him as a good friend.'

'And it didn't occur to you he was saying goodbye?' he demanded incredulously.

'Of course not.' Then she said swiftly, 'Well...yes. Yes, of course I realised that our *friendship* was over. His proposal changed everything—and I was going back to New Zealand in a few hours. But...if he loved me, why did he leave it so late to propose?'

Cade said nothing and she went on in a low, subdued voice, 'I did...I did love him, but not the way he wanted me to, and I still can't...'

Cade remained emphatically silent while she gulped back her emotions, eventually regaining enough self-possession to say in a voice drained of all colour, 'I d-don't know what I could have done to help him.'

'Nothing.' He was watching her so closely she took

a step backwards. In a level voice, he said, 'Although offering to return his money might have made some difference to his decision to kill himself.'

'Money?' She flushed when she realised what he was talking about. 'It had already gone to my parents. It was used to fit out the new yacht—and he wanted to give it to Mum and Dad, Cade. If you believe nothing else, believe that. He insisted on sending it to them.'

He shook his head. 'Not that—I know he donated it to your parents. As I said last night—you're a good daughter.'

Now she understood what he'd meant—and why he'd left her alone last night.

Numbly, she listened to him continue, shrivelling inside when he went on, 'Peter had every right to give his money to whoever he wanted to. No, the money I'm talking about is the rest of his advance for the sculpture he was commissioned to produce.'

His words rang senselessly in her ears, jangling around her head in meaningless syllables. She stared at him, met penetrating eyes that judged and assessed every tiny muscle flickering in her face.

'What are you talking about?' she asked numbly.

He lifted one eyebrow to devastating effect. 'Don't be coy, Taryn. As well as the donation for the clinic, Peter gave you a large chunk of that advance. Where is it?'

Deep inside her, some fragile, persistent hope shattered into shards, dissolved into nothingness, leaving behind a black bitterness and misery.

Cade had deliberately targeted her, tracked her down and made love to her—because he thought she'd taken money from Peter. A large amount of money. Peter had gleefully told her how much it was, and that it was to be used to buy the materials for his sculpture.

Everything Cade had done, he'd done because he was convinced she was a thief. He'd brought her here, made love to her, given her such joy—and it was all false, all lies…

Trying to speak, she discovered that her throat had closed. Her stomach turned and she clapped a hand over her mouth.

He said, 'Stay there.'

Taryn closed her eyes, shielding her misery from him. She heard a clink and felt a glass of water being put into her hand.

'Drink it up,' he advised.

Their fingers touched and, in spite of everything, a jolt sparked through her. Dear God, she thought wearily, how could her body betray her like that when she now knew exactly what he thought of her—a liar and a common thief?

She wished she could summon righteous anger at being so badly misjudged, but her only emotion was a deep, aching grief for a fantasy that had turned into a dark nightmare.

Although she was sure she'd choke if she tried to drink the water, her throat was so dry and painful she forced several gulps down.

'Thank you,' she said hoarsely, wishing he'd step back. He was too close, and she…she was as broken as though the very foundations of her world had been cut from under her.

Clutching the glass in front of her like a pathetically useless shield, she said, 'I don't have anything of Peter's—certainly not his money.'

'Taryn, if you don't have it, who does?'

He spoke quite calmly and for a brief, bewildered

second she wondered if indeed—somehow—she did have the money.

Then sanity returned, and with it some courage. 'I don't know,' she said. Her voice wobbled, so she swallowed and tried again. 'All I know is that he didn't give me any money. I'll furnish you with the records of my bank account so you can see for yourself.'

His lashes drooped. 'I want to see them, although if you took it you've had plenty of time to stash it away and cover your tracks.' He waited for a second and when she remained silent went on, 'It will be much easier if you just tell me where it's gone. Once it's returned, we'll forget about it.'

Fighting back against shock and fear and disillusionment, she drained the glass and set it down. She looked up, measuring him like a duellist of old, sensing that once again he was testing her, assessing her reactions to discern whether she'd stolen the money.

In other words, he wasn't sure.

The thought acted like a stimulant, but she forced herself to repress the wild hope that burst into life. Although her thoughts were still far from coherent, she said as calmly as she could, 'I swear to you, Peter didn't give me a cent all the time we knew each other.'

'Taryn, every financial transaction leaves a paper trail.'

When she shrugged, he finished softly, 'I can find those trails.'

It was a threat, but now she'd found a few shreds of composure she recognised it for an empty one. 'You'll discover that there's nothing to find. Cade, you'll never know how sorry I am that Peter's dead, and how sorry I am that I laughed when he proposed. I have that on my conscience, but not the loss of his money. And now I want to go home.'

Home? She didn't have a home, but if she didn't get away from Cade soon she'd crack. Now that she knew the depths of his betrayal, she couldn't bear to stay anywhere near him—let alone pretend they were lovers.

'We'll be leaving tomorrow,' he said inflexibly. 'Until then, I'll expect you to behave as you have been.'

'You must be joking!' she burst out, incredulous at his arrogant command.

'Far from it.' And when she started to speak again he said, 'You won't get off the island without my permission so don't try it.'

She stared at him, met an implacable gaze. He had to be lying—yet, perhaps not. Fleur Chapman might be a warm, compassionate woman, but her husband had the same air of effortless, uncompromising authority that marked Cade. They were also good friends.

And there were her parents—if the Chapmans were thinking of helping their mission, she didn't dare put that in question. Quietly, she said, 'Very well, I'll work for you, but that's all.'

'That's all I want,' he returned.

He turned away, stopping when she said, 'Why did you wait until now to tell me this?'

Without looking at her, he said, 'It had gone far enough.'

And he strode out of the room.

Taryn made sure she was in bed when he came back in the warm tropical night. Working had given her mind something to do—something other than returning endlessly to that moment when Cade had accused her of stealing money from Peter and stripped away her foolish, self-serving illusions.

Except that in bed, faced with the truth, her mind refused to allow sleep. Endless, scattered, anguished thoughts tumbled through her mind until she forced herself to accept that she couldn't love Cade. He'd deceived her and seduced her.

Actually, he hadn't seduced her. Besotted idiot that she was, she'd met him more than halfway there.

But she had too much pride to love a man who could deliberately lie to her—even though she accepted he had good reason to find out what had killed his brother.

Most nights a sighing breeze kept the mosquito nets breathing in and out, but tonight the sultry heat—and what felt perilously like a broken heart—kept her wide-eyed and sleepless.

On a half sob, she thought Cade had caused her more wakeful hours than anyone else in her life.

A pang of exquisite pain made her catch her breath. More than anything, she wanted to be able to blank him out, forget she'd ever met him, ever seen him. The memories hurt too much.

So she set her mind to the mystery of Peter's missing advance. He'd splashed money around a bit once he'd gained the commission, but he hadn't been extravagant. Certainly not enough to have spent it all…

She was still mulling this over when she heard Cade come into the *fale*. Her breath locked in her throat and her lashes flew up. For a few ridiculous seconds she hardly dared breathe, but of course he didn't knock on her door.

Once she left Fala'isi and Cade, surely she'd get over this aching emptiness, this sense of loss and loneliness, of being betrayed by hopes she hadn't even recognised?

Driven by a searing restlessness and a heart so sore it

felt like an actual physical pain, she got up and walked across to the window. It took her some time to realise that Cade was out there in the tropical night, a tall, dark form standing beside the pool.

Still, so still, as though he couldn't move...

Moonlight shimmered across the arrogant planes of his face, picking out in silver the sweeping strength of bone structure, the straight line of his mouth. Tears burned behind Taryn's eyes, clogged her throat. She blinked them back, focusing on the object Cade held in his hand.

A flower, she realised when he turned it and light glimmered across its silken petals. A hibiscus bloom. What intrigued him so much about the blossoms?

Wincing, she saw him throw it down as he had done before. Then she froze when he suddenly stooped and picked up the flower. Hardly daring to breathe, she watched him walk towards the *fale*.

Her breath sighed out slowly and she turned and made her way back to her bed, too heartsore to do more than wonder why he'd bothered to pick up the flower...

Eventually exhaustion claimed her, but only to dream, and wake with a start to wonder why her unconscious mind had brought her images of a friend of Peter's, famous for her artistic installations.

Peter had respected Andrée Brown as an artist and enjoyed her acid wit, but they'd had an odd, edgy relationship. Sometimes Taryn had suspected he and Andrée were lovers, and wished she could like the woman more. She'd found her heavy-going, a nervy, almost neurotic woman who lived for her art and made no secret of her disdain for people without talent.

Grimacing into the humid air, Taryn used every technique she could remember to calm her mind and woo the oblivion of sleep. But when it arrived it was disturbed by chaotic, frightening dreams so that she woke in the morning unrefreshed and heavy-eyed.

Work was penance; treating Cade with cool dispassion was hell. Doggedly, she plugged through the day, even went to the beach in the late afternoon when she judged everyone would be inside preparing for drinks before dinner.

Soon she'd be back in New Zealand; she'd never have to see Cade again, and this heavy grief that had lodged in her heart would fade. People recovered from the most appalling things; she'd recover too.

She had to…

Shaded by palms, Cade watched her swim towards shore, long arms stroking effortlessly through the water. When she stood, the westering sun kindled an aura of gold from the glittering sheets of water that poured from her. She looked like Venus rising from the Mediterranean, slender and lithe and radiant, no sign of stress in her lovely face, her hair a sleek wet cloak of red so dark it was almost crimson.

Hot frustration roiled through him. Had he just made the biggest mistake in his life?

His jaw tightened as she stooped to pick up her towel. In spite of everything, heat flared through him. Damn the woman; he'd spent most of last night lying awake, remembering how sweetly, how ardently she'd flamed in his arms.

In spite of everything, he couldn't reconcile the laughing, valiant woman he'd come to know with the woman he knew her to be.

His cell phone stopped him just as he was about to step out onto the hot sand. He said something fast and low, but the call was from his PA in London. Today was the day they were to get the results of a further series of tests his PA's three-year-old had endured.

'Yes,' he barked into the phone.

He knew the instant his PA spoke. Instead of the heavy weight of fears of the past month or so, his tone was almost buoyant. 'It's not—what we feared.'

'Thank God,' Cade said fervently. 'What's the problem?'

He listened for a minute or so as Roger told him what lay ahead for little Melinda. When the voice on the other side of the world faded, he said, 'So it's going to be tough, but nowhere near as bad as it could have been.'

'No.'

'OK, take your wife and Melinda to my house in Provence and stay there for a week. Get some sun into all of you.' He cut short his PA's startled objection. 'I refuse to believe you can't organise someone to take your place. I won't be back for another week, so things can ride until then. And buy Melinda a gift from me—something she's been wanting.'

He overrode Roger's thanks, but fell silent when his PA asked urgently, 'Have you heard from Sampson?'

'No.' Not since the investigator he'd set to track down the money from Peter's account had come to a dead end.

Cade stiffened as the tinny voice on the other end of the phone said, 'He rang on Thursday to say he might have something for you in a couple of days.'

An odd dread gripping him, Cade glanced at his watch, made a swift calculation and said, 'OK, thanks. And enjoy Provence.'

He stood looking down at the face of his phone, then set his jaw and hit the button that would get him

Sampson. As the investigator began to speak, his intent expression turned from hard discipline to shock, and then to anger. Swinging around as he listened, he strode back to the *fale*, the cell phone pressed to his ear.

An hour or so later, Taryn walked reluctantly into the *fale*, a *pareu* draped around her from armpit to ankle, only hesitating a moment when she realised Cade was already there.

He said harshly, 'I have something to tell you. Something about Peter.'

'I don't want—' She stopped, her eyes widening. He looked—exhausted. A fugitive hope died into darkness. It took her a moment to summon enough strength to say quietly, 'What is it?'

He closed his eyes a second, then subjected her to an unreadable examination. 'Did you know he was a drug addict?'

Shock silenced her, leaving her shivering. She put out a shaking hand and clutched the top of a chair, bracing herself while Cade waited, his face held under such rigid restraint she couldn't discern any emotion at all.

She whispered, 'No. Oh, no. Are you sure?'

'Yes. I've just been talking to the man I got to investigate the whereabouts of Peter's advance.' He paused, then said in a voice she'd never heard before, one thick with self-disgust, 'You'd better sit down.'

'I'm all right,' she said automatically. 'Go on.'

But he shook his head. 'Sit.'

And because her head was whirling and she felt nauseated, she obeyed, but said immediately, 'You can sit too.'

He said, 'I feel better standing.'

Taryn swallowed. 'All right.'

But he sat down anyway.

Slowly, painfully feeling her way, she whispered, 'I hate to say it, but it makes sense. Peter was mercurial—in tearing good spirits one day, then in the depths the next. I thought it was artistic temperament—made even more so when he got that commission. And asking me to marry him was so out of the blue! He was a great, good friend, but there had been nothing…nothing like…'

Nothing like the instant, unmistakeable reaction between you and me. A glance at Cade's stern face made her remember that only she had felt that wild erotic response.

Stumbling a little, she went on, 'Just nothing. Which was why I thought he had to be joking.'

Would Cade believe her now? She held her breath, her heart thumping so heavily in her ears she had to strain to hear his reply.

'He wasn't joking,' he said roughly. 'He loved you.'

But Taryn shook her head. 'He never made the slightest approach—never touched me except for the odd kiss on the cheek—the sort of kiss you'd give a child.'

'I imagine he was afraid to let you get too close in case you found out about his addiction.' Cade spoke with a control that almost scared her. 'And, although I can't be sure, I suspect he began to hope that if you married him he'd be able to beat the addiction.'

Taryn drew in a ragged breath, grateful he'd made her sit. 'It would never have got that far,' she said numbly. 'I loved him too, but not—' She stopped again, because she'd been so lost in Peter's private tragedy she'd almost blurted out *not like I love you.*

'Not in a sexual way,' she finished, acutely aware of his probing gaze. 'But, oh, I *wish* I'd known. I might have been able to help him. At the very least, I'd have known not to laugh when he proposed…'

'He would have been ashamed of his weakness,' Cade said.

'If I'd understood, I wouldn't have let him down so badly.' The words were wrenched from a depth of pain she could hardly bear.

Cade said, 'He didn't tell anyone.' He paused before saying without inflection, 'Our parents knew what addiction could do, and not only to the one with the problem. My birth mother was an addict—they'd seen what living with her had done to me. When I arrived at their house I was feral—wild and filthy and barely able to function on any level but rage. They worked wonders with nothing more than uncomplicated love and fortitude and their conviction that there was some good in me.'

She made a slight sound of protest and he went on harshly, 'It's the truth. They fostered me because they were told they'd never be able to have children. Peter was their miracle, but it appears he always felt they loved me more than him.'

He'd withheld so much about himself, so much she'd longed to know. The telling of it was clearly painful and now she wished he didn't feel obliged to. 'I'm so sorry,' she whispered.

'Damn it, I don't know why,' he said with a hard anguish that wrung her heart. 'I just don't know.'

But Taryn thought she understood. When he compared himself to Cade's compelling character and the success he'd achieved, Peter must have felt inferior.

As though driven, Cade got to his feet, moving awkwardly for so lithe a man. For once he seemed unable to find the right words. 'I thought we had a good relationship, but it appears it was not. He didn't come to me for help because he resented me.'

'No,' she said swiftly. This was something she could give him—possibly the only thing he'd take from her.

She steadied her voice. 'Whenever he spoke of you there was no mistaking his affection. He never said your name—it was always *my brother*—but he told me little incidents of his childhood, and he always spoke of you with love. He might have felt he couldn't measure up to you, Cade, but he did love you.'

He got to his feet and strode across the room as though driven by inner demons. 'Life would be a hell of a lot easier without love. It complicates things so damned much,' he said angrily. Then, as though he'd revealed far too much, he continued, 'I owe you an apology.'

Taryn's breath locked in her throat. If only he'd tell her he'd really wanted her, that it hadn't all been a fantasy…

One glance at his face told her it wasn't going to happen.

He went on in a cool, deliberate tone, 'I should have made sure of my facts before I taxed you with stealing the money. It's no excuse that I didn't want to believe it, but no one else seemed close enough to him to be a suspect. And he'd given you the money for your parents.'

He hesitated, and she waited with her breath locked in her throat.

But he finished, 'From what the investigator has discovered, it probably all went to pay off drug debts.'

Yet another thing to blame himself for, she thought bleakly, once more faced with a situation she was unable to help, unable to do anything but watch him with an anguish she didn't dare reveal.

In a softly savage voice that sent shudders down her

spine, he said, 'That supplier will be out of business very soon—just as soon as I find out who he is.'

'I might be able to help there,' Taryn said impulsively, immediately regretting her statement when he swung around, eyes narrowing. Choosing her words carefully, she said, 'Peter had a friend—an artist he respected—but it was a difficult relationship. Intense and vaguely antagonistic...'

As she spoke, she suddenly realised why she'd dreamed of the other woman. Torn, she hesitated.

'What was his name?' Cade demanded.

Taryn made up her mind and gave him Andrée Brown's name. 'I saw him handing her a wad of notes once. At the time I didn't think anything of it. It might have been perfectly innocent. Probably was.'

'But?' Cade said curtly.

She frowned, trying to put into words something that hadn't been suspicious but which she'd remembered. 'When he realised I'd seen he told me why—he had a perfectly logical reason, but his reaction was odd. Not for long, and not so much that I was at all suspicious, but just a bit *off*.'

Keen-eyed, he asked her to write the woman's name down, and when she hesitated once more, gave a hard, mirthless smile. 'Are you worried I might hound her too? I never make the same mistake twice,' he said brusquely. 'Taryn, I've treated you abominably. Whatever I can do for you I'll do.'

'Nothing,' she returned automatically, chilled to the bone but holding herself together with an effort that came near to exhausting her.

He said harshly, 'Don't be a fool.'

Taryn's heart contracted, but she steadied her voice enough to be able to say, 'I accept your apology. You had what you thought were good reasons for your mistake—and I understand why you wanted to punish someone who took away your brother's hope.'

'He could have asked for help, booked himself into rehab.'

'Poor Peter,' she said, her voice uneven. 'Would you have helped him?'

'Of course.'

She believed him. 'And surely your parents wouldn't have turned against him?'

He wasn't nearly so quick to answer this time. 'At first they'd have been shocked and intensely disappointed, but they loved him. They'd have tried to help him. I had no idea he thought he'd failed them, and I'm sure they didn't suspect either. If they had, they'd have reassured him.'

Something about his words made Taryn say, 'You speak of them in the past tense.'

He shrugged. 'My father died of a heart attack two weeks after Peter's funeral, and my mother walked out in front of a car a few weeks later.' After a glance at her horrified face, he said immediately, 'No, she didn't intend to. She'll be in a wheelchair for the rest of her life.'

More than anything, Taryn longed to put her arms around him, give him what comfort she could. She didn't. His tone was a keep-off sign, a message reinforced by the jutting lift of his chin, taut stance and steely eyes.

She said quietly, 'I'm so sorry.'

'You have nothing to be sorry about.' As though he couldn't wait to be rid of her, he went on, 'I'll get you back to New Zealand straightaway.'

Within twelve hours she was in Aramuhu, listening to

her landlord while he told her that the sleepout needed urgent repairs and she'd have to find somewhere else to live.

She nodded and must have appeared quite normal because he said, 'I'm sorry, Taryn. The roof's started to leak and I have to get it all repaired before the kiwi fruit pickers come in. You'll stay with us until you find somewhere else to live, of course.'

When he'd gone she sat down and let the slow, unbidden tears well into her eyes, farewelling the past, looking ahead at a future that loomed grey and joyless.

CHAPTER TWELVE

'TARYN, why won't you come with us?' Hands on her slender hips, her flatmate eyed her with exasperation. 'You're never going to get over The Mystery Lover by staying obstinately at home.'

Taryn's lazy smile hid the flash of pain that any mention of Cade always brought. 'I'm too tired to go halfway across Auckland for a concert—I walked up to the top of One Tree Hill this afternoon,' she said cheerfully. 'I'd be nodding off halfway through the first song.'

Isla grinned. 'You couldn't—the band's too loud. And you're not going to get over a broken heart by turning into a hermit.'

'I'm not a hermit,' Taryn told her. 'I'm an introvert. We enjoy being alone.'

Her flatmate wasn't going to be diverted. 'Piffle. It's just not *natural* for you to never go out with *anyone*.'

Taryn said with indignation, 'Stop exaggerating. I have gone out.'

'Friends don't count!' Isla flung her arms out in one of the dramatic gestures she did so well. 'Auckland has over a million people living here, half of them men, and quite a few of them looking for a gorgeous woman like you. But no, you ignore them all because you're still fixated on some man who did you wrong. You know how you're going to end up, don't you? You'll be an old maid, buying baby clothes for your friends' kids but never for your own. And it's such a waste because you're not only gorgeous, you're clever and nice as well, and you can cook and change a car tyre—the world *needs* your genes.'

'What's this about babies?' Taryn eyed her suspiciously. 'You're not trying to tell me you're pregnant, I hope?'

Isla snorted. 'You know better than that. Look, it's a fabulous night, just right for a concert in the Domain. I've got enough food and champagne to feed an army, and I happen to know that in our group there'll be one unattached, stunning man. You'll love the whole thing. And it will do you good.'

'Thanks for suggesting it, but no.'

Isla cast her eyes upwards. 'OK, OK, but I'm not giving up—I'll get you out sooner or later, just see if I don't. And that's both a threat and a promise.'

She turned away to gather up the picnic basket and a wrap, adding over her shoulder, 'Still, at least you're no longer looking quite so much like a ghost. You had me really worried for a while.'

'I'm fine,' Taryn said automatically. 'Go on, off you go. Have fun.'

'That's a given. See you.' Isla disappeared down the passage of the elderly villa she shared with her two flatmates. The other one, a man, was away for the weekend. Taryn liked them both and got on well with them, grateful for their uncomplicated friendship, just as she was grateful for the job she'd found in one of Auckland's smaller libraries.

She heard the front door open and Isla's voice, startled and then welcoming. 'Yes, she's here. In the living room—second door on the right. See you.'

Hastily, Taryn scrambled to her feet. She wasn't expecting a visitor.

The door opened and Cade walked in, somehow seeming taller than she remembered, she thought confusedly above the urgent clamour of her heart. Her stomach dropped and then a great surge of joy burst through her.

He stopped just inside the door, gaze hardening as he examined her. When her tension reached near-screaming point, he said, 'You've lost weight.'

Her head came up. Reining in the urgent need to feast her eyes on him, she said astringently, 'Thank you for that. *You* don't appear to have changed at all. How did you know where I live?'

'I've known since you got here,' he said, adding, 'and any changes in me are internal, but they're there. Are you going to ask me to sit down?'

Taryn cast a desperate glance around the room, furnished in cast-offs from Isla's parents, who were short. 'Yes, of course. The sofa, I think.'

Afraid to ask why he'd come, what he wanted, she sank into a chair, only to scramble up again. 'I'm afraid I haven't got anything to drink—not alcohol, I mean. Would you like some coffee? Or tea?' She was babbling and he knew it.

'No, thank you,' he said curtly. 'How are you?'

She managed to rake up enough composure to say, 'I'm fine. Thank you. Very well, in fact.' Struggling to control the wild jumble of emotions churning through her, she sat down again. 'How are things with you?'

Shrugging, he said in his driest tone, 'Fine. I thought you'd like to know that Peter's supplier is in custody now. And yes, the go-between was Andrée Brown—who cheated Peter by telling him the dealer was demanding more and more money. In effect, she drove him to his death. She's being investigated for fraud and drug trafficking.'

Taryn grimaced, relieved to have something concrete to fix on. 'I'm glad. It's been worrying me that Peter might never be avenged. It was kind of you to come and tell me.'

Cade said harshly, 'You deserved to know. And I don't consider bringing them to account to be revenge—it's a simple matter of justice.'

Taryn realised every muscle was painfully tight, and that she was holding her breath. Forcing herself to exhale, she said, 'You said you always knew where I was—how?'

'I had someone keep an eye on you.' His mouth curved as he met her seething glance.

'Why?'

He shrugged. 'To make sure you were all right.'

Taryn didn't dare look at him in case the hope that bloomed so swiftly—so foolishly—was baseless. She said steadily, 'I'm all right, so you can go. Nothing can take away the fact that if I hadn't laughed at Peter and refused his proposal he'd probably be alive today.'

'It's no use going over what can't be changed.' He shrugged. 'You weren't to know—he must have gone to incredible lengths to hide his addiction from you—from everyone—as well as his dependence on that woman for them.'

Something shifted in Taryn's heart, and the grief that had weighed her down since she'd left Fala'isi eased a little.

Uncompromisingly, he continued, 'We didn't understand how fragile he was because he took pains to prevent anyone from seeing it. Nobody could help him because he wouldn't let us see he needed it. We can wallow in guilt until we die, but it's not going to help Peter.'

Taryn swallowed. 'You sound so hard.'

He said harshly, 'I am hard, Taryn. I suspect the three years I spent with an addict mother toughened me. And the fact that she was an addict probably explains why Peter would have moved heaven and earth to keep me from finding out about his addiction.'

Taryn dragged in a deep breath. 'What happened to your mother?'

'She died soon after I went to the Coopers.'

'Your grandmother must have loved you,' Taryn said swiftly. 'Babies need love to be able to survive, and you not only survived, but you learned to love your foster-parents, and Peter when he arrived in the family. You're not that hard.'

He shrugged. 'That sort of love, yes, but until I met you I wondered if I'd ever be able to love a woman in the way Harold Cooper loved Isabel.'

Inside Taryn wild hope mingled with bitter regret. Heat staining her cheeks, she met his unwavering regard with slightly raised brows. 'And after you met me?'

'I decided to use the attraction between us to get the information I wanted from you.' He stopped, then went on as though the words were dragged from him, 'But I made love to you because I couldn't stop myself.'

Her heart leapt and the pulse in her throat beat heavily, but she didn't dare let hope persuade her into more illusions. Mutely, she waited for whatever was to come next.

'When we were together I didn't think of Peter.' He

spoke carefully, his face bleak yet determined. 'I was too concerned about hiding my response to you. Just by being yourself, you wrecked my logical plan to win your trust so you'd confide in me.'

'Logical?' she demanded, suddenly furious. 'Cold-blooded, more like.'

He frowned. 'Yes.' He paused, then said, 'I *am* cold-blooded. Cold-blooded and arrogant.'

In a shaken voice, she said, 'That's not true—you loved the Coopers. You set out on this…this charade… because you loved Peter. The time with your birth mother must have been horrific, but I'm so glad you had those early years with your grandmother and that the Coopers took you in. They must have been wonderful people.'

He said evenly, 'They were—my mother still is. And I don't want sympathy. But a background like that probably explains why—until I met you—I found it easier to talk of wanting rather than loving. It's no excuse. I had no right to do to you what I did. I should have told you who I was when we met.'

'Why didn't you?' she asked, almost against her will, and braced herself for his answer.

He said quietly, 'I expected someone like Peter's other girlfriends—like the lovers I've had, someone charming and beautiful and chic and basically shallow, I suppose. Instead, I saw a girl with a hose trying to put out a fire she had every reason to know would ultimately get away from her, possibly put her in danger. A woman who was beautiful under a layer of smoke and sweat, a woman who ordered me around.' He stopped, then said with an odd catch in his voice, 'A woman I could love. And every sensible thought went flying out of my head. Oh, I thought I was in control, but all I wanted was to get to know you, to find out what sort of person you were. I wouldn't—couldn't—accept that I'd fallen in love at first sight.'

Taryn went white. She stared at his controlled face, the only sign of emotion a tiny pulse flicking in his angular jaw. He *couldn't* have said what she thought she'd heard.

'I'm making a total botch of this,' he said curtly. 'I didn't believe I could love. But I did, even when I was telling myself that all I was doing was finding out why Peter had killed himself. And every day that passed I fell deeper and deeper in love with you without recognising it or accepting it. Although I told myself I needed to give you chances to talk about Peter, I really didn't want to know.'

He got to his feet. Unable to stay where she was, she too stood, but couldn't move away from her chair. He paced across to the window and looked out at the rapidly darkening garden.

In a level voice that somehow showed strain, he said, 'I love you, Taryn. Even when I was accusing you—I loved you. I sent you back to New Zealand because I needed time to accept what I'd learned about my brother. And I needed to see my mother. But I came here because I couldn't stay away.'

For long moments she stared at him, his face drawn and stark, a charged tension leaping between them. He didn't move and she couldn't take a step towards him, held prisoner by caution that ached painfully through every cell in her body.

But she believed him, although it was too soon to feel anything other than relief, and a fierce desire to see everything out in the open after all the lies and secrets.

She said, 'That connection between us—I felt it

too. I'd never have made love with you so quickly—so easily—if I hadn't somehow known that beneath the hunger and the excitement there was more. I didn't know what the *more* was, but it was always there, from the moment I saw you.'

He said her name on a long, outgoing breath, and covered the distance between them in two long strides.

But, half a pace away, he stopped and examined her face with a gaze so keen she had to fight the urge to close her eyes against it. His voice was deep and hard when he demanded, 'You're sure?'

'Yes,' she said with all her heart. 'Living without you has been a lesson in endurance, but it's made me utterly sure.' She gave a half smile and searched his beloved face. 'Are you?'

'Sure you deserve more than I can give you,' he said quietly. 'These past interminable weeks have shown me that without you my life is empty and useless, bleak and joyless. Taryn, I need you to make it complete.'

As though the admission opened some sort of channel he took that final step. Her eyes brimmed when his arms tightened around her to bring her against his lean, strong body.

'Don't,' he said in an anguished voice. 'Don't cry, my love, my dearest heart. I don't deserve you, but I'll spend the rest of my life making you happy. I feel like an alien, dumped onto a strange, unknown planet with no support. It's like nothing I've ever experienced before. Once I'd realised I was falling in love, I was scared witless.'

She gave a little broken laugh. 'I understand the feeling. It's beyond comprehension. These past weeks have been…bleak. Hollow—just going through the motions.'

'Exactly. And, as I'm being honest about my feelings,

I must admit I hoped I'd get over it.' His smile twisted. 'I tried to convince myself that loving you was an aberration, something that would die once you left. In fact, I felt like that feral five-year-old—at the mercy of something so much bigger than myself I had to protect myself in any way I could.'

'Oh, no,' she whispered, understanding for the first time why he'd fought so hard against this miraculous love.

'It's all right,' he soothed swiftly. 'And that's a stupid way of describing how I feel. How on earth do people deal with such an overwhelming, uncivilised need? I had to come and ask you if there was any hope for me.'

Every cell in her body cried out for the relief and joy of his arms around her.

But she said, 'I love you with all my heart, everything I am.' And pressed her fingers over his mouth when he went to speak. 'Cade—there's still the fact that, although I didn't intend it, I caused your brother's death.'

'You didn't,' he said simply. 'Possibly, he hoped you'd rescue him but, in the end, the decision to take his life was his, no one else's.'

'Your mother—'

'She knows I'm here, and why. She's not happy about this, and yes,' he said quietly, still holding her, 'I won't say that didn't affect me but, although I love her, this is none of her business. If you come to me, Taryn, I will do my best to make you happy, to make sure that you never regret it.'

His oddly formal phrases were enough to banish the final cowardly fear.

'Is it going to be so simple?' she asked softly. 'Because I will do my best to make you happy too. Is that all it takes?'

She felt his body stir against her and a leap of excitement pulsed through her.

'I hope so. It hasn't been easy for either of us,' he said quietly. 'I had to struggle with the knowledge that I'd done you a grave wrong, one I regret bitterly. Except that out of it has come this utter commitment to you—one without any reservations.'

Taryn's heart swelled and, lifting her face so she could kiss him, she said against his mouth, 'I love you so much.'

A year later, with small Teresa Rose Peredur sleeping in her arms, Taryn watched her husband come across the room.

Love misted her eyes. She'd never been so happy as in these past months. He'd supported her through her pregnancy and been with her during their daughter's birth, and he'd been wonderful in his dealings with her parents. Not only had he charmed them and won their respect, but he'd financed the trust they'd been trying to set up, so that by the time they gave up their practice there would be local doctors and nurses to take over.

Relations with his mother were still strained. She'd made her wheelchair the reason for not attending their wedding, and she wouldn't stay with them or visit them in the house they'd bought in Buckinghamshire, but Taryn hoped that time would ease Isabel Cooper's reservations.

'Our darling daughter is going to have your nose,' Taryn said happily, turning so Cade could look at the baby's face. 'It's stopped being snub and is turning into a definite aquiline.'

He laughed, scooping the baby from her arms. 'My poor little treasure,' he said in the voice he reserved for his daughter. 'Not that it isn't a perfectly efficient nose, but it's going to look a trifle odd in that beautiful face you've inherited from your mother.'

'It will give it character,' Taryn said firmly.

He laid the baby in her crib and came across and kissed his wife. 'My mother is coming up to London next week and asked if she could stay here a couple of nights,' he said, watching her keenly.

Elation filled her. 'I'm glad,' she said, hugging him. 'It's the first step, isn't it?'

'Yes, I think so,' he said without hesitation. 'She knows you a little better now, and she's accepted that whatever happened between you and Peter was not your fault.'

'I'm so glad.' It seemed inadequate to describe the relief she felt, but a glance at his face told her he understood.

He said, 'She'd been worried about him for some time, but he wouldn't confide in her. And she suspected drugs—that you might have introduced him to them. But when it came out at the trial that he'd been sleeping with that Brown woman, she accepted that your reaction to Peter's proposal wasn't as cruel as it seemed.'

Andrée Brown and the man who'd supplied her with drugs were both in prison.

Taryn glanced across at the sleeping baby. 'Even if we take Teresa to see my parents often, a child needs at least one grandparent close by. And your mother made such a brilliant job with you, I'm sure she can teach me a lot.'

He laughed and kissed her again, and they left the nursery for their own room. As he started to change out of his business clothes, Cade said, 'Ready for next week?'

'Just about,' she said cheerfully.

Next week they were visiting her parents in Vanuatu. It would be the first time they'd seen their granddaughter, and she was excited.

'I thought you might like to drop in on the Chapmans,' he said. 'They've offered us the *fale* in Fala'isi.'

Where they'd first made love, where they'd married and spent their honeymoon...

'Lovely,' Taryn said, and hugged him exuberantly. Happiness expanded inside her, filling her with delight, but she said a little wistfully, 'It's a pity everyone can't have an ending like ours, isn't it.'

'Happy ever after?' he teased. 'My romantic love...'

'Only it's not an ending, is it,' she said soberly. 'It's a series of beginnings too, and they won't all be happy ones.'

'We'll deal with anything.' They exchanged a long look, one of perfect trust.

Heart swelling, Taryn nodded. 'Yes,' she said, smiling at his beloved arrogant face with perfect confidence. 'Whatever happens, we'll cope because we love each other. It really *is* that simple.'

TEMPTING THE BILLIONAIRE

NIOBIA BRYANT

As always, for my mama/my guardian angel,

Letha 'Bird' Bryant

Chapter 1

September 2018
Cabrera, Dominican Republic

Thud-thud-thud-thud-thud-thud.

Chance Castillo heard the pounding of his sneakered feet beating against the packed dirt as he ran up the tree-lined path breaking through the dense trees and royal palms. He made his way up the mountains that appeared green and lush against the blue skies when viewed from a distance. He didn't break his pace until he reached the top. His lean but strong muscular frame was drenched in sweat, and his heart pounded intensely in that way after great exertion—which for him was sex or running.

I've had way more of the latter lately.

He pulled his hand towel from the rim of his basketball shorts and wiped the sweat from his face and neck as he sat atop a large moss-covered rock, propping his elbows on his knees. As his pulse began to slowly decelerate, Chance looked around at his tranquil surroundings. He was surrounded by shades of green, from vibrant emerald to the muted tones of sage and olive. The smell of earth and nature was thick. He inhaled deeply, knowing he would miss his morning run from his secluded villa down along the white sand beach of the shoreline of the Atlantic Ocean to the surrounding mountains and cliff side.

His mother, Esmerelda Diaz, had transplanted her love of her beautiful hometown of Cabrera to him. As a kid, he had loved her stories of growing up on a small farm in the hills overlooking the coast in the northern region of the Dominican Republic. Her family members were hardworking farmers of fruits and vegetables whose livelihood depended on their crops. She spoke of days more bad than good. Plenty of struggle. Sometimes just a small meal away from hunger. Money spent on nothing more than bare necessities. Her life was filled with more coastal tranquility than wealth, but her memories were of a small family working hard in humble surroundings and enjoying the simple life they led.

Chance squinted his deep-set chestnut-brown eyes as he looked around at the higher elevation of the small town that was ripe with hills, oceanfront cliffs and mountains as green as emeralds. Fortunately, the town had not yet been overtaken by traffic and congestion like neighboring tourist traps. Still, there were a good number of people from other countries living in the town, experiencing the vivid Latino culture and enjoying the excellent exchange rate of American dollars while retaining their citizenship to their home country.

Chance chuckled. *Technically,* I *am an expat.*

He was a United States citizen, and although he had been living in Cabrera for the last eight months, he had every intention of returning to the States. *Back to my life.*

His brows deepened as he frowned a bit and turned his head to look off in the distance. The sun was setting, and he could just make out the outline of his sprawling two-story beachfront villa. It was the epitome of luxury living, with its private beach and sweeping views of the surrounding mountain ranges, tranquil waters, and azure skies.

It was the best his money could buy.

And seeing the smile on his mother's face when he purchased it two years prior had been worth every cent. Never had he seen her so proud. It was everything she worked for as an Afro-Dominican single mother with a broken heart and a low-paying job as a nursing assistant who was determined her son not get lost in the shuffle of the tough streets of the Soundview section of the Bronx, New York.

He still shook his head in wonder at the sacrifices the petite beauty had made for him to have a better life. Chance was ten when Esmerelda began working double shifts as a certified nursing assistant to move them out of their apartment in the Soundview projects to a better neighborhood. It meant taking on higher rent and a longer commute to her job, but she felt it was worth the sacrifice to be closer to the fringes of the Upper East Side because she wanted him to attend the elite Manhattan private academy The Dalton School. Although she applied for scholarships, she fought hard to pay his annual tuition and fees while keeping them clothed, fed and with a roof over their heads.

Chance's heart swelled with love for his mother. He'd never forgotten or taken her sacrifice for granted. It motivated him. Her happiness was his fuel through the tough days adjusting to being the poor kid who felt different from his classmates. He went on to finish at Dalton and graduated from Harvard with a degree in accounting and finance. While making a good living in finance, six years later he became a self-made wealthy man in his own right after selling a project management app for well over $600 million. That, plus the dividends from smart investing, was rocketing him toward billionaire status. He had purchased a home in Alpine, New Jersey, for his mother and ordered her retirement—she gladly agreed.

That was three years ago.

I'm not the poor kid from the Bronx with the two uniforms and the cheap shoes anymore.

In the distance, Chance heard the up-tempo beat of Ozuna and Cardi B's "La Modelo." He looked back over his shoulder, and at the top of the hill there was a crown of bright lights. He rose from the boulder and flexed his broad shoulders as he jumped, bringing his knees to his muscled chest with ease before racing up the dirt-packed path of the hill as the darkness claimed the skies.

At the top everything intensified. The music. The smell of richly seasoned foods being cooked in the outdoor kitchen. The bright lights adorning the wooden planks of the large pergola. And the laughter and voices of his extended family all settled around the carved wooden benches, or dancing in the center of the tiled patio. The scent of the fruit of the towering royal palm trees filled the air as the firm trunks seemed gathered around the small farming property to offer privacy.

The three-bedroom villa with its one lone bathroom and barely an acre of land was modest in comparison with his beachfront estate, but it was here among his cousins, with the night pulsing with the sounds of music and laughter, that he felt warmth and comfort.

Mi familia.

He came to a stop, just barely shaded by the darkness, and looked at his petite, dark-haired mother whose brown complexion hinted at the history of a large majority of Dominicans having African ancestry due to the slave trade of the early 1700s. She stood before a rustic wood-fired oven, stirring the ingredients in a cast-iron pot as she moved her hips and shoulders in sync to the music. He chuckled as she sang along with Cardi B's part of the song and raised the large wooden spoon she held in the air.

Everyone cheered and clapped when she tackled the rap part, as well.

Esmerelda Diaz was his mother and everyone's beloved. Although only forty-nine, she was the last of the Diaz elders. The baby girl who grew up to lead their descendants.

His mother turned and spotted him standing there. Her dark, doe-shaped eyes lit up as if she didn't have her own suite on his estate and had not fixed him *pescado con coco* for lunch. His stomach grumbled at the thought of the snapper fish cooked in coconut sauce.

"Chance!" she exclaimed, waving him over. *"Mira. Mira. Mira."*

The nine members of his extended family all looked over to him and waved as they greeted him. His cousin Carlos, a rotund, strong man in his late twenties, came over to press an ice-cold green bottle of Presidente beer in his hand as he slapped him soundly on the back in greeting.

This was the home of Carlos, his wife and four small children. He owned and operated farmlands of just three acres only a few hundred yards from the villa and was proud of his work, like many other Dominican farmers, providing locally grown fruits and vegetables and taking care of his family. Chance respected his cousin's hard work ethic and enjoyed plenty of his harvest during his time in the country. In kind, he knew his family respected him for the success he had made of his life back in the Estados Unidos.

"Tough day?" Chance asked.

Carlos shrugged one shoulder. "Same as always. And you, *primo*?" he asked with a playful side-eye and a chuckle before he took a swig of his own beer.

Chance laughed. His days of finance work and the development of his app had never been physically hard, and now that he just served as a consultant to the firm that'd purchased his app, the majority of his time was spent maintaining his toned physique and enjoying the fruits of his labor. Life was good, with his private jet, his estate in Cabrera and his permanent one in Alpine, New Jersey, and the ability to do whatever he wanted, whenever he chose. And during this time of his life, he chose to travel, enjoy fine food and wine, and spare himself nothing.

His days of struggling were over. As were his days of feeling less than for having less than.

"Excuse me, I'm starving," he said, moving past his younger cousin to reach his mother.

She smiled up at him before turning her attention back to stirring the pot.

"Sancocho de mariscos," he said in pleasure at the sight of the shellfish stew rich with shrimp, lobster, scallops, garlic, plantains, pumpkin and potatoes.

"Sí," Esmerelda said, tapping the spoon on the edge of the pot before setting it atop a folded towel on the wooden table next to the stove.

Living in a town directly off the Atlantic Ocean had its privileges. Although Chance was no stranger to traditional Dominican cooking. On her rare days off, his mother would go shopping and spend the day cooking and then freezing meals for him to enjoy while she was at work.

"Como estas?" she asked in rapid Spanish as she reached up to lightly tap the bottom of his chin with her fingertips.

"I'm fine," he assured her.

She shrugged one shoulder and slightly turned her lips downward as she tilted her head to the side. Translation? She didn't agree with him, but so be it.

The radio began to blare "Borracho de Amor" by Jose Manuel Calderon, and Chance was thankful. His mother gave a little yelp of pleasure and clapped rapidly at the sound of one of her favorite songs from the past before she grabbed the hand of her nephew Victor and began dancing the traditional *bachata*.

Chance took a seat at a wooden table and placed his beer on it as he watched his mother, alive and happy among her culture and her family. But as everyone focused on their dance, his attention was on the words of the song. As was common with traditional *bachata* music that was about heartache, pain and betrayal, it was a song of a man who turned to drinking after the heartache and pain caused by a woman's scorn. It was said that the tortured emotions displayed in the song fueled *bachata* dancers to release those emotions through dance.

Chance knew about heartache all too well.

His gut tightened into a knot at the memory of his former fiancée, Helena Guzman, running off with her lover and leaving him at the altar. In the beautiful blond-haired Afro-Cuban attorney he'd thought he found the one woman to spend his life with. She'd even agreed to give up her career as a successful attorney to travel the world with him.

But he'd been wrong. And made a fool of.

His anger at her was just beginning to thaw. His mother referred to her only as "Ese Rubio Diablo." The blond devil.

Cabrera had helped him to heal.

But now I'm headed home.

This celebration was his family's farewell to both him and his mother.

The daughter of his best friend since their days at Dalton, Alek Ansah, and his wife, Alessandra, had been born and he'd been appointed her godfather. He'd yet to see her in person; photos and FaceTime had sufficed, but now it was time to press kisses to the cheek of his godchild and do his duty at her upcoming baptism.

In the morning they would board his private plane and fly back to the States. She would return to the house he purchased for her in New Jersey, and he would be back at his estate in a house he'd foolishly thought he would share with his wife and their family one day.

Chance looked over into the shadowed trunks of the trees that surrounded the property as his thoughts went back to the day he was supposed to wed the woman he loved...

"I'm sorry, Chance, but I can't marry you," Helena said, standing before him in her custom wed-

ding dress and veil as they stood in the vestibule of the church.

For a moment, Chance just eyed her. His emotions raced one behind the other quickly, almost colliding, like dominoes set up to fall. Confusion. Fear. Pain.

"I am in love with someone else," she said, her eyes filled with her regret.

Anger.

Visions of her loving and being loved by another man burned him to his core like a branding. The anger spread across his body slowly, seeming to infuse every bit of him as the truth of her betrayal set in.

"How could you do this, Helena?" he asked, turning from her with a slash of his hand through the air, before immediately turning back with his blazing fury.

And his hurt.

That infuriated him further.

"How long?" he asked, his voice stiff.

"Chance," Helena said.

"Who is he?"

She held up her hands. "That is irrelevant," she said. "It is over. It is what it is, Chance."

"Who?" he asked again, unable to look at her.

"My ex, Jason."

The heat of his anger was soon replaced with the chill of his heart symbolically turning to stone. He stepped back from her, his jaw tightly clenched. "To hell with you," he said in a low and harsh whisper.

Long after she had gathered her voluminous skirt in her hands and rushed from the church to run down the stairs, straight into the waiting car of her lover,

Chance had stood there in the open doorway of the church and fought to come to grips with the explosive end of their whirlwind courtship.

Chance shook his head a bit to clear it of the memory, hating that nearly eight months later it still stung. The betrayal. The hurt. The dishonor.

Damn.

"*Baila conmigo*, Chance."

He turned his head to find Sofía, the best friend of Carlos's wife, extending her hand to him as she danced in place. She was a brown-skinned beauty with bright eyes, a warm smile and a shapely frame that drew the eye of men with ease. They had enjoyed one passionate night together a few months ago after a night of dancing, but both agreed it could be no more than that, with his plans to return to the States. And his desire to not be in another relationship.

Accepting her offer, he rose to his feet and took her hand, pulling her body closer to his as they danced the *bachata*. "You remember what happened the last time we danced?" he teased her, looking down into her lively eyes.

Sofía gave him a sultry smile before spinning away and then back to him. "I can't think of a better way to say goodbye," she said.

Chance couldn't agree more.

"Lord, help me get through this day."

Ngozi Johns cast a quick pleading look up to the fall skies as she zipped up the lightly quilted crimson running jacket she wore with a black long-sleeved T-shirt, leggings and sneakers. The sun was just beginning to rise, and the early morning air was crisp. She inhaled it deeply as she stretched her limbs and bent her frame into a few squats before jogging down the double level of stairs of her parents' five-bedroom, six-bathroom brick Colonial.

Her sneakered feet easily ate up the distance around the circular drive and down the long paved driveway to reach Azalea Street—like every street in the small but affluent town of Passion Grove, New Jersey, it was named after flowers.

Ngozi picked up the pace, barely noticing the estates she passed with the homes all set back from the street. Or the wrought iron lamppost on each corner breaking up the remaining darkness. Or the lone school in town, Passion Grove Middle School, on Rose Lane. Or the entire heart-shaped lake in the center of the town that residents lounged around in the summer and skated on in the winter.

She waved to local author Lance Millner, who was in the center of the body of water in his fishing boat, as he was every morning. The only time he was to be seen by his Passion Grove neighbors was during his time in the water, tossing his reel into the lake, or the rare occasions he visited the upscale grocery store on Main Street. In the distance, on the other side of the lake, was his large brick eight-bedroom home with curtains shielding the light from entering through any of the numerous windows. He lived alone and rarely had any guests. The man was as successful at being a recluse as he was at being a *New York Times* bestselling author.

He waved back.

It was a rushed move, hard and jerking, and looked more like he was swatting away a nagging fly than giving a greeting.

Ngozi smiled as she continued her run. With one movement that was as striking as flipping the middle finger, he confirmed his reputation as a lone wolf with no time to waste for anyone. When he did venture from his lakeside estate, his tall figure was always garbed in a field jacket and a boonie hat that shaded his face.

Passion Grove was the perfect place to come to enjoy high-scale living but avoid the bustle, noise and congestion of larger cities. Home to many wealthy young millennials, the town's population was under two thousand, with fewer than three hundred homes, each on an average of five or more acres. Very unlike Harlem, New York. She had enjoyed living in the city, soaking in the vibrancy of its atmosphere and culture and the beauty of its brownstones and its brown-skinned people—until a year ago. A year to the date, in fact.

When everything changed.

"Damn," she swore in a soft whisper as she shook her head, hoping to clear it.

Of her sadness. Her guilt.

Ngozi ran harder, wishing it were as easy to outrace her feelings.

It wasn't.

She came to a stop on the corner of Marigold and Larkspur, pressing her hand to her heaving chest as her heart continued to race, even though she did not. She grimaced as she released a shaky breath. She knew the day would be hard.

It had been only a year.

Ngozi bit her bottom lip and began jogging in place to maintain the speed of her heartbeat before she finally gathered enough strength to push aside her worries and continue her morning run. She needed to finish. She needed to know there was true hope that one day her guilt and remorse would no longer hinder her.

She continued her run, noticing that outside of the echo of her colorful sneakers pounding on the pavement, the chirp of birds and errant barks of dogs occasionally broke the silence. With the town comprising sizable estates that were all set back three hundred or more feet from the streets—per a local ordinance—the noise was at a minimum.

"Good morning, Counselor."

Ngozi looked over her shoulder to find the town's police chief standing on the porch of the Victorian home that had once served as the town's mercantile during the early days of its creation in the 1900s. For the last fifty years, it had served as the police station and was more than sufficient for the small town. She turned, jogging in place as she looked up at the tall and sturdy blond man who looked as if his uniform was a size—maybe two—too small. "Morning, Chief

Ransom," she greeted him as she checked her pulse against the Fitbit. "Care to join me?"

He threw his head back and laughed, almost causing his brown Stetson hat to fall from his head. "No, no, no," he said, looking at her with a broad smile that caused the slight crinkles at the corners of his brown eyes to deepen. He patted his slightly rounded belly. "My better half loves everything just as it is."

Eloise, his wife, was as thin as a broomstick. Opposites clearly attracted because it was clear to all that they were deeply in love. The couple resided in the lone apartment in the entire town—the one directly above the police station. It was a perk of accepting the position as chief. It would be absurd to expect a public servant to afford one of the costly estates of Passion Grove—all valued at seven figures or more.

"You have any future clients for me?" Ngozi asked, biting her inner cheek to keep from smiling.

"In Passion Grove?" the chief balked. "*No* way."

She shrugged both her shoulders. "Just thought I'd ask," she said, running backward before she waved and turned to race forward down the street.

As a successful New York criminal defense attorney, Ngozi Johns was familiar with the tristate area's high-crime places. Passion Grove definitely was not counted among them. The chief had only two part-time deputies to assist him when there was a rare criminal act in the town, and so far that was limited to driving violations, not curbing a dog, jaywalking or the occasional shoplifting from the grocery store or lone upscale boutique by a thrill-seeking, bored housewife.

There were no apartment buildings or office buildings. No public transportation. Only stop signs, no traffic lights. There were strict limitations on commercial activity to maintain the small-town feel. Keeping up its beautiful aesthetic was a priority, with large pots on each street corner filled with plants or colorful perennial floras.

Like the police station, the less than dozen stores lining one side of Main Street were small converted homes that were relics from the town's incorporation in the early 1900s. She jogged past the gourmet grocery store that delivered, a few high-end boutiques, a dog groomer and the concierge service that supplied luxuries not available in town. Each business was adorned with crisp black awnings. She crossed the street to ignore the temptation of fresh-brewed coffee and fresh-baked goods wafting from La Boulangerie, the bakery whose delicacies were as sinfully delicious as the store was elegantly decorated like a French bistro.

She appreciated the serenity and beauty as she reached the garden that bloomed with colorful fall flowers, and soon was at the elaborate bronze sign welcoming everyone to Passion Grove. She tapped the back of it with gusto before taking a deep breath and starting the run back home.

Ngozi successfully kept her thoughts filled with upcoming depositions or cases. By the time she turned up the drive and spotted her parents' sprawling home, the sun was blazing in the sky and some of the chill had left the morning air. She felt less gloomy.

Thank you, God.

"Good morning, Ngozi."

Her heart pounded more from surprise at the sound of her father's deep voice than the run. She forced a pleasant smile and turned in the foyer to find her tall father, Horace Vincent, with deep brown skin that she'd inherited and low-cut silver hair, standing in the open door to his office. He was still in his silk pajamas, but files were in hand and he eyed her over the rim of his spectacles.

"Good morning, Daddy," she said, walking across the hardwood floors to press a tender kiss to his cheek. "I just finished my run."

Horace was a retired corporate and banking attorney who started Vincent and Associates Law over forty years ago. It was one of the top five hundred law firms in the country—a huge accomplishment for an African American man—and Ngozi was proud to be one of the firm's top criminal trial attorneys.

"Ngozi!"

The urge to wince rose quickly in her, but Ngozi was well practiced in hiding her true feelings from her parents. "Yes, Mama?" she asked, following her father into his office to find her mother leaning against the edge of the massive wooden desk in the center of the room. She was also still in her nightwear, a satin red floor-length gown and matching robe.

Even in her seventies, Valerie "Val" Vincent was the epitome of style, poise and confidence. Her silver bob was sleek and modern. She exercised daily and stuck to a vegan diet to maintain her size-eight figure. Her caramel-brown skin, high cheekbones, intelligent brown eyes and full mouth were beautiful even before her routine application of makeup. She was constantly mistaken for being in her fifties, but was regally proud of every year of her age.

And she was as brilliant as she was beautiful, having cultivated a career as a successful trial attorney before becoming a congresswoman and garnering respect for her political moves.

"I know today is difficult for you, Ngozi," Val said, her eyes soft and filled with the concern of a mother for her child.

As her soul withered, Ngozi kept her face stoic and her eyes vacant. She never wanted to be the cause for worry in her parents. "I'm fine, Mama," she lied with ease.

Her parents shared a look.

Ngozi diverted her eyes from them. They landed on the wedding photo sitting on the corner of her father's desk. She fought not to release a heavy breath. The day she wed Dennis Johns, she had put on a facade as well and played the role of the perfectly happy bride vowing to love the man she'd met in law school.

Until death do us part.

After only four years.

She was a widow at twenty-nine.

She blinked rapidly to keep the tears at bay.

"We want you to know there's no rush to leave," her father began.

Ngozi shifted her gaze back to them, giving them both a reassuring smile that was as false as the hair on the head of a cheap doll. It was well practiced.

I'm always pretending.

"When we suggested you move back home after Dennis's…passing, your mother and I were happy you accepted the offer, and we hope you'll stay awhile," Horace continued.

"Of course, Daddy," she said, widening her smile. "Who wants to leave a mansion with enough staff to make you think you're on vacation? I ain't going nowhere."

They both smiled, her show of humor seeming to bring them relief.

It was a pattern she was all too familiar with.

How would it feel to tell them no?

Her eyes went to the other frame on her father's desk and landed on the face of her older brother, Haaziq. More death.

She winced, unable to hide what his passing meant for her. Not just the loss of her brother from her life, but the role she accepted as defender of her parents' happiness. Losing their son, her brother, in an accidental drowning at the tender age of eight had deeply affected their family. Little six-year-old Ngozi, with her thick and coarse hair in long ponytails and glasses, had never wanted to be a hassle or let down her parents because of their grief. She'd always worn a bright smile, learned to pretend everything was perfect and always accepted that whatever they wanted for her was the right course of action.

"Let's all get ready for work, and I'm sure breakfast will be on the table by the time we're ready to go and conquer the world," Val said, lovingly stroking Horace's chin before rising to come over and squeeze her daughter's hand.

At the thought of another meal, Ngozi wished she had dipped inside the bakery, enjoyed the eye candy that was Bill the Blond and Buff Baker, and gobbled down one of the decadent treats he baked while resembling Paul Walker.

Bzzzzzz.

Ngozi reached for her iPhone from the small pocket of her jacket. "Excuse me," she said to her parents before turning and leaving the office.

She smiled genuinely as she answered the call. "The early baby gets the mother's milk, huh?" she teased, jogging up the wooden staircase with wrought iron railings with a beautiful scroll pattern.

"Right." Alessandra Dalmount-Ansah laughed. "The early bird has nothing on my baby. Believe that."

Alessandra was the co-CEO of the billion-dollar conglomerate the Ansah Dalmount Group, along with her husband, Alek Ansah. Ngozi served as her personal attorney, while corporate matters were handled by other attorneys at Vincent and Associates Law. The women had become closer when Ngozi successfully represented Alessandra when she was mistakenly arrested during a drug raid. She'd been in the wrong place at the absolute worst time, trying to save her cousin Marisa Martinez during a major drug binge.

"How's my godchild?" Ngozi asked, crossing the

stylishly decorated family room on the second level to reach one of the three-bedroom suites flanking the room.

"Full. Her latch game is serious."

They laughed.

The line went quiet just as Ngozi entered her suite and kicked off her sneakers before holding the phone between her ear and her shoulder as she unzipped and removed the lightweight jacket.

"How are you?" Alessandra asked, her concern for her friend clear.

"I'm good," Ngozi said immediately, as she dropped down onto one of the four leather recliners in the sitting area before the fireplace and the flat-screen television on the wall above it.

Liar, liar.

She closed her eyes and shook her head.

Then she heard a knock.

"Alessandra, can I call you back? Someone's at my door," she said, rising to her feet and crossing the room.

"Sure. See you at the baptism Sunday."

"Absolutely."

Ngozi ended the call and opened the door. Reeds, her parents' house manager, stood before her holding a tray with a large bronzed dome cover. She smiled at the man of average height with shortbread complexion, more freckles than stars in the sky and graying brownish-red hair in shoulder-length locks. "One day my mother is going to catch you," she said as she took the tray from him and removed the lid to reveal buttered grits, bacon, scrambled eggs and toast.

He shrugged and chuckled. "The rest of the staff wouldn't know what to do without me after all these years."

"I *know* that's right," Ngozi said with a playful wink.

"Just remember to at least eat the bowl of fruit at breakfast," Reeds said before he turned and began to whistle some jazzy tune. He stopped in the middle of the family room to glance back. "*Or* you could just tell your mother you're not vegan. Your choice."

Ngozi ignored his advice and stepped back into the room, knocking the door with her hip to push it closed.

Chapter 2

Alpine, New Jersey

The day of reckoning is here.

Chance splashed his face with water and pressed his hands to his cheeks before wiping the corner of his eyes with his thumb. He stood tall before the sink and eyed his reflection in the large leather-framed mirror above it. He released a heavy breath and studied himself, rubbing his hand over his low-cut fade haircut.

Today he would face his friends for the first time since what was supposed to be his wedding day. With the last bit of pride and bravado he could muster, Chance had stood before all those people and admitted that the wedding was called off. The swell of gasps of shock and whispers had filled the church as he strode down the aisle with nearly every eye locked on his stoic expression. He would admit to no one the embarrassment he felt, and didn't allow his head to sink one bit until he left the church.

He had instructed Alek to have the wedding planner, Olivia Joy, turn the reception into a party, but he had not attended the event. The idea of being pitied or ridiculed by Helena's betrayal was too strong for him to swallow. He spent what was supposed to be his wedding night ignoring all attempts at communicating with him as he nursed a bottle of pricey Dos Lunas Grand Reserve tequila, stewed in his anger and envisioned Helena being bedded by her lover.

Early that next morning, with a hangover from hell, he boarded his private jet and flew to Cabrera with no foreseeable plans to return. His consultant work for the same firm that purchased his app could be handled from anywhere in the world with Wi-Fi. All he knew was he had to get away. So he did.

Now I'm back.

He eyed his reflection, hating the nerves and anxiousness he felt.

It took him back to his school days as a poor brown-skinned Latino kid from the Bronx trying his best not to feel less than around students who were predominantly white and absolutely from wealthy families.

He flexed his arms and bent his head toward each of his shoulders, instinctively trying to diminish those feelings from his youth. "Let's get this over with," he mumbled under his breath, removing his towel and drying his body before tossing it over the smoothed edge of the cast concrete in the center of the dark and modern bathroom.

He quickly swiped on his deodorant and lightly sprayed on cologne from one of the ten bottles sitting on a long ebony wood tray in the space between the large tray sinks atop the concrete vanity.

Naked, he strode across the heated marble floors and through the opening in the tinted-glass wall to his loft-style bedroom suite. His motorized open-front closets lined the entire wall behind his king-size Monarch Vi-Spring bed, but the suit he'd already selected was laid across one of the custom chaise longues at the foot of it. His long and thick member swayed across his thighs as he moved to pull on his snug boxers, having to adjust it to comfort before he finished dressing in silk socks, his off-white wool-silk suit and a matching open-neck shirt. The fit against his athletic frame spoke to its custom tailoring and his desire for both quality and style.

Not wanting to run late, he hurriedly selected one of a dozen watches to buckle around his wrist while slipping on shoes that were almost as comfortable as his bed.

Life was good when it came to the creature comforts. The days of squeaky rubber-sole shoes from the dollar store were over.

I hated to walk in 'em, he remembered. *Felt like everyone heard me coming.*

He rushed through his opulent two-story villa-style mansion, which sat on two gated acres in Alpine, New Jersey, styled in muted tasteful decor with vibrant pops of color that were a testament to his dynamic Latino culture. Chance lived alone in the six-bedroom luxury home, and he usually kept music or his 4K televisions on to break the silence. Hip-hop from the 1990s played from the sound system, and he rapped along to Big Daddy Kane's "Ain't No Half-Steppin'" as he grabbed his keys from beside the glass-blown structures of nude women atop the table in the center of the foyer.

Soon he was out the double front doors and behind the wheel of his black-on-black Ferrari 488 Pista, taking I-280 to Passion Grove. He drove the supercar with ease with one hand, effortlessly switching lanes on the interstate as he lightly tapped his fist against his knee to the music playing. The commute was hassle-free because it was Sunday morning, and he was grateful as he finally guided the vehicle down the exit ramp and made his way through the small town. He didn't think he could find an upscale town more laid-back than Alpine, but Passion Grove proved him wrong.

A city without traffic lights in 2018?

Chance felt bored already. He still found it hard to believe that his fun-loving best friend, Alek—who was born into a billionaire dynasty—chose the small town to live in after jet-setting all over the world.

Real love will make you do unexpected things.

His and Helena's plans had been to travel the world and explore new adventures after they were wed.

And look how that turned out.

His hand gripped the steering wheel, lightening the color of his skin across his knuckles. He was glad to finally make it to Alek and Alessandra's, accelerating up the private mile-long paved street leading to the expansive twenty-five-acre estate until he reached the twelve-foot-tall wrought iron gate with the letter *D* in bronzed scroll in the center.

Alessandra had inherited the estate upon the death of her father, Frances Dalmount, who co-owned the billionaire conglomerate the Ansah Dalmount Group, along with Alek's father, the late Kwame Ansah. When Alessandra and Alek wed last year, they'd decided to make the Passion Grove estate their main home, while maintaining both his Manhattan and London penthouse apartments, and the vacation estate they built together on their private island in upstate New York.

After getting checked in by security via video surveillance, Chance drove through the open gates and soon was pulling up to the massive stone French Tudor. He hopped out and pressed a tip into the hand of one of the valets his friends were using for the day to park the vehicles.

He jogged up the stairs and accepted a flute of champagne from the tray being held by a servant. "Thank you," he said with a nod of his head as he entered the foyer through the open double doors.

"Thanks so much."

Chance paused and turned at the soft voice. He froze with his drink still raised to his mouth as he eyed the woman over the rim of the crystal flute. His heart began to pound, and his breath caught in his throat. *Well, damn...*

She was beautiful. Tall and shapely with skin as dark and smooth as melted chocolate. Long and loose waves of her beyond-shoulder-length ebony hair framed her oval face with high cheekbones, bright and clear brown doe-like eyes, and a nose bringing forth a regal beauty similar to the women of Somalia. The long-sleeved white lace dress she wore clung to her frame with a V-neck highlighting her small but plump breasts, and a wide skirt above long shapely legs. Her gold accessories gave her skin further sheen.

As she walked past the valet with a soft reserved smile, the wind shifted, causing her hair to drift back from her face as she moved with confident long strides that flexed the toned muscles of her legs and caused the skirt of her dress to flounce around her thighs. He couldn't take his eyes off her and had no desire to do so. She was a treat, and the very sight of her as she easily jogged up the stairs made him hunger for her.

He smiled like a wolf behind his flute as his eyes dipped to take her in from head to delicious feet displayed in open-toe sandals with tassels that were sexy.

Who is she?

He felt excited with each step that brought her closer to him. When she paused to take her own flute of champagne, his hawk-like eyes locked on how the flesh of her mouth pressed against the crystal, leaving a light stain of her lip gloss on the glass.

Who is she? And does she want to leave with me later?

The prospect of that made his return to the States completely worth it.

"There you are, Chance."

With regret, he turned from his temptress. "Here I am," he agreed, genuinely smiling at Alessandra Dalmount-Ansah as she walked up to him, looking beautiful in a white light georgette dress with perfect tailoring.

She grabbed his upper arms lightly as she rose up on the tips of her shoes to press a kiss to his cheek. "Welcome home, Chance," she said with warmth, looking up at him with sympathetic eyes as she raised a hand to lightly tap his chin. "You good?"

He nodded, hating the unease he felt. *How much more of this pity will there be today?* he wondered, purposefully turning from her to eye the beauty in peach as she stepped inside the foyer.

Her eyes landed on his, and he gave that lingering stare and slow once-over that was nothing but pure appreciation and a desire to know more. Her brows arched a bit and her mouth gaped as she gave him the hint of a smile that was just enough to give him hope.

"Hey, Ngozi," Alessandra said, moving past Chance to kiss her cheek in welcome.

So, this is Ngozi? Alessandra's best friend and attorney. Brains and beauty. Just as Alessandra had said to him so many times.

Her eyes left him, and Chance felt the loss, finally

taking a sip of the champagne he instantly recognized as Armand de Brignac.

"That's right, you two have never met," Alessandra said, reaching for one of Ngozi's hands and then one of Chance's. "Chance Castillo, godfather, meet Ngozi Johns, godmother."

She pressed their hands together.

Their eyes met.

As they clasped hands, Chance stroked the pulse at her wrist with his thumb, enjoying how it pounded. It matched his own.

Ngozi felt breathless.

Her first sight of Chance Castillo as she stepped inside the house had made her entire body tingle with excitement. He was tall with an athletic frame that could not be denied in his tailored suit. His stance as he stood there eyeing her over the rim of his glass spoke of unleashed power. A man. A strong man built for pleasure. Not just handsome, with his medium-brown complexion and angular features softened by lips and intensified by his deep-set eyes, the shadow of a beard and his low-cut ebony hair…but intriguing. Something about him had instantly drawn her in. Excited her. Made her curious. Forced her to wonder, *Who is he?*

And now, as Ngozi stood there with her hand seemingly engulfed by his with his thumb gently grazing her pulse, she shivered and sought control of her body. Her pulse. Her heartbeat. Her breaths.

The pounding of the sweet fleshy bud nestled between the lips of her core. *Damn.*

All of it surprised her. Never had she had such an instantaneous reaction to a man before.

Needing to be released from the spell he cast upon her, Ngozi pulled her hand from his and forced a smile that she hoped didn't look as awkward as it felt. "Nice to finally meet, Mr. Castillo," she said, proud of her restored cool composure.

It was all a sham, and she deserved an award for the performance.

"Chance," he offered, sliding the hand she once held into the pocket of his slacks.

"Right this way, y'all," Alessandra said, leading them across the stately round foyer, past the staircase and down the hall into the family room, where the glass doors were retracted, creating an entertaining space that flowed with people lounging inside or outside on the patio or around the pool.

Alek spotted them and excused himself from a couple he was talking with to cross the room to them. It was similar to watching a politician or other public figure as he spoke to each person who stopped him while still moving toward them. The man was charismatic.

Ngozi took a sip of her champagne as she glanced at Alessandra over the rim. The look in her friend's eyes as she watched her husband was nothing but love. She'd found her happily-ever-after.

A twinge of pain radiated across her chest, and Ngozi forced herself to smile in spite of it.

"Careful, Ngozi," Alessandra said, holding out her arm in front of her. "Don't get in the way of this bro love, girl."

Ngozi looked on as Chance took a few strides to meet Alek. The men, equally handsome, confident and strong in build, clasped hands and then moved in for a brotherly hug complete with a solid slap of their hand against the other's back. It barely lasted a moment, but it was clear they were close.

As the men talked quietly to one another, Ngozi eyed Chance's profile, surprised by her reaction to him. And she still felt a tingle of awareness and a thrill that ruffled her feathers. He smiled at something Alek said, and her stomach clenched as a handsome face was instantly transformed into a beautiful one.

"He looks happy," Alessandra said softly to herself.

Ngozi glanced over at her, seeing the hope on her face that her words were true. She remembered Alessandra explaining Chance's absence because he had been left at the altar by his fiancée and was in the Dominican Republic recovering from his heartache. That had been nearly nine months ago.

What woman would leave him behind?

Ngozi had never asked for any more details than Alessandra offered, but that was before she'd seen him. Now a dozen or more questions flew to mind with ease. Her curiosity was piqued.

"I'm going up to get the baby," Alessandra said. "Be right back."

Ngozi glanced around the room, raising her flute

in toast to those she knew professionally or personally. When her eyes landed back on the men, she found Chance's eyes on her. She gasped a little. Her pulse raced.

He gave her a wolfish grin—slow and devastating—as he locked his gaze with hers. They made their way toward her, and Ngozi forced herself to look away as she felt a shiver race down her spine.

"I wanted to finally greet you, Ngozi," Alek said.

She looked up at him with a smile. "I thought I was invisible," she teased, presenting her cheek for a kiss as she pretended Chance was not standing there, as well.

"Chance told me Alessandra already made the introductions between you two," Alek said.

She stiffened her back and glanced up at Chance. "Yes, it's nice to finally put a face to the name," she said.

"Same here," he agreed. "Especially since we're sharing godparent duties."

"Right, right," she agreed with a genuine smile. "We'll rock, paper, scissors for overnight stays."

He opened his mouth and then closed it, biting his bottom lip as if to refrain himself. He shared a brief look with Alek, who then shook his head and chuckled.

And she knew—she just *knew*—Chance was going to say they could have overnights together.

"Really, fellas?" she asked, eyeing them both like a teacher reprimanding naughty schoolboys.

"What?" they both asked innocently in unison.

Ngozi was surprised to see Alek, normally severe and businesslike, standing before her with mirth in his eyes. "So, we all have that one thing or one person—a vice—that makes us different. Today, Alek Ansah," she said before turning to face Chance, "I have met yours."

Chance's smile broadened as he looked down at her. "And what—or who—makes you different, Ngozi Johns?"

She loved how her name sounded on his lips. "Oh, is there something about me that needs fixing?" she asked, forcing herself not to quiver under his intense stare as she met it with one of her own.

"From what I can see, not one damn thing," Chance responded with ease, his voice deep and masculine.

"On *that* note," Alek said, clearing his throat as he looked from one to the other, "I'll take my leave."

And he did, leaving them alone.

"Ngozi!"

At the sound of her name, Ngozi broke their stare and turned to find Marisa Martinez standing beside her. She gave the petite woman with a wild mane of shoulder-length curly hair a warm smile. "It's good to see you, Marisa," she said, her eyes taking in the clarity in the woman's eyes and feeling sweet relief.

The former party girl who lived hard and fast off the allowance she received from the Dalmount dynasty had developed an addiction to alcohol and drugs that put both her and Alessandra's freedom in jeopardy. As the head of the family, Alessandra felt it her obligation to guide and protect the entire clan made up of her two aunts, Leonora Dalmount and

Brunela Martinez, her cousin Victor Dalmount and his bride, Elisabetta, and Marisa, Brunela's daughter. That sense of duty had led Alessandra to seek out Marisa at a house party and to get caught in the middle of a police drug raid.

Ngozi was called on by her client to represent them both. The charges were dropped, but Alessandra had forced Marisa to either attend the long-term rehab program Ngozi arranged or be disowned.

Marisa chose the former, and six months later, she'd returned drug-free.

"I just wanted to thank you for everything you did to help me," Marisa said, before lifting up on her toes to give Ngozi an impromptu hug.

"Well, I thank you for not letting my hard work go to waste," she said, returning the hug. "You look good."

Marisa released her. "I feel better," she said, her eyes serious before she forced a smile and walked away with one last squeeze of Ngozi's hand.

She watched her walk over to join her mother and aunt Leonora by the fireplace. With her work as a criminal attorney who insisted on pro bono work and tough cases, Ngozi was well acquainted with thankful clients.

"I've heard you're one of the best attorneys on the East Coast."

Him.

Ngozi took a sip of her champagne as she eyed him with an arched brow. "Just the East Coast?" she teased.

He chuckled.

"I'm kidding," she rushed to say, reaching out to grasp his wrist.

His pulse pounded against her fingertips. She released him.

"La tentadora," Chance said.

The temptress.

Her entire body flushed with warmth.

Chance was Dominican on his mother's side, and like many other Afro-Latinos did appear to be what was standardly thought of as such. Much like Laz Alonso, Victor Cruz and Carmelo Anthony.

"Me das demasiado crédito," she said, loving the surprise that filled his deep brown eyes at her using his native tongue to tell him that he gave her too much credit.

"Ah! ¿Tu hablas español?" he asked.

"Yes, I speak Spanish," she answered with a nod.

"¿Pero alguna vez te ha susurrado un hombre en español mientras te hace el amor?"

Ngozi gasped in surprise and pleasure and excitement at his question of whether a man had whispered to her in Spanish while making love. She recovered quickly. "No," she answered him, before easing past his strong build and imposing presence to leave.

"Usted tiene algo que esperar," Chance said from behind her.

Then you have something to look forward to.

Chance Castillo.

She gave in to her own temptation and glanced back at him over her shoulder. He had turned his attention to greeting Alek's younger brother, Naim. She pressed her fingertips to her neck as she turned away, admitting regret that his attention was no longer on her.

In truth, she couldn't remember feeling that affected by a man in a long, long time.

She pursed her lips and released a stream of air, intending to calm herself.

Ngozi stopped a male waiter and set her near-empty flute on the tray. "Thank you," she said. Her stomach rumbled, and she looked around with a slight frown, hoping no one had heard it. Quickly, she turned and tapped the shoulder of the waiter. "Is there another one like you with a tray of hors d'oeuvres? A sista is hungry."

He chuckled and shook his head. "Not yet," he said. "The food will be served after the ceremonies."

Damn. Ngozi checked her platinum watch as he walked away.

She crossed the room and made her way outdoors. During the day, the September air was still pleasant. It was the early mornings and late nights that brought on a chill that reminded her summer was drawing to an end.

As she neared the Olympic-sized pool, she felt an urge to jump in and sink beneath the crystal clear depths to swim to the other end and back. Instead, she settled for slipping off one of her sandals to dip her toes in the water, causing it to ripple outward.

Dennis loved to swim.

She felt sadness, closing her eyes as she remembered his looking back at her over his shoulder before he dived into the deep end of her parents' pool back in some of the rare moments of free time they had during law school.

She smiled a bit, remembering how happy they were then.

That was a long time ago.

"Excuse me, Ms. Johns."

She was surprised by the same waiter who took her drink, now standing beside her with a sandwich on his tray.

"Courtesy of Olga, the house manager, per the request of Mr. Castillo," he said.

Ngozi looked up and bit back a smile at Chance standing in the open doorway, raising his flute to her in a silent toast. Her stomach rumbled again as she bowed her head to him in gratitude. She assumed he had overhead her conversation with the waiter.

"One sec, please," she said, holding the man's wrist to keep her balance as she slipped her damp foot back into her sandal.

Once done, she took the sandwich and cloth napkin from him and bit into it. Her little grunt was pure pleasure at the taste of seasoned and warmed roast beef with a gooey cheese and a tasty spread on the bread. "Thank you," she said to him around the food, with a complete lack of the decorum she had been taught by her parents.

"No problem."

As he walked away to finish his duties, Ngozi turned her back to the house and enjoyed the view of the manicured lawns to avoid people watching her eat.

"Ngozi."

Him.

Her body went on high alert. Every pulse point on her pounded. *What is wrong with me? Am I in heat?*

"Yes?" she said, patting the corners of her mouth with the napkin before turning to face him. *Wow. He's fine.*

Chance was nursing his second glass of champagne and squinting from the sun of the late summer season as he eyed her.

"You shouldn't drink on an empty stomach," she said, offering him the other half of the sandwich still on the saucer.

He eyed it and then her. "My appetite isn't for food, Ngozi," he said before taking another deep sip of his drink.

"The only thing I have for you is half of this sandwich, Mr. Castillo," she said, keeping her voice cool and even.

He chuckled.

"Akwaaba. Akwaaba. Memo o akwaaba."

They both turned to find LuLu Ansah, Alek's mother, standing in the open doorway looking resplendent in traditional African white garb with gold embroidery with a matching head wrap that was simply regal. Both the Ansah and Dalmount families surrounded her, with Alek and Alessandra beside her with the baby in Alessandra's arms. Both she and Alek looked around before they spotted Chance and Ngozi, waving them over.

They rushed to take their place, Ngozi gratefully handing the saucer and the remainder of the sandwich to one of the waiters.

"Welcome. Welcome. We welcome you," LuLu

translated, looking around at everyone gathered with a warm smile that made her eyes twinkle.

Ngozi leaned forward a bit to eye her goddaughter, who was just eight days old. She was beautiful. A perfect blend of Alek and Alessandra, with tightly coiled ebony hair and cheeks that were already round. She couldn't wait to hear her name. Alessandra had not budged in revealing it early.

"Today we are honored to officially present a new addition to our family. We will have both a religious ceremony to baptize our little beauty to ensure she is favored by God, and then an outdooring, which is a traditional Ghanaian ceremony when a baby is taken outside the home for the first time, given a name and prepared with the love and wisdom we all hope for her. Is that okay with you all?" she asked, looking around at the faces of everyone in attendance with a sweet, loving expression.

People applauded or shouted out their approval.

"And so, we welcome into our world, our community, our village… Aliyah Olivia Ansah," LuLu said with pride. "May we all pray for her, guide her and love her."

Alessandra pressed a kiss to Aliyah's head, and then Alek pressed one to her temple.

She was so loved.

Ngozi was happy for them and couldn't help but smile.

Chapter 3

Two weeks later

"Congratulations, Counselor."

Ngozi finished sliding her files inside her briefcase and then raised her hand to take the one offered by the Brooklyn district attorney Walter Xavier. She had just served him a loss in his attempt to prosecute her client, an ex-FBI agent, for murder. "You didn't make it easy," she told him, matching his steady gaze with one of her own.

With one last pump of her hand and cursory nod of his head, the man who was her senior by more than thirty years turned and walked out of the courtroom with several staff members behind him.

Ngozi allowed herself a hint of a smile as she looked down into her briefcase.

"Ayyeeee! Ayyeeee! Ayyeeee!"

"Angel!" Ngozi snapped in a harsh whisper, whirling around to eye her newly appointed personal assistant at her loud cry. She found her arm raised above her head, as if she was about to hit a dance move, which took her aback. A win in the courtroom was not the same as getting "turned up" in the club.

Angel, a twentysomething beauty whose enhanced body made a button-up shirt and slacks look indecent, slowly lowered her hands and smoothed them over her hips.

"Get out," Ngozi mouthed with a stern look, seeing that other people in the court were openly eyeing them.

"What?" she mouthed back, looking confused as she picked up her fuchsia tote from her seat in the gallery and left the courtroom with a pout.

"Precious Lord," she mumbled, thankful her client had already been taken back into the holding cell by the court officers.

Ngozi often went above and beyond for her clients, including hiring a former stripper/escort as her personal assistant to meet the requirements of the probation Ngozi was able to secure. At the firm she had her own staff, clerks, paralegals and junior associates, plus an experienced legal secretary. The last thing she needed was a personal assistant—especially one like Angel, who lacked discernment.

Two weeks down, two years to go...

Ngozi gathered the rest of her items and finally left the courtroom. As she made her way through the people milling about the hallway, Angel and her junior associate, Gregor, immediately fell in behind her. Her walk was brisk. She had to get back to the Manhattan office for an appointment with a prospective new client.

She had a rule on no walking and talking outside the offices of Vincent and Associates Law, VAL, so they were quiet. Once they reached the exit on the lobby level, she saw the crowd of reporters and news cameras awaiting her. This was another huge win for her in a controversial case. She felt confident in the navy Armani cap sleeve silk charmeuse blouse, tailored blazer and wide-leg pants she wore. She had self-assuredly and correctly anticipated the win and made sure to be camera ready—which had included an early morning visit from her hairstylist/makeup artist.

"Angel, go mannequin-style and say nothing," she mumbled to the woman.

"But—"

A stare from Ngozi ended her statement before it even began.

They exited the building and then descended the double level of stairs, with Ngozi in the lead. She stopped on the street and the crowd created a semi-arc around them. "Hello, everyone. I am Ngozi Johns of Vincent and Associates Law. As you know, I am the attorney for Oscar Erscole, who has been successfully exonerated of the charges of murder that were brought against him. After a long and tenuous fight, we are thankful that the jury's discernment of the facts and the evidence presented in the case has proven what we have always asserted, which is the innocence of Mr. Erscole, who can now rebuild his life, reclaim his character and enjoy his life. Thank you all. Have a good day."

With one last cordial smile, she turned from them, ignoring the barrage of questions being fired at her as they made their way through the crowd and to their waiting black-on-black SUVs. Ngozi and Angel climbed into the rear of the first one. She pulled her iPhone from her briefcase and began checking her email. "Back to the office, please, Frank," she said to the driver, working her thumb against the touch screen to scroll.

"Now, Ms. J.?" Angel asked, sounding childlike and not twenty-one years of age.

It wasn't until the doors were closed and their tinted windows blocked them from view that Ngozi glanced over at Angel and bit the corner of her mouth to keep back her smile. "Now, Angel," she agreed.

"Ayyeeee! Ayyeeee! Ayyeeee!" Angel said, sticking out her pierced tongue and bouncing around in her seat. "Congrats, boss."

"Thanks, Angel," Ngozi said, laughing when she saw the driver, a white middle-aged man who liked the music of Frank Sinatra, stiffen in his seat and eye them in alarm via the rearview mirror.

They continued the rest of the ride in relative silence as Ngozi swiftly responded to emails and took a few calls. When the car pulled to a stop, double-parking on Park Avenue in midtown Manhattan, Ngozi gathered her things back into her briefcase as the driver came around to open the door for her. "Thank you, Frank," she said, lightly accepting the hand he offered to help her climb from the vehicle and then swiftly crossing the sidewalk with Angel on her heels and the rest of her team just behind her.

They entered the thirty-five-story beaux arts–style building complete with retail and restaurant space on the lower levels and corporate offices on the remaining thirty-three. Everything about the building spoke to its prominence and prestige. After breezing through security with their digital badges, Ngozi and the others traveled up to the twenty-second floor, where Vincent and Law Associates had occupied the entire twenty-two thousand square feet for the last twenty years, housing nearly fifty private offices, a dozen workstations, several conference rooms, a pantry, reception area complete with a waiting space and other areas essential for office work. The offices of the senior partners, including the one her father had vacated upon his retirement, were on half of the floor of the next level up.

Vincent and Associates Law was a force with which to be reckoned. Her father had begun his firm over forty years ago with his expertise in corporate and banking law. Over the years, he acquired smaller firms and attorneys with proven records of success in other specialties to expand and become a goliath in the Northeast and one of the top five hundred law firms in the country.

To know that her father spearheaded such power

and prominence made her proud each and every time she walked through the doors. It had been no easy ride for an African American man, and her respect for her father was endless. And she was determined to rightfully earn her spot as a senior partner and claim the office that sat empty awaiting her—when the time was right.

It was one of the few goals for her that they shared.

Ngozi moved with an Olivia Pope–like stride as she checked her Piaget watch. The team separated to go to their own offices or workstations in the bright white-on-white interior of the offices. Angel took her seat at a cubicle usually reserved for law interns. "Angel, order lunch. I want it in my office as soon as my meeting is over," Ngozi said as she continued her stroll across the tiled floors to her glass corner office.

"Champagne or brandy, boss?" her legal assistant, Anne, asked as she neared.

Champagne to celebrate. Brandy to commiserate.

Ngozi bit her cheek to keep from smiling. "Champagne," she said with a wink, doing a little fist pump before entering her office and waving her hand across the panel on the wall to close the automated glass door etched with her name.

She didn't have much time to marinate on the win. She took her seat behind her large glass desk and unpacked several files, her tablet and her phone from her suitcase. After checking the online record of messages sent to her by those at the reception desk, she tucked her hair behind her ear and lightly bit the tip of her nail as she stared off, away from her computer monitor, at a beam of sunlight radiating across the floor and the white leather sofa in her conversation area.

Bzzzzzz.

Her eyes went back to the screen.

A Skype call from Reception. She accepted the video option instead of the phone one. The face of Georgia, one of the firm's six receptionists, filled the screen. "Ms. Johns. Your one o'clock appointment, Mr. Castle of CIS, is here."

"Thank you, Georgia, send him in," she said.

Ngozi turned off her monitor and cleared her desk. She glanced through the glass wall of her office and then did a double take.

Him.

All her senses went haywire as she watched the handsome charmer make his way past the workstations in the center of the office with the ease of a well-trained politician. A smile here, a nod there.

And it was clear that a lot of the women—and a few of the men—were eyeing him in appreciation.

Chance Castillo was undeniably handsome, and the navy-and-olive blazer he wore with a navy button-up shirt and dark denim were stylish and sexy without even trying.

She hadn't seen him since the festivities for their goddaughter, Aliyah.

"What is he up to?" she mumbled aloud as she settled her chin in one hand and drummed the fingernails of the other against the top of her desk.

When Angel jumped up to her feet and leaned

over the wall of her cubicle, Ngozi rolled her eyes heavenward. Especially when he paused to talk to her. Soon they both looked down the length of the walkway, at her office.

His smile widened at the sight of her in the distance.

Ngozi raised her hand from the desk and waved briefly at him with a stiff smile before bending her finger to beckon him to her.

By the time he reached her office, there were many pairs of eyes on him.

She pressed the button on her desk to open the door as she rose to her feet. "Very slick of you, using the English version of Castillo, Chance," she said, extending her hand to him as she would any client—new or old.

"I didn't want to risk you canceling to avoid me," he said, taking her hand in his.

It was warm to her touch.

She gently broke the hold, reclaiming her seat. "So, you're clear on me wanting to avoid you, then?" she asked.

"Damn, you're smart," Chance said, walking around her office.

His presence made it seem smaller.

"Um, excuse, Ms. J."

Both Ngozi and Chance looked over to find Angel standing in the open doorway.

"Yes?" Ngozi asked, noting to herself that the young'un usually avoided work (in other words, coming to her office) at all costs.

"I wondered if you were ready for lunch?" Angel asked Ngozi with her eyes on Chance.

He turned his attention back to the bookshelves lining the wall.

"Yes, I already asked you to order lunch, remember? And is there something wrong with all the communication available between us…from your desk?" Ngozi asked, pointing her finger in that direction.

Angel smiled as she tucked a loose strand of her four bundles of waist-length weave behind her ear. She used to wear her hair in voluminous curls that gave her a hairdo like the Cowardly Lion from the *Wizard of Oz*. Ngozi had requested she wear it straight and pulled back into a ponytail while at work. Thankfully, she acquiesced.

"I also wanted to ask if you or your guest wanted somethin' to drink?" Angel asked, cutting her appreciating eyes on Chance again.

"No, thank you," Ngozi said politely, as she jerked her thumb hard a few times toward Angel's workstation.

With one last look at Chance's tall figure behind his back, Ngozi's young assistant reluctantly left them alone, but not before flicking her tongue at him in a move Ngozi knew had been a hit during her former profession. She added a long talk on not flirting with clients on the long mental list of things to school Angel on.

She closed the automated door.

Chance turned to eye it before focusing his attention on her. "She's…unexpected," he mused with a slight smile.

That she is.

Some of the partners were still not fully sold on her working there.

"No pictures," Chance observed, walking up to her desk.

"Too many reminders of death," she said truthfully, without thinking to censor herself.

"Death?" he asked.

"Nothing," she muttered, sitting back in her chair as she eyed him. "I'm sure you didn't set up a fake appointment with me just to survey my office."

Chance shook his head as he folded his frame into one of the chairs facing her desk. "Fake name. Real appointment. I would like you to represent me," he explained.

That surprised her, and her face showed it. She reached for a legal pad and one of her favorite extrafine-point pens filling a pink-tinted glass bowl on the corner of her desk. The firm had every technological advance available, but she preferred the feel of a pen on paper when assessing the facts of a new case. "Typically, I handle criminal cases," she began.

"I know," Chance said, smiling at her. "Congratulations on your win this morning."

"Thank you," she said graciously, wondering if his smile had the same effect on all women the way it did on her. "You saw the news?"

He nodded. "You looked beautiful, Ngozi."

Thump-thump-thump-thump-thump.

She fought for nonchalance as her heart pounded wildly, seeming to thump in her ears. "And smart," she added.

"Of course, but beautiful nonetheless, Ngozi."

Thump-thump-thump-thump-thump-thump-thump-thump-thump-thump.

She shifted her eyes away from his. "What type of trouble are you in?" she asked, seeking a diversion from her reaction to him.

"It's a civil matter," Chance told her, raising one leg to rest his ankle on the knee of the opposite one.

Ngozi set her pen down atop the pad. "I'm sure a man of your means already has proper representation for a civil case."

"I may be interested in moving all my business here to Vincent and Associates Law…if this case is successfully litigated," he said. "That's a revenue of seven figures, if you're wondering."

She had been.

Ngozi steepled her fingers as she studied him, trying her best to focus on the business at hand and not how the darkness of his low-cut hair and shadowy beard gave him an intense look that happened to be very sexy. The news of the Harvard grad and successful financier inventing a project management app and reportedly selling it for well over $600 million had taken the business and tech sectors by storm, but it was his backstory of claiming success in spite of his humble beginnings that made Ngozi respect his hustle. He retained a small percentage of ownership with the deal and served as a well-paid consultant on top, making several large investments beyond the sale of his app to only increase his wealth and holdings.

Chance Castillo was a man to be admired for his brains. He made smart money moves that even Cardi B could respect.

The senior partners would appreciate bringing his legal interests under the firm's umbrella, and it would take the assistance of other attorneys more equipped to handle matters outside her expertise...if she won the civil case.

"What is the case about?" she asked, her curiosity piqued as she reclaimed her pen from the pad.

Chance shifted his eyes to the window wall displaying the sun breaking through the heart of midtown Manhattan's towering buildings. "I'm sure you heard about the end of my engagement last year," he began.

Her eyes widened a bit at the hardness that suddenly filled the line of his jaw and his voice. Yes, she had heard. The story held almost as much prominence in the news as the sale of his app. Although she had avoided reading about gossip, it was hard to ignore as conversation filler at dinner parties and such.

"She was having an affair the entire time she planned a million-dollar wedding on my dime. The willingness to foot the bill was mine, I admit that," he said, shifting eyes that lacked the warmth and charm they'd once contained. "But doing so after she ends the engagement to be with another man, that I can't swallow. Not on top of the cost of the engagement ring, as well."

Ngozi paused in taking notes. "And the cost of the ring?"

"A million."

"Would you like that recouped, as well?"

"I wish I could recoup every cent I ever spent on her," he said, his voice cold and angry.

Ngozi tapped the top of her pen against the pad as she bit the corner of her mouth in thought. "You understand that gifts cannot be recovered."

He held up his hand. "That's why I said I *wish* and not I *want*. I understand those things are lost to me."

She nodded. "The name of your ex-fiancée?"

He frowned as if the very thought of her was offensive and distasteful. "Helena Guzman," he said, reaching into the inner pocket of his blazer to remove a folded sheet of paper to hand to her.

Ngozi accepted it and opened it, finding her contact information. She frowned a bit at her work address, recognizing it instantly. "She works for Kingston Law?"

"She's a real estate attorney," he said, rising to his feet and pushing his hands into the pockets of his jeans as he stood before the window. He chuckled. It was bitter. "I assume once she left her meal ticket behind, she put aside her plan to stop working."

He was angry. Still. It had been nine months or more.

She broke his heart.

Ngozi eyed his profile, feeling bad for him. Gone were the bravado and charm. This was a man dealing badly with heartbreak.

"Are you sure litigation is necessary?" she asked, rising from her desk to come around it.

"Yes."

She came to stand with him at the window, their reflection showing his stony expression and her glancing up at his profile. "Why the wait, Chance?"

He turned his head to look down at her, seemingly surprised by her sudden closeness. "I was out of the country," he answered, his eyes vacant.

This Chance was nothing like the man she'd met two weeks ago, or even the one he'd been when he first strolled into her office. Which was the facade?

She gave him a soft smile.

He blinked, and the heat in the depth of his eyes returned, warming her. "With you looking up at me, I could almost believe in—"

Thump-thump-thump-thump-thump.

"Believe in what?" she asked.

He shook his head, softly touched her chin and then turned his focus back to the view splayed out before them. "Will you take the case?" he asked.

Ngozi swallowed over a lump in her throat and put the distance back between them. "Is this about anger over her not marrying you—which is breach of promise to marry and is no longer a viable defense in certain states? Or do you feel you've been wronged and would like a cause of action for strictly financial remedy?"

Chance flexed his shoulders. "The latter" was his response.

Ngozi reclaimed her seat, not admitting that she

did not believe him. "I think a case of this nature is best presented before a jury. It will be a long way to go, particularly with Ms. Guzman being an attorney herself, but perhaps she will be willing to settle this out of court."

Chance nodded.

She made several notes on her pad before looking up at him again. "I will need the details of your relationship and its breakup, and any receipts and invoices you have pertaining to the purchase of the ring and the wedding should be provided."

He nodded once more.

"Chance," she called to him.

He looked at her.

Their eyes locked.

Thump-thump-thump-thump-thump.

"During the length of this case you are going to have to relive what was clearly a very difficult time for you," she said. "It may become fodder for the news—"

"Again," he injected.

"Right," she agreed. "I just want to be *sure* you want to pursue this."

He smiled at her. "I'm sure, Ngozi."

"And you're sure you want me to represent you?" she asked, ignoring the thrill of her name on his lips.

His smile widened. "I take any business or legal matters very seriously. Even the offer to move my interests to this firm was researched first. I joke and laugh a lot. I love life, I love to have fun, but I never play about my money."

She stood up and extended her hand. "Then let's get your money back, Mr. Castillo," she said with confidence.

He took her hand in his but did not shake it, instead raising it a bit to eye her body. "We should celebrate our future win with dinner and a night of dancing, *la tentadora*," he said.

Ngozi visibly shivered, even as she looked to her right through the glass wall of her office and, sure enough, discovered quite a few eyes on them, most widened in surprise and open curiosity. She jerked her hand away and reclaimed her seat as she cleared her throat. "Please make an appointment at the receptionist's desk for us to review the details of the case," she said, paying far too much attention to the notepad on her desk. "I will need that information to complete the summons."

Chance chuckled. "Was I just dismissed?" he asked.

"Yes," she said, glancing up at him with a smile.

"Hay más de una forma de atrapar al gato," he said, turning to walk out of her office with one last look back at her.

His words lingered with her long after he was gone, while she futilely tried to focus on her work.

There is more than one way to catch a cat.

It wasn't quite the proper saying, but nothing had been lost in translation.

Chance Castillo had made his intention very clear.

Ngozi put her chin in her hand and traced her

thumb across the same spot on her chin that he had touched.

Thump-thump-thump-thump-thump-thump.

She released a stream of breath through pursed lips.

This was uncharted territory…for the last year, at least.

This attraction. This reaction. This desire.

An awakening.

Ngozi swore as the all-too-familiar pings of guilt and regret nipped at her, seemingly an integral part of her DNA.

Her brother's death. Her parents' grief. Her husband's death.

She pushed aside her thoughts and focused on work, soon getting lost in the minutiae of motions, reviewing court minutes, and at the end of the day celebrating her latest win with a champagne toast from the senior partners.

That evening, behind the wheel of her caldera red Jaguar F-Type coupe, Ngozi put the five-liter V8 engine to good use once she was on I-80 West, headed to Passion Grove. The sky darkened as she passed the township's welcome sign. She was grateful for the panoramic roof as she made her way toward her parents' estate. She slowed to a stop and looked out into the distance at the town's heart-shaped lake. Soon the chill of winter would freeze it over and the townspeople would enjoy ice skating, but tonight the stars reflected against the gentle sway of the water and she found the serenity of it comforting.

Following an impulse, she parked the car on the street and then climbed out to swap her heels for the pair of running sneakers she kept in her trunk. With her key fob in her hand, Ngozi made her way up the street around the brick-paved path surrounding the lake. She took a seat on one of the wrought iron benches, crossing her legs and leaning forward to look out at the water.

Ngozi, come on. Come skate with me.

Ngozi smiled a bit, feeling as if she could see her late husband, Dennis, before her at the edge of the frozen lake, beckoning her with his arm outstretched toward her. It was not a dream, but a memory.

Christmas night.

Maxwell's "Pretty Wings" was playing via the outdoor surround system that streamed top pop hits around the lake during the winter.

Earlier, right after Christmas dinner, the lake had been crowded with townspeople enjoying snowball fights or ice skating, but now only a few remained as darkness claimed prominence and the temperature slid downward with the absence of the sun. Snow covered the ground, casting the night with an eerie bright glow as the moon and stars reflected down upon the sheen of the ice…

Ngozi had been happy just to watch Dennis effortlessly gliding upon the ice with the skill of an Olympian, but she slid on her ice skates and made her way to him, accepting his hands and stepping onto the ice. They took off together, picking up the speed they needed before gliding across the ice with Dennis in the lead and their hands clasped together.

When he tugged her closer, she yelled out a little until he held her securely in his arms, burying his head against her neck as she flung hers back and smiled up at the moon while they slid for a few dozen feet before easing to a stop…

A tear slid down her cheek, and she reached out as if to touch the all-too-vivid memory of better times.

Bzzzzzz.

She let her hand drop as the vibration of her phone brought her out of her reverie. Blinking and wiping away her tears with one hand, she dug her iPhone out of the pocket of her fitted blazer.

"Yes?" she answered.

"Ngozi?"

Her father.

She closed her eyes and fought to remove the sadness from her tone. "Hey, Dad," she said and then winced because it sounded too jovial and false to her ears.

"Hey, congrats on the win, baby girl," Horace said, the pride in his voice unmistakable. "I thought you would be home by now. You didn't say you had a meeting or event or anything."

Her interpretation of that: Why are you late?

She was as predictable as a broken clock being right at least two times out of the day. Predictable and perfunctory.

"I'm on the way," she said, delivering a half-truth.

"Good. Your mother had a council meeting and Reeds is serving up real food for us while she's gone."

Ngozi laughed. Her father disdained the vegan lifestyle as much as she did. "Steaks simmered in brown butter with mashed potatoes and two stiff bourbons on ice?" she asked as she rose to her feet and made the small trek back to her car, guided by the lampposts lining the street.

"Absolutely," he said with a deep chuckle. "Hurry!"

"On my way," she promised, turning and taking a few steps backward as she gave the lake one last look and released the memory.

Chapter 4

Two weeks later

Chance reached inside the jar of almonds he kept on his desk, gathering a few into his hand to toss into his mouth as he leaned back in the ergonomic chair. Since he'd hit his major windfall a couple of years ago and left behind his work in finance, he rarely used his home office, but for the last couple of days an idea for a new app had been nagging at him. So he took his morning run, returned to shower and then meditate, and then headed into his office to hammer out the details floating around in his head.

The normal blare of the music was gone. He needed quiet to focus, and his estate in Alpine provided him plenty of that.

Again, the app was a labor of necessity. Although he was no longer on an 8:00 a.m.–8:00 p.m. job, he still found a need to be productive. Unlike his wealthy friends who grew up with staff, Chance preferred to do without. Many were not aware that the staff seen during his lavish dinner parties were not full-time nor live-in. He used a household staffing agency on an as-needed basis.

But for someone who preferred solitude, yet also had an active social life, traveled frequently and at times conducted business on the go, to have a virtual personal or executive assistant was as good as the real thing—or with the right analytics and algorithms, even better.

Ding.

He glanced at the email notification on the screen. It was from Ngozi's firm. Another request for an appointment.

Chance ignored it with a chuckle as he rose from his chair and crossed the wide breadth of his office to leave it and enter the kitchen. He froze and frowned at the sight of his mother stirring a bowl at the island. She was so consumed with it that she didn't even notice him. He crossed his arms over his chest and leaned in the doorway before he cleared his throat.

Esmerelda looked up and smiled at the sight of him. "Hello, Chance. I thought you were sleeping," she said, moving about his kitchen with ease.

He released a heavy breath. He loved his mother. Adored her. He was so thankful for her contribution and sacrifice to his success. He loved to gift her whatever she wished for, except…

"Ma," he said, pushing off the doorjamb with his hand extended toward her. "Come on. Give it up."

Esmerelda stared at him.

He bent his fingers as he returned her stare.

She sucked air between her teeth and wiped her hands clean with a dish towel before reaching in her designer tote bag for her key ring. She mumbled things in Spanish as she worked one of the keys around the ring.

Chance didn't lower his arm until she came around the island and pressed the key against his palm with a jerk. "How many copies did you make?" he asked, sliding the key into the pocket of his cotton sleep pants. "This has to be the tenth key I have taken from you. It has to stop. One day you're gonna walk up in here and see *way* more of me and a lady guest than you want to."

Esmerelda waved her hand dismissively. "Nothing I haven't seen. I changed your diapers," she said, stirring a spatula in the large ceramic bowl again.

"Things are not the same," he balked.

"I hope not."

Chance shook his head, walking up to press his hands against the marble top of the island. "Ma, I *need* my privacy," he said, his voice serious.

Esmerelda avoided eye contact. "You need this stew," she stressed.

Bzzzzzz.

He reached for his cell phone from the pocket of

his sleep pants. Soon he smiled and then ignored the call from Ngozi's assistant.

Will you walk into my parlor? said the Spider to the Fly.

"How is your case coming?" Esmerelda asked.

"It's still in the early stages," he said, raising his arms above his head to stretch as he watched her.

"Have you heard from Ese Rubio Diablo?"

Chance shook his head. "And I don't want to," he said with honesty. "The time for talking is over."

Esmerelda nodded and glanced at him before she turned to set the bowl on the countertop next to the eight-burner Viking stove he rarely used. "It is no easy feat to overcome heartbreak," she said. "Nothing but time can do it. Time and…forgiveness, *mi amada*."

Chance had moved to the French door smart fridge for a bottle of water, but paused at her words and the softness of her tone. "You think I should forgive her and move on?" he asked in surprise.

Esmerelda turned from the stove. "In time, you will have to, for yourself if not for *that* witch," she said. "Trust me, I know."

He took a deep swig of the water before setting the bottle atop the island as he watched her. His mother was only in her late forties. Still young and beautiful, with an air and vibrancy that made her seem far younger than her years, but with a lifestyle of a woman twenty years her senior. As far as he knew, the only man in her life was his father, and that was a subject they rarely discussed. Yet it had not quelled his curiosity about the man he knew he favored in looks.

His mother had been just seventeen and fresh from a move to America from the Dominican Republic with her grandmother. She met and fell in love with Jeffrey Castillo, a young and handsome Afro-Cuban street dude whom she later found out to be more fabrication than truth and more lust than love. When she told him she was pregnant, he ended the relationship and began seeing another young woman who lived in the same Bronx apartment building as Esmerelda—something that caused her great pain and shame. In time, that relationship of his ended as well, and he soon moved out of their neighborhood. She never saw him again.

"¿Has perdonado a mi padre?" he asked of her forgiveness of his father, using Spanish to connect to the Latino heritage in them both—the mother he knew and the father he did not.

Esmerelda's face became bitter. "For breaking my heart? Yes," she said. "For breaking yours? *Never.*"

Chance came around the island to hug her petite frame to his side, pushing aside the pang of hurt he felt at the truth of her words. He'd never spoken of the hurt of not having a father in his life. The questions. The curiosity about him. The regrets. At times, the anger. "I'm good, Ma," he reassured her.

"You are better than good, *mi amada.*"

My beloved.

Bzzzzzz.

His phone vibrated atop the island. He moved away

from her to retrieve it as she turned back to the stove. Flipping it over, he looked down at the screen. *Jack-pot.*

"I gotta take this," he said to his mother, picking up the phone and padding barefoot across the tiled floor back to his office. "Hello, Ngozi."

"Mr. Castillo, my staff has been attempting to reach out to you to set an appointment to come in and discuss the facts of the case you want to take to court," she stressed, her tone formal and indicating clear annoyance.

He held the phone to his ear with one hand and massaged his bare chest with the other as he stood at the windows behind his desk and looked out at his pool. "I apologize for that. My schedule has been hectic. In fact, I'm in the middle of something right now but I didn't want to miss your call."

"Chance," she said, in warning.

"Can we meet this evening? I know it's last-minute, but I will be flying out of the country later tonight—"

"Chance," she repeated slowly.

"Yes?" he asked.

"Where are you?"

He paused. *Should I lie? No, never lie.* "I'm home."

"Do you have the information I requested?"

"Yup," he said, eyeing the folder of information he'd had prepared for her the day after their first appointment.

"I'll be there by seven to pick it up."

Even better than his original plan to have her meet him at the airfield.

Click.

Whistling, he left his office and reentered the kitchen. "Ma, I appreciate the food," he said.

"No problem," she said. "I felt like some oxtails, and I like your kitchen better than mine."

"Do you want to have it remodeled?" he asked, always wanting to spoil her.

"No, Chance, it's a new house and I lied. I love my kitchen, but I love my son more," she stressed, giving him a stern eye to let him know she meant it.

"How long before you're done?" he asked with feigned nonchalance.

Esmerelda raised a brow and rolled her eyes. "A girl."

"A woman," he corrected with emphasis.

She shook her head. "You're kicking me to the curb for some noony-knack," she said, glancing back at him over her shoulder.

"I don't think sending you home to your four-bedroom French Tudor is kicking you to the curb," he drawled, crossing his strong arms over his chest.

"I could go get a mani-pedi at seven," she said.

"Throw in a massage and be gone by six," he bartered.

"Deal. No cash. I'll charge it," she assured him, patting her pocketbook.

"Same difference," he said.

He gave her a weekly allowance, paid her monthly utility bills and gave her an unlimited credit card—that she refused to use without his permission.

"I'm glad you're dating, Chance. You deserve to

be loved again," she said as she emptied a bowl of diced onions into a pan that soon sizzled.

He frowned deeply. "Love?" he scoffed. "No, I'm not looking for the lies of love again. You can forget about that. Helena taught me a lesson I will never forget. Trust no one. Nah."

Esmerelda pointed the tip of the spatula at him. "You're smarter than that. No one can live without love forever," she said.

"Says the woman who has only loved one man in her life," he rebutted.

Esmerelda looked at him as if he had suddenly grown a horn in the center of his handsome head. "Says the silly man who thinks his mama has only loved—or been loved—by one man in thirty years," she said, widening her eyes at him as she released a short laugh. "Silly Chance."

His mouth opened in shock.

"Just because you didn't see it, baby boy, don't mean it wasn't going down, o-*kay*?" she said, her Spanish accent thick. "I wasn't hot to trot, but I got *me*. O-*kay*? And that wasn't any of your business. O-*kay*?"

Chance frowned, shaking his head as if to clear it. "I'm done with this conversation," he said, tilting his head back to drain the last of the water in the bottle into his mouth.

"Yeah, I thought so." Esmerelda chuckled. "Ain't nothing dead on me."

"Let yourself out, Mama. Love you," he said over his shoulder as he left the kitchen.

"Bless his silly heart."

Chance pushed aside thoughts of his mother having a sex life and made his way through the massive house, then jogged up the stairs to his master suite. Standing before the walls of his closet, he admitted to feeling excited at seeing Ngozi again as he selected an outfit.

You deserve to be loved again.

He paused.

He desired Ngozi. He liked her spunk and cleverness. Being around her made him feel good.

But love wasn't in the equation.

Love—or what he thought was love—led to him being made a fool, and a public one at that.

"Nah, I'm good on that," he said to himself, selecting an outfit. "A brother's just trying to have fun with a beautiful lady. That's it. That's all."

Right?

"Right," he said, as if to reassure himself while he laid the clothes on his bed and made his way to his bathroom.

When he returned downstairs, fully dressed and subtly smelling of Creed Viking cologne, the scent of the stew permeated the lower level of the house. He headed to a large framed mirror on the wall beside the front doors, opening it to display the security monitors. He was scanning each room and both three-car garages to make sure his mother had taken leave when one of the monitors showed a red sports car pulling to a stop in front of the secured gate.

The driver's side window lowered, and Ngozi sat

behind the wheel with rose-gold aviator shades in place.

Chance smiled at the sight of her as she reached out and tapped the touch screen. *Just beautiful.*

His security system was automated, but he tapped the pad on its wall base anyway. "Come on in," he said, watching as the gate slid open, and soon she was on her way up the short driveway to him.

He closed the mirror front and then checked his appearance in it, smoothing his beard and adjusting the lightweight V-neck silk sweater he wore with linen slacks. He pushed the sleeves midway up onto his forearms before opening the door and walking down the steps to his stone-paved courtyard.

She parked at an angle before climbing from the car.

With his hands pushed into the pockets of his pants, he watched her, loving the way her hair was pulled back into a sleek ponytail that showed off her high cheekbones. The gray metallic sheath dress she wore fit her frame and complemented her shapely legs. The sun was just beginning to set, and the white uplight began to glow, casting a gleam against her deep brown complexion as she walked up to him.

"Nice ride, Ms. Johns," he said. "You sure you can handle it?"

Ngozi slid her shades on top of her head as she glanced back at her vehicle and then looked up at him. "I'm not giving you an opening for a double entendre," she drawled.

He chuckled before giving her a smile. "Welcome to my home, Ngozi," he said.

"And a beautiful home it is," she said, looking around at the manicured lawn and the wrought iron accents on the French villa exterior.

"Would you like a tour?" he asked, surprised that her opinion mattered to him.

Ngozi crossed her arms over her small bosom and tapped one toe of her shoe against a stone paver. "Nope. I'm not falling for the banana in the tailpipe again, Eddie Murphy," she said. "Over the last two weeks, you have been elusive. I have suggested meetings in every *possible* location except my office."

Chance nodded.

"And yet, each and every time I have been unsuccessful," she said, undoing her arms and splaying her hands. "Do you have the paperwork and the timeline of your relationship—including its demise—with Helena Guzman?"

"Yes," he said, fighting hard not to smile because he knew her annoyance with him was genuine and understandable.

She clapped a few times and then clasped her hands together. "Thank you, Lord. Now…do you have it *here*?"

"Yes. It's in my office."

She arched a brow. *"Here?"* Ngozi stressed again.

"Yes."

"Would have been so lovely if you had it in your hand to give to me right now, and send me on my way," she said.

He reached down for her hand, clasping it with his own before turning to walk up the steps. "What fun would that be?" he asked.

She followed him up the stairs and into the house, but when they stepped inside the grand foyer, she eased her hand from his. "Wow," she said, turning on her heels to look around at the elaborate metal chandelier and the towering height of the ceiling. "Nice."

He watched her as she walked up to the sculptures of the nude figures. He didn't miss when her mouth opened just a bit as she reached out to trace from one clavicle to the other on a few of the figures. Chance's gut clenched at the subtle and seemingly innocent gesture.

Damn.

"This is a lot of house," she said, glancing back at him as she withdrew her hand.

"Big house for a big man."

Their eyes met.

His heart pounded.

She looked away with a lick of her lips as if they were suddenly parched. "The…the paperwork," she reminded him gently, raising her hand to smooth the hair pulled up into her ponytail.

There were things Chance knew for sure, and other things he could only assume or guess—but his gut instinct rarely let him down. And there were two things he knew for sure over the time they'd spent together in the last two weeks. He desired Ngozi with an intensity that was distracting.

And Ngozi Johns wanted him just as badly.

The thought of striding up to her and pressing his lips against hers captured his attention at random moments throughout his day, and curiosity if her attitude in bed was as fierce as it was in court dominated his nights.

All of the telltale signs were there.

Long stares.

Little licks of her lips.

Catching her watching him.

Hunger in her eyes.

Moments where the will to resist him was seemingly weak.

But each time, she fought and won over her desire for him, leaving him disappointed and craving her even more.

But this chess game of desire between them was always her play. Her move. Her time.

Releasing a short breath that did nothing to quell the racing of his pulse, Chance pointed beyond the wrought iron stairs. "This way," he said, clearing his throat and leading the way into the chef's kitchen.

"Whatever that is smells so good," she said, eyeing the stove as they passed the massive island. "Kudos to your chef."

"My mom made oxtail stew," he said, opening the door to the office and turning on the ceiling light.

"You live with your mom?" she asked from behind him.

Chance picked up the folder and looked at her in disbelief. "I am a grown-ass man," he said as he handed it to her. "I live alone."

She held up her hand as if to say *my bad* before taking it from him and flipping through it. "I have people on staff and couriers on call to pick up stuff like this, Mr. Castillo," she said, chastising him.

He leaned against the edge of his desk, crossing his legs at the ankles. "I enjoy your company, Ms. Johns," he countered smoothly. Honestly.

Again, their eyes met.

That vibe between them pulsed, electrifying the air.

"I don't mix business and pleasure, Chance, not with clients nor coworkers," she said.

He wasn't sure if she was schooling him or reminding herself about the line she had drawn in the sand.

He eyed her, finding himself unable to stop. His eyes dropped to her mouth.

"Show me your beautiful house," Ngozi offered, turning from him to leave the office.

Her invitation to remain in his company both surprised and pleased him.

"You think I can get a to-go box of some of your mama's stew?" she asked with a coquettish smile that brightened her eyes.

"Or you could stay and have dinner with me," he offered, coming to a stop before where she leaned back against the island.

Ngozi swallowed hard as she looked up at him. "Chance," she whispered softly, her eyes dropping to his mouth as she licked the corners of her own. "Come on, help me out."

He put his hands on either side of her, leaning toward her, feeling drawn into her as he inhaled the warm scent of her perfume in the small and intimate space between them. “Help you what?”

He saw her tremble. It made him weak. That attraction—an *awareness*—throbbed between them. It was hard to resist. Passion. Chemistry. Electricity.

“Fight this,” she implored, her eyes soft and filling with the heat rising in her.

“Nah,” he drawled slowly and low in his throat as he lowered his head and pressed a soft kiss to the corner of her mouth.

It was softness. Sweetness.

“Chance,” she sighed with just a little hint of aching in her tone.

He shook his head as he smiled and then pressed his lips against hers.

The tip of her clever tongue darted out to lick at the little dip in the center of his bottom lip.

He grunted in hot pleasure, feeling his entire body jolt with an unseen surge, a current. This power created by a connection between them had been stoked over the last two weeks, taunting and tempting them with a force that could not be ignored.

There was no woman he'd ever wanted so much in his life.

When she brought her quivering hands up to clutch at the front of his sweater, he followed her lead—her unspoken acceptance—and gripped her hips to pull their bodies close together as they deepened the kiss and gave in to the passion that could not be denied.

It started out slow, as if they were trying to savor every moment.

Chance brought his hands up to her back, massaging the small of it as he drew the tip of her tongue into his mouth and suckled it. She whimpered as she brought her hands up to hold the sides of his face.

He felt her hunger and matched it with his own, relinquishing control as he gently broke their kiss to press his mouth to her neck. He inhaled deeply of the warm scent of her perfume, and he enjoyed the feel of her racing pulse against his lips. And when he suckled that spot, she gasped and flung her head back.

"Yes," she whispered hotly, her hands rising from his cheeks to the back of his head to press him closer.

Chance felt a wildness stir in him as he suckled her deeply, not caring if he left a mark as he brought his hands down to pull her body from the edge of the island and glide his hands to her buttocks. Cupping them. Massaging the softness. Loving the feel of his hardness pressed against her stomach as he ached for her.

"Ngozi," he moaned against her neck, feeling lost in her. Her scent. Her presence. Her vibe. Her energy.

Her being. Her everything.

He grabbed her by the waist and hoisted her up on top of the island as he undid the zipper on the back of her dress. Eased the top of her dress down, moved back to take in the sight of her small but plump breasts in the black strapless lace bra she wore before he quickly jerked off his sweater and flung it away.

Chance stood there between her open thighs with

the skirt of her dress up around the top of her thighs, eyeing her. The hint of her lace bikini panties peeked out between her legs, with her chest slightly heaving as her hard nipples pressed against the barely there lace, her eyes glazed and the gloss on her swollen lips smudged from his kisses. He had never seen anything sexier.

Ngozi Johns was allure personified.

And when her eyes took in the sight of his chest and abs, and moved down to his hard curve tenting his linen pants, he saw both her appreciation and anticipation. Never had he wanted so much to live up to expectations.

One small move forward and she was back in his arms, her flesh against his as she wrapped her arms around his neck when their lips met again with one kiss and then a dozen more. Small but satisfying, and leading to more as he offered her his tongue and she touched it with her own with a hungry moan.

The sound of one shoe and then another hitting the floor echoed in the moments before Ngozi wrapped her legs around his waist. The heel of her foot dug into his buttock, and Chance couldn't care less. He kissed a trail down her body until he lightly bit the edge of her bra to jerk it down below one breast with his teeth. The first stroke of his tongue against her nipple caused Ngozi to arch her back.

"Yessss," she cried out. "Yes. Yes. Yes."

He sucked harder. Deeper. Pulling as much of her breast into his mouth as he could.

Ngozi reached down between them and began to undo his belt with rushed movements.

Chance stepped up onto the foot rail lining the island to make the job easier for her. And when she pressed her mouth to the hard ridge between his biceps, it was his turn to tremble. She kissed a trail to one hard nipple to circle it with her tongue.

That move surprised him, and the moan of pleasure he released came from his gut.

She guided her lips to the other, and this time she sucked that nipple into her mouth before lightly grazing it with her teeth as his loose-fitting pants fell down around his ankles.

He was so anxious for her that he could hardly think straight. His lengthy manhood was so hard that his loins ached to be surrounded by her, deeply stroking until satisfied. He removed his boxers, freeing his thick curving member. It lay atop the island between her open thighs, the coolness of the marble surprisingly arousing to him.

"Oh…oh my." She sighed in pleasure as she looked down at his inches and then up at his eyes.

"Look," he said, gesturing downward with his head.

She did.

With no hands, he raised it off the cool marble and brought it back down upon it with a light thud.

Her jaw slowly dropped. "You…uh…you really have great control of that," she said.

"Imagine when I use my hips," he forewarned with a sultry chuckle.

Ngozi licked her lips and swallowed hard. "Why imagine?" she asked, sliding backward along the smooth marble until she was in the center of it. She lay back, her eyes on him as she slid her pinkies inside the edge of her lace bikini panties and raised her buttocks to ease them down until they lay in a pile by her feet.

Chance quickly retrieved protection for them from his wallet and sheathed himself with it before he climbed atop the island with her, his erection leading between her open legs. As soon as he lay on top of her, her hands were on his back and then his buttocks, gripping his firm cheeks as he arched his hips and guided his hardness inside her with one firm thrust.

He looked down into her face as her eyes widened, and she gasped before she released a tiny little wail and arched her back. He could feel her walls throbbing against his hard length. He buried his face against the side of hers as his body went tense. "You're so tight, Ngozi," he said near her ear, the strain in his voice clear.

"I feel you. I… I… I feel it," she whispered with a breath. "I needed this. I *needed* this."

Her words seemed like a revelation to herself… and they were pure motivation to him.

Chance was more than ready to give her *exactly* what she needed.

He eased his hands beneath her buttocks and raised her hips up a bit as he began to stroke inside her, seeking and finding her mouth to kiss her.

"Yes, yes, yes," she panted in between kisses with an urgency.

He felt her body against him. Wet. Hot. Throbbing. Her moans of passion were a catalyst. Her hands switched between gripping or massaging his back and buttocks, pushing him closer and closer to the edge of his climax. But he was not ready for the ride to end, and so he would pause in his strokes many times as it eased.

"We're moving," she said.

He raised his head from where he was biting down on her shoulder and saw that each of his thrusts had propelled their bodies down the length of the slippery island. A few more inches and her head would be over the side. He looked down at her, and they shared a smile. "I want to make you come, not give you a concussion."

Her eyes warmed over before she lifted her head and licked hotly at his mouth as she raised her arms high above her head and gripped the edge of the island tightly. The move caused her breasts to spread and her nipples to point to the ceiling, drawing his eyes. He shifted his body to pull one and then the other with his mouth.

"Mmm," she moaned, arching her back again.

He looked up at her. "Still want it?" he asked, his voice deep.

She matched his look with dazed eyes. "Still *need* it," she stressed, working her hips so that her core glided down the length of his hardness.

Chance crushed his mouth down upon hers as he

drove his maleness in to fill her again and again and again. His pace quickened. His erection hardened. His thrusts deepened.

Her cries of wild abandon fueled him.

The sight of her breasts lunging back and forth with each hard thrust or circular motion of his hips excited him.

And the feel of her walls tightening down on him with white-hot spasms of her own release pushed him over the edge. He willingly fell into the abyss, tumbling into pleasure and excitement that blinded him to everything but the feel of her body and the look of surprise and rapture on her face.

And when he saw that tears filled her eyes as she trembled, he kissed them away and held her tightly, turning them over so that her body was now atop his and her head was nuzzled against his chest. He could feel her heart pounding as hard and as fast as his own. He looked up to the towering custom coffered ceiling as he waited for his equilibrium to return.

"I… I…have to go."

Chance jerked his head up as Ngozi rushed to rise, standing up on the island and then stepping over his legs to climb down off it. Not even the delectable sight of her bare bottom could distract him from the sudden shift in mood. "Hey, Ngozi, what's wrong?" he asked, quickly jumping down to grab a wad of paper towels from the countertop holder.

She jerked her strapless bra up over her breasts and fixed her dress so that she wore it properly but leaving the back unzipped. "This was a mistake," she said.

Oh hell.

He removed his condom inside the towels as he watched her frantically gather her discarded panties into a wad in her hand. "Ngozi," he said again, reaching for her arm as she struggled to step into her heels.

"Just let me leave, Chance," she pleaded, jerking out of his grasp and bending down to grab both shoes by the heels with one hand instead.

"What the hell happened?" he asked, confused by her behavior.

"Bye, Chance," she said, turning away with an awkward wave to leave the kitchen.

Naked and uncaring, he followed behind her. "Ngozi, at least put your damn shoes on," he said.

She stopped in the foyer, looking back at him. Her eyes darted down to his now-limp member, and she whirled away from him to hold the edge of the table as she slid on each of her shoes.

"Not exactly sure how you go from *I need this* to needing to get the hell away from me," he said.

She continued on to the door, her perfect ponytail now mussed and her makeup smeared. She opened the door and paused. "It was amazing, Chance, but a mistake," she said, not turning to face him. "You're my client. You *were* my client. I can't represent you now—"

Chance scowled. "So not only are you making me feel bad for giving you exactly what you said you needed, but you also won't rep me anymore. You know what? Unnecessary drama, Ngozi. Just…unnecessary. If that's how you want it, then fine."

She turned. "You got what you wanted, right?" she asked.

No, I got more than I asked for.

"Whatever you say," Chance said, turning to walk away.

When the front door closed, he paused, wiping his bearded chin with his hand as he shook his head. *Damn.*

Chapter 5

"You're so tight, Ngozi."

"I feel you. I... I... I feel it. I needed this. I needed *this."*

Ngozi shivered at the hot memory and then was flooded with embarrassment, raising her hands to press her palms against her cheeks. She had begged the man to please her. Making love with Chance atop that island had been so out of character for her. Not Miss Prim-and-Proper. Not Miss Perfect.

But…

It had felt so right. So good. So *necessary.*

But that didn't take away from her unprofessionalism. She had broken her one rule of not mixing business with pleasure. For that, she was disappointed in herself and ashamed.

But…

At odd moments through the last few days and each night, she had thought of him, inside her, riding her, pleasing her…and she wanted more.

"Whoo," she sighed, releasing a shaky breath as she leaned back in her chair in her office at VAL and closed her eyes, hoping to abate the steady throb of her femininity and the hardening of her nipples as her arousal came in a rush at the very *thought* of Chance Castillo and every delicious, long, curving inch—

"Mmm."

She popped up out of her chair, her eyes wide, and pressed the back of her hand to her lips, surprised by her own moan of pleasure. She looked out the glass wall of her office and was happy no one had noticed her startled reaction. She smoothed the fitted black lambskin dress with embroidered pocket she wore before reclaiming her seat with a shake of her head.

"Come on, Ngozi. Gather yourself," she said, reaching for her conference phone to hit the button for the speakerphone before she dialed an extension.

"Yes, Ms. Johns?"

"Hello, Roberta. Can Larry take a quick call?" she asked the legal secretary of Larry Rawlings.

"Sure thing. Hold on, I'll transfer you in."

Beep.

He was on the line within a second. "Yes, Ngozi?"

"Hey, Larry, I just wondered if Mr. Castillo followed up with you," she said, shifting her gaze out at the sun beginning to set beyond the towering Manhattan buildings.

"Yes, he did. Matter of fact, a messenger just dropped off a folder of receipts with a detailed outline of dates," he said. "We have an appointment to meet next to get the ball rolling."

In her haste to leave Chance's home she had left the folder of information behind.

"Good," she said, confused by her disappointment. "Thanks for picking up the ball for me, but I know you will get the job done, and hopefully the firm will be able to cover some other interests for Mr. Castillo, as well."

"I'm on it."

"Thanks, Larry. Enjoy your weekend."

She ended the call.

Chance had moved on. There had been no calls or attempts to finagle more of her time. There was no more chasing to be done.

Ngozi winced as she thought of his annoyance at her. She could understand.

So not only are you making me feel bad for giving you exactly what you said you needed, but you also won't rep me anymore.

Glancing at her watch, she rose and retrieved her black wool and lambskin belted jacket from her closet before grabbing her clutch and portfolio, as well. She quickly began packing files into the crocodile briefcase.

"Good night, Ms. J."

She glanced up at Angel with a smile. "Have a good weekend," she bid her assistant, before returning to her task. Suddenly, she looked up. "Not *too* good. You're on probation."

"Yes, I know. You remind me *every* weekend," she said. "What do you have planned? Any fun?"

Ngozi looked taken aback. "I have fun, Angel," she said.

Three days ago, I had plenty of it atop an island in the middle of a kitchen.

Her personal assistant looked disbelieving.

"As a matter of fact, tonight I am attending a charity dinner and I'm looking forward to it," she lied.

Alek and Alessandra had purchased a few tables in support of a charity benefiting inner-city youth. The odds were in favor of Chance being in attendance, as well. Their seeing each other was inevitable. They shared a godchild and friends.

What if he brought a date?

Ngozi came out from around her desk. "I am headed home to find just the *right* outfit," she said as they walked down the length of the office together to the elevator.

Chance stood at the entrance of the open brass door leading into the grand ballroom of midtown Manhattan's Gotham Hall and took in the sight of the elegant decor with bluish lighting that highlighted the gilded ceiling with its stained glass center and the oval-shaped room's marble flooring. It was as beautiful as every other gala event. Tables set. Flower arrangements centered. Candles lit. Music playing.

Gourmet food ready to be served. Drinks prepped to be poured. Attendees mingling in their finery.

He was bored.

He was better with writing the check and wishing the charity well, and didn't need the pomp and circumstance surrounding it. It all was a bit much for the boy from the wrong side of the tracks, but alas, he had long since learned to play the role. To show up. Write the check. Rub shoulders. Advance.

And then find his fun elsewhere.

He spotted Alek at the large bar and made his way toward him, weaving his way through the crowd of people filling the large room. "Good to see familiar faces," he said.

Alek turned, and they shared a handshake.

"Right," Alek said. "Thanks for coming. I know this is not your thing. Why'd you change your mind?"

Chance shrugged before leaning against the bar and looking about the room.

"No date?"

At that moment, Chance spotted Ngozi as she stepped into the open doorway of the ballroom. His heart instantly pounded at the sight of her in the floor-length illusion gown with a fringe skirt and plunging neckline lined with lace scalloped edges that made her décolletage all the more appealing. *Damn.*

Memories of nuzzling his face in that soft spot between her breasts as he made love to her came in a rush. Flashes of hot moments they shared in his kitchen replayed—the same memories that had plagued him since that evening. In that moment, she brushed her sleek hair back from her face and entered the ballroom. Any hints of the anger he once held for her faded like a fine mist.

He missed her.

He wanted her.

And it took every bit of strength contained within him not to call her. To accept that the heated moments they shared had been a mistake, just as she had said.

He didn't believe that. The energy and excitement he felt in her presence was like nothing he had ever experienced with any other woman. Not even Helena.

And the sex?

His gut clenched.

He thought he'd gone mad in those furious moments as he climaxed inside her.

His eyes were on her as she made her way across the room. He watched as she reached the table. Alessandra rose to greet her, and the two women hugged each other, exchanged words and shared a laugh.

Alek turned and pushed a double shot of tequila into Chance's hand.

"Huh?" he said, looking down at the drink in surprise before taking it from his friend.

"There's Ngozi," Alek said, sipping from his drink with one hand and holding a flute of champagne with the other. "Wow, that dress is unforgettable. I wonder who she's trying to tempt tonight."

"Me," Chance answered, looking on as both Ngozi and Alessandra looked across the room toward them.

"Huh?" Alek said, frowning. "Am I missing something?"

"Plenty," Chance said before taking a deep sip of his drink.

"Care to fill me in?"

"Nope."

"Cool," Alek said, motioning for the bartender. "Another flute of Dom, please."

With drinks in hand, Chance eyed how the blue lights reflected so perfectly against her dark complexion and highlighted her back in the low cut of the dress. "Why is she so damn fine?" he asked, accepting that his nerves would forever be shot in her presence as he neared her.

"I couldn't answer that because I got a hella fine one my damn self," Alek said, giving his wife an appreciative eye in the strapless white dress she wore with a large statement necklace of gold.

"Hello, Ngozi," he said.

She turned and looked up at him. "Chance. How are you?" she asked, accepting the flute he handed to her.

Their hands lightly grazed each other, and their eyes locked.

And there it was again. Big. Bold. Undeniable. Constant.

Chemistry.

Ngozi barely heard the live band's rendition of Minnie Riperton's "Loving You" as she tried her best not to stare at Chance, but they both seemed to be failing at it. She would look at him, he would look away. She would feel his eyes on her, like heat, but when she glanced in his direction, his attention was elsewhere.

Several times she caught both Alek's and Alessandra's eyes shifting back and forth between them. Her heart was pounding so rapidly that she feared it would outpace her and send her into a total blackout. And when Chance rose, tossing his linen napkin on his untouched food, and came around the table to extend his hand to her, she pursed her glossy lips and released a breath filled with all her nervous anxiety.

She looked up at him, down at his big beautiful hand, and then back up at his face, knowing that sliding her hand in his was much more than an invitation to dance.

"Come on," he mouthed.

She couldn't resist.

"What am I missing?" she heard Alessandra ask from behind her.

"Hush, baby," Alek suggested.

Ngozi hung her beaded egg-shaped clutch around her wrist and accepted Chance's offer. Her hand was warm where they touched as he led her onto the dance floor beneath the oscillating lights. He stopped and gently tugged her to pull her body close to his. She settled her arms across his back as he settled his around her waist. The top of her head came to his chin, and as they danced, their bodies seemed to fit. To work. To click. Like lock to key.

He dipped his head. "Still don't need me anymore?" he asked near her ear.

She leaned back to look up at him. "Chance," she whispered, her resolve sounding feeble to her own ears.

"I came here tonight looking for you," he admitted.

"Really?" she asked, acutely aware of how warm his hand was against her bared lower back.

"And you wore this dress tonight for me, *la tentadora*. Right?"

The temptress.

Yes, her dress fit that bill.

She looked away from him and licked the corner of her mouth. "In case you brought a date," she confessed, arching her brow as she tilted her head to look up at him once again.

He chuckled. It was deep and rich.

"Your hand feels good rubbing my neck."

Ngozi lowered her hand to his back once more, not even realizing she had been stroking his nape with her fingertips. It felt natural showing affection toward him.

He held her arm high in the air and slowly danced around her before pulling her back into his embrace and then spinning her out and reeling her back in to him. "You should smile more often, Ngozi Johns," he said.

"I haven't had much to smile about in a really long time," she admitted, surprised by her candor.

"Me either," Chance said. "So let's have fun together. Nothing serious. No ties. Just fun."

Why does that sound so good to me?

"Your caveat about not dating clients no longer fits, because you no longer represent me," he reminded her.

That's true.

"I don't know, Chance," she said, allowing herself to stroke his nape again.

"Okay, think about it, but let me offer this?" he began, trailing his finger up her spine.

Ngozi shivered and her nipples hardened as all of her pulse points throbbed—including the now-swollen bud nestled between the lips of her core. "What?" she whispered, her eyes falling to his soft mouth.

"Let's have fun tonight and worry about tomorrow when it comes."

Ngozi always put what was right before what she wanted. Always. With her parents. With her marriage. With her career.

Sometimes being so damn perfect was so damn tiring.

"I need it," he moaned near her ear, his breath lightly breezing against the lobe.

She feigned indignation. "Really, you're playing the need card?"

"You played it first. Remember?"

"I haven't been able to forget."

They shared a laugh that was all too knowing.

"It was *fun*," Ngozi acknowledged, her body trembling.

"Damn right it was."

"Let's go," she said, stepping back from him.

"We're gone," Chance agreed, grabbing her hand as they made a hasty retreat toward the door.

Ngozi sat up on the bed and ran her hand through her tousled hair as she looked down at Chance's nude body sprawled out beside her. The contours of his body were defined by the silver moonlight through the open curtains of the hotel suite's balcony doors. The soft buzz of his snores was thankfully muffled by the pillows over his head.

He deserves his rest.

She shook her head in wonder at his skill as she reached for her iPhone on the bedside table. She held the lightweight cover across the front of her body as she rose from the bed gently and stepped over her $3,000 gown carelessly left on the floor in their haste. As she made her way to the open balcony doors, she dialed her parents' landline phone number, tapping the tip of her nail against the rose-gold sequin as it rang.

"Hello."

"Hey, Reeds," she said, hating that she felt like a high schooler sneaking out for the night.

I am a successful over-thirty-years-old attorney—

"Is everything okay?" the house manager asked, his voice filled with concern.

"Everything's fine, Reeds. Everything okay there?" she asked, looking out at the moon shining down on the New York skyline.

"Same as always. Your parents already turned in for the night."

"Thank God. I thought they would wait up for me."

"They asked me to do it," Reeds admitted with a chuckle. "No one is roaming about this time of night but me and one of your father's Cuban cigars."

"Enjoy your cigar and go to bed," Ngozi said. "I'm staying in the city tonight."

"Okay. Be safe. Good night, Ngozi."

"Night," she said softly, hating the relief she felt that she had dodged talking to either of her parents.

"Should I be jealous?"

Ngozi whirled, causing the blanket to twist around her legs as she eyed Chance rising from the bed to walk over to her. She ran her hand through her hair, failing to free it of the tangles created during their love play. "No," she said, looking up at him as he stood before her, naked and beautiful in the moonlight. "Because this is only for the night. Remember?"

"Give me the weekend," Chance requested. "We can fly wherever you want in the world. Name it. It's yours."

Ngozi shook her head, lightly touching her kiss-swollen lips with her fingertips. "I can't."

He bent his strong legs and wrapped his arms around her waist to heft her up. She had to look down into his upturned face, and gave in to the urge to stroke his cheek. "Paris. Dubai. Italy," he offered. "Ibiza, Antigua, French Riviera, Bora Bora…"

Chance paused and smiled.

"Your life is different from mine, huh?" she asked.

He bent his head to press a kiss to her clavicle, then drew a circle there with his tongue.

Ngozi let her head fall back, the ends of her weaved tresses tickling the small of her back. "I haven't had a break in a long while," she admitted with a sigh. "And I do carry my passport in my wallet."

Chance carried her over to lay her on the bed, and then grabbed the blanket to pull off her body and fling onto the floor.

Feeling flirty, she rolled over onto her stomach and glanced back at him over her shoulder as she raised her buttocks. Her smile spread as he became erect before her eyes. *He really is all kinds of perfection.*

Chance lightly held her ankles and slid her body across the bed until she was bent over it. He reached onto the bedside table for one of the dozen foil packets of condoms. She watched him roll the ribbed latex down his length before she closed her eyes and sighed in pleasure. The warmth of his body radiated as he knelt behind her and curved his body against hers as he licked a hot trail up her spine and then lightly bit her shoulder. And when he spread her open and guided every inch of his hardness inside her, she grimaced and clutched the sheet in her fist as her body tried to conform to the fit and hard feel of him.

"Chance?" she said, looking back at him as he stroked inside her, slowly enough for her to take note of each inch as it went in and out of her.

"Yeah, baby," he said, looking down at the connection before tilting his head to the side to give her his attention.

"Not so deep," she said, closing her eyes. "I don't need all of it. I'm good."

He chuckled a little as he pulled out some. "Better?" he asked, biting the side of his tongue.

She relaxed her body with an eager nod.

He slid his hand around her body and pressed his fingertips against her moist and swollen bud, gently stroking it as he thrust inside her.

Ngozi's eyes and mouth widened.

"I thought making you come a couple times make up for it," he said thickly.

"A couple?" she asked with a lick of her lips.

"Oh *yes*," he stressed.

"Oh my."

She chose Italy.

Chance eyed Ngozi standing there on the balcony of the sprawling villa he rented in Sorrento off the Amalfi Coast. Her arms were splayed as she gripped the railing of the private balcony off their palatial bedroom as she overlooked the gardens, the grass-covered mountains and the nearby bluish-green waters of the Mediterranean Sea. Her hair was loose, and she wore a red strapless maxi dress that clung to her body when the wind blew.

He found her so breathtaking that he paused his steps as his pulse raced and his heart pounded.

She turned and smiled at him at the exact moment that the sunlight framed her from behind, bringing to mind dark chocolate lightly dusted with gold powder.

Ngozi Johns was trouble.

Forcing a smile, he continued over to her, handing her the goblet of white wine he carried. "A little fun isn't so bad, right?" he asked, leaning back against the railing as he sipped from his snifter of tequila.

"Yes, but too much is not for the best either," she countered.

"Here's to balance," he said, raising his snifter.

"To balance," she agreed, touching her glass to his.

Chance looked beyond her to the downtown area

of Sorrento in the far distance. "I still can't believe you agreed to stay through Monday," he said.

"I can't believe you made it worth the extra work I will have on Tuesday to catch up with my crazy workload," Ngozi said, moving away from him to lie on one of the lounges.

He watched her drape her hair over one shoulder before extending one leg and bending the other as she closed her eyes and let the sun toast her flawless skin a deeper shade of brown.

From the moment they had arrived in Italy on his jet, they had squeezed in as much sightseeing, fine foods and fun as they could during the days, and fell into that heated abyss they created throughout the nights. They were scheduled to leave tomorrow afternoon, and for him it was a mixed blessing.

He didn't trust how she made him feel.

The stain Helena had left on his life and his belief in his instincts was ever present.

"Can I ask you something?" he called over to her, seeking refuge from his thoughts.

Ngozi waved her bent leg back and forth as she looked over at him. "I'm a lawyer. Questions are my life," she said.

Chance took a sip of his drink, looking at her over the rim of the crystal as he closed the short distance between them to sit on the lounge beside her. "The first time, in my kitchen, why did you run away like that?" he asked. "We were both lying there caught up in a *damn* good moment, and it made you run?"

She reached for her wine and took a deep sip as if stalling for time or gathering courage.

He said nothing, patiently waiting for an answer to a question that had remained with him since the moment she fled.

"In that *damn* good moment," she began, not meeting his eyes, "I felt guilty that the first time I ever climaxed in my life was with someone other than my husband."

First time?

"It felt like a betrayal," she continued. "It felt like that *damn* good moment overshadowed my entire sex life with him. So, it was glorious and shocking and damn good and…hurtful."

"And now?" he asked, not really sure what to say.

Ngozi leveled her eyes on him. "Still damn good," she admitted with a smile, sliding her leg onto his lap.

"Still hurtful?" Chance asked as he turned to straddle the lounge chair facing her. He ran his hands up the smooth expanse of her legs, from her ankles to the V at the top of her thighs.

"I'm getting better with it," she said softly, her chest rising and falling.

He took note of her reaction to him and tossed the edge of her dress up around her hips, exposing her clean-shaven mound and her core to him. "And are you satisfied?" he asked, bending to bless each of her soft thighs with a kiss.

He felt her tremble as she softly grunted in pleasure.

"Each and *every* time," Ngozi confessed, setting her wineglass down before she reached over to smooth one hand over the back of his head.

"Then let me go for a perfect record," he said, his words breezing against her core in the seconds before he suckled her clit into his mouth.

Ngozi descended the stairs from Chance's jet, giving him a smile of thanks when he extended his hand to help her down off the last step. Hand in hand, they walked across the tarmac to the two black-on-black SUVs awaiting their arrival.

The extended weekend was over.

She could hardly believe the whirlwind of it. The shopping for clothes and undergarments, the long flight to Italy, the sightseeing, the delicacies, the lovemaking and so much more. It seemed like much longer than three days.

It was over, just as they had agreed.

At the first SUV, she turned and faced him. "Thank you for the escape. Thank you for giving me what I didn't know I needed, Chance Castillo," she said.

"Same here."

His eyes dipped to her lips.

She licked them.

"Can we say goodbye to what we shared with a kiss?" he asked.

She stepped toward him and rose up on the tip of her toes to cover his mouth with her own.

He moaned as he wrapped a strong arm around

her waist, picking her up to level their mouths as he deepened the kiss.

With regret, and a few soft touches of their lips, Chance and Ngozi ended it, both stepping away.

With one last look at him, she turned and allowed the driver to open the rear door so that she could climb onto the leather seat. With one last wave, she faced forward and was proud of herself for not looking back as the driver closed the door and drove the vehicle away.

Chance's mansion was quiet and dimly lit. He found the setting necessary as he struggled with his thoughts. From the time he was a poor kid with wealthy classmates up until the moment he sold his app, he had always relied on his guts. That all changed when the woman he thought loved him revealed her betrayal.

The last thing he wanted was another relationship. Another opportunity to be burned and betrayed. Embarrassed. Disrespected.

But I miss her already. I miss Ngozi.

He wasn't ready to pretend that nothing had happened between them. With her, there had been no thoughts of Helena and the havoc she'd wrought on his life. With Ngozi, he had felt lighthearted again. He'd had fun.

Security check. Front exterior gate.

At his alarm system sending out an alert, Chance picked up the tablet on the sofa where he sat in the den. He checked the surveillance video. At the sight of the car sitting there, he squinted even as he tapped the screen to unlock the gate.

Dropping the tablet back onto the couch, he rose and made his way across the expansive house to the grand foyer. He pulled one of the front double doors open and stood in the entrance as he watched her climb from her car and walk over to the front steps to look up at him.

"I thought maybe for a little while longer, we could have some more fun together," Ngozi said, climbing the steps to lightly trace the ridged grooves of his abdomen with her finger.

Without a word, Chance captured her hand in his and turned to walk back inside his home with Ngozi close behind him.

Chapter 6

Two months later

"Hello, Aliyah," Ngozi cooed to her goddaughter as she held her in her arms where she sat on one of the chaise longues in her nursery.

Alessandra sat in the other, smiling as she looked on at her friend and her baby daughter. "You ready for one of those?" she asked.

Ngozi gave her a side-eye. "No, I am not," she stressed, moments before she bent her head to press her face in the baby's neck to inhale her scent.

"Lies," Alessandra drawled with a chuckle.

Ngozi shrugged one shoulder before shifting the baby upward to rest against her belly. "Okay, maybe one day, but not now."

"And not Chance?"

Ngozi frowned in confusion. "What about Chance?"

"What exactly is going on with you two?" Alessandra asked.

A hot memory of her biting down into the softness of a pillow with her buttocks high in the air as he gripped her fleshy cheeks and stroked deep inside her from behind played in Ngozi's mind.

Her cheeks warmed and the bud between her legs throbbed to life.

"Just fun. Nothing serious," she said.

But I miss him even right now.

"I figured that when you two spent Thanksgiving and Christmas apart."

Truth? She had thought of him on both holidays, and their texting had not sufficed to slay her longing for him.

"And there won't be any kissing at midnight on New Year's Eve either," Ngozi said. "Neither one of us are looking for anything more than what we have, which is nice *private* fun to pass the time."

More truth? He had become a new normal in Ngozi's life.

Ding-ding.

As a notification rang out, Ngozi picked up her iPhone from the lounge to read her text. She smiled as her heart raced. *Chance.*

He'd spent the holidays with his mother and family in Cabrera.

Chance: Coming home 2night. Can I see u?

Yessss, she thought.

"Pass the time until what?" Alessandra asked.

"Huh?" Ngozi asked, pausing in answering his text with one of her own.

Alessandra arched a brow and looked pointedly down at her friend's iPhone. "You and Chance are passing the time until what?" she asked again.

Ding-ding.

"Until it's not fun anymore," Ngozi said as she opened his text.

Chance: I can send a car.

Aliyah began to stir and cry in her arms.

"It's time for her to eat," Alessandra said, rising to walk across the large room to gather her baby in her arms.

Ngozi rose with her phone in her hand and walked over to one of the bay windows. She paused at the sight of Alek's mother, LuLu, talking to Alessandra's longtime driver, Roje, in the rear garden. Her eyes widened when he pulled her body close to his by her waist, and she pressed her hands to his broad chest to resist him even as her head tilted back to look up at him.

Ngozi's eyes widened when they shared a passionate kiss that lasted just moments before LuLu broke it and wrenched out of his grasp.

Feeling small for peeking into other people's lives, Ngozi whirled from the window.

Alessandra was breastfeeding Aliyah with a lightweight blanket over her shoulder and the baby to shield herself. "What's wrong?"

"Nothing," Ngozi said, respecting LuLu and Roje's privacy even as her curiosity over the extent of their relationship shifted in overdrive.

As far as she knew, LuLu had never remarried or even dated after the death of her husband, but there was clearly something between her and the handsome middle-aged driver.

Ngozi flipped her phone over.

Ngozi: Welcome back. I can drive. Time?
Chance: 7? I can fix dinner.
Ngozi: Dinner at 7? Dessert by 8? ;-)
Chance: And breakfast in the a.m.?
Ngozi arched a brow at that.
Ngozi: See you at 7, Chance.
Chance: K.

She looked up when the door to the nursery opened and LuLu entered. Only hints of her bright red lipstick remained, with some a little smudged outside the natural lines of her lips. Ngozi bit back a smile. Passion had ruined many lipstick or lip gloss applications for her, as well.

Humph.

Throughout her marriage and for one year after the death of her husband, Ngozi had lived without the passion Chance evoked. And now, just two months into their dalliance, she hungered for him after just a week without it.

"Hello, ladies," LuLu said, setting her tote bag on the floor before heading straight to Alessandra and Aliyah.

"She's all full, LuLu. You can burp her," Alessandra said, rising to hand the baby and a burping cloth over to her mother-in-law.

"How are we doing, ladies?" LuLu asked, lightly patting upward on Aliyah's back as the baby struggled to hold her head up.

Feeling flirty, Ngozi texted Chance.

Ngozi: Panties or no?

Ding-ding.

Chance: Yes...if I can tear them off.

Hmm...

"We were just talking about finding love again after the death of a spouse," Alessandra said, readjusting her maternity bra beneath the rose-gold silk shirt she wore with matching slacks.

Ngozi froze and eyed her client and friend.

Alessandra gave her a deadpan expression.

LuLu looked at Ngozi with a sad smile. "I lost my Kwame six years ago," she began, shifting Aliyah to sit on her lap. "It felt like a piece of me died with him, so I understand how you feel."

Ngozi looked away, unable to accept her sympathy when the truth was unknown to everyone but herself, shielded by her long-practiced ability to hide imperfections and present what was palatable to everyone else. Guilt twisted her stomach as if its grips were real.

"But our stories are different because I am limited by *obligations*...to children, to the dynasty he helped create, to a marriage of more than twenty years, to class, to my age," she admitted.

Her sadness was clear, and it drew Ngozi's eyes back to hers.

"You have a freedom I do not, Ngozi," she said, raising the baby and pressing her cheek against hers. "Do not waste it."

And right then, Ngozi knew that LuLu Ansah loved Roje and wanted nothing more than to be with him, but felt she could not.

Alessandra stooped down beside where LuLu softly sang a Ghanaian song to the baby and lightly touched her knee. "LuLu," she said softly.

The older woman looked down at her.

"Your obligation as a grown woman who has successfully raised her children and mourned her husband is to yourself," Alessandra said, her eyes filled with sincerity and conviction. "You deserve to be loved again, and I *know* there is a man out there who can and will love you just as much if not more, and nothing—not children, business, class or age—should keep that from you."

LuLu's eyes filled with a myriad of emotions, but above all she seemed curious as to just what Alessandra knew of her life.

Ngozi wondered the same.

Ding-ding.

Chance: I really missed you Go-Go.

Her pulse raced. *Go-Go* was short for *Ngozi.* She had no idea why he insisted on giving her a nickname. She'd never had one.

And secretly she liked it. It was something just for them.

Ngozi: I missed you 2.
Chance: Not fun.
Ngozi: Not expected.
Chance: Not a part of the plan.
Ngozi: No. Not at all.

She awaited another text from him. None came. She checked the time. Three more hours until she was with Chance again. It seemed like forever.

You have a freedom I do not, Ngozi. Do not waste it.

Dinner was forgotten.

Food would not sate their hunger for each other.

Chance feasted on her body like it was his own buffet, kissing her skin, licking and lightly biting her taut nipples, massaging the soft flesh of her buttocks as he lifted her hips high off the bed to bury his face first against her thighs and then her plump mound, before spreading her legs wide to expose the beautiful layers of her femininity. Slowly, with more restraint than he had ever shown in his life, he pleased her with his tongue as he enjoyed her unique scent. His moans were guttural as he sucked her fleshy bud between his lips gently, pulling it in and out of his mouth as if to revive her, but it was her shivers and her moans and the tight grips of her hands on his head and shoulders and the way she arched her hips upward, seeking more, that gave him renewed life.

His body in tune with hers, he knew when her release was near and did not relent, wanting to taste her nectar, feel her vibrations and hear her wild cries. With no compassion for wrecked senses, as she was still shivering and crying out, he entered her with one hard thrust that united them, and he did not one stroke until his own body quivered and then stiffened as he joined her in that sweet chasm, crying out like a wounded beast as he clutched her body. He bit down on the pillow beside her head to muffle his high-pitched cries as he forced himself to continue each deep thrust even though he felt near the edge of madness.

Long afterward they lay there, bodies soaked in sweat, pulses racing, hearts pounding and breaths harshly filling the air as they waited for that kinetic energy they'd created to dissipate and free them.

Snores—evidence of their exhaustion—soon filled the air.

Chance awakened the moment he felt the weight of her body shift the bed. She was already reaching for her clothing. "No, Ngozi," he said, his voice deep and thick with sleep.

She paused in pulling on her lingerie to look back at him over her shoulder. "Huh?" she asked, as she clasped her bra from behind.

"Stay the night," he said, sitting up in bed and reaching over to turn on the bedside lamp.

She shook her head, causing her now-unkempt hair to sway back and forth. "No," she said.

The silence in the room became stilted.

"We haven't shared a night together since Italy," he began, finally broaching the subject he'd wanted to for weeks. "You run home to your parents like a little girl with a curfew."

Her brows dipped as she eyed him over the wrap dress she held in her hands. "What...what—what is this?" she asked, motioning her hand from him to her several times. "When did the rules change, because no one told me."

Chance eyed her, knowing she was right.

"I'm not a little girl with a curfew. I am a grown woman with respect for my parents' home," she said.

"Then maybe it's time for a grown woman to have her own home," he said, bending his knees beneath the sheets and setting his arms on top of them.

"Says the grown man who spends his days frolicking," Ngozi said, her tone hard as she jerked on her dress.

Chance stiffened at the judgment. "Frolicking?" he asked, kicking his legs free of the sheets before he climbed from the bed to stand before her.

"Yes, Mr. Italy today and Cabrera tomorrow and... and...and skiing and sailing...and not doing a damn thing else but working on your body and deepening your tan," she said, motioning with her hand toward his sculpted physique.

"Because my work doesn't look like what you think it should, then I'm just a loaf?" Chance asked. "Because I work smarter and not harder, then I ain't shit because I increased my wealth by a million dollars just yesterday. Did *you*?"

"No. Nope. I did not, Mr. Billionaire, but I spent my holidays working to get the bail reduced on a hundred different pro bono clients of nickel-and-dime crimes so they could spend that time with their families, and for those whom I failed, I paid their bail out of my own pocket," she said, her voice impassioned as she looked up at him. "So, you tell me, Mr. Million-Dollars-in-a-Day, what the hell are you doing with your wealth—and your time and your brilliance—besides creating more opportunities to play and have fun?"

"You have no idea what I do because we don't share every aspect of our lives with each other," he spouted, feeling insulted and belittled.

Ngozi raked the tangles from her hair. "Right."

"And when your life is exhausted and time flies because you are so busy working your nine-to-five—excuse me, your six-to-eight—that you haven't lived, then what?" he asked. "You spend the last years of your life with damn regrets. Well, no thank you. I will live and let live."

"You know what, you don't have to justify your life of leisure to me. Just don't judge me for how I choose to color within the lines," she said, dropping down on the edge of the bed to pull on her heels.

Chance turned from her. "All we do is either fuck or fight," he said, wiping his hand over his mouth.

"Then maybe this has run its course," she said.

He looked at her over his broad shoulder. Their eyes locked. "Maybe it has," he agreed.

Ngozi finished gathering her things. "Goodbye, Chance," she said softly, moving to the door.

He followed behind her, saying nothing but feeling so many things. At the front door, he reached out past her to open it for her, even though the chill of December sent goose bumps racing over his nude form. He stood there looking down at her. "It was fun," he began.

"Until it wasn't," she finished.

He bent his head to press a kiss to her forehead and her cheek. "Goodbye, Go-Go," he whispered near her ear.

And with that, she left his home without looking back.

He stood there until she was safely in her car and had driven away from him.

"Five…four…three…two…one! Happy New Year!"

Ngozi took a sip of her champagne from the second floor of her parents' home as all of the partygoers began to either kiss their mate or join in singing "Auld Lang Syne." The charity dinner/silent auction was an annual event for her parents, and Ngozi had attended for many years with Dennis by her side. Now she turned away from the festivities and the emotions it evoked, making her way to her bedroom suite and gratefully closing the door.

She crossed the sitting room to her bedroom, setting the flute on the eight-drawer dresser. The maid staff had already cleaned her room and turned down the bed. She could barely make out the sounds of the party down below as she stepped out of her heels and unzipped the black sequin dress she wore to let it drop to the floor around her feet.

After washing the makeup from her face and wrapping her head with a silk scarf, she sat on the edge of the bed. Soon the quiet was disturbing. Her thoughts were varied. She shifted between grieving the loss of Dennis and feeling guilt over missing Chance.

Needing an escape from her own thoughts and emotions, Ngozi turned off the lights and snuggled beneath the covers. Her line of vision fell on her iPhone sitting on her bedside table. She snaked her arm from under the thick coverlet to tilt it up. No missed calls or texts.

She rubbed the screen with her thumb, fighting a small inner battle over whether to reach out to Chance or not.

The latter won.

There was no happily-ever-after for her and Chance, so why be with someone you were so very different from? It would be fine if their different outlooks on life didn't cause conflict, but Chance wanted to fly out of the country on a whim and would expect her to be able to do the same. And when he drove them somewhere, his lack of respect for the speed limit was another point of contention. Ngozi Johns the attorney most certainly was not a rule breaker testing the boundaries and risking wasting money on speeding tickets.

Their moments together were either filled with passion or skirmishes.

It was tiring.

She returned the phone to its place and released a heavy sigh as she closed her eyes and hoped that her dreams were a distraction from Chance and not filled with memories of him as they had been over the last week since their divide.

"Five…four…three…two…one! Happy New Year!"

Chance pressed a kiss to the mouth of a woman he'd met just that night at the multilevel Drai's Nightclub on the Las Vegas Strip. He couldn't remember her name, and her mouth tasted of cigarettes and liquor that had soured on her tongue. *Serves me right.*

He turned from her just as the fireworks shot off from Caesar's Palace across the street began to echo around them as they lit up the sky. When he felt her tugging at his arm, he gently disengaged her, closed out his tab with the bottle service girl and made his way out of his own section, leaving her and her friends to have at the abundance of liquor he'd already ordered.

Bzzzzzz.

He paused on the dance floor of the club as his

cell phone vibrated against his chest from the inner pocket of his custom black-on-black tuxedo.

Ngozi?

Chance looked down at the screen. "Mama," he mouthed, accepting his disappointment as he answered her call and made his way to the elevator.

"Feliz Año Nuevo, hijo!" Esmerelda exclaimed.

He smiled. "Happy New Year to you, too," he replied, pressing a finger in his ear to help hear beyond the music and noise of the club and the commotion coming through from his mother's boisterous background. She had remained behind in Cabrera after the Christmas holidays.

Chance looked down at his polished shoes. He'd planned to do so as well, but he'd traveled back to the States because he longed for Ngozi. *And then we fought.*

"I'll call you tomorrow," he said, ending the phone call.

He stood there with the colorful strobe lights playing against his face and the bass of the music seeming to reverberate inside his chest, looked around at the gyrating bodies crowding the space and accepted that it would take more than that to make him forget Ngozi.

Two weeks had passed since Ngozi last spoke to Chance. Fourteen days. Three hundred and thirty-six hours. Twenty thousand one hundred and sixty minutes.

She shook her head and rolled her eyes at her desk

in her office as she looked out at the snow falling down on the city.

She'd been so steadfast in her avoidance of the dynamic Dominican that she'd avoided Alessandra and Alek's estate. She was determined to get Chance Castillo out of her system.

And she was failing at it miserably.

Chance increased the speed and incline on one of the three treadmills in his state-of-the-art exercise room. He picked up the pace as he looked out of the glass wall at the snow steadily piling high on the ground and weighing down the branches of the trees in his spacious backyard. He'd spent the last two weeks cooped up in the house, alternating between exercising and working on his app.

Nothing worked to keep Ngozi out of his thoughts.

Or memories of her out of his bed.

With a grunt and mind filled with determination, he picked up the pace, almost at a full sprint now.

It did absolutely nothing toward his outrunning his desires to have Ngozi Johns back in his life.

"Ngozi."

"Chance."

They shared a brief look before moving away from each other after exchanging stilted pleasantries at a charity art exhibit. She hadn't expected him to be there, and from the look on his face when he first spotted her, he had been just as surprised by her appearance. Her heart felt like it was trying to push its way out of her chest.

Wow. He looks sooo good.

Ngozi gripped the stem of the glass of white wine she sipped, fighting the nervous anxiety she felt. She barely focused on the exhibit as she moved about the gallery. Her eyes kept seeking Chance out. And several times, she'd found his gaze on her already.

That thrilled her beyond measure.

Why are we mad at each other again?

That familiar hum of energy and awareness she felt in his presence was still there. Across the room. Across the divide. When their eyes met, it seemed no one else was in the modern gallery.

Not a soul.

She released a breath into her glass as she trailed her fingertips across her collarbone and turned from the sight of him. She soon glanced back. He was gone. She took a few steps in each direction as she searched for him.

What if?

What if they never argued?

What if they were not so intrinsically different?

Then what?

Sex, sex and more sex. And fun.

She couldn't deny that Chance had brought plenty of joy into her life. With him, she had laughed more and done a lot more *things.*

Her clit throbbed like it agreed with her naughty thoughts.

Humph.

Ngozi shook her head. "Where did he go?" she mouthed to herself.

She could clearly envision herself walking up to him and requesting that he take her home. And then staying there with him for days on end, whether making love or watching those 1990s action movies they both enjoyed or jogging together or cooking together. Anything. Everything. With him.

Maybe I should go.

Her longing was so strong, and she wasn't quite confident in her willpower.

She took a final sip of her wine and stopped a uniformed waiter to set the goblet on his tray with a smile of thanks. Tucking her gold metallic clutch under her arm, she turned and walked right into a solid chest. "Sorry," she said as a pair of hands gripped her upper arms to steady her.

Warm masculine hands.

She inhaled the scent of cologne.

Both were all too familiar.

Chance.

She knew it before she tilted her head back and looked up into his handsome face.

Chance couldn't remember Ngozi ever looking so beautiful to him. She was stunning in the winter-white jumpsuit she wore with her hair pulled back into a sleek ponytail. The contrast against her skin was amazing.

He hadn't been able to take his eyes off her.

Nor could she him.

Finally, he had to close the distance between them. Now he hesitated to take his hands off her.

And he knew in his gut if he pulled her into a dark secluded corner and pressed his lips to that delicate dip above her collarbone—her spot—that she would not resist him. Once again, she would be his. But for how long? A few stolen moments? One night?

"We can't avoid each other," Chance said, finally dropping his hands from her arms as his heart beat wildly.

"We spoke," she said, taking a step back from him as she smoothed her hand over her head and dragged it down her waist-length ponytail.

Chance nodded. "We did."

They fell silent.

"I thought this wasn't your type of thing?" Ngozi said.

"Art?" Chance asked.

"No, charity," she said with a sly lift of her brows and a "so there" look.

Chance frowned. "Still throwing jabs, huh?"

"Yes, that was childish, Chance. My bad," she admitted.

"As a matter of fact, I am sponsoring this event," Chance said, trying his best not to sound smug or give her the same "so there" look.

She looked perplexed. "Did the Ansahs know about that?"

He nodded. "Yes. I wish they could be here. Alek helped me arrange the connection."

"Well, they claimed they couldn't make it so I was

pressed to use their ticket…with no mention of your involvement, of course."

Chance rocked on his heels and looked up at the well-lit ceiling as he chuckled. "Scheming, huh?" he asked, looking back at her.

Their eyes locked before she looked away with a bite of her bottom lip that stirred naughty thoughts in him.

"It seems so," Ngozi said, her nervousness clear.

"You were right," he said.

"About?"

"Me needing to do more. Care more. Focus more on what's right," he admitted, his eyes searching her face for a sign that she understood this shift in his thinking was due to her.

She looked surprised. "You did this for me?" she asked.

He shook his head. "No, I didn't know you were coming, remember, *but* I took your advice, Ngozi, and it feels good to give back more, Mrs. Pro Bono."

Her shoulders slumped a bit as she looked up at him in wonder.

Chance balled his hands into fists behind his back to beat off the temptation to stroke her face. "What's that look about, Ngozi?" he asked.

Tears filled her eyes, and his gut felt wrenched. She tried valiantly to blink them away before turning to quickly stride away.

He fell in step with her and placed an arm around her shoulder to guide her into an office. "Ngozi," he said softly, wanting her to open up to him.

She shook her head. "I feel silly, but… I appreciate your taking my advice and listening to me even though I voiced it out of anger. Outside of my career, what I care about, what I think…what I *feel*," she stressed, letting the rest of her words fade as she pinched the bridge of her nose and closed her eyes.

Chance could no longer resist, stepping close to pull her into his embrace. When she allowed him to do so and rested her forehead against his chest as she released a long breath before her body relaxed, he enjoyed being someone she could rely on for comfort and support.

"You just don't know, Chance," she admitted softly.

He set his chin on her head lightly. "Tell me. You can talk to me about anything, Ngozi. I promise you that," he swore, surprised by the truth of his own words.

He wanted so badly, in that moment, to inquire if her husband had been that for her. Her protector. Her warrior. Her shoulder to lean on.

But he did not.

"Chance Castillo, I don't know what to do with you," she professed.

The same struggle he felt between what he wanted and what he needed was there in her voice. "Help me become a better man."

She looked up at him. "And what will you do with me?" she asked, her hands snaking around his waist to settle on his back.

"Help you color out of the lines a little bit more."

She smiled. "And somewhere in the middle—"

"We have amazing sex."

"Chance," she chided softly.

"Ngozi," he volleyed back.

She chuckled.

He looked down at her, studied her, enjoyed the beauty of her. *She is not Helena.*

The truth was Ngozi Johns was not the type of woman built for frivolity. She was "it"—fun, brilliant, sexy, loyal, reliable, empathetic…

He could go on and on.

But what if I'm wrong?

"Let's stop fighting this, Ngozi," he implored, touching his index finger to the base of her chin to lift her head high as he bent his legs to lower himself and touch his lips down upon hers.

Her answer, he was pleased to note, was to tightly grip his shirt in her hands as she kissed him back with the passion he had craved and missed.

Chapter 7

Ngozi was exhausted.

From the moment they left the art gallery together, she and Chance hadn't been able to keep their hands—or anything else—off each other.

In the office at the gallery.

In the car.

Against the wall of the living room.

On the bench of his nine-foot Steinway grand piano in the music room.

In the shower.

And the bed…where he held her nude body closely as he united them with deep intense strokes and whispered to her how much he missed her until they climaxed and cried out in sweet release together.

And she was spent as she straddled Chance's

strong thighs as he sat in the middle of his bed with his back pressed against the headboard. Her sigh was inevitable when he gripped her thighs to massage them. She rested her hands on his shoulders, gently kneading the muscles there.

"We're really doing this?" Ngozi asked, pressing kisses to his brow as he lowered his head to her chest.

"I don't think we can resist," Chance said, turning his face from one side to the other to plant a warm kiss to each curve of her breasts.

She eased her hands from his shoulders and up his neck to grip his face to tilt upward until he was looking at her. The room was dimly lit by a corner lamp across the room, but the light of the moon and the brightness of the white snow reflected a light in his eyes that she felt herself getting lost in. He met her stare and she lost her breath, feeling something tugging at her heart and claiming a piece of her soul.

She kissed him lightly. "Chance," she whispered, her eyes searching his as she felt a lightness in her chest.

Bzzzzzz.

They both looked to his iPhone vibrating on his bedside table.

Ngozi was thankful for the intrusion. She had started to feel spellbound.

Chance held one of her butt cheeks with one hand and reached for his phone with the other.

She felt his body stiffen. "What's wrong?"

"The attorney notified me that Helena has been officially served her summons," Chance said, his voice hard as he turned the phone to show her.

Ngozi winced. *Helena.*

She moved to rise up off him, but he wrapped his arm around her waist and held her closer. "Don't answer that, Chance," she advised, putting on her attorney hat.

She visualized the blonde Cuban with whom he'd been ready to share his life. Ngozi, educated woman and accomplished attorney, had looked up the woman's Instagram account weeks ago. She was gorgeous. J-Lo level.

"Helena," he said, his tone chilly enough to make her wish for a sweater.

"You have got to be kidding me, Chance. Are you serious? Suing me?" she railed.

He had her on speaker.

Ngozi successfully freed herself from his hold and rose from the bed, not interested in eavesdropping on their conversation.

"Racking up a million dollars' worth of bills for a wedding while screwing another man? Are *you* serious?" he countered, his anger and annoyance clear.

Ngozi paused in the entrance to his bathroom and looked back at him over his shoulder. Something in him needed this moment with Helena.

She squinted as he began to slash his hands across the air as he rose from the bed and paced, and they began arguing heatedly in Spanish.

Her entire body went warm and she leaned against

the frame of the doorway as she accepted what she was feeling. Jealousy. Pure and simple.

And she knew that when she looked in his eyes and saw the moonlight in the brown depths, that the emotion that took her breath was the same one that made her warm with envy.

Her heart pounded so loudly it felt like it thudded in her ears.

Ngozi gripped the door frame tightly and released a long, shaky breath as the truth of her feelings settled in…and scared her.

I love him. I love Chance.

"Go to hell!" Helena screamed.

Ngozi refocused her attention on them.

"I will see you there," Chance returned coldly, holding the phone close to his mouth.

Ngozi stiffened her back and pushed off the door frame to walk across his expansive bedroom and calmly slip the phone out of his hand to end the call. She turned and tossed it onto the middle of his bed. "It is hurtful to your case to argue with Ms. Guzman," she said, turning away from him so he couldn't see how hurtful it was to her, as well.

How did I let this happen?

"You're right," he said.

She glanced at him as she gathered her clothing, taking note with a critical eye that he stood before the floor-to-ceiling windows with his hands on his hips as he looked out at his backyard. His back was to her, but in his reflection in the glass, she took in both his nudity and the pensive look on his face.

He looked lost in thought.

She was tempted to dress and walk out, leaving him lost.

Instead, she set her clothes down on the edge of the bed and walked over to him to press her body against his back and wrap her arms around him as she pressed a kiss to his spine.

Chance brought one hand up to cover hers as he looked down at her over his shoulder. "I'm glad you're back," he said.

Ngozi eased her body around his to stand before him with her bare bottom, her upper back and head against the chilly glass as she looked up at him. "You sure?" she asked, reaching up to stroke his low-cut beard.

Chance cupped her face with his hands, tilting her face up as he bent his head to kiss her. "Honestly?" he asked, as his eyes searched hers just as hers had searched his earlier.

She wondered if he felt the same breathlessness that she had in that moment. "Always," she finally answered, her voice whisper soft.

"I wasn't looking for anything serious and…and I'm not sure I'm ready," Chance admitted. "In fact, I don't think either of us are."

She nodded with a slight smile. "True," she confessed, enjoying the feel of his hands.

Chance stroked her lip with his thumb. "But I don't know how to be without you, Ngozi. I've tried and failed. Twice."

More truth.

The hour was late. Later than she'd ever stayed at Chance's home, but when their simple kisses filled with heat and passion, she didn't dare to resist. Once she stroked him to hardness, in tune to her soft sucking motions of his tongue, the chill of the glass against her body faded as the heat of their passion reigned. She wrapped her arms around his neck and her legs around his waist after he hoisted her body up, centered her core above his upright hardened length and lowered her body down on each inch until they were united fully.

Ngozi gasped and released a tiny cry as she arched her back, pushing her small but plump breasts forward. Chance licked at each of her taut brown nipples with a low growl as she rotated her hips in an up-and-down motion like a rider on a mechanical bull. She kept looking at him, enjoying the glaze of pleasure in his eyes, the grimace of intensity and the quick shallow breaths through pursed lips as he fought for control.

"Ahhhh," she sighed, her eyes still locked on him as she released his neck to press the back of her hands against the glass and slid them upward as she continued to wind her hips.

Chance's grip on her hips deepened, and she felt him harden even more inside her.

"Yes," she sighed with a grunt of pleasure, closing her eyes as she tilted her head back.

Never had she felt so bold, so sexy, so powerful as she did with Chance. The look in his eyes, the strength of his hold and his reaction to her moves pushed her beyond her normal limits with her sexuality. It was new and refreshing and satisfying in every way.

With him there was no shame. No inhibitions. No denial of her wants and desires.

With him she was free.

With the strength of her thigh muscles from her daily runs, Ngozi gripped his waist tighter and lowered her body down the glass until they were face-to-face. They locked eyes and shared what seemed to be a dozen small kisses as he took the lead, alternating between a deep thrust and a circular rotation of his hips that caused his stiff inches to touch every bit of her feminine core and drag against her throbbing bud.

And there against the chilly glass, with the heat they created steaming away the frost, Chance stroked them to another explosive climax that shook Ngozi to her core with such beauty and pleasure that it evoked tears.

She felt like she was free-falling.

It was amazing.

Still shivering, she clung to Chance and buried her face against his neck as he walked them over to his bed. She relaxed into the softness of the bed and snuggled one of the down pillows under her head. She closed her eyes as the exhaustion of her emotions and her climax defeated her.

"You're staying?" Chance asked, his surprise swelling in his voice.

She nodded as he curved his body to hers and

wrapped a strong arm around her waist after pulling a cool cotton sheet over them.

Ngozi snuggled down deeper on the bed, content that she didn't have the will or the energy to leave him.

It was early morning before Ngozi made the short trip home from Alpine to Passion Grove. She entered her security code on the side entrance in the massive kitchen, pushing it open as a yawn escaped her mouth. Chance had gifted her another mind-blowing, energy-sapping, eyes-crossing orgasm before she left him.

"No sleep last night?"

Startled, she paused in the doorway at her father sitting at the mahogany island, still in his plaid robe and pajamas, drinking from a cup of what she presumed to be coffee from the heavy scent of it in the air. "Sir?" she asked, by way of stalling as her nerves were instantly rattled.

"We're not trying to heat the outdoors, Ngozi."

Her head whipped to the right to find her mother at the breakfast nook, also in her nightclothes as she drummed her clear-coated fingernails atop the round table.

Double trouble.

Ngozi turned to close the door, pausing to lick her lips as she furrowed her brows. She felt like a child about to be scolded.

"Reeds was kind enough to let us know you called and told him you were staying in the city for the night at the firm's apartment," her father began, ever the attorney—retired or not.

Late last night, she had dug her phone out of the pile of clothing on the floor and texted Reeds to cover for her yet again. "Good, I wouldn't want you to worry," she said, striding across the kitchen at a pace that could have won a speed-walking race with ease.

"Ngozi," her mother said, all simple and easy.

Deceptive as hell.

Ngozi paused and turned, uncomfortable with her face makeup-free and her hair disheveled, dressed in the same white outfit she'd worn to the art gallery the night before.

"Your father is retired from the firm but he's still the majority owner, my daughter," Val said, turning on the padded bench to fold her legs and look across the distance at her daughter. "And that includes the firm's apartment—"

Oh damn.

She was a gifted attorney as well and knew exactly where she had made a wrong calculation. Her eyes shifted from one to the other. Her father took another drink, and in that moment, Ngozi wished he would stir his spoon in his cup so the floor would open and send her to her own special sunken place.

They know I wasn't there.

"Who is he?" Horace asked, setting the cup down on top of the island.

Ngozi opened her mouth to lie. When it came to her relationship with her parents, subterfuge was her first line of defense.

Val held up a hand. "Let's remember that anything less than the truth is disrespect," she advised before shifting her focus back to her husband.

"Who is he?" Horace repeated.

I don't want to lie. I don't want to deny Chance. I don't want to.

"Chance Castillo," she said, physically and mentally steeling herself for a long list of questions and reminders of obligations to Dennis even beyond his death.

Silence reigned.

Their faces were unreadable.

"Invite him to dinner," her mother said.

Ngozi grimaced. "But—"

"Soon," her father added before returning his attention to his coffee.

"Horace, we better go up and get ready," Val said, rising from her seat. "We have that breakfast meeting with possible donors for my upcoming campaign."

Ngozi looked from one to the other, her mouth slightly ajar. She couldn't hide her shock, even as they eased past her to leave her in the kitchen alone.

Chance carefully steered his silver Bentley Bentayga SUV over the busy New Jersey streets, being sure to stay focused with all of the snow and ice on the ground. As he pulled the vehicle to a stop at a red traffic light, he looked over at Ngozi sitting beside him in the passenger seat. He smiled at all the nervous gestures he spotted. Swaying her knee back and forth.

Twisting the large diamond-encrusted dome ring she wore on her index finger. Nibbling on her bottom lip.

He had picked her up from work, fresh off yet another trial win, and she was dressed in a claret ostrich feather coat with a turtleneck and pencil leather skirt of the same shade that was beautiful against her mocha complexion, particularly with the deep mahogany lipstick she wore.

"Mi madre no muerde, sabes," he said, giving her thigh a warm rub and squeeze as he steered forward under the green traffic light with his other hand.

"She doesn't bite, huh?" Ngozi said, translating his words. Inside the dimly lit interior of the SUV, she glanced at him with a weak smile. "I told you my parents want to meet you as well, so let's see how easy-breezy you are when I finally get the nerve to serve you up to them."

"I'm ready," Chance said with a chuckle as he turned onto the short paved drive of his mother's two-story brick home just a few miles from his estate. He pressed the button to open the door of the two-car garage and pulled into the empty spot next to her red convertible Mercedes Benz she called "Spicy."

"And the deposition tomorrow—are you ready for that?" Ngozi asked.

Chance shut the SUV off and looked over at her. The overhead motion lighting of the garage lit up the car, offering him a clearer view of her face. "Yes, I am."

"That's good," she said. "Just be sure to keep your cool."

He frowned. They rarely discussed his lawsuit against Helena. "My cool?"

Ngozi reached for the handle to the passenger door. She looked nonplussed. "Same advice I would give if you were still my client," she said matter-of-factly with a one-shoulder shrug.

"But you're not my attorney, you're my woman," he reminded her.

Ngozi relaxed back against the seat. She stroked the underside of his chin, letting the short beard hairs prick against her hand. "Your woman, huh?" she asked.

He smiled as he leaned in and pressed his lips to her own as he reached down to use the controls to lower her seat backward.

"Don't...start...something...we...can't...finish," she whispered up to him in between kisses as her eyes studied his.

"Who says we can't—"

"Chance! Are you coming in?"

They froze before they sat straight up in their separate chairs again.

Chance looked through the windshield at his mother standing in the open doorway leading from the garage into her kitchen. She was squinting as she peered into the car with a frown.

Ngozi covered her face with her hands, feeling the warmth of embarrassment that rose in her cheeks. "Oh God," she moaned.

Chance chuckled before he opened the driver's side door. "We're headed right in," he called out to her.

She turned and walked back into the house, leaving the door ajar.

"Great first impression," Ngozi drawled, before he climbed from the car and strode around the front to open the passenger door.

"No worries, *mi tentadora*," he said, closing the door when she stepped aside.

"Your temptress?" she asked, looking back at him as she climbed the brick staircase.

Yes, you are.

A relationship had not been in the cards for him after Helena, but Ngozi had drawn him in from their first meeting and he hadn't been able to shake his desire for her ever since. She was his temptation. His temptress.

And in time, his acceptance of that truth shook him to his core.

"Ready?" he asked, seeing the nervousness in her eyes as she waited for him to pull the glass door open for her.

She nodded before stepping inside.

Chance eyed his mother as she turned and walked across the spacious kitchen with a wide, warm smile.

"Welcome, welcome," Esmerelda said, grasping Ngozi's shoulders as she kissed both of her cheeks. "It's nice to meet you."

Chance eyed Ngozi as she returned the warmth, and her shoulders relaxed.

Their exchange pleased him.

"We can go in to eat since you were running a little behind," she said, with a meaningful stare at Chance.

He gave her a wide smile. Her disapproval vanished.

"What do you want me to carry, Ma?" Chance asked.

"Nothing, just go on in."

Chance led Ngozi out of the kitchen and through to the dining room. The large wood table, covered with a beautiful lace tablecloth that looked out of place among the modern design of the home, was set for three with his mother's favorite crystal drink ware and a large floral arrangement. "She went all out," he said as he pulled back the chair for Ngozi at the table.

She took the seat, smiling up at him when he stroked her neck before moving around the table to take the chair across from her.

"Relax," he mouthed as his mother began carrying in large ceramic bowls in bright colors to set on the table.

The smell of the food intensified, and Chance's stomach rumbled.

"I'm too nervous to eat," she admitted.

"Nervous? Why?" Esmerelda asked, setting down a bowl of white rice and a pitcher of amber-colored liquid with fresh fruit pieces.

"Nothing, Ms. Castillo," Ngozi said.

Chance fought not to wince as his mother gave her a stiff smile. "It's Ms. Diaz," she said with emphasis. "Castillo is the name of his father, who didn't choose to share it with me by marriage."

Ngozi remained silent, giving Chance a pointed

stare as his mother took her seat at the head of the table.

"She didn't know, Ma," he said, reaching to remove the lid from the bright turquoise tureen. "*Tayota guisada con longaniza.* I love it."

"This is a popular dish from my country," Esmerelda said, scooping a heaped spoonful of rice into each of three bowls stacked by her place setting. She handed each bowl to Chance to ladle the sausage and chayote cooked in tomato sauce, onion, garlic, cilantro and bell peppers. "I hope you don't find it *too* spicy. Sometimes the palate of those not raised in our culture is delicate."

Chance frowned. Traditionally, there wasn't much heat to the dish.

"I'm sure it's fine. Everything looks delicious," Ngozi said, using both of her hands to accept the bowl he handed her.

He picked up his spoon and dug in, enjoying the flavor of the food. There was a little bit of a spicy kick that tickled even his tongue.

Ngozi coughed.

He glanced across the table at her. Sweat beads were on her upper lip and forehead. Her eyes were glassy from tears.

She coughed some more.

Chance rushed to fill her glass with his mother's homemade fruit juice, standing to reach across the table and press it into her hands.

Ngozi drank from it in large gulps.

"I'm so sorry, Ngozi. Perhaps I can fix you something else if that is too much for you," Esmerelda said, sounding contrite.

Ngozi cleared her throat. "No, this is delicious," she said, setting the glass down before dabbing her upper lip with the cloth napkin she'd opened across her lap.

Chance shook his head. "You don't have to—"

"This is fine," she said, giving him a hard stare and his mother a soft smile before taking a smaller bite of the dish from her bowl.

As their meal continued in silence, Chance eyed Ngozi taking small bites of food followed by large sips of juice. It was clear she didn't want to offend his mother.

"Ngozi, Chance tells me you're an attorney," Esmerelda said, covering her nearly empty bowl with her cloth napkin as she placed her elbows on the table and looked directly at Ngozi.

"Yes, I'm a junior partner of the firm my father established," she answered.

"My Chance seems to have a soft spot for attorneys," she said.

Ngozi licked her lips as she set her napkin on the table.

"Helena and Ngozi are nothing alike," Chance offered into the stilted silence.

"Espero que no, por tu bien," Esmerelda said. *"Ella debería estar llorando a su esposo y no buscando uno nuevo. Los buscadores de oro huelen el dinero como tiburones huelen a sangre."*

"Ma," he snapped sharply as he sat up straight in the chair and eyed her in surprise and disappointment.

He could hardly believe her words and could only imagine how harsh they sounded to Ngozi: *"I hope not for your sake. She should be grieving her husband and not looking for a new one. Gold diggers smell money like sharks smell blood."* Ngozi rose to her feet, looking down at his mother. Chance rose, as well.

"Se equivoca acerca de mí, Señora Díaz," Ngozi said.

His mother's jaw tightened, and her eyes widened in surprise to find Ngozi speak in fluent Spanish to proclaim that she was wrong about her.

Chance shook his head. He agreed with Ngozi that his mother was mistaken about her.

"I am not a gold digger nor am I on the prowl to replace my dead husband with a new one," she said in his mother's native tongue, her voice hollow.

Chance eyed his mother in disbelief. He could tell she felt his stare as she avoided his look.

"My apologies if I offended you," Esmerelda said, reverting to English.

"Thank you for dinner," Ngozi said before quickly turning to walk into the kitchen. Soon the alarm system announced the opening and closing of the side entrance door.

Chance's eyes continued to bore into her.

"What?" she asked.

"You have never taught me or shown me the example of how to be rude and mean to anyone," he began. "I'm just trying to figure out who is sitting before me."

Esmerelda turned in her chair and looked up at him. "I watched you recover from heartbreak by Ese Rubio Diablo for almost a year, so what you see now is a mother willing to fight to make sure you don't go through that heartache again," she said, her voice impassioned and her eyes lit with the fire of determination.

"I know you mean well, but Ngozi should not have to suffer for what Helena did to me," Chance insisted, forcing softness into his tone. "All I ask is that you give her the same kindness you give strangers. Even a dog deserves respect, Ma."

She shrugged and turned her lips downward.

He stepped near her and bent at the waist to press a kiss to the top of her head. "Thank you for dinner," he said and then frowned deeply as he rose to look down at her again in skepticism. "Did you spice the food on purpose?"

Esmerelda sucked air between her teeth and threw her hands up. "It didn't kill her," she said.

"Ma!"

"What?"

"I'll see you later," Chance said, walking around her chair. He paused. "Do you need anything?"

"Just for you to be happy," Esmerelda said.

"I'm a grown man. My happiness is in my hands now," he said. "You don't have to work double shifts to take care of me and send me to private school. I will love you and spoil you because of your sacrifice, but your time putting me before yourself is over. I got it from here."

She remained quiet and studied her nails.

He could tell she was hurt, but the truth of his words could not be retracted to save her feelings. He gave his mother the world, but he was a man who had no desire to be babied and coddled by his mother.

"Te amo, Ma."

"I love you, too, Chance."

With that he took his leave.

Ngozi was sitting in the SUV. He eyed her through the windshield as he made his way over to the driver's side door. He climbed inside. Unspoken words swelled between them.

Chance licked his lips and reached over to take one of her soft hands in his. "Say it," he urged. "I'm listening."

"It's nothing. I'm fine," she said, looking to him with a smile as fake as the plastic one pinned onto a Mr. Potato Head toy.

"Don't ever deny your feelings for the sake of anyone—not me or anyone else—because they matter," he said.

She smiled again. It was soft and genuine. "I wouldn't know what it feels like to put myself first," she admitted.

Chance leaned over to press kisses to the side of her face. "Try it," he whispered into her ear.

"I want you to know that I am not looking to replace Dennis," she said, turning on the seat to face him. "Hell, I don't even feel I have the right to move on and be happy when he's dead."

Chance took a moment to properly frame what he said next. "I never expect you to let go of Dennis."

She began to stroke his hand. "Not of him, of my guilt," she acknowledged before closing her eyes and releasing a breath.

He wondered if talking about him was like releasing steam to dissolve the buildup of pressure.

"We've never spoken of his death," he offered, being sure to tread lightly to avoid stepping on or disrespecting her feelings.

"I've never talked about it with anyone."

Her sadness was palpable, and his gut ached for her. "And do you want to talk now?" he asked.

Ngozi shook her head. "Not yet, but thank you for letting me know that someone is there to finally listen to me."

"Sounds like a lot to unload from that clever brain of yours," he said, his eyes searching his.

"It is. Think you can handle it?"

With a final kiss, he turned his attention to starting the car. "For you I will do anything," he said, letting the truth of his words settle in his chest as the engine roared to life.

Chapter 8

No, Ngozi. No.

Determined not to give in to her own curiosity, she pushed back from her desk and crossed her arms over her chest. Her eyes stayed locked on her computer monitor, though. She had to tighten her fingers into a fist, hoping to stop herself from reaching out and pulling up the video recording of the deposition of Helena Guzman in Chance's lawsuit against her.

No.

Ngozi had been in court all morning and missed when Helena and her attorney arrived. She considered it a mixed blessing.

Grabbing the edge of her desk, she rolled the few inches forward and picked up her pen. Even as she reviewed the case file in front of her, her attention kept shifting to her monitor. *To hell with it.*

Ngozi reached for the keyboard.

"Ms. J."

She jumped like a startled deer, rising and then dropping back down in her seat. Angel looked at her in bewilderment. She cleared her throat and pressed her palms down on the desk. "Yes, Angel?" she asked, thankful for the black shirt and simple wide-leg slacks the young lady wore.

She'd really been making an effort of late to tame her wild ways and boisterous unprofessional behavior. Ngozi took note, appreciated it and was proud of her.

Angel walked in the room, looking nervous as she set an envelope before her.

"What's this?" Ngozi said, opening the flap to find a check.

"I finally saved enough to repay you for my fine and the bond that you paid," Angel said with a wide smile. "And that's the first check I ever wrote from my new checking account, ya heard me."

Ngozi was stunned and she sat back in her chair, letting the check and the envelope drop to the desk as she pressed her fingertips to her lips. There was no denying the pride on Angela's face. And it was the reason she fought just as hard for her pro bono cases as all her others. The hope of giving someone a second chance to better their lives. To find a better way. And in truth, out of all the clients she went above and beyond her attorney duties for, she wouldn't have guessed that Angel would be such a success story.

"If it wasn't for you, I would still be stripping and tricking. Now I'm looking up to you, and I ain't gonna never be no lawyer or nothing, but I want to go back to school…because of you. So thank you for seeing something in me 'cause it taught me to see more in myself, Ms. J.," Angel said.

Ngozi felt emotional, but she kept her face neutral. Maintained her professionalism.

Stuck to her routine—her facade.

Don't ever deny your feelings for the sake of anyone—not me or anyone else—because they matter.

Taking a breath, she rose from her seat and came around the desk to pull Angel into a tight hug. "I'm so proud of you," she said, letting her emotions swell in her tone. "Keep it up."

"I will, Ms. J. I won't let you down," she promised.

Ngozi nodded, releasing her as she stepped back. "I believe that. Thank you," she said, turning to reclaim her seat behind her desk.

Angel took her leave with one last little wave.

"Shut the door, please," she requested, already turning her attention back to her wireless keyboard.

Ngozi was left with her curiosity about the deposition still nagging at her. With a bite of her bottom lip, she logged on to the company's server and searched for the video file of the deposition. She stroked her chin and released long steady breaths at the sight of Chance and his attorney, Larry Rawlings, entering one of the three conference rooms in the offices of Vincent and Associates Law.

Her heart raced at the sight of Chance. The night before, they had lain naked together in front of his lit fireplace as she worked on a new case and he read a book. Leaving him to return to Passion Grove had not been easy, especially because she knew his deposition was the next day.

Now here she sat looking on like a Peeping Thomasina at his ex, a blonde and beautiful golden-skinned Afro-Cuban, entering the room with her attorney. She was rattled. She and Helena were completely different in looks, and although Ngozi was a confident woman, it would be hard to deny Helena's stunning beauty…or the way Chance stared at her with such livid intensity.

Ngozi's heart was pounding as she looked on.

"Ms. Guzman, were you actively involved in a relationship with Jason Young while planning your wedding to my client, Chance Castillo?" Larry asked, looking across the table at the woman over the rim of his horn-rimmed glasses.

Larry's slightly disheveled appearance and his brilliance didn't align, which caught most people unfamiliar with him off guard.

Helena conferred with her attorney before giving Larry a cool look. "No. It was not a relationship," she said, her accent present.

Chance loudly scoffed.

Helena continued to ignore him.

Ngozi nibbled on her bottom lip.

Larry made a note on his notepad. "Were you and Mr. Young intimate during that time? Did you share meals? Did you vacation together? Did you have conversations about life? Did you ever discuss your future with him?"

Helena again conferred with her attorney, a tall silver-haired woman with an olive complexion. "Per the advice of my counsel, I am invoking my right under the Fifth Amendment not to answer, on the grounds I may incriminate myself."

Ngozi winced when Chance jumped up out of his seat. "If I were you, I wouldn't admit to being a scheming two-timing—"

Larry rose to his feet and whispered in Chance's ear.

Both men took their seats.

Ngozi barely heard the rest of their words because of her focus on how Helena barely glanced in Chance's direction, but he never took his eyes off her. His hostility toward Helena seemed to swell and fill the room. Long after the deposition ended and the video faded to black, Ngozi couldn't forget the look in his eyes or the tense stance of his frame.

Sadness and jealousy stung with the sharpness of a needle. His demeanor gave credence to Helena's response that the motivation for Chance's lawsuit was irrational hurt brought on by a broken heart, and even more, injured pride.

His anger was immense, and she felt his hurt was equal to it. As was the love he'd once had for her.

Love he doesn't have for me.

His anger leaves no room in his heart for anything else.

For a long time, she sat staring out the window with that thought foremost in her mind.

The dry heat of the sauna radiated against their nude frames as Ngozi sat astride Chance's lap on one of the cedar benches lining the large infrared sauna. The red light cast their bronzed bodies with a glow meant to be therapeutic, but which also gave the warm interior a vibe that was sexy.

"Talk to me, Ngozi."

Chance was stroking her back. He felt her stiffen for a millisecond before her body relaxed against his again. They'd decided to enjoy a sauna while a three-star Michelin chef who now worked exclusively as a private chef prepared them a romantic dinner. It was clear to him that her mind was elsewhere from the moment she had arrived at his estate.

As much as he enjoyed the feel of her soft body pressed against the hard muscles of his frame, it was clear that a conversation was more needed than another session of fiery sex in a steamy room beneath a red light.

She took a large breath that caused her chest to rise and fall as she sat up straight to look down into his face with serious eyes. "I don't think I have a right to ask, because I know that I'm not where I should be with the death of my husband…and who am I to expect something from you that I can't seem to claim for myself?"

Chance felt lost in her gaze. "And what is that?" he asked, massaging her buttocks.

"Moving beyond. Letting go," she admitted with several soft nods as if to reaffirm her words to herself.

He remembered the moment they shared in his SUV the night he brought her to dinner at his mother's. "About your guilt?"

She looked unsure. "Yes…my guilt about Dennis… and whether you could drop your lawsuit against Helena?" she asked, forcing her words out in a rush because of the courage it took for her to finally voice her worries.

Chance frowned, and his hands paused on her bottom. "You want me to drop the lawsuit?" he asked, his surprise clear.

Ngozi looked away from him as she nodded.

He gently touched her chin and guided her face forward so that their eyes were locked once more. "What's going on? Do you think I'll lose? Is this about us? What…what's going on?" he asked, his tone soft.

Ngozi gave him a soft smile, looking up at the red light before glancing back at him. "Did you mean it when you said I could tell you anything?"

"Absolutely, Ngozi. Anything," he emphasized, as a dozen or more questions about the legal validity of his case raced through his head.

"I have never told anyone that my marriage was not at all what it appeared to be," she began, withdrawing her hands from his body as she bent her arms and pressed her hands to the back of her neck. "I think we were meant to be friends rather than spouses, because in the end this person with whom I had once enjoyed spending time began to feel like an…an…adversary."

Ngozi tilted her head, exposing the smooth expanse of her neck as she closed her eyes and released a long breath.

He remained quiet, wanting her to unload her feelings.

"In law school we worked together to study, pass tests and graduate, but soon our careers seemed to take us in two different directions, and all of a sudden, we were cold and distant with each other, and the only heat was in arguments, but then we would put on the greatest show alive like circus monkeys and pretend in public. All smiles. All kisses. All lovey-dovey bull. Nothing but icing covering up shit."

She looked off into the distance, but the pain in her eyes was clear. "We were in our apartment one Sunday and we were both preparing for cases the next day. He was in our office, and I was in the living room on the floor in front of the fireplace. I was feeling weary and decided to make coffee. I made him a cup just the way he liked, black and sweet, in this huge Superman mug that he'd had since like high school," she said softly, as if back in the moment. "I took the coffee in to him and he didn't look up at me or say thank you. I don't know, in that moment I was so sick of the silence and the distance and the way we were with each other. I missed my friend and I *felt* like I hated my husband—and they were one in the same man."

Chance noticed she was raking the tips of her fingernails against her neck, and he reached up to take her hand into his. She seemed so lost in her thoughts that he wondered if she even noticed.

"In that moment I just wanted him out of the apartment, out of my sight. Just gone," she said, her expression becoming pained. "I asked him to go get lunch, just to get him out...and...and he *never* came back."

Her body tensed, and she winced as a tear raced down her cheek, quickly followed by another and another.

Chance's heart ached for her. "What happened, Ngozi?" he asked, his voice tempered.

"A car crash," she said. "I wished he was gone. I wanted our marriage over. I sent him out. And he never came back. And I have never told a soul," she admitted in a harsh whisper.

"Oh, baby, you can't put the weight of his death on your conscience or your shoulders like that," Chance said, pressing his hands to her face.

She nodded. "My brain understands that, but I still feel like I don't deserve to be so happy."

"With me?" he asked.

Ngozi looked at him. "You were the last thing I was looking for, Chance Castillo," she admitted. "And now I wonder just what I would do without you."

His heart swelled and filled with an emotion for her that had become familiar of late. An emotion he was still hesitant to claim but was finding hard to deny.

I love her.

His heart pounded furiously.

"Do you still love Helena?"

His brows dipped. "No," he said unequivocally.

I love you.

"Then why the lawsuit, Chance?" Ngozi asked. "It keeps you connected to her. It keeps you angry at her."

He stiffened, feeling uneasy. "I'm not—"

"I saw the video of the deposition, Chance."

He swallowed the rest of his denial, closing his eyes to avoid her gaze on him. Yes, Helena had infuriated him earlier in the deposition. That was undeniable. "It was my first time seeing her since she walked out on me before the wedding," he admitted, giving her the same glimpse into his vulnerability that she'd given him. "All I could think about when I was looking at her is how much she'd fooled me. Made a fool of me. It took me back to being the poor kid at school with the rich kids, with girls who looked a lot like Helena, who wouldn't give me the time of day."

Damn.

The thought that childhood issues still affected him stung like crazy.

Ngozi stroked his face and he turned his head toward her touch, enjoying the warmth, care and concern he felt there.

"I'm not dropping the case, Ngozi," he insisted, waiting for her touch to cease.

It didn't.

But she released a heavy breath. "Chance?"

"I don't want her back. I am glad that she didn't marry me and have me financing her side relationship, but it was wasteful and vindictive to push for a huge wedding on my dime when she knew she wasn't all-in, Ngozi. She doesn't just get to walk away with no consequences. She left me holding the bag regarding that wedding."

Ngozi said no more as she rested her forehead against his.

He knew she still held her doubts about his feelings for Helena, and he wanted nothing more than to admit that she had captured the heart he swore he would never entrust to another woman again. But the moment didn't call for it. It would seem more of a ploy than a revelation of his true feelings, so he held back, admitting that he needed time to adjust to the truth himself.

I love Ngozi.

The sound of utensils hitting against flatware echoed into the quiet of the stately dining room as Chance, Ngozi and her parents enjoyed their dinner of prime rib, potatoes au gratin and sautéed string beans.

It was *so* awkward.

Ngozi took a sip of plum wine—a deep one.

"So, Chance, tell me more about your work?" Horace asked, settling back in his chair as he eyed the man sitting to his right.

Ngozi went tense. *Work? Chance spent his downtime planning what to do during his free time.*

"Once I sold my app, I shifted away from finance full-time, and now I have a few different irons in the fire," he said, sounding confident and proud. "I'm a consultant and minority owner of the firm that purchased the app I developed. I do freelance investing for several clients that insisted I continue to work on their portfolios. And I'm currently finishing up a new app to help productivity for businesspeople on the go."

Ngozi sputtered the sip of wine she just took, her eyes wide in surprise. Was he lying to impress her parents? *Why don't I know about any of this?*

All eyes shifted to her as she grabbed her cloth napkin and cleaned up the small splatter she had made on the tabletop.

"Ngozi, since you don't drink alcohol much, maybe you should take it easy on that wine," Valerie said.

Chance frowned deeply. "She drinks—"

Ngozi kicked his shin under the table, silencing him.

He grunted as he eyed her with a hard stare.

"You're right, Ma. I better stick to water," she said, setting the goblet of wine aside as she avoided Chance's confused stare.

Their conversation continued, and the air became less tense as the questioning of Chance subsided. Ngozi sat back and observed her parents and her man as the conversation switched to politics. She had *never* imagined introducing her parents to a man other than Dennis—and definitely assumed they would resent him because of their fondness of her deceased husband.

This isn't bad. Not bad at all.

"So how long have you been interested in my daughter?" Valerie asked, before sliding a bite of food in her mouth.

Ngozi sat up straight. *What now? Weren't they just talking about the president?*

"Not long, really," she said, purposefully vague.

Chance gave her another odd expression. "From the first day we met, I wanted to know more about her other than her beauty," he said, resting his eyes on Ngozi.

She swallowed a sudden lump in her throat, finding herself unable to look away from him.

"I have discovered that she is as brilliant, caring, empathetic, loyal and funny as she is beautiful," he added.

Her entire body warmed under his praise. It was hard to deny that in time she had not felt appreciated or respected in her marriage. It was as if the success in her career had to be diminished to soothe the ego of a man used to being in the lead.

With Chance, it was different. He was her biggest champion.

After dinner and some more polite conversation over coffee and drinks, Ngozi looked on as Chance shook her father's hand and offered her mother a polite hug. "It was good to meet you both," he said.

"Same here," her father said with a nod, turning his attention to his nightly ritual of smoking a cigar and reading the local newspaper, *The Passion Grove Press*, which was mostly news and tidbits about the small town and the achievements of its residents.

"See, I survived," Chance said as they walked together to the front door.

Ngozi nodded, wrapping both of her arms around one of his. "Yes, you did," she said, looking up at him.

At the sound of footsteps, she quickly released him, but relaxed when she turned to find Reeds carrying Chance's leather coat. "Thank you, Reeds," she said.

"No problem," he said, undraping it from over his arm and handing it to Chance with a warm smile. "Drive safe, sir."

"Thank you."

Ngozi looked up at Chance but was surprised by the troubled look clouding his handsome features. "What's wrong?"

"Nothing," he said, outstretching each arm to pull on his fur-lined coat to defeat the arctic northeaster snow still dominating the March weather. "Are you coming back to Alpine with me?"

Her hands paused in smoothing the collar of his coat. "No, not tonight."

"You haven't stayed over except that one time," he said, his brows dipping as he brought his own hands up to cover hers.

Ngozi forced a smile, remembering her parents' ambushing her that next morning. "I will again," she said, conciliating him.

"Not with me, Ngozi," he said. "No, ma'am. Save the show for those who purchased a ticket. Me? I want nothing but the real. So, no, not with me. Never with me."

Ngozi withdrew her hands from his and rubbed them together as she looked into his eyes. "You're the only one who makes me feel like I can be me, whatever that may be. Shit show and all," she said, moving to take a seat on the bottom of the staircase.

Chance walked over to stand in front of where she sat, his hands now pressed into the pockets of his coat.

"I just would prefer my parents not know we've... uh...we're...intimate," she said.

He frowned as he looked up at the large chandelier above their heads. "Or that you drink. Or how long we've been together. Or a dozen other things I saw you outright lie or skirt the truth around tonight," he said.

"Really, Chance?" she asked, leaning to the side a bit as she gave him a stare filled with attitude.

"Really," he affirmed, looking down at her. "It was quite a performance."

Ngozi rose and moved up two steps so they were eye level with each other. "Don't judge me, Chance," she warned.

"Like you did about the lawsuit?" he asked, his voice chiding.

Wow.

"I'm wrong for making sure I'm not wasting my time trying to build something with you?" she asked.

"No, definitely not. Just like it's okay for me to now be skeptical about moving forward after seeing you so willingly—and so easily—present yourself as whatever is needed in the moment," he countered.

"You don't trust me, Chance?" she asked, her feelings hurt by the thought of that.

He shook his head. "I didn't say that," he insisted.

"But I do wonder if you even trust yourself to be who and what you truly want to be, if you are so busy playing the role of Ms. Perfect."

Ngozi arched a brow. "That's not playing perfect—it's providing respect," she countered.

"And who were you respecting by staying in an unhappy marriage—"

Ngozi held up both hands with her palms facing him as she shook her head vigorously. "No, you don't get to focus on issues you think I have and ignore the emotional baggage sitting on your own doorstep."

They fell silent. The air was tense. Gone was the joy they usually had just being in each other's company.

"It seems we both have some stuff we need to fix," Chance finally offered.

She nodded in agreement. "Maybe we should work on that before trying to complicate each other's lives further," she said, unable to overlook her hurt and offense at his words.

He looked surprised, but then he nodded, as well. "Maybe," he agreed.

What are you doing, Ngozi? What are we doing?

She descended the few steps, moving beyond him to stride across the space to open the front door. The chilly winter winds instantly pushed inside. She trembled as goose bumps covered her.

Chance looked at her over his broad shoulder before he turned with a solemn expression and walked over to stand before her. "We never can seem to get this right," he said, wiping away a snowflake that blew in and landed on her cheek.

Ngozi had to fight not to lean into his touch. "Maybe one day we'll both be ready for this," she said, sadness filling her as she doubted the truth of it.

They had taken a chance on each other and failed.

"Maybe," Chance agreed.

With one final look shared between them, he turned and left.

Ngozi gave not one care about the brutal cold as she stood in the doorway and watched him walk out of her life at her request.

A warm hand touched her arm and pulled her back from the door to close it. She turned to find Reeds just as a tear raced down her cheek. Her feelings were not bruised because he had pointed out what she knew about herself—she flew under the radar in her personal life by putting on a facade to make everyone but herself happy. Having it presented to her on a platter by the man she loved had been embarrassing, but the true hurt was his inability to release Helena from his life and move on. That stung like crazy, and she'd be a fool to risk her heart when she wasn't sure his wasn't too bruised by another woman to love her in return.

"It's just a mess, Reeds," she admitted, wiping away her tears and blinking rapidly to prevent any more from rising and falling.

"You've been hiding your tears since your brother's death, Ngozi," he said, his wise eyes searching hers. "Shrinking yourself. Denying yourself. You were a child taking on the role and responsibility of an adult by trying to adjust her life for grown people. Now you're grown, and you're still doing it. And I'll tell you this—I'm glad *somebody* finally said it."

Ngozi was startled. "Say what now?" she asked.

"Listen, my job around here is to make sure the house operates well and the staff acts right. It's not to cross the line and interject myself between the people who pay me and their daughter whom I adore, but I will tell you this—since your young man opened the door. They feel they are protecting you just as much as you feel you're protecting them, and I think you're all wrong for the way you're going about it. Avoidance is never the answer."

And now Ngozi was confused, because she knew Reeds wouldn't speak on personal family matters—especially if he wasn't sure about his opinion.

"Well, since it's clear you overheard my conversation with Chance," she said, kicking into attorney mode, "why should I risk my heart for a man who won't let something go for me?"

Reeds smiled. "And if he did? If he readily agreed to drop this lawsuit you're so worried about, would you have been prepared in that moment to be the woman he is requesting of you—to stand up for yourself and demand your happiness in whatever way *you* see fit?"

Ngozi quickly shifted through emotions. *How could I love someone when I haven't learned to fully discover and love myself?*

"I believe you have just put me at a rare loss, Reeds," she admitted as he chuckled.

"Now that is high praise, Madam Counselor," he said, reaching over to squeeze her hand before he turned and walked away toward the dining room, presumably to ensure the staff had cleaned the area.

She crossed her arms over her chest and rubbed the back of her upper arms as she made her way back to the den. Her parents were lying on the sofa together watching television. Her eyes shifted to the spot on the floor in front of the polished entertainment center. An image of her and her brother, Haaziq, sitting cross-legged replayed in her mind. They were dressed in nightclothes and laughing at some TV comedy as their parents snuggled.

It was a memory that was hard to forget because of its regular occurrence in their life as a family.

In the image, he slowly faded away and she was left alone.

God, I miss my brother. I miss him so much.

"Ngozi? What's wrong?" her mother asked, rising from where she had been resting her head against her father's chest.

She smiled and shook her head, falling into her all-too-familiar role. "Nothing," she lied, sounding fine but feeling hollow.

"Okay," Valerie said, reclaiming her spot. "You had an odd look on your face."

And just like that, a hiccup in their life, a spot of imperfection, was corrected.

"Is your friend gone?" her father asked.

Maybe forever.

Ngozi nodded, feeling overwhelmed. *When do my feelings matter?*

"Mama," she called out, wringing her hands together.

Valerie looked over at her. "Yes?"

"I lied before," she admitted.

"About what?" her mother asked, rising from her husband's chest once more.

"I was thinking about...about...how we all sat in here every night, me, you, Daddy and... Haaziq, and watched TV before you would send us to bed," she admitted, wincing and releasing a harsh gasp as one tear and then another raced down her cheek. "And how much I miss him."

Her parents shared a long, knowing look before her mother rose to come over to her and her father used the iPad to turn off the television.

And at the first feel of her mother's arms wrapping around her body and embracing her, Ngozi buried her face in her neck and inhaled her familiar scent.

"We knew this was coming, we just didn't know it would take so long," her father added, coming close to massage warm circles on her back.

Ngozi enjoyed the warmth of their comfort, and cried like she had never cried before.

Chapter 9

Three months later

Chance leaned against the wall of the hospital with his hands pressed deep into the pockets of the dark denim he wore. As hospital personnel moved past him in completion of their duties and he ignored the scent of illness and antiseptic blending in the air, Chance eyed room 317.

On the other side of the closed door was his father.

Jeffrey Castillo.

He'd never seen him. Never met him. Never known anything about him except he was his father.

Over the last ninety days, he had made his life one adventure after another. Helicopter skiing in Alaska. Diving with sharks on the Australian coast off a megayacht. Shopping at the House of Bijan in

Beverly Hills. Kayaking in Norway. Watching the grand prix in Monte Carlo. Skydiving in Dubai.

And then he'd received an inbox message on Facebook from a woman introducing herself as his father's wife and letting him know his father was terminally ill and wanted to finally meet his eldest son. That was the day before, and now here he was. Chance hadn't even told his mother.

I don't know why I'm here.

Pushing up off the wall, he walked down the length of the corridor to the window, looking out at the cars lined up in the many parking spots and at the traffic whizzing past on the street.

He froze when he spotted a tall dark-skinned woman climb from a red car and make her way toward the hospital's main entrance. His gut clenched until the moment he realized she was not Ngozi.

"Chance?"

He turned from the window to find a pretty round-faced woman with a short silvery hairdo paused at the door to his father's hospital room. It was his father's wife, Maria. She gave him a warm smile as she walked up to him.

"You came," she said.

"I haven't gone in," he admitted.

Her eyes showed her understanding of his hesitation. "If you decide not to, I won't tell him," she said. "The man he is today is not the man he was before. Life has caused him to change, but that will never top how you must have felt growing up without his presence in your life."

Chance liked her. Empathy was always a bridge to understanding and respect.

"Does he know you reached out to me?" he asked, looking down the length of the hall to the closed door.

She shook her head. "No, I didn't want to disappoint him if you—or the others—chose not to come."

Chance went still with a frown. "Others?"

Maria nodded, bending her head to look down as she opened her purse and removed a folded, well-worn envelope with frayed edges. She pressed it into his hands.

Chance allowed his body to lean against the wall as he took in the list of three names in faded ink—his and two more. "And these are?" he asked, looking at the woman.

"Your two brothers," she said, offering him a gentle smile.

Chance deeply frowned. When he was younger, he was optimistic enough to wonder if he had sisters and brothers. Age and the passing of time with no such knowledge had led to him not caring and then not wondering about it all.

"Jeffrey and I also have a daughter, Chance," she said gently. "Her name is Camila."

His father. A stepmother. And three half siblings.

Chance shook his head, not quite sure of anyone's intention and whether he was ready for a new family. "I need time," he admitted, folding and shoving the envelope in his back pocket.

"I understand," Maria said. "Please keep in mind that your fath—that Jeffrey is very ill, and this may be your last opportunity to see him alive."

He nodded as his emotions whirled around like a tornado.

"Ma?"

He looked down the hall at a tall, slender woman in her midtwenties, with short jet-black hair and a shortbread complexion, standing in the open doorway to room 317. He knew from the lean beauty of her face and the similarities in their look that she was his sister, Camila. Camila Castillo.

"I'm coming," Maria said, giving him one more smile filled with her desire for him to meet his father before she turned and walked to her daughter.

"Who is that?" Camila asked, swiping her long bangs out of her face as she eyed him in open curiosity.

"Someone who knows your father," Maria said, offering a hint at the truth but successfully evading it.

Both women gave him one final look before entering the hospital room and closing the door behind them.

Quickly, Chance strode down the middle of the hallway, his height and strength seeming to make the space smaller. He felt pressure filling his chest as he pressed the button for the elevator with far more vigor than necessary. Coming there had become more than he bargained for. Once on the elevator, he pulled the frayed envelope from his back pocket and lightly rubbed the side of his thumb against the faded block lettering that he assumed to be that of his father.

A name on an envelope wasn't much, but it was more of a thought than he'd ever imagined his father to have spent on him.

Chance stopped the elevator doors from closing

and stepped off, making his way back down the hall to room 317. The door opened, and Camila exited. He stepped out of her path, but she stood there looking up at him even as the door closed behind her. "Excuse me," he said, moving to step past her.

"You look just like my father. Are we related?" she asked in Spanish.

Chance froze and then stepped back, causing a nurse to have to swerve to avoid bumping into him. "My bad," he apologized.

The pretty blonde gave him an appreciative look. "No problem," she stressed before continuing on her way with a look back at him over her shoulder.

The door opened again, and Chance's eyes landed on the gray-haired man lying on the hospital bed. He had but a brief glimpse as the door closed. He was surprised his heart pounded with such vigor.

Maria eyed Chance and then her daughter.

"Camila, I thought you went down to the café," she said, reaching to press a folded bill into the younger woman's hand. "Bring me something sweet to nibble on."

"But, Ma—"

"Adios, Camila," Maria said, gently nudging her daughter on her way.

With one last long look at Chance, she turned and walked down the hall to the elevators.

"You came back," Maria said, squeezing his hand. "Come, Chance. Come."

Gently, he withdrew his hand, but he followed her into the room.

"Mi amor, mi amor," she said gently in a singsong fashion. "Look who is here, *mi amor*. It is Chance, your son."

Chance stood at the foot of the bed and looked at the tall and thin man whose gaunt features could not deflect that he looked like a younger, fuller version of his father. Jeffrey opened his eyes. They were slightly tinged with yellow and glassy, but he couldn't deny when they filled with tears.

Jeffrey reached out his hand to Chance and bent his fingers, beckoning him.

For so long, when he was younger, he wondered about the moment he would meet his father. Never had he imagined it happening on his deathbed with cancer winning in the fight for his life. His hesitation was clear as Maria eyed him and then her husband. His father's hand dropped some, as if the effort exhausted him.

That evoked compassion from him, and Chance moved to the side of the bed to take his father's hand in his own. His grip lacked strength. The scent of oncoming death clung to the air around him.

"Forgive me," Jeffrey said, his Spanish accent present even in the weakened state of his tone.

Chance remained stoic even as he looked down into his father's face. He didn't know if his heart could soften to him. His mother had worked double shifts to make up for the help she did not receive from him. Even now, he didn't know if she would feel betrayed by his coming to his father's bedside.

"Forgive me?" Jeffrey asked this time.

Chance glanced across the bed to find Maria had

quietly left them alone in the room. He shifted his gaze back down to his father. It was amazing that he could look so much like a man he had never met. His imprint was undeniable.

Chance released a breath and looked up at the ceiling as the emotions from his childhood came flooding back to him. He clenched his jaw.

The grip on his hand tightened.

Chance looked down. "Why?" he asked.

Jeffrey squeezed his eyes shut, and tears fell as he shook his head.

Chance hoped to be a father one day. He knew he would do better than his own sire because he would be present, scolding when needed and loving always, but *if* he made a misstep, he would hope on his deathbed he would be forgiven. He believed you had to give what you hoped to receive for yourself.

"Te perdono," Chance said, offering this stranger the clemency he requested.

His father pulled his hand to his mouth to kiss the back of it and then made the sign of the cross as he gripped it. *"Gracias,"* he whispered up to him.

He had learned through the loss of the woman he loved that vengeance was a drawback he refused to let hinder his life again.

Passion Grove was truly home.

Ngozi adjusted the large oil painting she'd hung above her fireplace and then stood back to observe her handiwork. The artwork was alive with the vibrant colors and matched the decor of her new home in the affluent small town. It was a rental, but the Realtor said the owners may be interested in selling the four-bedroom, four-bathroom Colonial early next year.

Regardless, for the last month it was home.

"When did you get so Afrocentric?"

Ngozi sighed at the sound of her mother's voice behind her. "I don't know, Ma, maybe my name inspired me," she said as she turned and eased her hand into the pockets of her oversize coveralls.

Her father chuckled from his spot relaxing on her bright red leather sofa.

Valerie gave him a sharp eye that only made him laugh harder. "With the new hair and all this artwork everywhere, you really are taking us back to the motherland," she said, touching a large wooden African ceremonial mask that hung on the wall by the door.

Ngozi touched her faux locks, which were twisted up into a topknot. "My house, my way, Ma," she said, coming close to kiss her cheek before moving past her to close the French doors and unfortunately cut off the breeze of April air drifting in from outside.

"You know, this new and improved Ngozi is a lot chattier," Valerie said.

"Well, I like it," Horace said, rising from the sofa.

"Me, too, Dad," Ngozi agreed, looking around at the spacious family room, which had been the last of the areas she decorated.

For the first time in a long time, longer than she could remember, Ngozi had the same confidence and tenacity that made her a conqueror in the courtroom in her personal life. She enjoyed living her life by her gut instincts and not just by what she thought others wanted her to do or to be. Not living to please others was freeing.

Her parents, particularly her mother, were adjusting to discovering just who their daughter truly was.

Valerie winked at Ngozi. "If you like it, I love it," she said.

Ngozi had discovered over the last ninety days that her parents weren't as strict and judgmental as she'd thought growing up. She'd never felt so close to them.

The night she'd opened up about Haaziq, they'd discussed the impact of his death on their lives. She'd discovered that they tiptoed around her just as much as she placated them. In the end, they were a family trying to cope with a death and just didn't know how to do it.

Now if a memory of Haaziq rose, no one shied away from the thought, and instead they would share a laugh or just reminisce on the time they did get to have him in their lives. And if they were moved to a few tears, that was fine. They grieved him and got through the moment.

"Horace, you ready?" Valerie asked, reaching for her designer tote bag sitting on one of the round end tables flanking the leather sofa. "The town council is cutting the ribbon on the Spring Bazaar, and I do not want to be late."

He eyed his wife as she smoothed her white-gloved hands over the skirt of the pale apricot floral lace dress she wore. It was beautiful and fit her frame well, but it was completely over the top for a local bazaar being held on the grounds of the middle school that offered the works of artists and crafters with plenty of vendors, good food, rides and live music.

"Has she always been so extra?" Ngozi whispered to her dad as her mother reapplied her sheer coral lip gloss.

"Yes, and I love every bit of it," he said with warm appreciation in his tone.

Ngozi looked at him, clearly a man still enthralled by his wife.

I want someone to look at me that way.

Not someone. Chance.

Ngozi pushed thoughts of him away.

"I never wanted to marry until I met and eventually fell in love with your mother," Horace said, walking over to wrap his arm around his wife's waist and pull her close. They began to sway together as they looked into each other's eyes.

"Right," Valerie agreed. "And I was so career driven that at thirty-nine I began to assume I would never find love and have a family of my own…until your daddy put on the full-court press for my attention. I never assumed this man I competed with in the courtroom for so many years would turn into the love of my life."

"Same here," he agreed, doing a little shimmy and leading them into a spin.

"I tamed that dog," she teased.

"The dog tamed himself," he countered.

"So I guess your always loving that Vincent and

Associates Law also spells out VAL isn't proof enough that you're sprung?" Valerie stroked his nape.

"And you're not?" he asked, with a little jerk that pulled her body closer.

They shared an intimate, knowing laugh.

"Respect your elders, Horace," she said. "You're lucky I don't make you call me Mrs. Vincent."

"Two whole years older than me. Big deal," he said.

Ngozi looked at them with pleasure at their happiness and a bit of melancholy that she didn't have that, as well.

Her parents were in their early seventies but lived life—and looked—as if they were far younger.

"You're going to wrinkle my dress, Horace," Valerie said, not truly sounding as if she cared.

"Wait until you see what I do to it when I get you home," he said low in his throat before nuzzling his face against her neck.

Ngozi rolled her eyed. "*Hellllooo*, I'm still here. Daughter in the room," she said.

"And? How you think you got here, little girl?" Valerie asked, ending their dance with a kiss that cleared her lips of the gloss she'd just applied. "Your conception was *not* immaculate."

"But it was spectacular," Horace said.

"Don't you make us late," she said in playful warning.

Ngozi walked across the spacious family room. "Okay, let me help mosey y'all along," she said over her shoulder as she left the room and crossed the foyer to open the front door.

They followed behind her.

"Any chance you're going to change?" Valerie asked, eying the overalls.

In the past, Ngozi would have found a pretty spring dress to wear to please her mother, complete with pearls and a cardigan. "No, ma'am."

"Leave her be, Val," Horace said before leaving the house and taking the stairs down to his silver two-door Rolls Royce Wraith sitting on the paved drive.

Valerie quietly made prayer hands in supplication as she left.

"See you later at the bazaar, Ma," Ngozi said, closing the door.

She turned and leaned against it, looking at her home. She was proud she had taken a large space and infused it with warmth and color. Not even the apartment she'd shared with her husband had her personal touch. She had chosen what she thought he would like.

No, this is all me.

Ngozi closed her eyes and just enjoyed being in her own place and her own space for the first time in her life.

Ding-dong.

The doorbell startled her. Ngozi's heartbeat was racing as she turned to open the door. She smiled at Josh, one of the high school kids who served as deliverymen for The Gourmet Way, the grocery store on Main Street that specialized in delicacies.

"Hello, Ms. Johns, I have your weekly delivery," the tall freckle-faced blond said with a smile that showed off his Invisalign braces.

"Come on in," she said, closing the door when he obeyed and then leading him with the heavy black basket he carried through the family room, which opened into the gourmet kitchen.

Josh set the basket on top of the marble island.

"Are you going to the Spring Bazaar?" Ngozi asked as she removed a twenty-dollar bill from the billfold sitting with files and her laptop on the large kitchen table before the open French doors.

"As soon as my shift is over," he said, accepting the tip with a polite nod.

"See you there," she offered as he turned to leave.

"Bye, Ms. Johns."

Ngozi opened the basket and removed the perishables to place in her fridge or freezer, deciding to leave the little things like chutneys, a canister of caviar, bottles of cordials and black garlic. She did allow herself a treat of thinly sliced *soppressata*, broke a small piece off the ball of fresh mozzarella and wrapped both around a garlic-stuffed olive.

"Vegan who?" she said before taking a bite.

Mmm.

After popping the last bite into her mouth, she cleaned her moist fingertips on a napkin before reclaiming her seat at the table. She had an office upstairs in one of the spare bedrooms, but the light was the brightest and the breeze from outside the best at the kitchen table. It was Saturday, but she had a court case to prepare for in defense of an heir charged with murdering his parents.

The Skype incoming-call tone sounded from her tablet.

Ngozi eyed it, reaching over the open files with pen in hand to tap the screen and accept the video, then propping the tablet up by its case. She laughed as her goddaughter's face filled the screen and she released a spit bubble that exploded. "Hello, Aliyah," she cooed.

"Hewwoo, Godmommy!"

Ngozi arched a brow. "Really, Alessandra, I thought you were a co-CEO of a billion-dollar corporation, not offering voice characterizations for the cutest baby in the world," she drawled.

Alessandra sat Aliyah on her lap in her office and smiled into the screen over the top of her reading glasses. "I do both. I'm complex," she said with a one-shoulder shrug.

"A woman's worth," Ngozi said.

"Right…although Alek is pretty hands-on with her. I can't really complain. In the boardroom, bedroom and nursery, we are getting the job done together."

"Why can't we all be that lucky?" Ngozi said wistfully.

"*We* all could," Alessandra said with a pointed look.

Chance.

Her friend had thankfully agreed not to mention him, but it was clear from the way Alessandra stopped that his name almost tumbled from her lips.

Ngozi looked out the window at the trees neatly

surrounding the backyard without really seeing them. At a different time in their lives, what they shared could have blossomed into that lifetime of love her parents had. She smiled at the thought of Chance—older, wiser and more handsome—lovingly teasing her as they danced to their music no one else heard.

"I thought we could ride to the bazaar together," Alessandra offered.

"I'll probably walk. The school isn't that far from here," she said.

"Alek and Naim, his brother, are in London on business…so you won't be third-wheeling, as you call it."

Ngozi smiled.

"I'm on the way."

She ended the Skype call and rose to close the French doors before she grabbed her wallet and billfold. She dropped those items into the bright orange designer tote bag sitting on the half-moon table by the door. She used the half bath off the foyer to freshen up before sliding her feet into leather wedges and applying bright red lip gloss.

On the security screen, she saw the black 1954 Jaguar MK VII sedan that had belonged to Alessandra's father. Ngozi slid her tote onto the crook of her arm and left the house. Roje, Alessandra's driver, climbed from the car. The middle-aged man with a smooth bald head and silvery goatee looked smart and fit in his black button-up shirt and slacks as he left the car to open the rear door for her.

The scent of his cologne was nice, and Ngozi bit

back a smile as she remembered the private moments he had shared with Alessandra's mother-in-law. She could easily see how the man was hard for LuLu to resist.

"Thank you," Ngozi said to him before climbing in the rear of the car beside Aliyah's car seat.

"Soo…does Alek know about his mother and your driver?" Ngozi asked as she allowed six-month-old Aliyah to grip her index finger.

Alessandra gasped in surprise.

Ngozi gave her friend a look that said *deny it.*

"I plead the fifth."

"You can plead whatever. I *know* what I saw," Ngozi said, eyeing Roje coming around the front of the vintage car through the windshield mirror.

"What?" Alessandra asked.

Aliyah cooed as if she, too, was curious.

"You tell what you know, and I'll tell what I know. Then *we'll* keep their secret," she said.

Roje climbed into the driver's seat and eyed the women in the rearview mirror before starting the car. "Ready?" he asked, his voice deep and rich.

They both nodded and gave him a smile.

Roje eyed them oddly before pulling off down the driveway.

They rode in silence until they reached Passion Grove Middle, a stately brick building with beautiful ivy topiaries and a large playground surrounded by wrought iron finish with scrollwork. Like most community events in the small town, attendance was high, with those from neighboring cities attending the annual affair, as well.

"The elusive Lance Millner is doing a book signing?" Ngozi asked after reading the large sign as Roje pulled the car to a stop before the open gate.

"That's a first around here," Alessandra said.

"Hell, I have never seen him without that damn hat on," Ngozi said. "I have got to see this."

"Ladies, you go in and I'll search for some parking on the street," Roje said, climbing from the driver's seat to open the rear door and then retrieve the folded stroller.

"Good idea. Thanks," Alessandra said, unsnapping Aliyah from her car seat.

Ngozi climbed from the car and looked at the crowd milling around the artwork and crafts on display, the vendors selling their wares, food trucks offering tasty treats, live music offering entertainment, and a few carnival rides on the athletic fields for the children.

"Roje, I'm sure you don't want to hang around for this, so you can go and come back for us in a few," Alessandra said.

Ngozi turned just as Roje smiled and inclined his head in agreement.

"I would like to run a quick errand," he admitted.

"To Manhattan?" Alessandra asked.

LuLu Ansah lived in a beautiful penthouse apartment on the upper east side.

Roje's expression was curious as he pulled mirror shades from the front pocket of his shirt and slid them on his face. "Would you like me to pick up something for you in the city?" he asked, sidestepping her question.

"A little happiness for yourself," Alessandra said.

"I wish," he admitted. "Sometimes life gets in the way."

Ngozi thought of Chance. Her love had not been enough to stop life from getting in their way.

Chance sat on his private plane, looking out the window at the clouds seeming to fade as darkness descended. In the two weeks since he'd met his father, he hadn't returned to see him again. Instead, he had continued his tour around the world. Paris. London. China. And now he was headed to his estate in Cabrera.

He pulled his wallet from his back pocket and opened it to remove the well-worn envelope.

More than anything, it was his siblings he was avoiding. He wasn't ready. Chance was well aware that he was a man of considerable means, and he had no idea what Pandora's box of problems he was setting himself up for with the inclusion of so many new people in his life. Suddenly. And perhaps suspiciously.

Was his father's sudden need for reconciliation more about his guilt as death neared, or his discovery of his sudden billionaire status?

I'd be a fool not to consider that.

He was just as aware he was in a position to help people who were his family by default. By blood.

I'd be an asshole not to consider that.

Chance put the envelope back in its safe spot inside his wallet before rising from his ergonomic reclining chair to walk to his bedroom suite. He was exhausted from his quests and ready to settle down in one spot to rest and relax. Nothing spoke more of relaxation to him than being on his estate in Cabrera.

Except making love to Ngozi.

He thought of her. Moments they had shared in fun or in sex. Her smile. Her scent. Her touch.

Damn. When will I get over her?

He flopped over onto his back and unlocked his iPhone to pull up a picture of her in his bed, her body covered by a sheet as she playfully stuck her tongue out at him.

When will my love go away?

He deleted the picture and dropped his phone onto the bed, wishing like hell it was that easy to erase her from his thoughts and his heart.

"Congratulations on another win, Ngozi."

"Do you even know what an L is?"

"Congrats."

"Ngozi, good win."

"District attorneys hate to see you coming, Counselor."

Ngozi kept her facade cool, like it was just another day at work, accepting each bit of praise as she made her way through the offices of Vincent and Associates Law. She smiled, thinking of her parents' inside joke about the acronym. This was the house Horace

Vincent had built, and his love for his wife was in the name.

And now I'm making my mark.

Instead of heading to her office, Ngozi turned and rode the elevator up one story to the executive offices of the senior partners. "Good afternoon, Ms. Johns," the receptionist for the senior partners greeted her.

"Good afternoon, Evelyn," she said, always making sure in her years at the firm to know the name of each staff member.

To her, that was one of the true signs of leadership.

"Can I get anything for you?" Evelyn asked.

"Not a thing but thank you. I just want to hang out in my dad's office for a little bit," she said softly, moving past the reception desk.

"Actually, he's in today."

Ngozi paused and looked back at her in surprise. "Really?" she said, unsure why she suddenly felt nervous.

Evelyn nodded before turning her attention to the ringing phone.

Large executive offices were arranged in a horseshoe pattern around the reception area, but it was the office dominating the rear wall of the floor toward which she walked. Her briefcase lightly slapped against the side of her leg in the silk oxblood suit she wore with matching heels. Reaching the white double doors, she knocked twice before opening the door.

"Getting my office ready for me, Pops?" she quipped, but the rest of her words faded as all five managing partners of Vincent and Associates Law turned to eye her.

Ngozi dropped her head abashedly. "My apologies, I thought my father was here alone," she said, moving forward to offer her hand to each partner.

"It will be yours one day, Ngozi," her father said as she came to stand beside his desk. "Just as soon as you're ready."

She nodded in agreement. Her father offered her no shortcuts to success, and she never expected any. She would become the principal partner of the firm her father started by consistent wins and proven leadership, bringing in high-level clients with strong billable hours. She was just thirty, and although she was making good headway, she had a long journey ahead of her.

Ngozi didn't want it any other way.

"More wins like today definitely doesn't hurt," Angela Brinks, a sharp and decisive blonde in her early sixties, offered.

"Thank you," Ngozi said, holding her briefcase in front of her. "It was a tough acquittal, but my staff pulled it out and the client is heavily considering moving some other corporate business our direction."

"I understand you played a role in Chance Castillo putting VAL on retainer to oversee his corporate and business matters," Greg Landon said.

Chance.

Her heart seemed to pound against her chest.

She hadn't known that. She made it her business to avoid even discovering the outcome of his case.

"Everything okay?" her father asked.

Get it together, Ngozi.

"Yes," she said. "Actually, I'm going to leave you all to the meeting I interrupted. I actually have another case to prep."

"Federal, right?" Monique Reeves asked. She was the newest managing partner—and the youngest, at forty-five.

Ngozi found the woman smart, formidable and tenacious—her role model, particularly as an African American woman.

"I would offer you my expertise in that arena… but I don't think you need it. Still, the offer is on the table," Monique said.

"Thank you, Monique, that's good to know," she said before moving toward the door. "Have a good day, everyone."

As soon as she exited and closed the door, Ngozi dropped onto the long leather bench against the wall, letting her briefcase land on the floor as she pressed one hand to the side of her face and the other against her racing heart.

Chance. Chance. Chance.

Just when she had a nearly complete day without his invading her thoughts and creating a craving… BOOM! Nearly four months since their breakup and she was not over him.

Not yet.

Ngozi cleared her throat and stood with her briefcase in hand as she stiffened her back and notched her chin a bit higher, then made her way down the long length of the hall.

But I will be...one day.

I hope.

Chapter 10

One month later

Ngozi brought her swift run to an end as she came to Main Street of Passion Grove. She released puffs of air through pursed lips and checked her vitals and mileage via her Fitbit. She waved and smiled to those townspeople she knew as she continued to move her feet in place while she waited for her heart rate to gradually decline.

Feeling thirsty, she walked down the block toward the bakery, pausing a moment at the display in the window of the high-end boutique, Spree, that offered the latest trend in designer clothing. A beautiful silver beaded sheath dress with a short hem caught her eye, and she knew if she wasn't still sweaty and hot from a run, she would have gone into the boutique to try it on. "Another time," she promised herself, continuing on her way.

The large black metal bell sounded as she opened the door to La Boulangerie. The scent of fresh-brewed coffee and decadent sweets filled the air. There was a small line of customers awaiting treats in the pastry shop decorated like old-world Europe, with modern accents and brick walls. It was a warm Saturday in June, and the townspeople were out and about, milling around their small downtown area.

She checked incoming messages on her phone as she waited her turn. Soft hairs seemed to tickle her nape and she kept smoothing them with her free hand, also aware that she suddenly felt a nervousness that made her wonder if she'd caught a flu bug or something. When the hairs stood on end, she turned but didn't recognize any of the people in line behind her.

"Welcome to La Boulangerie. How may I help you?"

Ngozi faced forward. Her eyes widened to see Alessandra's cousin and her former client behind the counter. "Marisa, you work here?" she asked, her surprise clear.

Alessandra's family, the Dalmounts, was a super-rich family of prominence. She doubted her salary matched the weekly stipend Alessandra allotted her entire family, following the tradition her father had started when he was the head of the family.

Marisa, a beautiful young woman in her late twenties with a massive head full of natural curls that rested on her petite shoulders, smiled and shrugged one shoulder. "I've never had a job and I have to start somewhere," she said, her voice soft and raspy as if she could bring true justice to a soulful song. Although Ngozi recalled that her deceased father was Mexican, there was no hint of a Spanish accent.

"That's true, but I'm surprised Alessandra couldn't get you something entry level at ADG," Ngozi said, taking a small step back to eye the desserts on display in the glass case.

"I'm just starting to think a handout from your rich family isn't the best way for me," she said, sounding vague.

"Not many young women would feel that way," Ngozi said, pushing aside her curiosity. "I'm proud of you," she offered, feeling odd giving praise to a woman not far from her own age.

"Thanks," Marisa said.

"Hey, Bill," Ngozi said, smiling at the man with shoulder-length blond hair pulled back in a ponytail. As always, his black apron with Bill the Pâtissier embroidered on it was in place.

"Afternoon," he said, his tone appreciative as he gave her a slow once-over in her pink form-fitting running gear.

Bill wants some chocolate in his life.

"Marisa, I'll take a bottle of water and a fresh fruit cup for my walk home," she said, politely ignoring his flirty look. She was used to it. Bill had long ago let his intentions be known, and she had always turned him down gently.

He just chuckled at her deflection before heading back to the rear of the bakery.

"Coming right up," Marisa said, using the back of her hand to swipe away a long tendril that escaped from her top knot before pulling on gloves.

Ngozi was tempted to purchase a mini walnut Danish ring, able to tell it was packed with cinnamon sugar. She wasn't ever going vegan, but she did try to fit in healthy eating when she could. *Still...that Danish is looking like a treat.*

"Let me get a walnut Danish ring, too," she said, pulling her credit card from the zippered pocket on the sleeve of her running jacket.

Marisa gave her a knowing smile as she used tongs to slide the treat into a small brown paper bag with the bakery's logo. She took the card and handed Ngozi her treats and a small foil packet with a wet wipe for her hands. Soon she returned with her receipt. "Thank you and come again," she said.

"Bye, Marisa. I will," Ngozi said, turning away with a smile.

She tucked the water bottle under her arm and the Danish in her pocket before opening the wet wipe packet to wipe her hands.

"Ngozi."

Her body froze, but her heart raced a marathon, and those hairs on her nape stood on end. Now the nervous energy was familiar.

Chance.

Turning toward his voice, she spotted him sitting at a bistro table in the corner of the pastry shop with Alek. She hadn't even noticed them there. Chance unbent his tall frame—his tall, well-proportioned, strong frame—and waved an inviting hand to an empty chair across from him.

Ngozi hesitated.

They had done so well avoiding each other for all these months. And now, just like that, out of the clear blue sky, here they were.

Fate?

Perhaps.

Finally, she moved toward him, and it was as if everything else in the bakery outside of her line of vision on him blurred. With every step that brought her closer to him, her nerves felt more and more frayed.

Alek tossed the last of his powdered doughnut into his mouth before wiping his hands with a napkin and rising. "Good to see you, Ngozi," he said.

She just nodded, never taking her eyes off Chance.

Alek looked between his friend and his wife's best friend before walking out of the pastry shop as if he knew his presence was suddenly forgotten.

Chance reached around her to pull the chair out.

"Still the gentleman," she said, offering him a polite smile before she sat down and crossed one leg over the other.

"Of course, of course," Chance said, offering her a charming smile as he sat back down.

Ngozi set her water and the plastic container of fruit on the table as she eyed how good he looked in a navy tracksuit with one of his dozen or so Patek watches on his wrist. "You look good, Chance," she admitted, picking up the bottle to open and take a sip.

"So do you," he said, eyeing her before shifting his gaze out the window of the storefront.

They both fell silent.

Then they spoke at once.

"Ngozi—"

"Chance—"

They laughed.

"Our goddaughter is growing up fast," Ngozi said, searching for a neutral topic.

Chance nodded. "I got her a baby Lambo car. She'll be driving around their courtyard in no time."

"Only you would buy a baby a mini-Lambo," she said. "Is it pink or bright red?"

His smile widened. "Fire red, of course."

"Of course," she agreed.

More silence.

So many questions were sitting on the tip of her tongue, ready to tumble out.

"You're still running?" Chance asked.

Ngozi looked pensive. "Running from what?" she asked, instantly nervous an argument would ensue.

Chance shook his head. "No, I meant running. Exercising. Jogging," he said, making back-and-forth motions with his fists as if he were running.

"Oh," Ngozi said. "My bad. Yeah. I'm still running, addicted to the high of it. You?"

He nodded. "I did ten miles this morning," he said.

"I did like five around the lake and then came here for a little snack before I head back to my house," she said.

"Your house?" he asked.

Their eyes met.

Ngozi looked away first, opening the container to pop a grape into her mouth. "I moved out of my parents'," she said, lifting the container toward him in offering.

He picked it up and poured a few grapes into his hand. "How is it?"

"The house?" she asked.

"Living alone for the first time."

They shared another look.

"Necessary," she admitted. "It was time to trust myself to be who and what I truly want to be. Right?"

Those were the words he had given to her that night they'd ended their relationship. She could tell he caught the reference instantly.

"I only wanted the best for you," he explained.

Ngozi leaned forward to grasp his hand atop the table. "No, I'm not throwing shade. I needed to learn to want the best for me, too," she said.

He looked down at their hands clasped together and stroked her thumb with his.

Ngozi shivered, feeling a rush she could only guess was like an addict getting their first hit of drugs after a long break of sobriety. Not wanting to stir up the desire for him for which she was still in recovery, Ngozi gently withdrew her hand.

Chance instantly felt the loss of her touch. He looked down at his empty hand for a few beats before closing it into a fist.

He hadn't expected to run into Ngozi today. Even

with sharing godparent duties for baby Aliyah and each of their best friends being married to each other, they hadn't crossed paths. When she walked into the bakery, he'd watched her, but he wasn't even sure he wanted to make his presence known to her. They had moved on from each other. Survived the breakup.

He was so intent on letting her go about her day that he never let Alek, who had his back to the door, know that she was there. But he never lost sight of her. Never took his attention off her. He couldn't deny that he was pleased to see her again. And the jealousy sparked by Bill the Surfing Dude flirting with her could not be denied.

And when she reached for the door handle to leave, he had to stop her.

Now she pulled away from his touch.

"I saw they did a news story on your pro bono work," he offered, shifting away from sensitive subjects.

Ngozi nodded. "Recently, I've been doing more of that, but I think it's necessary. Not everyone is as privileged as we are to afford proper legal representation."

"People forget I grew up in the hood, but I have never forgotten, and I remember young dudes getting locked up for small crimes but staying in jail for months or longer because no one could afford bail or owned property to put up as collateral," he said.

"Maybe you could donate to help the underserved with that issue," Ngozi offered, tearing the label off the water bottle. "I'm thinking of setting up a non-profit to do just that."

Nervous?

The thought that he still affected her made him anxious.

"Yes, or you could refer such cases to Second Chances, the nonprofit I've already set up to do that," he said, remembering all of her urgings for him to give back more with his wealth.

Remember, to whom much is given, much is required, Chance. God didn't bless you so that you can buy thousand-dollar burgers and million-dollar cars.

She looked taken aback. He gave her a wide smile, enjoying it. "Growth," he pointed out.

"Right," she agreed. "I will definitely send some referrals your way. Maybe I could talk to the partners about making an annual donation. It would be a good look for the firm."

Chance looked around the busy little pastry shop to avoid getting lost in her deep eyes. "So, we're teaming up?" he asked.

"For a noble cause? Definitely," she said without hesitation.

His heart hammered, and he could hardly believe that this woman still had the power to weaken him at the knees. "And more?" he asked.

Now, that caused her to noticeably pause.

"You know what, forget it," he said, shifting in his seat as he took a sip of the cup of Brazilian coffee he'd purchased. "You may have met someone."

"I haven't."

He cut his eyes up at her over the rim of his black cup. She didn't look away.

Chance set the cup down as he wrestled with the myriad feelings now swirling inside him, creating their own little storm.

"Have you?" she asked, her voice soft.

He shook his head. "How could I? When I *love* you, Ngozi," he confessed.

Her eyes widened, and she covered her mouth with her hand that trembled.

"I dropped the lawsuit when I realized that not having you in my life hurt far more than losing a million damn dollars on a stupid wedding I shouldn't be having anyway because she was *not* the love of my life," he said with such passion, leaning forward to take her free hand in his.

"You are, Ngozi. You are the love of *my* life."

Her grip tightened around his hand.

"I have tried to forget. Tried to move on. Tried not to dream about you. Tried like hell not to miss you. And until I saw you today, I convinced myself that I succeeded, but I didn't," he said, licking his suddenly dry mouth as his breaths quickened. He pressed a hand to his chest over his pounding heart, patting it. "You are in here. All of it. And I don't know what to do but love you. To have you. To fight for you. To take care of you. To make love to you. To be happier than I have ever been…with you."

Again, she tugged her hand, freeing it of his clasp as she rose, gathered her items and strode away.

His heart ached at her denial of his love. He clenched

his jaw and curled his fingers into a fist to fight the regret that filled him as he watched her walk away from him. She tossed the water bottle and the fruit cup in the trash can before walking back over.

He stiffened his spine and cleared his throat, preparing for another of their epic arguments—those he did not miss. *Especially in public.*

"Let's go," Ngozi said, extending her hand.

His confusion showed on his face. "Where?"

"To my house, to show you just how much I *love* you, Chance Castillo," she said with a sassy and tiny bite of her bottom lip.

His desire stirred in an instant.

As he grabbed his keys and took her hand to follow her, he was thankful that his heated blood didn't rush to his groin and leave him to walk out of the shop with a noticeable hard-on.

They barely made it through the front door.

Ngozi gasped as Chance pressed her body against it with his, holding her face with his hands as he kissed her with unrelenting passion that left her breathless and panting. And when he lowered his body against hers, layering her with hot kisses to her neck and the soft cleavage he revealed as he unzipped her jacket, she spread her arms and foolishly tried to grasp the wood of the door, looking for something to cling to as her hunger for him sent her reeling.

With each press of his lips or lick of his tongue against her skin—the valley of her breasts in her lace sports bra, her navel, the soft skin just above the edge of her undies—she lost a bit of sanity.

And cared not one bit.

Chance stripped her free of her clothing and her undergarments, leaving her naked and exposed to his eyes and his pleasure. And he enjoyed her long neck, rounded shoulders, long limbs, both pert breasts with large areolae surrounding her hard nipples and clean-shaven vulva with plump lips that only hinted at the pleasures it concealed.

With his hard and long erection pressing against the soft material of his pants, Chance hoisted Ngozi's naked body against his and carried her the short distance to the stairs, laying her on the steps and then spreading her smooth thighs as he knelt between them.

"I'm sweaty," she protested, pressing a hand to his forehead when he dipped his head above her core.

Chance looked up at her. "I don't give a good goddamn," he said low in his throat before brushing her hand away and dipping his head to lightly lick and then suck her warm fleshy bud.

He ached at the feel of it pulsing against his tongue, and when she cried out, arching her hips up off the steps as she shifted her hands to the back of his head, he sucked a little harder. Feeling heady from the scent and taste of her, Chance stroked inside her with his tongue.

"Chance," she gasped, her thighs snapping closed on his shoulders as she tried to fight off the pleasure.

He shook his head, denying her, not caring if he pushed her over the brink into insanity as he pressed her legs back open and continued his passionate onslaught with a deep guttural moan.

"Please...please," she gasped.

He raised his head, his eyes intense as he took in hers brimming with pleasure, and her mouth gaped in wonder. "Please what? Please stop or please make me come?" he asked, his words breezing across her moist flesh.

The sounds of her harsh breathing filled the air as she looked down at him. "Make me come," she whispered. "Please."

Chance smiled like a wolf as he lowered his head and circled her bud with his tongue before flicking the tip against the smooth flesh with rapid speed meant to tease, to titillate, to arouse and to make his woman go crashing headfirst into an explosive orgasm. He had to lock his arms around her thighs to keep her in place as she wrestled between enjoying the pleasure and being driven mad by it.

And while she was deep in the throes of her climax, he rose from her just long enough to shed his clothes and sheathe himself. To be as naked as she. To relieve his aching erection. He hungered for her and could not wait one more moment to be inside her.

Chance thrust his hard inches inside her swiftly. Deeply.

Ngozi reached out blindly and gripped the wrought iron railing of her staircase, not caring about the hard edge of the step bearing into her lower back or how each of his wild thrusts caused her buttocks to be chafed by the wood.

Chance lifted up his upper body to look down at her as he worked his hips back and forth. Each stroke caused his hardness to slide against the moist ridges of her intimacy. She was lost. To time. To place. To reason.

"Here it comes," he whispered down to her.

She gasped as his inches got harder right as he quickened his thrusts and climaxed inside her, flinging his head back, the muscles of his body tensing as he went still and roughly cried out in pure pleasure.

Wrapping her ankles behind his strong thighs, Ngozi worked her hips in a downward motion that pulled on the length of him.

Chance swore.

Ngozi had a devilish little smile, taking over as she worked her walls and flexed her hips to send him over the edge into the same mindless pleasure he brought her. And when he gave a shriek similar to the falsetto of an opera singer and tried to back out of her, she locked him in place and continued to work every bit of his release from him.

"Please," he begged, wincing and biting his bottom lip.

"Please what? Huh? Please stop, or please make me come some more?" she asked, her tone flirtatiously mocking in between hot little pants of her own.

"*Please* stop," he pleaded.

She stopped her sex play, but with him still inside

her, she sat up and pulled his face down to kiss his mouth a dozen or more times. "Don't you ever forget that I love you, too," she whispered against his lips, searching his eyes and seeing that all her doubts of his feelings for her had been for naught.

The next weeks for Chance and Ngozi seemed to fly by. Happiness and being in love had a way of snatching time. And they were happy. Their time apart had brought on changes both needed to be able to love someone properly.

Life was good.

Ding-dong.

Ngozi was lounging on her sofa reading through briefs. She picked up her tablet and checked the security system, frowning at the sight of Chance's mother, Esmerelda, standing on her front doorstep.

Well, life was almost good.

She dropped the tablet and the back of her head onto the sofa as she released a heavy sigh. *What could she possibly want?*

Ngozi avoided Esmerelda at all costs. Although she and Chance had reconciled, they'd never discussed his mother or her clear dislike of her son's choice for love. "Hell, I'm not the one who left him at the altar," she muttered, rising from the sofa to pad barefoot out of the room and over to the front door.

Ding-dong.

Ngozi paused and frowned with an arched brow. "A'ight now," she warned.

She allowed herself one final inhale and exhale

of breath with a prayer for patience before opening the door with a smile that felt too wide and too false. "Hello, Ms. Diaz. How can I help you?" she said.

Esmerelda was a beautiful woman of just her late forties. Having had Chance at such a young age, she physically did not look that much older than him. She stood there in a strapless red dress with her hair in a messy topknot. Ngozi couldn't deny that she was beautiful.

"May I come in?" she asked, looking past Ngozi's shoulder.

"Chance isn't here," she immediately explained.

"Yes, I know," Esmerelda said. "He's at the offices for Second Chances."

Very true. Yes, he was. Of course, she would know that. Esmerelda and Chance were very close, Ngozi knew, but she also felt they were too close. *Hell, does she think anyone is good enough for him?*

"So, may I come in?" Esmerelda asked again.

Ngozi nodded and stepped back, pulling the door open along with her. "Right this way," she said, closing the door and leading her into the family room.

"That is a beautiful painting," Esmerelda said, moving to stand in front of the fireplace and look up at the artwork Ngozi had hung there the day of the Spring Bazaar.

Three svelte women in floral print dresses with large wide-brimmed hats that covered their faces sat in a field of flowers. "It is *The Gossiping Neighbors* by—"

"Juan Eduardo Martinez," Esmerelda provided,

turning to offer her a smile. "I am very familiar with his work."

"Chance introduced me to him and some other Dominican painters with the art he has at his house," Ngozi said, crossing her arms over her chest in the strapless woven cotton jumpsuit she wore.

"Yes, *I* introduce *him* to our culture any time we are back in Cabrera," she said with pride.

Ngozi nodded. "We flew there last weekend and it really is a beautiful city, Ms. Diaz," she said.

Esmerelda looked around at the room, taking in the vibrant colors and artwork. "Do you mean that or are you just saying it?" she asked.

"I mean it or I wouldn't have said it," Ngozi said, feeling offended.

Esmerelda looked surprised by Ngozi's push back. "I don't know," she said with a shrug and downturn of her ruby red lips as she dragged a finger across the edge of the wooden table.

The hell...

"Ms. Diaz, I love your son. I r*eally* do. I mean, I thought I would never be blessed with happiness after losing my husband. At first I didn't know what I did to deserve a second chance. I actually thought I didn't, but now I know I am just as good and decent and caring as he is. We are *good* for each other," Ngozi stressed. "And if you can't see that I make your son happy, then you just don't want him to be happy with me or maybe anybody else. I just really wished you had been this vigilant with Helena and saved him the heartache and shame."

Esmerelda's eyes lit up and she rubbed her fingers together, like she was excited by Ngozi's spunk and candor. "Hello, Ngozi Johns, it's nice to finally meet the *real* you," she said, extending her hand.

Ngozi looked down at it guardedly. "Huh?" she asked.

"I thought you were a phony blowhard like the Blonde Devil, and it's good to see a difference in you," she explained, her hand still offered. "I fed you the spiciest meal I have ever cooked, and you still swallowed it down to avoid angering Chance's mother. You wouldn't even speak up for yourself. I saw you as docile and weak. That is not the type of woman my son needs."

Ngozi was surprised at the woman's discernment. They'd met just once, and she saw right through the facade.

"I told him this and my Chance kept insisting that you were fiery, strong and had no problem telling him when he was wrong. I wanted to see this for myself and I didn't…until just now," Esmerelda said, actually offering Ngozi a smile. "I know my son. Sometimes, not all the time, but *sometimes* he needs to be challenged and pushed. Push him to be the best man he can be, and then my job can be done, Ngozi."

She nodded, feeling relief as she finally took Esmerelda's hand into her own. "I will because he does the same for me."

"Good," Esmerelda said, releasing her hand and turning to open her tote to remove a teal canister with delicate flowers. She handed it to Ngozi. "Recipes of my son's favorite Dominican dishes. Learn to feed him something besides sex. *Bueno?*"

Ngozi took the can and laughed. *"Si,"* she said, holding the canister to her chest.

Esmerelda reached for her purse and headed out of the room, pausing at the entrance. "The only two secrets I want you to keep from Chance are that you have those recipes and that I was here today," she said before turning and leaving.

Ngozi didn't have a chance to walk her to the door.

Instead, she opened the canister and sifted through the recipe cards. They were photocopies of the originals Esmerelda obviously wasn't ready to part with.

Feed him something besides sex.

Ngozi could only laugh.

Chance was watching television as they lounged in Ngozi's master suite, having decided to spend the night at her home in Passion Grove instead of at his in Alpine. He glanced over at where she had been reading Colson Whitehead's *Underground Railroad.* The book was lying on the lounge chair in front of the window, and she stared outside at the late summer night.

"Something wrong?" he asked.

Ngozi glanced over at him with a soft smile. "Today would have been my brother's birthday," she said.

Chance used the remote to turn the television off and then rolled off the bed in nothing but his sleep pants to walk over and straddle the lounge as he sat closely behind her. He pressed a kiss to her shoulder and then her nape. Finally, she had shared more with him about her brother's death and its impact on her family's life, just as he told her about meeting his father and discovering he had three half siblings—none of which he was prepared to deal with in the manner it called for. Ngozi had made sure he knew that she wanted him to reach out and meet his siblings sooner rather than later. It was clear her longing for her deceased brother intensified her feelings on his relationship, or lack thereof, with his siblings.

"If he was here, what would you give him for his birthday?" he asked, redirecting his thoughts back to her as he leaned to the side to watch her beautiful profile.

"Oh wow, I never thought about it," she said, looking reflective. "He used to love comic books, so I would've bought out a whole theater and watched *Black Panther* with him," she said, nodding. "He would've loved that movie."

"Or you could have just brought him over to my theater at the house," Chance reminded her, massaging her upper arms.

"True," she agreed. "Sometimes I forget you're a billionaire."

"And that's one of the reasons I want to marry you," he said, meaning to surprise her with his admission.

He felt her body go stiff before she turned on the lounge to face him.

"Chance," she said.

"Ngozi," he returned, digging into the pocket of his pants and removing the box he had placed there.

The plan had been to slip it under the pillows and propose after making love to her, but the moment seemed perfect.

"Whoo," she exclaimed as she caught sight of the large diamond solitaire atop a band of diamonds.

"Are you saying yes?" he asked, feeling so much love for her and no fear of laying his heart on the line once again.

"Are you *asking* me?" she said gently with a pointed look at the floor.

"Right," he agreed, chuckling as he rose from the seat to lower his body to one knee and take her hand in his.

"Marry me, Ngozi, and love me just the way I need you to, and I promise to love and to cherish you just as you need to be loved and cherished. I want nothing more than to create a family with you. To love and be tempted by you for the rest of my life," he said earnestly, hiding none of his love for her.

Ngozi nodded. "I will love you forever and always, Chance Castillo," she swore as he slid the hefty ring onto her finger.

"Mi tentacion," he whispered to her as he rose and pulled her body up against his and kissed her with enough love and passion to last a lifetime.

Epilogue

Three months later

Ngozi felt sexy as she came down the stairs of Chance's mansion in Alpine in the beautiful silver beaded sheath dress she'd seen in the window of Spree the very same day she reconciled with Chance. She had returned to the upscale boutique and purchased the dress the very next day. She now finally had just the right opportunity to wear it.

A celebration.

She looked over at Chance, looking ever so handsome in his black-on-black tuxedo as he awaited her. *Life is good.*

Chance's foundation, Second Chances, had just received a multimillion-dollar grant to help fund its philanthropic efforts toward underserved and sorely underrepresented lower-income defendants unable to afford bail or bond. With Ngozi's involvement as cochair of the board, the foundation's efforts would also expand to recruit skilled attorneys for pro bono work, including helping innocent men serving time for crimes they did not commit. Together, Chance and Ngozi were determined to effect change with the unfair treatment of people of color within the judicial system.

"Ready?" Ngozi called over to him, striking a pose.

Chance turned, and his eyes instantly went to the short hem lightly stroking her legs midthigh. "Worth the wait, Ngozi," he said, now looking at her face as he came over to her.

They shared a brief but passionate kiss.

When his hands rose to grip her buttocks, she reluctantly shook her head. "We have a whole party and all our family and friends waiting for us at Alek and Alessandra's," she reminded him, using her thumb to rub her crimson gloss from his lips.

"To *hell* with that party," he growled low in his throat.

"Don't you want to celebrate the sale of your second app, Mr. Tech King?" she teased.

He smiled, and it slowly broadened. "Tech King, huh?"

She shrugged one bare shoulder. "*Forbes*' words, not mine," she said, accepting his hand as they crossed the foyer together.

"Not bad for a kid from the projects?" Chance asked as he opened the front door for her.

She glanced up and stroked his cheek as he passed. "Not bad at all," she assured him.

The sun had disappeared, but the summer evening was still warm as they made their way to Chance's new white Lamborghini—a celebratory gift.

He deserves it.

She looked around at the beautiful grounds of his estate before climbing inside the car. "You sure you're not going to miss all this?" she asked him once he was behind the wheel in the driver's seat.

"We're building from scratch. I'll be fine," he assured her.

Ngozi covered his hand on the stick shift with her own. "Good, because I really want our home base to be in Passion Grove," she said as she eyed the ornate bronzed for-sale sign just outside his exterior gate.

She had gladly given up her rental. Its purpose in her newfound independence had been served.

Chance chuckled. "Can you believe I used to make fun of Alek for moving to a small town?" he asked, accelerating the sports car forward.

"Yes, but Passion Grove is no ordinary small town," she said, thinking of the ability to maintain its charms but still perfectly blend with luxury.

"Damn straight it's not."

Chance pulled the car to a smooth stop at a red light. His hand went to one of her exposed thighs.

She released a little grunt of pleasure. "I can't wait to let everyone in on our secret, Mr. Castillo," she said.

Chance smiled as he looked over at her. "Me either, Mrs. Castillo," he said.

Just that morning they had followed their impulses and flew to Vegas to get married. Neither longed for a huge event after their past experiences with such—his nuptials never happened and hers led to anything but marital bliss.

They chose to focus on their marriage and not the wedding.

"My *tentadora*," Chance said, indulging himself with a kiss.

"Will I always be your *temptress*?" she asked, her voice and her eyes soft with her love for him.

"Until death do us part."

"Now *that* sounds tempting."

* * * * *